BUILD

UNIVERSES

Shine Enyinnaya Nwosu

Sold Kin

© 2024 **Europe Books**| London
www.europebooks.co.uk | info@europebooks.co.uk

ISBN 9791220152181
First edition: August 2024

Sold Kin

*This book is dedicated to the children,
men and women who were considered slaves and
who died as slaves during the Atlantic slave trade.*

May your memories never perish

Acknowledgements

Often times it is not the last person that is mentioned in a list that is the least, neither the first person mentioned the most important. But it is hardly ever perceived not to be so by the persons involved. So on that note I wish to stress that the first person I mention is not the most endearing to me or most important neither the least in any way whatsoever, but the first contact or beginner, so he comes first.

Having said all these, the first person that gave my book a chance is Angelo Emo who first read my manuscript and saw worth in it and gave me a lifeline. I must say I am forever grateful.

And the second contact I had is Andrea Pietromarchi who continued from where Angelo left off and was super calm to all my disturbances. The book had no future without you.

By no stretch of the imagination would the book have been a possibility without the Angelic presence, professionalism, empathy, kindness and dedication of Veronica Parise. She took the large hit of all my troubles and was calm through it all. I can never repay you.

And to the entire crew that made the book a possibility may your cups of blessings never run dry.

From a grateful heart I say thank you.

Fact

The Atlantic slave trade Started officially from 16th to 19th century. In the Igbo hinterland Slaves were gotten by raids, kidnapping, and some were sold by their family members. Those who shipped the slaves regarded them as cargos and they were treated as such. They were to work on coffee, tobacco, cocoa, sugar and cotton plantations, gold and silver mines, rice fields, construction industry, and as domestic servants. It is estimated that over 20 million Africans were enslaved and sold in the transatlantic slave trade.

The Igbos were a major export, it is estimated that 1.4 million Igbos were transported. And they were exchanged for wine, guns and other commodities by the African slave traders. This is a story of slave trade in the Igbo hinterland and coastal parts of what is presently known as Nigeria.

CHAPTER 1

"Dad I can't stay here, this is not what I bargained for, I am not finding it easy or good to look upon," Mary said.

"You know what, I won't do this again, this is my last time," Mary's father promised.

"No I don't want to hear it," Mary said, adamant.

She picked her hat and put on her overcoat, stepping out of the cabin she moved onto the deck, down she went on a canoe, travelling a little distance to the riverbank just trying to get away from the things that reminded her of what was going on. It was inhuman and she just couldn't find it in her nature to continue to witness it.

"Pick up your things John and give me that," she said to John and collected her umbrella from him. He had been sitting down, dutifully waiting for her on the riverbank. Now walking with her every step of the way. She walked kicking everything on her path. She was restless, everything along the way and around her irritated her, they were making her uncomfortable.

"Madam White what the matter?" John asked, trying to be helpful.

John called Mary 'Madam White,' she seemed okay with it. It didn't really matter to her. He had always been quick in learning things. Calling her Madam White he was referring to her skin colour. John was above average when it came to intelligence, he had proven to be smart and creative, able to assimilate and manage so many things at the same time. Despite most of them new and strange. His skin colour was the opposite of that of his madam. His skin was radiantly dark, every inch of it. With a good muscle build and a nice white teeth well packed together John was an exception. The name John was not the name given to him at birth. But he had grown to accept the name given to him by his master. When he was opportune to ask about the name he was only told it was a name from their religion. And he had never bothered to ask more questions about the name. Following his madam diligently, since she climbed down from the great *Pegasus*: It was a mighty ship indeed. She tried finding a shade along the riverbank, she had come to learn about her environment. She walked a little further along the riverbank, the cleared portion; it was all white sands and the cool air of the river coming up against her skin. She was feeling the cold bite of the forces of nature at work here. Just a little further with Pegasus out of sight, the only living thing, less troubling around her was John, others were afar off. He had been assigned to her and he kept watch over her. She didn't need it now, she wanted to be alone, she needed time to think about which way she wanted her life to take. Things were not going well, she was feeling empty, and there was a great void in her.

Nothing made sense, back home in Liverpool, she had nothing worth it over there. Only a house and a sea loving father, her mother was late, lost to tuberculosis. Over here it was nothing but hurting, just as she was feeling this way the bartering began. She could see them now, men and women in chains almost naked and ready to be sold for gun and wine. Her throat felt irritated as the scene sickened her. It made her stomach cold, her revulsion continued, it was endless for her with everything happening. She couldn't bear the sight so she looked away to her left. It was her second time and she was not going to witness what she witnessed before on the last trip again. As she looked away she turned and looked at John who had been standing beside her all the while, she was surprised at the show of lack of concern on his face. She moved to the tent made by the slavers of her kind on the riverbank, now it seemed a better thing to do. The time for loading would soon begin, and then it will be more horror for her. The wailing, the flogging, children screaming in pain, the pleading with tears unending from humans to humans.

*****

"Sire, we are done with the loading," a slaver said, with his clothes all roughened, he was sweating profusely, with scars on his arms, a mark to show the struggles slavers go through to instill fear and obedience into the slaves.

"Aye, let's set sail then. Where is Mary?" the captain asked.

"She is not on the ship, Sire" the slaver answered.

"Oh! Please look for her."

"Aye, Captain."

After searching the ship, just to be sure, by the captain's order, Mr. Henderson couldn't find her, now there was a frenzy and a frantic search had commenced. They looked everywhere and then on the riverbank John was sighted, getting to him.

"Hey John, where is your madam?"

"Madam White in tent," he answered, pointing to a tent behind him.

"Aye God be praised." They said.

Those searching for her went back and told her father the captain. He ordered for her to be brought back to the ship. Their attempt failed. She was not going to be on a ship filled with humans as cargo again. That was not the bargain with her father. A ship was not a place for a woman, but her father loved her dearly, not wanting her to be out of his sight or far from him, he had brought her onboard the Pegasus this second time. He had told her he was to trade in other commodities, but now the truth was out, he was once again demanded to ship slaves to the new world instead of other commodities. This made her disgusted, why has she found herself in such a world? It was not a world a person like her would want to live in.

"Captain she will not come onboard," Mr. Henderson the slaver reported. "We have pleaded but she won't heed."

"Alright then." The Captain answered.

The captain climbed down from the ship to the riverbank. They were done loading and now they awaited the Captain's return to set sail. Getting to Mary.

"Mary," he called to her. "We've been waiting for you. Howdy young lady?" he asked trying to smile to her. She was not buying any of it. He went on to assure her it would be the last trip and he would be coming back to the bight, not to buy slaves but do another business which would give her comfort.

"Alright then father, when you are back you would come pick me, I'm not going onboard that ship." Mary said.

Her father loved her dearly and would do anything to see her happy.

"But on whose account would you stay here?" he asked.

"I will stay with John."

He didn't want to argue with her so he let her be.

She would be okay on the shore, John was a good lad who would look after her. The Pegasus set sail and she was all alone in the bight. But she felt no different, she had been feeling unwanted by all humans around her.

Nothing gave her the happiness or contentment that she was craving for. It was almost dark and she would be staying in the tent, there would not be any disturbances at least, as also there were not too many ladies around. She might as well be the only lady. Her father it seemed, must have been smuggling her. Then again he was the captain and he should be the one to decide the crew. On the riverbank she wondered what it would be like in the hinterland, she had never been to the hinterland and she didn't know any of her kindred who had been to where these slaves come out from. She didn't even know what it looked like despite it being behind her. As for the slaves she had always been told that they were criminals or outcast in the villages where they were gotten from.

Wondering what life was like over there she discussed this with John. He gave a good detail of how these slaves were captured. But he pretended to be dumb and went silent, when the African slave dealers claimed that they were outcast and criminals or those not wanted in the society. John had always said this to be false but always got ignored. He himself was and still was a slave, though serving Mary made him feel he was not.

"John I wonder what it is like in the hinterland?" she asked after much thought.

"Madam it is not very good place for you." John said, his English was not perfect but to Mary it was outstanding, she rarely stressed to understand him.

"I know, but to fill my curiosity. It is one a dangerous mission worth taking." Mary said.

There and then with little effort, they concluded to take a trip into any of the villages around the riverbank. John was delighted. He missed so many things, though he had warned her of the dangers in going into the hinterland. She seemed not to care, she wanted to know what that world was like. She was not finding contentment in the world she was in, and she wanted something different. Her father didn't need to know, before he made his voyage back she would be out. As quickly as possible.

Nobody not even the slavers needed to know she was gone. John still remembered the route into the hinterland, his father was a slaver on the coast, but now he was no more. Through his father, he got to know about the Captain and came into the services of Mary. He had ever since been satisfied with his life. Remembering his father gave him mixed feelings. How it was that he came to be amongst the men that sold their brothers into slavery and found no fault or problem with it. Still with it, he still got to be who he was. A free black man, serving a white man on the African coast. He liked his job and it made him feel that he was better off his fellow black men and even the women, including men like his father. Now he was to take a journey back to some of the places his father took him to. He could not go back to his village because he didn't know his village. His father never told him where he was from. As a young man he only remembered waiting for him at the shore and when he came with the slaves, he gave him things (a lot of gifts). He couldn't ask his father about his history, until death took his father away. Neither did he ask him about his mother and siblings.

*****

"I'm ready." Said Mary to John.

"Okay Madam White, me too ready" John said.

They both had been on the shore for four days. They were backpacking to the hinterland, and they had to sneak out. It couldn't be possible that Mary's father didn't charge one of the slavers to keep watch on the both of them. Their journey would have to be in the night, they moved out through the night. The moon shining its light, the weather with a biting cold, and the river before them swayed calmly. Mary led the way, stealthily with her crouching, they both moved out. Now down the path, it was John to lead, as he led they made their way through the path made by the slavers. There was no one on the path, by this time everyone had returned to their respective villages or places of abode. As they walked a little they got to a point where they had to enter a canoe that obviously belonged to no one. The people close to the river area made canoes and left them for the white slavers should they want to use them. They made their way it couldn't be far. As John paddled, the plan was also to avoid the site of the barracoon, but get close to it because from it, the path into the hinterland began. They could not start making a new path now. Where they were going they knew not what they sought they knew not. Mary had an emptiness in her, she was not enjoying her life, she didn't like the things she had seen, most nauseate her and made her feel sorrowful. Maybe all she was trying to do was get away from the life her father had introduced her to. As they made their way, they got to land and the path was lonely. Tall bushes covered the way both to the right and to the left. It was a foot path threaded upon by the free and bound. They moved a while, walking freely, they were out of sight to those at the riverbank, with it they increased their pace. As they matched onwards, Mary was cut on her right leg. She was wearing her boots, but it was not covering her upper leg just below her knees, her legs mostly the shin area were exposed. She looked down as she was in pain, she was only able to muffle her words as she cursed out loud "Damn bad luck." John tried attending to the wound. They looked at what had caused the cut, it was a split tree trunk lying beside the road. She cursed even more. John tried to stop the bleeding aware it needed to be treated immediately to avoid infection. He didn't know how to help her. Mary had to lean on him or something to walk the remaining distance before they could find a suitable resting place. They shouldn't be putting pressure on the leg.

It was almost dawn, they had been walking for long and Mary was in an excruciating pain. In a while they could see a light, the light was a torch made with local materials. The indigenes had a way of making fire with palm oil. Mary had been walking with the help of a stick John found on the ground. John called out for help from the man coming towards them, not knowing if he was a friend or a foe. With his lamp he heard the call and walked faster towards the direction where the voice was coming from. With his machete in his hand, he saw them and was startled when he saw Mary. The man had heard that there were white men at the shore, but had never seen any. Seeing Mary he couldn't believe his eyes, how fair she was even in the dark. Seeing Mary and John's condition the man offered his help. The man led the way to his hut as he could do nothing about Mary's injury. His hut was in the village, the three made it to the hut and he introduced them to his wife and grandson and rushed out.

John thought he had gone to bring herbs. Instead after a few moments away, he came back with a young man. The young man saw Mary, he had seen her like before. He approached her, removing her boot with him uncovering her leg, he revealed a skin so perfect, a skin colour like nothing they had ever seen. He applied leaves grounded together that he had prepared in their presence.

Mary felt the moist grounded leaves touch her skin and the cut. At first it was cold, then she felt the pain. He had warned her it would be painful now she understood what he meant. It was painful, but a pain she could endure. After a while, she couldn't pretend any longer, she was exhausted. They advised her to lie on the bamboo bed. She obeyed and before she knew it, she dozed off.

CHAPTER 2

Adanna couldn't wait. Her brothers were nothing but weaklings. She had to do this alone, she was certain her brothers wouldn't come. She couldn't wait any longer. Amadi was on the farm that her father had warned him never to step onto again. With her creeping up on him, she carefully picked up a club, she looked around no one was in sight. Amadi was unaware of her presence, slowly Adanna with the club in her hand struck Amadi who was bending down and weeding on the head. He screamed and dropped down to the ground, fuming in his mouth. With his blood on the club she walked away, buried the club in the ground and made her way home. When her brothers arrived at the farm, they couldn't find anyone only Amadi with his face down on the ground and blood all around him where he was lying. They were sore afraid. They ran into the village to tell the people. Once the news went round, the village messenger announced for an urgent meeting at the village square. Amadi was dead and the family of Ubiakwa was summoned together with the whole village. The elders of the village knew that Amadi and Ubiakwa had been struggling over that parcel of land, now Amadi was dead on that farmland. Who killed him?

As the whole village gathered, Adanna's brothers were summoned to give an account of what they had seen. They answered the elders narrating what had happened. How it was that a passerby was asked to tell them to come to their father's farmland in dispute with Amadi's family. The messenger who was a passerby pointed to Adanna, saying she was the one who sent him to call her brothers. Adanna was summoned, she had the skin of a goddess, her skin radiated the beauty that can only be bestowed upon one, only by the gods. She was tall almost the same height with men in her village. She came forward, Odichi one of the oldest in the village spoke up.

"Adanna, what happened to Amadi?"

"I don't know," she answered looking bored.

"But you were the last to see him alive?"

"I was not the last, I saw him like that, the same way my brothers saw him, I went away to tell others also."

Odichi shook his head in disbelief, "How is it possible you saw him like that, how could you have seen him lying on the ground and went to call your brothers, you must have seen him standing, and not on the ground?"

Everyone was perplexed after hearing her account on how she saw him enter the farmland before she went after him, after waiting a long while for her brothers. No one knew what to do. They had to wait for their god, to avenge the death of Amadi. A search was ordered to be carried out whoever was responsible had been ordered to come forth. It couldn't be anything else but murder.

Somebody must have hit him on the back of the head with a big stick and that resulted in his death. Nobody was being suspected more than Ubiakwa, he was the one that had been fighting over that parcel of land with Amadi. Now his enemy was dead. To some it was not possible that it was him, he didn't seem to be a murderer.

Adanna on getting home felt unperturbed, nothing bothered her. Ubiakwa got home and summoned his children, one after the other, he asked them if they were the ones responsible. He knew his sons, the three of them that stayed with him in his compound. As the others had dispersed, they had the heart of a nursing mother, they rarely ventured out of the compound, not to talk of murdering someone. The thought was doubtful for Adanna her father's favourite. She had been his backbone, doing valiantly where the boys had failed. Ubiakwa's compound had numerous huts and the largest barn. He was the richest in Akom. No one could match him in wealth. He had slaves those captured in war and those bought with money. He had numerous sons and daughters from seventeen wives, and he planned to marry another. They didn't all stay with him as only the fourth wife stayed with him and that would be Adanna's mother. Every woman that had set foot in the compound had met Adanna and had to contend with her, and they always lost. She was the one with a man's heart in the compound, men feared her and her ways and that didn't concern her. It was none of her business whether you liked her or not, as long as she had her way and did what she wanted. The sun was setting and nobody in Ubiakwa's compound had accepted the responsibility for the murder of Amadi.

"The gods shall surely break the neck of the man responsible for the death of Amadi" Ubiakwa proclaimed.

And they all agreed. Adanna stood up, not talking to anyone she moved into her hut. The night's sleep would be a pleasant one. The enemy of Ubiakwa's compound was now sleeping with the gods. The Chief Priest had been told and tomorrow the family of Ubiakwa would swear before the god of the land 'Utte.'

*****

In the shrine of the Chief Priest, Adanna swore of not being responsible. The sons of Ubiakwa all were made to swear. They all swore including the slaves, to having nothing to do with the death of Amadi. After that, they all went home. The slaves took their water vessel and went to the stream to fetch water for the family of Ubiakwa. They had to do so, Adanna supervised their work and they wouldn't find it funny if they didn't do their normal chores. On getting to the stream Oka broke his water vessel, and he cried all the way home. Getting home Adanna heard of it, she took a part of the broken vessel and pierced his leg, as a mark that he wouldn't forget, so that he wouldn't break a water vessel again.

CHAPTER 3

Mary was feeling a little better now, the initial pain was gone but she still felt something at that spot. Something discomforting. She walked on her own also. A white woman in the hinterland. Many who came to see her in the compound of Okri were all astonished. They had heard of the white man at the shore but most of them had never seen any.

Now it was like they were seeing a ghost. Mary would like to see the Herbalist to appreciate him for his kind gestures. She had not thanked him since recovery, indeed she had not even seen him. It was dark when she first encountered him. She was feeling a little different but a lot scared, she had never been to this part of the world before. Maybe she had, had her curiosity fed. She brought up the idea of going back to John. They had been away for almost three days now, and the riverbank was not afar off. They had to go back, she just wanted to be in another world where people were not sold or exchanged for items.

But she had to be thankful to Okri, he had been a source of blessing to her, had he not agreed to help them, maybe they would be telling a different story now. To Mary, staying with Okri would make her feelings worse. Okri was a man in his sixties she could guess. He had a wife and a grandson, he had lost his two sons. Now he was staying in his compound with his only grandson. Mary wished she could change the world for him. His grandson was autistic. The villagers believed Okri to be cursed. He had no one left to him and now a white woman from another world was in his compound.

Okri didn't understand a lot of things going on, but he knew that one day things would get better. His name may be wiped off from the face of the earth but he would still remain who he was, 'Okri' that was who he was and would continue to be.

*****

Today they were visiting the farm and Mary felt she would like to come along, she could do it, she couldn't just stay alone in Okri's compound with John. Both of them were unfamiliar with the environment. However, something was terribly wrong. They couldn't find Ojani. He had wandered off again. Every now and then he wandered off, going around the village seeking no one or thing in particular. His grandfather Okri had always had to search for him. Ojani was born before the sudden disappearance of his two sons. Ojani's mother was late. She died while giving birth to him. Okri had known heartbreak and he was too familiar with loss of loved ones. He had lost so many things in his time on earth and nobody could survive the disappearance of two sons and the death of a daughter-in-law. If Ojani got lost, like his father he may never find him again. However, Ojani had wandered to the village market.

The market was well populated with people. It was a busy day and most village people came out to sell or exchange their wares and food items. Ojani never stayed in his hut, on this day he had gone to look at the people passing by in the village market square. There are a lot of things that bothered a man and he was calm about it. Okri did not know if the loss of Ojani would make him calm or finally take his life. To what was he fighting for, he had lost those that would have kept his name on the earth, his current existence was on the one who was sick. He had nothing to fight for, no love on earth. His wife was just as tired of life as he was. Yet there was still a little space in their heart to help a foreign woman and her servant, there was still hope for the goodness of mankind in the heart of Okri.

The path to the market square was dusty. Mary had not seen what the market of a black man in the hinterland looked like before. She was following Okri, his wife and John to the market square to search for Ojani. It was their destination because he had often wandered to it, and those who saw them along the way informed them that indeed he had been seen wandering aimlessly to the market square. Okri at the market square saw the brutal black slavers were back. This time they were parading those to be sold at the shore to the white man. These men claimed that those selected for sale, were those that were captured during the war or they were criminals, but it was not all the truth, some have been kidnapped and sold. Who knows? Maybe Okri's sons were not torn to pieces by wild beast, maybe they had been kidnapped. Ojani was still nowhere in sight. Mary was horrified, this couldn't be happening. She knew where these people in chains would end up, they would be bound hand and feet until they were loaded on a ship going to the new world and other parts. It sickened her that her father did this. He was one of the people that would end up carrying this people to their destinations. To Mary, man was not supposed to be sold as cargo. How would the slaves see the world? Mary was contemplating this, as she continued to search for Ojani. She couldn't believe it, how easy she had settled, but not the same for the villagers, as they were all staring at her. They had never seen her type before, her skin colour was different. There he was moving through the paths of the market, Okri was the one who saw him. The slavers had also seen Ojani, he was not the type they wanted. They wanted able bodied men and women those that could survive the perilous journey of the sea, make it to the new world and do whatever it was they did there. Okri took Ojani by the hand, they all converged, Okri spontaneously began to tell Mary as John interpreted.

"I don't have any one in this world except him and my wife, with this his constant wandering off I don't know how I can survive. There is no one to look after us, it is a future that holds nothing that I see. I curse the day I was born, look at me I'm close to the grave, I don't have a son or daughter that I know is alive. My sons went to the farm, I have never set eyes on them ever since then. My daughter-in-law died while giving birth. I can't afford marrying more than one wife because I can barely feed myself. My eyes are already dim, just what is it that the gods want from me? Who will take care of Ojani for me when I'm gone?"

Mary had no words to console him, only to stare at him and wish that he felt better. What was it that she was going to do to make everything alright for him. They returned home, no more farming for the day. John was disappointed. He had wanted to farm. He had already put on his khaki trousers and shirts his father gave to him.

*****

The day was a disturbing one, Mary couldn't sleep at night as she turned and turned around on the bamboo bed she was lying on. She had thought of moving on, she was already weakened. The sight of what she beheld today was exasperating, the slave dealers handled the slaves with cruelty, and she couldn't stop them on her own.

In the morning once again she decided to move on from everything. It was better to go back and await her father. She had already asked John if they were to return to the shore. He didn't know what to answer, all he wanted was to please her. It had been four days since she arrived at Okri's compound. 'The Herbalist' as she had come to know had been coming to visit her from time to time. He seemed eager to learn about her way of life and what she believed in. She had taught him all she knew about the world where she came from and about the world she had found herself in. She discussed about everything with him, and he was eager to learn. John cherished the experience as he was made to be the interpreter. He tried his utmost best to interpret all to the Herbalist. The Herbalist himself was quite a fine young man. He had learnt his line of work, the true calling of being a herbalist from his father, a renowned herbalist, in his village of Mkpunki. Now he was getting knowledge of another world from a strange woman. He had a lot to offer now that he understood her world.

CHAPTER 4

Only men were hunters in the village of Akom, while women were allowed to set traps. Other neighbouring villages like Nkor, Akuta, Okpete and others, respected and revered the people of Akom. They were known for their prowess in war. Already their men were revered, now they had a woman who was becoming known. Adanna had been able to challenge all that a man could accomplish. No one had found it in his heart to ask for her hand in marriage. She seemed to not care about the things of the world, the way they were craved for by women. Her concern was to be the one to dominate her father's compound. Her father had always seen her to be the one to dominate and it scared him. "Where have you ever seen a woman ruling in a compound?" Adanna was ruling in the compound. She did things that most men wouldn't want to do. She had joined her brothers to go hunting, after some pleadings for her to turn back. She refused adamantly. It was time for her to show them yet again, what she could do and she was going to do it again and again. Indeed they went hunting and she caught an antelope. No man in her compound had been able to do so, she must continue to prove herself. But the truth remained no one was in contention with her. She challenged herself and indeed she didn't want to see herself as a woman, she had a lot to prove. Hunting was her favourite occupation and she was going to keep it that way. Ejide her brother caught nothing and he was the first son of their mother. His father pitied him, he should be the one everyone was looking up to but instead he preferred to spend his time weaving basket.

"Is that not a woman's job Ejide?" Adanna would tease. But it didn't bother him, he loved his craft. His father had slaves and those that worked for him. Why should he bother himself with odious jobs as hunting? He would rather stay home and weave baskets and mats. He enjoyed manoeuvring palm fronds to meet people's needs. Odika and Obeli also caught nothing in active hunting but Odika's trap caught bush rat, at least they didn't come home empty handed. Once again Adanna had acted as the one who would forever uphold the name of her father Ubiakwa.

It was almost sunrise a wail was heard by Ubiakwa at the entrance of the compound. It was late Amadi's widow, she had returned from her journey. She went to visit her people only to come back home, to hear the dreadful news from her only daughter, of her husband's demise at the hand of a wicked soul. Amadi married two wives but one was late and had no child for him, his only surviving wife had only one daughter and now she was wailing at Ubiakwa's compound, asking for the god 'UTTE' to avenge her husband's death. She had warned him to ignore that parcel of land since it was causing strive between him and Ubiakwa. Now someone had murdered him on the land. 'Who could have done such a dreadful thing?' she asked still crying.

"Shut up your mouth." Adanna's voice loomed across the compound. Nobody was out yet to console her. They had just come back from hunting with the first break of light. Ubiakwa ran out of his hut to know who was crying and appease the person. Adanna would have none of it. She picked the wailing woman by the hair as she sat on the ground with her calico wrapped around her loosely. Adanna dragged her by the hair out of the compound. Amadi's widow struggled to let loose of Adanna's firm grip on her hair. She had uncovered her hair which was not plaited. Adanna continued to pull her by the hair until she finally dragged her out of the entrance of the compound. Ubiakwa had seen Adanna violently dragging her. When he got to them he saw Amadi's wife by the side of entrance screaming and rolling on the ground with tears flowing freely.

"Adanna what is it?" he asked.

People in the compound were gathering.

"Is it not this wretched witch that is accusing Ubiakwa's family of killing her husband." Adanna said.

"You should console her not drag her like that." Ubiakwa said. Everyone in the compound was out now, looking on.

"I don't have time for that, I need rest and she is making noise, somebody should get her out of here or I will cut her with machete, and when I cut her I will cut her into pieces." She said.

Ubiakwa shuddered, he stepped out to Obirika, the widow of Amadi who was still crying and cursing. He knelt down in front of her, raised his hands up and swore to "Utte" that he had never and never had anything to do with her husband's death. Ubiakwa pleaded with her to stop crying and come into his hut, as he assured her that the person responsible for her husband's death would surely be found. She stood up and walked with him after much pleading from everyone. Adanna disgusted at the sight spat on the ground with anger, she had wanted to spit at her, but for her father's sake she did not. She went into her hut, while Ubiakwa and his sons consoled the crying widow.

In a short while Adanna would be heading to the farm, she was not afraid of hard work. When she returned she would be joining her age group. The new yam festival was approaching and everyone was preparing, there would be celebrations, as all groups prepared to participate. The women would dance, the village masquerade would be out to perform. Adanna would only attend the preparations but she was not going to dance. Why would she want to waste her time with a thing like dancing, to her dancing was for women who were shameless. She would visit where they practice only because her father told her to, after she visited them she would be going to meet her hunting group in Okpete, they would go hunting and they must prepare.

On her way to the farm with her father's slaves and brothers they saw a young man being dragged by two hefty men. They didn't bother to stop the men to ask what was going on. Such was how debtors were treated, maybe they would sell him to the slavers to recover their debt.

CHAPTER 5

In Mkpunki where John was staying with Mary, they heard about the upcoming event. The people of Erom were going to celebrate their new yam festival. It was going to be the talk of the villages, the people of Erom, knew how to celebrate, even though all the villages would be celebrating likewise but John wouldn't want to miss the celebration in Erom, he had learnt about it from traders coming from Erom. Now if only he could convince Mary about it. It would be an amazing event to witness. How would he survive the torture to hear the sounds of their drums and smokes from their bonfire, their loud voices when celebrating and not attend when Erom was but a stone throw from there?

"Madam White," he called to her "festival in Erom, you come?" he asked wishing for luck.

He thought she wouldn't want to, but surprisingly to him she agreed whole heartedly. She had been waiting patiently for an event to come up, she had been wanting something to help her forget about a lot of things. As the day came they all made it to Erom to witness their new yam festival event. On getting to Erom after a day's journey Mary had never known anything like this before, she had never witnessed such an event, the masquerades were out and soon the chief masquerade was out, with it out, some women and children ran away. The masquerade was a dreadful thing with awesome powers. The women that couldn't run and also didn't have the heart to stay, fainted and the men gladly carried them away to avoid them being stepped on, and to recover. The event was everything John imagined it would be and he was glad to have witnessed it. Mary was confused especially with the women fainting, at the same time she was also glad to have witnessed a different part of the people and also learn a new thing. Indeed it was a tale she would always tell about the time she went to the African hinterland.

CHAPTER 6

In Akom similar event was occurring, the main masquerade Mbgounku would soon be out. The uncanny thing about this masquerade was that the people who crafted it, had made it to look like a white woman. Soon it would be out and everyone would witness its spectacular action, it was even more dreaded, more than that of Erom. After the masquerades, the women would be out to perform at the village square everyone was standing around while some followed them, dancing along with them as they danced. The masquerade moved away, they would dance from every corner then they would finish their dancing at the village square. Everyone who was not at home would be at the village square after the dance the men's competition would follow. Odika Adanna's brother, could not afford to miss this one, here the strongest men came forth.

After this, it was the event where strength, skill and ability was witnessed. In this one the man with the favour of the gods was chosen, here a he-goat's head was cut off at one attempt. The men would file out, the one chosen amongst the lot, would dance brandishing his machete, after dancing he would proceed to cut off the goat's head at one attempt. If he failed he was regarded as a failure and cursed by the gods but if he succeeded he would be the next village champion. The lot fell on Anyanaelu, he danced and danced around brandishing his machete. Rumour had it that he sharpened it seven times. The goat was brought out, it was time to prove whether the gods were with him. If the gods allowed him to cut the head of the goat at once it would mean another fruitful harvest come next season.

Anyanaelu knew this was the only time he would do this. Odika was gripped with apprehension. They were all watching intently Anyanaelu still dancing, once he saw that the goat had stretched its neck. Swiftly with one strike he cut off the goat's neck. There was uproar and a celebration as if the initial dancing was nothing. Adanna was present, she had seen Odika and wondered what was happening to him. Someone had a body contact with her, bringing her attention back to the village square. She had also thought about the event of new yam festival, surely a woman should be allowed to do the goat head cutting and dancing, women were not allowed but Adanna fancied her chances at performing. All other women were dancing but she was not, everyone now was with a palm frond celebrating the recent achievement of Anyanaelu. He was carried on the shoulder by his peer group as they all celebrated his victory. It was not an easy thing to cut off the head of a he-goat at once. The celebration continued, the masquerade danced round the village and his companions, those playing the flute, drum and gong also followed him round the village. The people were happy with the outcome of the events that were taking place. Adanna knew there would be another day for her as she fancied doing the things the men did. The village heads had picked up the remains of the harvest goat, it was time for them to prepare it and have Anyanaelu to be the first to taste its meat.

*****

With the main event celebration over at the village square everyone went back to their homes, to continue the celebration privately. It was twilight and Adanna went to visit her hunting group, it was time for hunting again. She met with Okanka, Uja and Aroro, it appeared she was late. On their way returning from hunting with their catch they saw an antelope on the ground along the way into the hunting forest. Adanna sighted it first, it must have been dropped by someone and the person must have dropped it in a hurry, the footprints indicated there was a scuffle as Aroro pointed out. The four were startled as to what this could mean, trying to be brave they followed the footprints and lost it after a while as the footprints moved into the deeper part of the forest. They would never know what could have occurred, who could have abandoned an antelope. It was clearly a hunter, the four made it back to the village to announce their findings because the dead antelope had not been lying there for long, as everything about it still looked fresh. When they got to the village they went to meet Odichi who was already in a meeting that early morning with other village heads, all elderly men in the village were in the compound of Odichi except Ubiakwa, they had been discussing the impending war with Akuta. Adanna on getting to the presence of the elders, after greeting wanted to speak.

"My dear don't speak, there is an older man with you let him speak up you are in the presence of the elders," one of the elders said. Turning to his fellow elders he looked at them with surprise. "I wonder what they teach our children these days, a girl wants to speak before the elders, not only that there are men with her." The man said still surprised, others concurred with him.

Indeed Okanka was the eldest but it didn't matter to Adanna, reluctantly she allowed him to speak. Okanka narrated their story to the elders facing them as they were seated in the compound. Odichi had many huts in his compound as he married nine wives and had fifteen children all surviving, he had no trouble feeding them as he had one of the largest farmlands in the village of Akom. Okanka narrated his story to the elders and they noted that this was not the first mysterious disappearing report that they were receiving, so many people had come forth to give accounts of the disappearance of people both strangers and their family members. Akom was blaming Akuta. The people of Akuta had never been friendly with the people of Akom now there were people disappearing in Akom, it must come from the people of Akuta. Elder Oname the brave one dismissed Okanka and his companions. Oname was known as the brave one because he always never feared war, he was reputed to have been fearless in front of battle, a fact well known. They continued with their deliberation as to whether they would have war or peace with Akuta.

After being dismissed Adanna picked up her kill as she made her way home. Her father would be thrilled for her kill, he loved her meats and the soup she made with them.

CHAPTER 7

Mary and John made it back to Okri's compound who was relieved. And welcomed them profusely, he was so elated because he was worried for Mary and her safety, her kind had never been to that part of the world. As they got to the compound it had been days that they journeyed to Erom and back. Approaching the village men had already gathered at the compound of Okri as they had never seen a white woman before now there was one living at Okri's place and they were demanding to know who she was. It was a dangerous thing to bring in a strange person into the village, a person who did not know their ways of life. They doubted the king knew about her presence.

John was having the best time of his life with all the attention that he was getting, things were better now, no more the days where all he saw was a white man and slaves, the few of his race he saw were those bartering and to be bartered.

CHAPTER 8

The people of Akuta had heard about the rumours of war from Akom and they were preparing themselves adequately. They were not afraid as long as Oja dike the mighty one would led them. Oja had learnt about war from his father who was a revered warrior and hunter. The gods of Akuta seemed to always favour them when it came to taking life. Be it the life of an animal or human and the lives of Akom warriors would do just fine. Let them come. Oja had led them to war before capturing warriors and leading them to the white man at the shore as slaves he knew what it was like to take another's life. His wealth had increased tremendously since he started selling slaves, now Akom wanted to challenge Akuta. It meant more captives for Akuta and slaves for the white man. Akuta had just ended a war that it embarked on against Ogi people, whom they captured and left none alive. It was high time that another war came their way so they could make more sales of slaves. Oja had married six wives and had numerous slaves, he was planning to embark on another raid to get more slaves, his taste and desire for more blood and wealth was insatiable. No man was like Oja when it came to war. He was not a man of peace, he never denied the fact that he knew that the hands of the gods were with him, that was why he always had victory and was always standing in the crowd with his head above everyone else's. So many people feared Oja both in the time of peace and in the time of war. The village messenger had gone out to call all the able bodied men to the village square to come out for an important meeting, the people of Akuta all responded, now in the village square all had gathered and it was the time for Onuka to speak.

"My people of Akuta, I greet you all." He said this three times as the custom demanded, then he went to the reason why the meeting had been called.

"We are gathered here to discuss about the people of Akom where our messengers got a report that they are seeking war with us, they have been witnessing disappearance of their people, and now they blame the people of Akuta for the disappearance. We the people of Akuta are never afraid of war. If it is war they want I think we should give it to them, I have spoken." Onuka said. Turning to Oja "What do you have to say?"

Oja stood up with the skull of a dead man hanging on his neck, when he stood all became silent, the mighty warrior had stood. Then he spoke,

"My people I greet you all." He greeted three times then he began to speak, "I have in a single battle killed three hundred men with my sword, I have in a night killed a wild pig with my bare hands by crushing its skull. When we fought with the people of Ogi I single handedly ended the lives of about two hundred men and sent their wives, sons and daughters to the white man as slaves, now the skull of the strongest warrior in Nfuta land hangs around my neck, these are recent happenings I am recounting for those who are new and know nothing about Oja, I need not tell the stories of past deeds. People of Akuta are you scared?"

"No!" they all shouted.

"Good then, let war come. I will also destroy this people of Akom and end their incessant irritation forever."

"Yes!" they all shouted jubilating.

Oja turned to elder Onuka "Let war come we are ready." The people started singing a war song praising Oja and his prowess.

"Oja you are the only strong one we know.

Oja you are the man of Akuta.

Who is strong like you the beautiful One.

Your hands are as strong as that of our god.

Your teeth can crush the strongest rocks.

Who knows the beauty of Oja come let us show you."

When they finished singing about Oja they began to sing for the village Akuta.

"Akuta has sons and daughters filled with every art and craft.

We are the people of Akuta, wonderful is our god, who has given us the ability for war.

When our peace is disturbed we fight till we regain it.

We are Akuta, only blood can bring peace."

Abanajo raised his hand, then he asked them to be quiet, he asked for peace, he didn't want war.

"My people of Akuta let us not be hasty in going to war, instead let us have peace. We have gone to war many times but this time I suggest we ask the village priest before we sing songs of war."

"Abanajo sit down." The elders shouted with the people murmuring with displeasure.

Then Onuka spoke again, "If it is another people we will ask for peace but not from the people of Akom. If it is war they want we will have war." The people supported and cheered.

"Let us ask the Chief Priest." Oja demanded. The Chief Priest who was already amongst them was summoned and he answered in the affirmative giving assurance for war. Once again they started their war songs and every one dispersed waiting for the day they would be summoned for war, Oja went home and beckoned his slave Annuela.

"Go to the farm, go and release that goat Abiam."

Abiam was Oja's first slave but he still treated her like nothing. He had tied her to a tree in the farm for two days as punishment for her not preparing his food early. In the compound of Oja all his wives that he married none could birth a child for him, so he sent them all away. Of all things Oja had accomplished not having a child was the one thing that humiliated him the most. It haunted him to the extent he believed everyone was making fun of him for not having an offspring. But it was a lie unknown to him, his not having children was not fooling the people. Because they still believed he was a force to be reckoned with. That his six wives bore no child for him meant nothing. Abiam had been faithful in serving him, it was during war with her village that Oja took her, she was but a child when it all happened. She couldn't even remember what her parents looked like. It was Oja that she had always known, and she had served all his wives. Oja had a belief that bringing yourself low to love and respect a woman was a thing for the weak. He once slashed the head of his third wife for no reason other than she did not greet him, even though she had pleaded she didn't see him. Annuela got to the farm, Abiam was motionless, he sprinted to her, untying her, he called her name she didn't respond. The farm was deserted, so he couldn't call any one for help, she had been tied to a palm tree and her back was bleeding. It must be from too much struggle with the rope trying to free herself. Annuela laid her on her back and started fanning her, he didn't know what to do when someone was unconscious. She was still breathing, he opened her eyes, it was a normal colour, he tried to wake her but to no avail. He picked her up and carried her on his back, back to the compound of Oja. He thanked the gods that no wild animal had attacked her for two whole days. He got to the compound and took her to the hut of Mkpeshi, the oldest slave of Oja, she knew how to treat their wounds. For she had been the one treating them, when Mkpeshi saw them she quickly ran towards them. She had been expecting sad news since she heard that Abiam had been treated to Oja's punishment, by being tied to a tree in a farm but thank the gods she was still breathing. Other slaves who had witnessed similar punishment from Oja were torn to pieces by wild animals, they never survived to tell the story. Quickly she went inside her hut and asked Annuela to bring her inside, where she laid her on a mat and started sprinkling water on her after which she took some herbs and applied on her back, then in a little while she tried to give her water to drink. In doing so Abiam resuscitated, she coughed out loudly vomiting the water that had gone into her throat. As she opened her eyes she tried to flee but was held down, as she woke up like one in a bad dream it must have been a nightmare for her. She saw Mkpeshi who was calming her down, then she let out tears. She was finally home, she continued crying. When Oja heard her crying he got out from his hut and went to the slave's quarters where Mkpeshi's hut was.

"Shut up!" he shouted at her, "Before the gods strike you dead."

Abiam had no option but to keep mute before he decided to treat her to another punishment. As Oja was stepping away from Mkpeshi's hut he was met by a messenger from the Chief Priest. Oja was startled, what could a messenger from the Chief Priest be doing in his compound?

"Wise one hope all is well?" he asked.

"All is not well Oja, you are needed at the shrine, the Chief Priest has a message for you, if you can come immediately please do, it is important it has to do with the war with Akom."

"I will be there right away."

Oja thanked the messenger and went into his hut not long after he was out and dressed on his way to the shrine. He met four boys going to the stream when they sighted him they all dropped their water vessels and prostrated on the ground to greet him. He acknowledged their greeting and went his way. The boys continued to the stream discussing how fortunate they were to have met Oja dike the mighty warrior of Akuta. Oja was almost leaping in an attempt to walk faster, a message from the gods. It had to be important, he was almost running down the footpath, the way to the shrine was only known to but a few. When you passed the part commonly treaded by the people then you would get to the path where only few knew. The sides of the footpath were all covered and flanked by trees, Oja made his way, on getting to the shrine he announced his presence to the Chief Priest who summoned him into the shrine.

"Oja I have seen what the mouth cannot speak of, a faint hearted man cannot take the message that the gods have passed along, should I continue to speak?"

"Speak wise one, I am listening. Oja has the heart to hear, speak."

The Chief Priest cleared his voice, "Akuta will not win this war and to make matters worse you shall not return from this war."

Oja was stunned but showed no outward expression, he waited for some moment, drawing air in from his mouth he scratched his head and patted his chest, trying to reposition himself but still wore a stern face.

"What will happen, wise one?"

"Akom will win the war Oja and the people of Akuta will have to surrender to them"

"But how could this happen?"

"I don't know."

"Wise one do not worry since you do not know Akuta will not fail. But at the meeting you said Akuta will win."

"I only affirmed I never said so besides I never consulted the gods before I spoke, it was a mistake on my part and I'm sorry Oja, I'm now fearful for the gods have spoken and they never speak lies."

"Oja will change the course of destiny you can be rest assured of that."

He stood up and left with a heavy heart but he believed in his strength. In his mind he asked where were the gods when we defeated the people of Ogi, we will defeat the people of Akom and the gods will come to respect us. Oja believed in his own arm to bring him victory he had never tasted defeat in battle. Though he had no children which he had been wanting for long. His father had eighteen sons and twenty daughters, him he had none. His brothers who were mostly farmers were not a match for him for he was the first son from his mother and he was the most famous amongst them all. He was the mighty one of Akuta, he would never back down. He was returning to his compound, getting home he kicked the wooden barrier that served as a gate that led to his compound open, no time to open it gently. What do the gods mean? he already had no children to give him joy that he lacked, the only thing that gave him joy they were about to take away, how could they take away war from a warrior must they make him handicapped, leaving nothing to keep him happy. Why must it be in the hands of the people of Akom that his strength would fail him, he could not back down the war must go on as planned and he was going to have his victory. No matter what it cost, nothing would stop it. This time his food was ready and waiting for him but he had no time for a meal, there were urgent matters that needed to be attended to. Oja picked up his staff, he had to speak to the village heads to ascertain if they had heard about the impending doom awaiting to befall Akuta. As he walked to the place of Onuka, he met with daughters of Akuta playing a game along the foot path and it touched him. He couldn't allow these ones to suffer. They all seemed happy what would happen if Akom won the war and took all of them away into slavery. He moved along the footpath both sides were covered with farmlands another harvest would come and there would be no one to enjoy the harvest because Oja failed in war. It would never happen, Oja would know no failure in battle, ages to come stories of his victory against all that came against him shall be told and songs would continue to be sung in his name. He made his way to the compound of Onuka on arriving he met Onuka eating his afternoon meal.

"Come and join us Oja, you are welcome indeed, the great son of the soil, you came well."

"I'm not here for food Elder Onuka something is bothering my spirit because all is not well."

"Ah! Is it the message from the Chief Priest?"

"So you have heard?" Oja wanted to ask how it could be that he was having appetite to eat.

"What can one do, what the gods wills let it happen" Onuka said.

"No it shall not happen, we cannot be defeated, I Oja will not be defeated."

"Hmm. It is said that the gods control the affairs of men, if they have spoken, they have spoken, even asking for the spirits of our ancestors to protect us may not work."

"I don't need ancestors to protect me, I will protect myself."

Without saying goodbye or waiting for Onuka to speak Oja turned and started towards his compound.

CHAPTER 9

The people of Akom knew what was awaiting them with the people of Akuta, they had heard about the strength of their warriors. But they were not disturbed, they believed that their god would give them victory. Ubiakwa's first son Ejide from his fourth wife was preparing to do double celebration. He was going to do a child's naming ceremony and also get married to his second wife. Ubiakwa had chosen a perfect bride for him, from the family of Banuju his best friend and close friendly rival in terms of wealth. Though the news of war loomed Ejide was not concerned or letting it deter him from doing what he wanted to do. The ceremony came, Ejide invited all his friends to witness his happy day, men in Akuta heard that the most wealthy man in Akom had his son celebrating. Oja too heard this, he had never been to Akom, now was a perfect time to know who to kill and who to let live. After days of preparation the ceremony began, men and women from all walks of life attended amongst them was Oja. He needed to know who was who to determine why the gods had said that Akom would defeat Akuta. In witnessing the event he couldn't help but be in awe, the men of Akom were not warriors. The richest man in Akom was supposed to have the best warriors in sons and slaves but all he was seeing were revellers making merry and drinking to stupor. How could this people be the ones to defeat Akuta? His face was not showing it but Oja was happy at what he was seeing. The men of Akom were not warriors he had not seen any whose arm was strong enough to match his. They were slackers and looked paunchy. Oja witnessed the ceremony, no one asked him questions since

Ubiakwa's wealth was known and people from every corner attended the ceremony. After the sun went down Oja made his way back to Akuta in high spirit. He had not seen not one person who could match him and the people who attended the ceremony were indeed all that Akom could offer. He got to his compound this time he gently opened the wooden gate and stepped in. He called for a slave to put his water for bath. He had his bath whilst whistling with his mouth the song that the villagers sang about him.

CHAPTER 10

Mary now fully recovered had the Herbalist still visiting to make sure her healing was perfected. His work had earned him a lot of respect from the people of Mkpunki, maybe one day he would go to see the land where Mary was from. It would be a thrilling thing to happen. She told him about the man they call Jesus in a faraway land she said this man died and rose again on the third day. Indeed it was hard to believe, as Mary spoke about a dead man, coming back to life, the Herbalist looked at her more intently. He had heard people having strange spirits that made them say unreasonable things, unknown to him in Mary's land such people were known as mentally challenged. For the Herbalist personally, he had witnessed that when people got hit in the head they said abnormal things with slurred speech, but Mary spoke fine only she was saying unreasonable things elegantly. The Herbalist also suspected John, maybe he was the one with the issue, Mary continued her explanation when he couldn't bear it any longer he cut in abruptly.

"You didn't hit your head anyway in the forest did you?"

John interpreted and Mary touched her head in surprise as if not sure.

"No," she said, "Why do you ask?"

The Herbalist didn't respond but simply shook his head and continued listening to Mary. Even if it were possible he didn't know but surely he would like to find out someday but now he was content with the gods that he knew and to practice his trade the way he knew best. Wanting to know more about this Jesus may lead him into trouble and he didn't want to get into trouble not now and not anytime soon. How can someone die and then rise again? It must be magic like none ever seen before, he gave her herb to rob on her leg. The life she sought was not what she was getting, she had wanted to spend this time away from her father in peace now she was in a place she knew nothing about and she was in it with an injury she had sustained. The only solace now being the discussions she did have with the Herbalist. She cherished talking to him, she liked his demeanor and the fact that he had a good heart and the urge to learn. The Herbalist sat down to ask her about her believe in this Jesus she talked about, he had been thinking about it and he didn't think it was possible for someone to die and then rise again from the dead.

"Well that is what happened," she said. "You can't see it with your eyes but you must believe with your heart that is the only way."

"How about someone becoming born again how is that possible?"

John was doing the interpretation and he himself couldn't believe the words that were coming out from his mouth. He had said them many times and had observed Mary but he would never understand what she was talking about.

Mary answered the Herbalist but he still didn't understand, he shook his head and marvelled at Mary's words then he packed up his bag and left believing he had heard enough for the day. Being born again was not something he intended doing anything soon, his plan was to get old not start afresh. The woman's ways of teaching and the things she taught were very strange. Maybe one day he would tell her about his own god. After he left, in a little while Mary and John stepped out into the compound where Okri's wife was pounding yam for dinner, Mary was making do with only meat and some local foods that she could manage, the fruits were helping too. John was enjoying the ones that Okri's wife served, they were both outside to enjoy the fresh air. Okri had gone to the farm alone, Ojani was sitting alone near the almost empty barn in the compound, as soon as they tried to sit outside people who were passing by began to stop to stare at her, they didn't know what to do with her. Already it had been days since she arrived at Okri's compound and he had not allowed anyone to see her except the Herbalist. Mary noticing that she was being stared at in an unfriendly way moved back into her hut, the people had gathered before she didn't want them to gather again. She had told John to prepare for them to go back. Okri had insisted she healed first before she embarked on such a journey again, but indeed the people were becoming increasingly disturbed. Mary still had not heard tales of her people coming to this part of the world, for all she knew she might be the first to have ever made it to that part. She had heard the Portuguese where the first to discover the area but surely did they enter the villages she didn't know, indeed she was not surprised that it had to be them. However she thought it to be better she left before curiosity moved the people to do something no one expected. John she had noticed was enjoying the attention he was getting, nothing made him more happy than people calling him to ask about the white woman he was with. He would explain to them but making sure not to reveal all to them at once so that they would come back wanting more. Okri returned from the farm, he had caught a bush meat in his trap and he was announcing how well he was going to feast with it much to the delight of his wife Olaedo. They both had much in common. And Mary believed it was the same with her own parents how they loved each other and was at each other's side through the pain and suffering. Her parents really loved each other before she lost her mother to the cold hands of death she could still see the fire of love in her father's eyes when they talked about her, it was a wonderful thing to behold. Her own life she wished would be likewise, when she settled down it would be with one who understood her and wanted to be by her side at all times. Okri moved towards the kitchen to give his wife the catch and Olaedo motioned to Mary to come see what her husband had brought home while she sat to prepare it. Olaedo decided to tell Mary a story. It had been only the Herbalist that she had been having conversations with, though Olaedo had been content and believed everything her husband told her about Mary now she wanted to have a conversation with her and also let her know about their own way of life. She motioned to John who was now seated to interpret for her to Mary, it was going to be a long tale she explained to Mary, also that it was their custom to tell stories. She told her that she used to tell her children stories, something moved in Olaedo when she mentioned her children but she shook it off trying to focus on the present and forget the past.

"So Mary" she began "I want to tell you about how our world was created." As Olaedo's story lasted it was almost time for dinner and Okri's bush meat was now boiling, he had promised everyone a taste including Mary telling her how it was that he was using herbs that would soothe her soul. John was enjoying all both the story from Olaedo and the aroma from the bush meat.

CHAPTER 11

Ubiakwa was always thrilled for her kill, he loved bush meat, waving goodbyes with promises of meeting again as usual, Adanna not afraid of any evil befalling her, should she walk alone despite what she had seen, took solid steps, with boldness and marched home. She even relished the prospect of an Akuta indigene coming up, upon her, she would rip the individual into pieces. She knew what she was capable of, gone were the days of a believe that a woman was weaker, she could and would show strength, fearlessly, she marched home. She had a lot to do for the day, so much to do that could weigh down a lazy person, with her appointments lined up, it simply meant, the day was going to be one of the days she missed to sleep again. She had done so before, going two days without sleep, and the good thing was, she wouldn't feel it, she never had. The biting cold continued to chill her skin, people may not have noticed but she cherished things such as the early morning calmness, it transferred to her mind, calming all that was in her heart, she enjoyed the freshness, it also freshened her inner self, for her it was the most beautiful part of the day, and a period one should learn to cherish.

When in her father's compound, she purposely woke in the very early part of the morning, that very moment when it was obvious the birth of a day had occurred, she would sit in front of her hut she shared with no one, and somehow the dews made her feel things, it filled her with hope, she thought about the possibilities of the whole day, and would believe that definitely good things could come out of it. Walking home, she inhaled deeply, pushed the thought of slavers from Akuta away from her mind, and took in the beautiful fresh air of the day, it was so clean and sweet, it had a soothing assurance of life. Few people recognised the beauty of early morning she reasoned to herself, most of the paths in Akom were all cleared, her hunter's torch was still on, clearly it illuminated the path, the early morning breeze gently blew the dried leaves on the ground from one corner to another, the leaves made cracking noise which added to the sweet melody of the early morning, the environment was so blissful to cure anyone of any ills. Adanna took in the moment, she knew what people thought about her, and how they perceived her, but she walked knowing they knew little, though she walked alone, she was okay being alone, the wet air, fresh gentle air cool and smelling sweet, made her journey a memorable one. She had her weapons, she had her kill, getting to the compound of Ubiakwa she entered the entrance, looking around as usual. She could notice that majority, were awake in their huts, preparing to come out and do the day's chores, definitely, waiting for daylight.

Adanna walked solidly and strongly then again Mother Nature had made it possible for her to walk with grace. "She is a woman." It must have said. Feeling the newness of the day, Adanna proceeded to prepare her kill, the palm oil lamp would serve well, with it she did all the necessary things. She had one thing in mind, to finish cooking it before Ubiakwa woke up. She would certainly serve it to him, when he woke up, still on the verge of finishing up, she had come to know, just about everything concerning the men she regarded as company, the word friends would be too strong. She had no desire to get to the level of friendship with anyone, the sort of power she wanted was the ability to revenge or kill anyone without thinking twice. For her that would be freedom. Gbokubi knew her hut, and where she would be, since he was talking to her he was also entitled to some privileges, like not following the entrance to get to Adanna's hut, despite the guards he could still walk around as he was well known in the family of Ubiakwa. Because of the business they always got involved in they needed haste and unimpeded access to each other should information be needed to be passed.

Gbokubi from behind her hut skillfully meandering through the surrounding bushes emerged and met up with her as she was fast into cutting up the bush meat. Soon she would need fire to burn out the furs, Adanna seeing him knew immediately that something was up that needed action. She was being informed because it involved her and her family. Gbokubi, would not lie to her, he needed the welfare she provided for those working for her in her destructive and wicked acts, it was none of her concern, she knew that was how people saw it, but not her, to her she was protecting her family, the regrets of not starting early to protect all that she loved still haunted her. Gbokubi, making his way to her, whispered into her ears and she knew she was going to have a filled day ahead. Gbokubi made haste and left after she had given him some orders. Adanna looked around she had never needed her father's slave's help in preparing a bush meat, they would simply irritate her with the fact she would have to talk too much before they could do anything right for her, as such she had decided to always do it alone. The day was maturing she had to work faster, despite what Gbokubi had just told her all that was the main concern and primary target was making sure the first thing Ubiakwa saw and ate was her bushmeat. She was certain he wasn't lying when he said, just the thought of eating her bush meat made him beg the gods to make him live longer. One meal made a craving for another, definitely she could do it. Adanna hurried up, by the time Ubiakwa came out, rinsed his mouth and expected to see a lot of visitors that disturbed him, because many of them were what he called.

"Please sir, please sir," visitors, they would kneel and use twenty pleases in a sentence of twenty-five words when saying what Ubiakwa knew they were going to say in words before they said them. They simply needed his help. Ubiakwa smiled when he heard rumours that some of them followed one way while coming and followed another when going because of Adanna. In certain days she was around and occasionally less busy enough to monitor them. She would make sure they got enough more than they bargained for. Ubiakwa out now, knew he had a limited time to take in the morning air, he sat outside in front of his hut, looking around, and returning greetings from the members of his household. He sighted Adanna approaching, his salivary glands came to life, Adanna had done it again, she was a stone that knew his soft spot. Getting to him Adanna greeted and proceeded to serve Ubiakwa the bush meat both sauce and pepper soup, Ubiakwa's brain tingled, the anticipation of a fulfilling pleasure. Adanna sat before him as Ubiakwa with smiles said a lot of kind words to Adanna, how she was the only one that understood him and was always at his rescue, the gift the gods had given him, the reason he was alive and happy. Adanna took the words with smiles, Ubiakwa too had forgotten how Adanna's action against the villagers of Akom, subtracted from his wealth all the time. He had lost count how many times he had to make restitution, by paying heavy fines, on her behalf. Perhaps it was worth it, he paid fines so that he would be able to witness such mornings as this. As Ubiakwa ate, Adanna sat and looked at him, while Ubiakwa devoured the delicacy, taking huge bites that expanded his cheeks, stretching it to unimaginable limits. Adanna had seen it before but it still intrigued her, the fact Ubiakwa nodded repeatedly while chewing, sometimes closing his eyes, and tilting his head. He had said little, Adanna sat still and glanced around, almost everyone looked already harried and the sun was not up yet. Adanna felt no pity for the occupants in her father's compound, they were living in the compound of a successful man, one of the richest if not the richest in Akom, he worked hard, they too must work hard. Ubiakwa ate trying to be as quiet as possible but couldn't resist the occasional smacking of the lips. Before he would take the white man's wine, he bought from slavers, but now he used them occasionally, preferring to drink palm wine rather. He motioned to Adanna as he gnawed on a bone. Adanna attentive now, with his left thumb he pointed to his hut behind him.

"Palm wine," he said trying to swallow, he cleared his throat.

Adanna rushed into his hut they were two gourds there, she couldn't tell the old one from the fresh one, she proceeded to get the light finally she could identify it, she brought it and poured for Ubiakwa who emptied a wine horn, and belched loudly with a sigh of relief. He relaxed a bit, and nodded again, thanked Adanna and praised her some more.

"You are light," he said to her "In my darkest times, when my enemies attack and design for my end, I feel no one cares, all want my wealth and not me, then I remember you and joy like a river cools my heated heart, thank you Adanna," Ubiakwa said with all forms of sincerity. Adanna nodded.

"Thank you father," she said, and began clearing the plates.

Ubiakwa relaxed now, took sips from his palm wine, Adanna left and he thanked her some more. With her leaving, a man approached, Adanna ignored him and passed. The man was led by Ubiakwa's slave, the man didn't look important neither did he look poor, he was a lucky man indeed, no matter what he said now it would be difficult for Ubiakwa to get angry. He would have become angry should it be that he was on an empty stomach.

Adanna quickly got herself ready and left, she had a lot to do and accomplish for the day, taking all necessary forms of weapons as usual, like one going to war. Several times she had explained she needed to be able to protect herself at all times. Adanna walked with haste in her steps, she took two turns and was headed to a forest area. She met an old woman, who apparently had struggled to tie her firewood together, she was labouring to put it on her head when Adanna was passing. Relieved the woman called to her.

"My daughter, the gods brought you this way, please come and help me with the firewood, I've been struggling with it," the woman said, laughing and pleased to see help. Adanna looked at her with disdain, as if she was disgusted just by the sight, she cursed the woman in her heart, 'It is the gods that will kill you,' as she walked by. The old woman was surprised but didn't bother much as two things came to her mind, maybe Adanna was deaf or maybe she did not understand the language, but both seemed unlikely she knew what she saw. The old woman stared at Adanna as she walked boldly and in a hurry, if only she could see a man, she would report that there was a stranger in Akom, everyone had got to be careful now, with the reports of evil turning up, every now and then.

The old woman looked at her firewood on the ground and sighed if only she was younger, unless someone came she would struggle a bit, she had packed it with the hope of seeing someone help her. Taking the firewood in small quantity was much labour for her and more dangerous as her home was too far to make a to and fro journey twice. Adanna moved on with her mind already imagining the situation of things and why she was needed, she took a left turn all around her were nothing but trees and bushes soon the part she was getting to nobody was going to be in the area, legs rarely passed through it. It was just perfect for the kind of purpose that it served. Adanna met up with those that had called her, the men were five in number she made them six, complete and certain they could proceed in unison. Guinta, greeted all and declared the reason they had gathered, all agreed and he ushered in Adanna to speak. She decided how much they earn, simply because she was the one that made the payment, and it was her that sustained them, and they took Adanna seriously, because their living depended on Adanna, with all five of them, looking at Adanna, she gave the orders.

"Nini." she called, "You will keep watching the family, and find out, anything we have missed let us not be caught unawares, you know our signal right?" Adanna asked.

Nini nodded, "Yes" he said later on.

Nini was the youngest in the group, his elder brother Guinta, was also in the group, and stood beside Adanna. Nini had a lot to learn about their business, before Guinta could introduce him to the group he had assured Adanna that Nini had the heart of a warrior. Adanna was still watching to be proved right that Nini was too frail to belong in their group. Nini's head was bowed as he took orders from Adanna, making sure not to look anyone in the eyes. His first test would be humility, then the test of loyalty to Adanna. Having received the full instructions, Nini dashed out, the remaining four men plus Adanna went on to re-strategize. Guinta had already made the plans, they would soon move out immediately.

Woku and his family were the people Adanna was after, the plan was to catch them or him unawares. In the group were Guinta, Jindeh, Hutushi, Kinlindim, Adanna would lead the pack, Guinta would be the last man, they had decided their strategic positions and in no time they made their plans certain and they moved out. Unlike Nini, the other men were matured and strong bodied, rarely looked like people that couldn't surmount any challenge, they wouldn't be following the main path, they didn't need to be seen by anyone, at least not yet, jogging as they went along, they said little in-between, they dodged as much trees, shrubs, twigs et cetera, as they could. Adanna was certain of her plans, when she planned and worked hard towards it, it rarely failed, they jogged with all haste. When they got to Woku's compound, they went round towards the bathing area, Woku was the target, not seeing him Adanna questioned the information she had been given, that Woku's hut was in the middle of the compound, there were two huts in the middle and Adanna wondered which one. She looked at Guinta who understood the look as if he could read her mind.

"The first one," he said.

Adanna watched from the bush, people outside were much, it was early morning and everyone busied themselves to get the day going, this meant they would take the second plan. The first was to adopt him in his compound, now it was to lure him outside, with few witnesses, that was the second plan the third and fourth were too dicey, the third which should have been the second as suggested by Guinta was to wait for him leave and then while outnumbered and exposed, he would be caught and dealt with. That would be a gamble, village heads do not go out alone, they move with a lot of slaves guarding them to showcase their affluence. Seeing the man sit in front of his hut, after Adanna took a better position which enabled her to see him more clearly, her heart expanded with hate, she just hated the man, the anger and bitterness towards him, made her increase his punishment in her head. Nini from his post in the bush directly facing Woku, saw him and was filled with pity, if only he knew what the day held for him, and the pain he was going to witness in a short while. The treacherous life we live, sitting in front of his hut, oblivious of what the day held for him. Nini had a duty, he had been instructed by both Adanna and Guinta and he knew his job. Woku was unfortunate. Sitting, Woku rinsed his mouth, he was making an attempt to wash it, and get ready for his meal, after which he would set out for the day's affairs. Nini saw from his lookout, a young girl approached, from the description given to Nini she must be the one, she passed Nini's lookout and went into the compound, just as was described to him, it played out exactly before him. Nini saw the girl greet Woku, Woku answered and in haste, walked after the girl out of the compound. Woku looked healthy and full of life, he was favoured by aging, despite his accomplishments, he still was a young man. Hurrying after the girl they both left the compound with Woku so much in a hurry, he didn't tell anyone where he was going. The distance from his compound to the next compound was a considerable one, no one would be in sight once they took the left turn, they entered the path, and Nini gave his signal, it was just a confirmation. Adanna was not going to let her operation rest on the competence of an amateur, she had seen Woku and the little girl take the left turn. Woku's mistake was allowing a bush in front of his compound, from there anything could happen. Woku being a man of affluence, wanted a secluded environment but then again not far from other people, he got a new land, made a path to it and went on to leave a bush in front, going to his compound you would walk through a path, then take your right, the small bush was by the right, then the compound had its entrance broadly cleared, also, you would cross this broad cleared path before entering the bush or Woku's compound. To Woku the bush gave aid to the seclusion he needed, but now it gave a surveillance area to Nini. Adanna and the other four were in the bush now, passing through the bush was faster. Nini saw them pass and maintained his position, he now had to watch for anyone, exiting the compound. Woku moving faster, without any weapon, did not suspect anything, the plan was to walk fast, meet up with the call, return home, prepare and then go out, while out, re-visit properly. Woku urged the girl to walk faster, enumerating all the reasons why she had to. The sun was not out, he could not have seen a shadow, all he saw was a figure move swiftly from his left and fall upon him, snatching him away from the ground, with another hand covering his mouth.

Woku did not see a face, and was now certain he was not going to see any, he was being gagged, and blind folded, his resistance amounted to nothing, those against him were stronger. Woku tried to scratch around but could not, he wriggled like a tied goat with its throat being slit. Adanna and her men secured him firmly. Kinlidim, another Veteran in the group, scouted the area once more to make sure no one saw what happened nor would see them run off with Woku, all was in place he ran to the junction wherein taking right would be moving to Woku's compound, he threw a stone forward, into the bush close to Nini, the rustling sound was supposed to inform Nini, they were moving out, that was the signal expected by Nini. Quickly they all turned right and left the place, the little girl had run home, unknowingly she had done her part, it was a marvel to the men at how well Adanna was able to trail her and carry out her plan, more marvellous, that she was, but a child. Adanna actually could talk to children but maybe it was only when they were needed for her use in perpetrating sinister and nefarious acts. Should the girl be seen by anyone, all she was to do was tell the person the truth. Indeed Woku was needed by his ailing friend, Adanna had monitored, when the friend would call for Woku, Adanna's informant had noticed the little girl to be the one to always bring message to Woku and they monitored her, today it worked out perfectly well, but then again, no one would care to ask the little girl what happened. She didn't even see a thing as she had been threatened to run and not look back. Adanna stealthily with her men meandered through the forest, almost running, Guinta carried Woku on his shoulder. He was the only one Adanna could trust, others flanked him and protected them from the sides. Adanna led the way, dealing with Woku now would be easy, they had done the difficult part of kidnapping him, very often Adanna reassured herself of how self-controlled she was, in the sense that all she wanted to do now was drop down Woku, and deal with him right there and then. The plan to take him to a safe place was good but at the same time not all that necessary, but a plan was a plan, and it would be good to always follow it the way they had planned it, that would re-affirm the bond, and make them stronger. Nini was now in his elder brother's position, he was the last, guarding those in front, Adanna thought little of it, he wasn't there because of his worth at least not yet. Guinta was training him to take over as he himself took up another post in the group. They ran to the agreed spot, a considerable distance from Woku's compound, all this while Woku had remained still on Guinta's shoulder, his choices were, stay quiet and be carried in peace, or disturb and be knocked out unconscious, that also meant he would be carried in peace. Woku had chosen to stay quiet, to him he would be able to imagine and guess their distance, all the while he had been calculating how far and what part of Akom they were in, but most importantly who were the captors. Slavers would turn on him should it be he had enemies known, but as such a man like him had unknown enemies, it couldn't dare be slavers, he knew almost all, till the seacoast, if these were slavers, they were new in the business. A man like Woku shouldn't be trifled with, especially when it came to the business of human cargo, to Woku, his silence was him being calculative, to Adanna, his silence was him being arrogant, with the belief that no one could harm him. This infuriated Adanna, she increased his punishment in her head, Woku must be taught a lesson this day, all that Adanna wished to do, was to bring him down, Woku had exalted himself and gone too far with it, just bring him down plus other things Adanna wished to add to it. She was not jealous of him, she had more than all Woku's wives combined together. When they got to their destination, they brought down Woku, the man was calm, now his calmness had turned to anger, he had frowned his face, a man who had achieved what he had achieved, should never be kidnapped or humiliated, Woku was sore infuriated. It was expected that there was a level you would get to and then, robbers and their likes would respect you, knowing that attacking you would only bring them harm and regrets because of your fame or notoriety, the world would rally to you should you call them to action. Woku believed with his actions he had struck so much fear into many that he was supposed to be revered and avoided now these nitwits had the audacity to kidnap him from his home. Still blindfolded but now ungagged and tied to a tree in the forest, Woku pushed away all fear and spoke boldly.

"Who are you people?" he asked.

He was not answered. He attempted to ask again, but before he could speak again a slap landed on his right check that momentarily stopped his hearing from that ear. Woku was stunned but got himself composed.

"You people are making a terrible mistake, stop this before it is too late, I am Woku, so I advise again, stop this and let me go…"

He received another slap on the same cheek, the ear carnal shut up again, at this rate it would stop working completely should it receive more slaps. The palm striking him was heavy and thick. Woku kept silent for a while, summoned up the courage and spoke again, with expectation of another slap.

"What do you people want?" he asked.

Another slap on the same cheek, this time the cheek bruised inside as it collided with his molars and premolars, the outside itched and was very hot. Whoever invented slapping on the cheek was a savage, and "woe" to the first person that was slapped. Woku was losing courage, and boldness, his questions were responded to with slaps, he attempted again.

"I can pay you people and help you also in this business."

Another slap on the same cheek, Woku was certain his left cheek was softened now, and the right palm of the person slapping him was getting hotter. Woku unsure of the next word to use, tried again, "I will dest…" before he could finish the word "Destroy" a heavy slap again this time the force was so heavy it almost pulled his head off from his shoulder. Woku lost all confidence, and almost his consciousness, he remained silent, since talking brought a hand upon his cheek. After he was quiet for long, another slap landed on his cheek, this sent Woku into confusion, Woku was now aware, it was not his talking but definitely they wanted something, he remained silent as the numerous tinkling sounds like a small bell continued ringing in his ear, after a while another slap landed on his cheek, Woku blurted out.

"Please, I beg you, please don't hurt me please, please I am begging you people, please."

Nini almost smiled, but counted his day a lucky one, he didn't, all were stone faced, Guinta now spoke.

"Now you understand your position Woku," he said, with an intimidating baritone, "You are not blindfolded because we are scared of you seeing us, rather because we want you to live, do you understand?" Guinta asked.

"Please, yes sir," Woku answered sobbing.

Woku was scared now, the good thing was he now knew his worth, the people against him were from Akom, their accent said it all, Woku was attentive, not hearing a word could be catastrophic to his cause.

"Woku." Guinta continued.

"Please, yes," Woku answered.

"You crossed the line, we all know your activities in Akom, how you pilfer our human resources, to enrich yourself, we ignored it all but one thing is certain, you have your limit and you crossed it, you stepped on toes, which is unfortunate for you, since last five market days your sons and daughters now go about threatening to send people as slaves to the white man, what do you say about that?"

Woku was confused, "Please, I will talk to them," he said.

His right cheek was reddened, soft and sore, yet a slap still visited it again, the pain rushed through Woku's body and lingered on his cheek after going round his body.

"Please I will punish them, if possible send them away, please."

"Good, very good," Guinta said, "that will be all Woku, this was easy indeed very easy, now we have an understanding and an agreement, all that remains now, is us beating you up and dropping you where you can be taken home, but remember, should you fail, to hold your own side of the bargain, we can do this again and again, so do not think of revenge."

"Okay. Let the beating begin," Guinta instructed.

Immediately, Woku was gagged again and untied, in no time kicks, punches, and sticks were raining down on him in heavy torrents. Woku expected death. Adanna stood aside as the commander, watching all unfold, she called Guinta to herself, when he was close.

"Give him an indelible mark, and inform him it is to remember this day, and his worth," Adanna said, Guinta turning back.

"And that should be the last thing," Adanna added.

Guinta, nodded and went back, he brought out his dagger and waited.

Woku still had so much life in him, as he wrestled and wriggled, till he was subdued, the scar would wait.

"Hurry up," Guinta ordered.

They had a lot to accomplish for the day. Woku gasped for breath and was choking, Guinta sensed this and ungagged him fast, the man gasped strenuously and for a moment coughed out violently, he was still blindfolded, he revived a little and was gagged again, lying almost lifeless. Nini couldn't believe his eyes and how he had played god in someone's life. Woku had slept and woken up with different thought and issues, definitely different plans for the day, he had not anticipated what had befallen him. But for Nini he had planned to change Woku's life, give him an experience, now they were set to mutilate him and make him remember the day men played his god. It was nothing to Adanna, we are all gods, his smooth skin was all dirty and roughened. Woku was a changed man, never to become the same again. Nini believed they had changed Woku's life, as humans, and they did it to perfection, how much then can the gods decide. They talked about it, they planned it, and now they did it. Life is treacherous, who played the part and took the actions? He took up his position as they prepared to move out, it was the last phase that they were on, and that was dropping Woku where he would be seen, and carried home to tell his tale. Adanna took up the leading role, the drops of blood on the ground were covered with earth, the area re-arranged to hide any sign that humans were there, satisfied, they moved out, four men carried Woku this time, two with each limb, two with the legs, another two with the arms. Adanna and Nini were the ones with weapons and acted as look outs. Going half the distance to Woku's house, Woku himself unconscious, Nini did his job again, scouted the area, and the path right to left, came back and gave a positive feedback, the men dumped Woku beside the foot path and untied his blindfold, ungagged him, and walked away.

CHAPTER 12

Matu, sat together with his peers in his hut as they strategized on how to compete with Ubiakwa, and if possible surpass him. Well they took it as a joke their main discuss had been on how to pay back Ubiakwa on what they owed him. Now they had harvested, he would be expecting payments from them and also gifts, it was not a secret that those who owe Ubiakwa in anyway, knew themselves and always gathered together at the end of a harvest to pay him. Ubiakwa was so resourceful that he had labourers for hire, not only that, he was constantly introducing new ways to farm, he had cultivated most of the new foods brought by the white man and was successful cultivating them. It was not a secret that other farmers concentrated on yam, cocoyam and the likes that their forefathers cultivated, but Ubiakwa had been able to cultivate maize, even foods which were weird but all the same delicious, not to mention the new fruits and vegetables.

"Ubiakwa feeds us," an elder once said.

There was no stopping or surpassing Ubiakwa, they had a lot to learn, but then again what Ubiakwa had was a gift from the gods and not the work of mere men. Matu who had only one wife went into his compound, with only three huts, his son was with his mother he met the two of them, probably chatting, he came in to inform them, they could come to his hut to greet his friends.

"What are you people even discussing with such mirth?" the wife asked.

Matu laughed, "Ubiakwa and his family of course."

The wife was surprised, when you hear Ubiakwa, then you certainly will hear Adanna, you can't escape it, and to the wife she had heard about Adanna, and they were not pleasant. She was like a disease or scourge you pray not to get in contact with, something you loathe with the mere mention of it.

"Just to clarify, are you people talking about Adanna?" she asked.

The man laughed, "Who will talk about her, no one does, when you talk about something, sometimes it seems to hear and materialize, so to avoid her, you just don't," Matu said.

The wife was laughing now. "We will join you soon," she said.

And her husband left and went towards his hut, to join his friends.

CHAPTER 13

Adanna got to the village square and noticed people had gathered, she wouldn't bother to stop there, she would get the information later, they were heading to her home, there was still a lot to be accomplished for the day, no one bothered to greet her and surely she wouldn't be greeting anyone. Woku had gotten what he deserved, the man allowed his children, take pride in his job, threatening people with slavery, now they would know their father was not as strong as they thought, seeing him in the condition that he was in. They had actually threatened to sell Ubiakwa's slave, and that was an affront not to be accepted, every man should know his or her worth, Adanna believed. If the rumours were anything to go by, Adanna had to prepare and get ready for the upcoming events, it wouldn't be easy, but she still had to try and make things easy for herself and family. She had a duty and an obligation, to her family and that was it, nothing else. She was not doing it out of care but obligation, her men followed her and they walked diligently towards her compound, when they arrived they knew, they would have to get refreshed which was the point. Adanna ushered them to her hut, when seats were brought they sat, in a short while food was flying in from two or three slaves, the men ate their fill. Nini tasted his first white man's wine, it was a strong drink indeed, he also saw the mirror, many travel distance to see themselves in the mirror and witness the magic, they ate and drank and congratulated each other. Adanna had remained her bush meat for them, Nini had never tasted such meat, Adanna also had fish but would save it for them for next time, let them not get all the goodies once.

Guinta ate calmly, he knew he was welcome to enjoy such and would continue to for a long while. Adanna excused herself from their presence to check on her father, it was farfetched that he would still be home now, but it was not impossible. She got to his hut. Surely he was not in, she scouted the enormous compound, she would have walked round, but it would delay her and her plans, looking around and returning to her hut, she saw Odika her brother lost in thought and soliloquizing. Adanna thought of ignoring him but, something pushed her, she didn't know what made her take the decision, she got to him, unsure on how to start with him, she didn't even know the words to say or use. It was not her fault she did not know how to relate with people to the level of 'Asking how are you,' those words were not natural to her, she didn't use them often.

"Why are you here?" she asked.

Odika looked at her, no words were coming forth. Did Adanna just ask him a question? With much labour.

"Nothing" he said, looking at her, Adanna wanted to say, 'I saw you looking distraught and murmuring to yourself,' but decided against it. Instead she said, "I am in my hut if you want to talk" she said and left. She did not look at him again till she got to her hut, with her men drinking fresh palm wine with pieces of meat in their hands. A lot of empty dishes were before them, "Men and meal." Before Adanna never discussed her dealings with anyone in her hut, now they had changed patterns, and she discussed it everywhere and anywhere. She gave them time to relax and let the food settle down a bit, waiting for them, Odika barged into her hut, panting, he surely did not run.

"It is Ekume, he swore to kill me, should I go ahead to present Eku to wrestle against him, Eku is my slave, and I believe..."

"Stop your nonsense" Adanna shouted, and Odika kept mute, and became rigid.

"Let us go" she said to her men, they all stood.

"Go back to your hut" Adanna said to Odika. The young man obeyed and left with a hurry, there was no need to disobey Adanna. Adanna's men moved swiftly with her, not knowing which way they were going they already had a plan to follow, but with Odika's information, Adanna may be headed towards Ekume's direction. She knew she had to hurry, with the thought she ran off, when she had taken two turns they realized where she was going, it was to Ekume's place. Ekume was still living with his parents, and was the same age with Odika, he had taken to wrestling because he had a huge body frame. Others called him fat, he was extremely difficult to throw to the ground, lifting him up alone was nearly impossible, and he had the strength of a youth. For Adanna bringing him down to size would be an easy task, it was just a misguided puffing up on his part, he certainly should know his worth, threatening or imagining to kill a son of Ubiakwa was a high crime. They got to Ekume and did to him what they did to Woku his own case being that they maimed him. By the time they were done, brutally battering Ekume they let him loose and as usual dumped him where someone would see him, recognize him and definitely take him home. Satisfied they had done their job they went after the original purpose, they wouldn't be thinking about Ekume, his right foot was dangling as they carried him to the path, that meant their work was successful.

They hastened to Igoko's residence, they actually ran to it, according to the information gathered, he was preparing to travel out of the village.

Adanna ran like a man, she acted like a man, most times she spoke like a man, but she didn't look like a man, she had the graceful beauty of a woman. When they got to his residence which was a single hut, in a new large compound, with the help of Adanna he had been able to acquire a land, and build his first hut with plans to build others and also settle down, he was a longtime associate of Adanna who acted as the treasurer of the group. Unfortunately for him, he was now on Adanna's enemies list and ranked high in the selection order. He had disobeyed a simple instruction. In the group, Adanna had given them their payments, he would be the one to collect the money from Adanna and hand it over to the other members, when he got the money he refused to pay Fugrigo. Another member of the group on suspension, Igoko had cited insolence from Fugrigo as the reason he didn't pay him, however, he did not withhold the money only decided to delay paying Fugrigo. Adanna decided to punish him too, for the same insolence, he should have told her and not try to be a lord in the group, besides he also disrespected her by not obeying her instruction to pay everyone. Igoko's punishment was to forfeit his payment, by returning it to her, and meanwhile paying Fugrigo. Fugrigo wouldn't escape punishment, he was on suspension which meant he wouldn't earn or do anything for a while till Adanna decided to call him back. Igoko's only problem was that he had spent his own money and had nothing to pay Adanna back with, and it would rather be his head than his land or hut. When the due date to return the money had elapsed, Adanna decided to go after him, at least she needed to know how far his insolence had grown to. Igoko knew all their tactics on getting people but that was not an assurance, nobody he believed, in the group knew his new residence, but he was wrong, Adanna had discovered a long time ago even before he bought the land. When Adanna got to his compound there was no need for any tactics on luring him out, they simply rushed into his hut and caught him, he was indeed preparing to run, but had to wait for an acquaintance to come take his place, before he left. Only a few people knew him as the owner of the compound, if he left it empty and unoccupied another person could come to claim it. When he saw Adanna, he knew what awaited him and he confirmed what awaited him, when they dragged him towards a tree, he pleaded for mercy from Adanna. Experience made him believe he was wasting his time, but his mind encouraged him to plead on, as they dragged him on, he lost sight of his compound that was more tragic to him than his pending punishment, he would die for that land and hut. When they got to a tree they proceeded to tie him to it, Igoko pleaded some more, he knew the pain that would follow, after much pleading and assurance to Adanna he asked for more time, that did not stop Adanna, what stopped Adanna, was the fact Igoko had soiled himself. Nini was the first to notice he was urinating on himself the young man didn't point it out but ignored it and pretended he had not seen it.

"I am sorry" he said "Please forgive my mistake, I was planning of ways to pay back the money, I have spent the one given, I will get it back," he pleaded.

Adanna noticed liquid dropping from him, it was not any other liquid but urine. They cut him loose and left him no one said a word to him. Nini was a bit confused, did Adanna leave Igoko because he was scared of Adanna to the point of soiling himself or did Adanna consider it disgraceful that a man of his caliber soiled himself, if it was that, then Igoko wouldn't be joining the group again. They had gone a considerable distance back to Adanna's place, they passed the village square again. Matu's son who had heard in the morning that Adanna never laughed or smiled, saw Adanna smiling to herself also the men with her all wore a grin, and chatted. To many it was not a smile, to the boy Grini, Matu's son it was a smile. Adanna's lips were drawn to one side of her cheek, making her cheeks form arcs, the boy had heard it said that 'Adanna does not smile' long ago, before his father said it this morning, all his father did was confirm his hearsay that Adanna did not smile. The boy seeing her smile, was playing and chatting with his friends, when he saw her and the smile he ran off towards home, he ran with all his might back home, when he got home his mother was the first person he saw. She rushed to him terrified.

"Grini! what is it?" the mother asked, the boy panting.

"Mother I saw Adanna smiling" he said.

The woman was confused, "Okay, is that why you ran home?" she asked, he nodded in affirmation.

"Well she is human okay," the woman said, "She is just human, now go back to your friends" she said.

When the boy ran off, she quickly went to her husband who was at the barn arranging his wealth.

"My husband" she called, "Grini said, he saw Adanna smiling," Matu's countenance changed from gay to sadness.

"When?" he asked.

"Just now" she answered.

He shook his head in disbelief "What a pity" he finally said, and returned to attending his barn. His wife waited for an action from him but was certain none was going to come forth.

"Won't we do anything?" she asked.

"So that what will happen?" the man chided his wife when she brought the option to go to the elders and report it.

"So that people can start looking for their loved ones, Adanna does not laugh or smile for no reason, she only does so, when she has carried out a sinister act against someone."

To the Matu's what it meant was that someone, somewhere was hurting and in great pain at that moment because of Adanna. The man Matu, ignored his wife, he didn't want any trouble not with Adanna and certainly not with Ubiakwa whom he was owing. Whoever it was that was in pain because of Adanna was unfortunate, Matu himself did not want to be the reason why Adanna would smile.

CHAPTER 14

Adanna sat with her men waiting for the evening time, the village messenger gave an urgent message. Everyone was expected to turn up at the village square immediately, every single person was expected to turn up, the messenger shouting from outside concluded by saying "If you want to live and also any of your family members. You must attend and call your loved ones to attend with you."

He left to another location to deliver the same message till the whole villagers heard it. Adanna and his men looked amongst themselves and had a moment of silence, each person revisited the scene of all their actions. Could there be any way they made a mistake? They believed they had been impeccable in their dealings. Nini became uneasy, this was the part he hated so much, the part that marred the perfection he found in the group, each of them was completely certain, they would be among the reasons for the impromptu gathering. Guinta was not agitated, they wouldn't be caught, if they were, Ubiakwa would do his magic, it was a win/win situation for him, he had told Nini. Looking at Nini he had forgotten. They wouldn't be the first people to get there, though they didn't have much doing they sat and discussed about other things, most assuredly their plans for the evening if it wouldn't be able to be carried out because of the new development, though it was anticipated. Certain everyone must be there now, they strolled to the village square and made sure a handful of people saw them arrive, the elders had already sat and deliberated, an elder stood to speak, this was a very large crowd, more than was anticipated considering the short time notice, this was not for the oldest elder to speak, but the youngest not only the youngest but the loudest, when he motioned to the crowd, everywhere became quiet.

"People of Akom we won't be observing formalities, terrible things are happening," he said.

As if it was a new phenomenon, in Akom the people were now accustomed to terrible things. News of the evil acts of men against other men, only scared them, but didn't surprise or shock them, they have seen, heard, and imagined it all happening.

"There are reports that people are missing in Akom, this is not a new thing rather it has increased in proportion and frequency and we will not allow our own neighbours to insult us, by thinking we are weaklings who cannot defend themselves, this we all know and is already planning for. The disturbing one is the fact as has been announced and deliberated upon previously, we do not know who it is that always takes justice into their hands by attacking the indigenes of Akom, the same pattern has been recounted by almost all. The ingredients of being taken into the forest, severely punished in the forest and brought out to the footpath, left for dead and nothing, prior we have warned that such actions should you be the one carrying them out, your punishment is banishment, ostracizing or enslavement, the perpetrators have gone too far this time, attacking a noble man of Akom, a young promising talent all in the same day, dear people of Akom we will no longer tolerate such, if you are here."

As the man spoke, Adanna and her men wore a straight face unconcerned by the rhetoric, Nini was agitated but held his head up high, he knew Adanna had been doing what she was doing for a very long time and could not remember any time she got into trouble or was caught. The man was still speaking.

"Your punishment is death," the man said, "I repeat, should you be found out to be the perpetrator of this dastardly act you shall be killed, people of Akom, I greet you all" he said and stepped down, the people shouted in agreement and made a great noise at the decision, they were okay with it, the crowd dispersed. Adanna and her men were not the first to leave the crowd, neither were they the last rather they acted casual and was like everyone else, they wouldn't talk about it, no need to, the pronouncement brought great joy to Adanna, those she would deal with next would be paralyzed with fear, when they would realize despite the law against the act being carried out someone was still willing to take the risk which meant the person was above the law, and she was certain she was.

The day wouldn't require much anymore the sun would stay a while longer before going down. Adanna went home and gave her men food provision for the day, she knew they had food in their various homes, but she had to make sure they were well fed, they needed all the energy and no one would give her an excuse. They knew their job and they would do it, their priority was the Ubiakwa family, Adanna so many times had told them that the Ubiakwa family had enemies and she was out to protect her family, whoever came in the way, paid the price, most time with torn flesh, broken bones, loss of blood, when required, death. Adanna now in Ubiakwa's compound after all necessaries were done sent them home for the day. Adanna intended to plan herself and see about her journey. In all her travelling Guinta had been charged to maintain the group and keep their priority in her absence. Ubiakwa could summon warriors, and had guards both physically and spiritually, still the part she played was vital to his survival, as a great and the most wealthy man in Akom and its environs.

CHAPTER 15

Adanna with the hut all to herself, recounted all to be dealt with to secure peace till she returned, closing her eyes to have peace and calm herself, a slave knocked at the entrance, she ordered him to speak.

"It is a message from our master Ubiakwa" the slave said.

Adanna ordered him to come in, should it be something else it would have been delivered outside.

"Master Adanna, our great master wants you in his quarters now" the slave said again.

Adanna who had been reclining, sat up on her bamboo bed with her fingers she waved him away from the hut, as he was leaving Adanna was behind him, walking towards her father's hut with haste. Approaching it she could hear laughter and hearty chatters, he must have important guest. Why he would call for her was a question in her mind she couldn't answer, as she got closer their chatter and obviously, banter, grew louder, escaping the surrounding noises from other inhabitants of the compound to be more noticeable. Adanna had trained herself to be fearless, this should be a walk over, she may have fears of being around her father's friends sometimes, when she got to the hut of Ubiakwa where he entertained guest, she had already shaken off the fear, the anxiousness. Would she disgrace her father by her countenance and demeanour and also the attitude she had acquired? Ubiakwa seemed elated when Adanna arrived.

"That is her" he said to his friends, smiling. The two men nodded with smiles, they could confirm Adanna's beauty and grace for themselves now. She greeted the men with respect but not with the shyness and humility of girls her age. Which Adanna attributed to naivety and gullibility of the said girls.

"How are you my dear?" one of the men asked.

"Fine" Adanna said. Both men looked wealthy, they had adorned themselves with many jewelries, and they donned the clothes brought by the white men from the shore. Ubiakwa had such clothes but preferred to wear the traditional ones his father once wore. Surprisingly behind the men were three girls, also looking wealthy with the features of daughters of a wealthy man, well pampered and cultured, their physical structure to Adanna looked a bit modern just like her own. They were a bit slender in stature, unlike their past mothers, Ubiakwa proceeded to introduce the men, Adanna stood and nodded at every word.

"This is Ogo a Chief and the greatest, a humble farmer like myself but also an industrious man, with so many achievements he is a humble man I say, a humble man," Adanna greeted once again and "Thus" also Ubiakwa said, pointing to the second man,

"The man is Oko the names are similar he is also a farmer, a noble and wealthy man," Ubiakwa taking pride in knowing such people, as if to whisper it, he lowered his voice, "these men have dined with the white man" he said "In fact they have more white men as friends, than black men, also they have been to the white man's land and have seen what their place looks like, they have also seen our people over there, these men are not to be trifled with," Ubiakwa continued praising them. Adanna nodded and acted awed by their accomplishments, she wasn't only envious, she would like to do such, but did not know a woman who had been able to do such. After Ubiakwa was done with the praising, he turned to Adanna particularly now.

"How are you my daughter?" Ubiakwa asked.

"Fine father" Adanna answered, Ubiakwa nodded. Ubiakwa from time to time asked his children about their welfare and how they were faring, but Adanna was certain, he did not know what their huts now looked like, only occasionally did he visit, which Adanna was sure was not more than three times since she came into this world, her brothers could remember maybe only once, but they knew their father to be a caring man, who was after the good of his children. He pointed Adanna's attention towards the girls seated behind the men.

"Your friends are here to see you" he said.

Adanna couldn't hide the surprise and confusion on her face, she had no friends, she had never had any friends, if she had ever had, Ubiakwa did not know about it. Adanna looked at the girls again, she had never seen them not even in her dreams, Adanna looked at Ubiakwa again, unsure what to say or do, her bane, the situation she hated most being in a state of weakness and confusion, she stood, rigid. Ubiakwa eased her pain.

"Go and sit," he said pointing to another seat by the right which was opposite the girls'.

"Wait for me" he said.

Adanna obeyed and sat gently straining not to look at the girls.

"I have no friends and I need no friends," she said to herself. Ubiakwa continued discussing with his friends, this time they made conversations in low tones, and to Adanna they were wrapping up the day's business, in a short while they greeted each other warmly, the discussion was over. The men smiled and made promises, Ubiakwa's smile was the broadest, to Adanna he just wrapped up another business deal to make himself richer. The men turned and waved at the girls, Adanna included, the four girls bowed and bid them farewell. When they were out of the hut, Ubiakwa called the four girls to come forward with smiles. It was a long bench carved out from a tree trunk the three girls sat together and Adanna made sure to give enough space between her and them while sitting on the same bench. Ubiakwa smiled when he noticed their sitting arrangements, he drew closer to the three girls.

"I have lost my voice, business is a hard thing to do" he said. He was lying his voice was perfectly fine, he wanted Adanna to come closer. Ubiakwa when he wanted to talk to her considering her distance raised his voice, the one he had lost, but talking to the girls he went back to a low voice sometimes whispering, so that Adanna would get closer. Adanna could hear him from her position, he noticed it and lowered his voice even more, Adanna now stretched her neck to hear him. Ubiakwa sensing the pattern wouldn't work, she would rather not hear him, than mingle with the girls, took action, the girls all looking cheerful and attentive to Ubiakwa had heard much about Adanna but knew little about her.

"Adanna" Ubiakwa called, "Why not come and sit here" Ubiakwa pointed to the space directly before him, occupied by Gbetu, the tall beautiful one who sat in the middle.

"My daughter please adjust" Ubiakwa pleaded.

Gbetu was happy to, and she gracefully obliged. The position made Adanna uncomfortable, that meant she would sit in between two girls. It had never happened to her before, with Adanna seated in between, Ubiakwa began introducing them all for the benefit of Adanna, the three girls already knew themselves.

"From my left is Rimma," Ubiakwa said. All four women occupied the highest echelon in all ramifications for women, nobility, beauty wealth, status, privilege, talent, gift and affection from admirers. In more than one way, they were equal, to a high degree.

"And the second is, Adanna, my daughter," Ubiakwa said, with pride smiling at Adanna.

"Ladies" he said to the other girls "You all must know she is my backbone, her benefits to me are innumerable," the girls nodded.

"The next is Gbetu," Gbetu smiled, Adanna looked at her and guessed her weak point, Gbetu loved praises and appreciation and constantly needed people's recommendation to feel beautiful and worthy. A day she went without anyone praising her, she would feel she had become ugly or not wanted, constant praise and adulation was her wine.

"And the last but not the least, is Fima," she smiled shyly too, "This is how far I can go with the introduction, with time you all will get to know better, about yourselves and all, any way my beautiful girls."

They adjusted themselves, Ubiakwa, took a long time to come up with this idea, on how to start the discussion and even what to discuss about, though it was still a pathetic attempt it still had merit in it.

"My daughters" he said, "I am an old man, I have convened you people here to ask you people a disturbing question. You know we elders do not know it all, so let us say, I am seeking your perspective and advice on a particular matter that is worrying and disturbing not only to me but to all the communities involved. Our men do not believe women can reason or make an intelligent suggestion, there are abundant misogynist in our days and male chauvinist also, but I was guided to the right part by a woman, whose advice I took and have not regretted since then, it was not only my mother but also my wives whose advice, not once but innumerably have changed my life for the better. So here is the problem, we have a terrible situation, a group of people are going about, inflicting injury and grievous bodily harm to people of this village, they go about hurting people as such no one is safe anymore, their victims end up shattered, and beyond repair by our physicians. A young man who was unfortunate to have encountered them today was a promising wrestler, but now with his injuries he will never wrestle again and he has threatened to commit a sacrilege by taking his life. You are future mothers, and you will have children, we must protect ourselves, so I have called you beautiful ladies here to give me your ideas, thoughts and insights towards this menace so that we can safeguard ourselves, our people are dying like chicken and at this rate, we will be wiped out, if nothing serious is done to arrest the situation. Now over to you girls remember the knowledge you give me I will present same to the elders for a better deliberation, now over to you, what do you think?"

Ubiakwa said all not looking at Adanna, the question he had asked was the secondary reason he convened the girls, he had a primary reason. Adanna was unaware of Ubiakwa's motive, everything he said was reasonable.

Fima was the first to indicate intention to answer, already the girls were feeling out of place, they had never bothered themselves to think such things, as the men handled such matters. Others would think a bit harder, before making an attempt to answer. Fima, clearing her throat, greeted everyone her courtesy was spotless.

"Thank you our master for the privilege, for me I will say, let our warriors work non-stop, let us have permanent warriors who will patrol our borders and foot tracks, they can divide themselves, some should be watchmen, some guard the forest paths, if possible, seeing it has almost all part of it as an exist and entrance. Let them also investigate, and fight should war break out, then more and all members of the village can join in the war but if we have men walking around, this evil people will not have such a free time and easy access, that is my humble submission our master," Fima said.

Ubiakwa felt glad he asked this, this could make him forget his primary intention. Gbetu ready to speak now, indicated her interest, Ubiakwa gave her the opportunity to speak.

"Our master, I think it all lies in the Chief Priest, let him make more potent medicine to expose this people, also let him call the spirits to guard and effect punishment immediately. I believe the spirits are omniscient and omnipotent let them fight for us, if I may be so bold, though I will take your rebuke with gratitude, we can ask for potent medicine from other villages to add to our own, only gods can fight this battle, thank you our master for this privilege." She said.

Adanna was looking at something, deep, deep, inside the ground, Ubiakwa had been glancing at her, her eyes had been fixed to a particular spot on the ground, and she was fully concentrated on the thing. Ubiakwa himself even had to look at the spot on the ground himself, he saw nothing that his daughter was seeing. He was certain she was seeing something. Rimma indicated her interest in contributing and appreciated Ubiakwa like others.

"For me master, people should be stopped from entering the forest, they are to only enter with permission, or at an appointed time, with that anyone entering or exiting on the prohibited day will be questioned, this evil people will find it hard to carry out their objectives on the allowed days should they find out a lot of people are also in the forest with them. And again only a designated portion should be allowed for everyone, other portions should be restricted with potent medicine and guarding spirits." Rimma said.

Ubiakwa felt a mixture of pride and sadness, sadness because most men wallowed in ignorance for ignoring the women in their lives and pride because the women made a considerable and intelligent contribution. Ubiakwa turned to Adanna she was the last person, and was still staring at that spot intently.

"Adanna do you have anything to say about your acti... the actions I meant to say, the actions we are discussing," Ubiakwa almost let himself out, that would have been a terrible slip of tongue, thank the gods he caught himself at the word your 'action', Adanna was aware he knew, she couldn't believe her father's attempt at playing a con artist. Previous accounts showed it was her pattern of serving justice, the only difference was that her recent victims were now blindfolded and gagged, nothing else. As such they did not know who their captors were and no one had verbally pointed towards her, some inwardly did. For the prior accounts Adanna had argued, those were blackmailers and slanderers, backbiting and wishing to do her harm. On those days, by the time Adanna was done defending herself, her accusers began to question their sanity, could it be they had been hallucinating? They would be certain it was Adanna, however her adamant refusal and display of innocence made them confused. She had so refined her acts now that no witnesses came up anymore. Ubiakwa was accustomed to paying her heavy fines, thank the gods, he didn't become poor because of her. Adanna removed her eyes from the ground, an ignorant person that knew nothing about her would think, the eyes were showing she was thinking. She was not thinking, she was saddened at Ubiakwa's attempt to play a con artist or trickster. Business acumen and wealth acquisition "YES", but not subtlety or apt at playing mind games, he was just not good at it. She knew Ubiakwa had a part of him assuring him, she had a hand in the events. Re-adjusting herself, she decided to answer. "For me," she said, "Father I think our people should always gather and people be taught certain things that can help them. For example, not meddling in other people's affairs, or being troublesome or quarrelsome, even threatening people arbitrarily and so much more, people should be called together and taught these things." Adanna said.

There was nothing Ubiakwa had not heard or seen in his lifetime, if there were, they were very few, and this just made the list smaller, subtracting hugely from it. Adanna returned to staring at the ground.

"My daughters," Ubiakwa said after recovering from Adanna's shocking statement. "You have more thinking ability than most of the men in Akom, I tell you majority has not thought about the suggestions you all made. I will quickly run to them with these ideas, I won't tell them they are from women, lest they treat it with contempt, I will only tell them afterwards that the knowledge of women rescued them, you all are blessed and wonderful. I appreciate you all, for what you have done, indeed I am grateful, please I must run to my fellow chiefs with haste. To our visitors your coming is impromptu, and once again I appreciate. I would have asked you spend the night, seeing the sun will soon go down but the truth is we didn't arrange such for you, seeing Otindu is not too far. However do you wish to stay, my daughter has clothes and I myself have so many that no one has ever worn and I have several huts for you, I am sure we can arrange that."

Adanna quickly cut in "They can go father, I myself will be amongst their escort, I will personally escort them," she said smiling.

Ubiakwa had never seen such an ugly smile before, again he subtracted from the few things he had not seen, or heard, he took a while to consider Adanna's proposition. It may even serve the purpose better he reasoned.

"Alright then Adanna shall escort you, then come back, I believe six of my guards and the six that brought you, plus my daughter is enough escorts to guard one safely to his or her destination, alright," he said, checking if he has forgotten to say anything.

"Please" he said remembering one, "I will ask that you people plan amongst yourselves, for a day to come and spend a week with my daughter," looking at Adanna "I know you are busy but I demand you stay and spend a week indoors with your friends. I believe it will be a worthwhile experience for all of us, please my daughter."

Adanna still wore the ugly smile, her saving grace was her beauty. To Ubiakwa he had seen people smiling and he was certain what Adanna was doing now, was not smiling. He looked at her.

"Are you alright with everything?" he asked, Adanna nodded and changed the pattern of her smile, but one thing remained, it was another pattern of having an ugly superficial smile.

"Great we have an agreement then," Ubiakwa said ignoring the smile, "Please come back quickly you know we live in a very dangerous time, things are dangerous and pitiful now," he warned.

Ubiakwa stood up and left. The ladies all assembled and marched towards Adanna's hut. She had requested to get her equipment. When she came out, everyone was ready the twelve guards were with them, the girls smiled at her, but she knew it was not genuine, she felt peace when they spoke, showing they were not going to hide anything from her, or be dubious with her, not having any form of secrecy. She preferred open people with nothing to hide.

"Why do you need so many weapons?" Gbetu asked.

Adanna looked at her with a surprised face, "For protection what else."

Gbetu didn't agree, with her reasoning, "It is the gods that protect, look," she said, showing Adanna a bangle, "The Chief Priest gave me this for protection, so believe me, if anyone wants protection they should seek the Chief Priest" Gbetu said.

"Very soon even the Chief Priest will be sold into slavery," Adanna said.

Everyone was offended, with Adanna's statement.

"The Chief Priest is too powerful to be seen as a mere man," Fima protested.

Adanna knew where they were going, she did not answer the question asked by Gbetu, if she didn't believe in the gods, such discussion wouldn't help anyone, especially her. She ignored all their protest and accounts of the Chief Priest's prowess, how he disappears, heals people, cannot die, can cause sickness, and so much more. Seeing Adanna had ignored them, they imagined they had defeated her.

"Let us say more lovely things." Rimma suggested as they all walked gracefully and gallantly. Adanna's footsteps had no difference with the guards. The guards sharing themselves, into four groups were allowed to surround the women. Where the path was too narrow they stayed ahead and behind, with their pace, they would get to their destination by twilight, which would disrupt Adanna's plans. She had to protect her father's image, not only by fighting or violence but also extending his warmth. He considered the girls to be valuable as such she must treat them with care, for her, she would have made great advancement walking to their destination, but with the girls walking with leisure pace, it would not be possible.

Rimma deciding to put cordiality into the group, "I believe we do not know much about ourselves, so I suggest we introduce ourselves, and say something about ourselves, I will go first" Rimma said, "I am Rimma Uboku, my father is the great Uboku, he majorly farms, as I have been told he was the first to farm the crops brought by the white man and given to our fore fathers of at least the past four generations, my father growing up was a dancer."

The girls applauded except Adanna, she wouldn't be faulted, her hands were occupied. She had a machete in her right hand, machete and not sword, and in her left hand she had a spear, should fight ensue she would sheath the machete and use the spear, she also wore her bow and arrow quiver with two daggers on her waist, these were the ones the guards could see. They were certain there were more weapons in her animal skin bag, they wondered why they bothered to protect her. Rimma continued.

"Though my father is predominantly a farmer his other times he spends as a dancer, my mother is his fifth wife, and he has close to thirty children, I have not counted all, I see new ones every day, my mother is also a dancer, and she sings also, I am from Otimbu that is all, Oh and I have six siblings, three girls and three boys, I believe that is all," Rimma said.

Gbetu said hers, "Well also I am from Otimbu region of Akom and have heard about the Uboku's and believe they are a wonderful family, a wealthy and noble family, for myself my father is relatively young. I am his first daughter, my name is Gbetu Aduome, my father is a merchant he sells only the white man's goods, their guns, their drinks, their jewelries, almost anything they fancy to bring to us for our human cargo, my father sells them all. Sometimes the chiefs give to him to sell and return the proceeds to them, while also taking a share from it. My father also farms, mostly yam and he is also a herder we can boast of more animals than we can of food, just like everyone else our farming sometimes is subsistence. Unlike other people, who farm for others."

To Adanna she must have missed the question or the reason that originated the talk, she politely demanded an opportunity to ask a question, she was obliged.

"Are we talking about ourselves or about our parents, for me, we wish to know ourselves not our fathers, for that I will show an example," the girls were lost at this, they may have never thought about it that way. Gbetu was certain she had no identity of herself, sometimes she thought she was everything sometimes she realized how empty she was. Adanna was beginning to give an example with herself "I am Adanna," the other name was not necessary, besides they already knew it, "Am a hunter I have been able to hunt, since I started becoming a woman and now I have passed my target of how many animals I wanted to kill, I have hunted and killed all sorts, and I have no preference for hunting a particular animal. I dance but I have only danced when my father forced me to, aside that I have never done it on my own, I like to travel, my favourite meal is cocoyam in any form I can eat it, but I eat other foods too, and I can eat almost any kind of animal and I drink palm wine, only the fresh one I detest the fermented one, I won't see myself as a farmer or any other thing, that is all for now," Adanna said.

Fima smiled, "Okay I guess it is my turn," she said, it took her a while "I am Fima Kogie and I like the white man's yellow colour, I like to weave, I in fact make hand fans, but I don't sell them myself, my slaves do, and I also dance. I have not seen most of the things I crave to, but I know, I will one day like to go to the white man's land and see their world, nobody talks about their world," Gbetu and Rimma, rejected it making the 'gods forbid it' sign, it was an unimaginable prospect.

Fima continued "I only prefer drinking water, my father is a farmer so is my mother and all my household but I have chosen to weave, I have a secret I want to share," the word secret peaked the girls' ears, even the guards came closer, Fima had a secret who wouldn't want to know about it, Adanna was attentive now.

"I heard there is a village that has a blacksmith and for a long while I made attempts to abscond and go join him, but I never did, because I am a woman and I have my limits. Again, anyway," she hesitated, "this is supposed to be news for another time but we can start talking about it now, I will be getting married soon."

The girls cheered again, except Adanna, what is the fuss about marriage she always wondered, people do it every day and every time. With the new direction the girls now talked about themselves and not their fathers. Adanna was beginning to notice something, their voices were getting louder, and their graceful noble demeanours were evaporating little by little. They were beginning to feel the air of freedom, carefree lifestyle; hopefully they wouldn't forget to observe their gracefulness when in a formal setting.

"I know we have asked before," Gbetu said, "But don't you think carrying these weapons, makes you look like a man?" she asked looking at Adanna who was now laconic.

"I have a womb to sustain a child and birth it, also I can give suck to a child, that makes me woman enough. Nobody is exempted from seeking long life or protecting herself, men won't always be around to fight for you, my weapons in no way stops me from being a full woman," Adanna said.

Gbetu agreed with Adanna for a flit of a moment, thoughts of her carrying weapons, and being like Adanna crossed her mind, but it was farfetched.

Rimma wished to go further, "But we all have our roles to play," she said, "We should concentrate on being women, doing the things women do, like, loving, caring, parenting and helping, being beautiful and graceful. While the men keep to their violence and work and fighting and every unnecessary stress meant for them. The children keep to their role of only being obedient and making their parents happy. The elders, the aged and weak, keep to releasing all the experience they have gathered and increasing the knowledge of the young. In such a way the society will function better, everyone to his own space allocated by the gods," Rimma said.

Gbetu was in conflict now, she just supported Adanna and her opinion on doing like a man, now Rimma was making sense, finally she decided to be like Fima and be neutral.

"Listen," Adanna was about to counter her argument, when the guard in front made a sign for them to stop, and be quite. He was hearing something, a rustling in the bush, he waited a while to hear it again but didn't. Everyone heightened their sense of hearing now,

Adanna's was akin to a dog's but she had been discussing with the girls, and paid no attention, after a long while walking slowly, Adanna could sense something was wrong she ordered them to stop. The path they were on, was a single file pathway, they all lined up, one after the other, at both sides were tall bushes with no trees in sight, the trees were further inlands, she couldn't see anything but the air had changed and she sensed evil hovering over them.

"Everyone on guard" Adanna commanded, she balanced the machete's handle well in her palm and was ready to strike, the three girls huddled together with four guards circling them, all weapons drawn, everyone quiet and looking around, Adanna gave a command.

"If anything happens everyone should run towards Akom," she said.

Rimma agitated suggested otherwise, "We are too close to Otimbu" she said, "We have passed halfway, why go back a longer distance?" Rimma asked.

Adanna wanted to answer, that 'Akom was safer,' for Otimbu they don't know what may have become of it. It may have been raided since they left it, besides she was confident in Akom warriors other than anyone else. If nothing they had "OBIAGU" in Akom, but before she could answer and counter Rimma, twelve men with great speed, force, a tremendous incontestable accuracy, rushed out from the bush like air, with spears in their hands, they went through the guards, killing eight of the guards instantly. The girls took to flight; they ignored Adanna's instruction and ran towards the direction they were facing, which was Otimbu region of Akom instead of the main (central) Akom as they called it. The guards with them, the four remaining guards, were Ubiakwa's guards, Adanna for a split moment was shocked and frightened, frightened because the men's precision, was uncanny and extremely professional they were not ordinary men. The two extra attackers had gone for Adanna, they wanted to guard the front and rear, blocking the girls exist to either direction, the girls were however able to run past him, because, one of Ubiakwa's guard had challenged him, throwing his spear towards the attacker, once again, the attacker knocked it off course, another display of great skill. The guard ran past him, with the girls making a head way also, the attacker re-adjusted himself trying to make a better stand, and stage another offensive. The guard picked up his spear and ran back to meet the attacker. Two of Ubiakwa's guards were left to fight the twelve men, they wouldn't necessarily be fighting but would block the way, allowing Adanna and others to escape, and that was exactly what they did, blocking the way, and moving backwards slowly. This time their back was facing Otimbu, they were not allowing the attackers to encircle them. As men they always refused to go into battle with bow and arrow, Ubiakwa's men, showed great skill and intelligence themselves. The twelve attackers split themselves and eight ran into the bush to move undetected, it would be a handful for the guards, but they could still delay, seeing the men run into the bush, they too ran into the bush each into the opposite direction. The remaining four on the path couldn't pass also, because they could not see the where about of the two guards, neither could they hear anything. For the four, looking at the bush didn't help much, because should one make a movement in the bush, anyone could see the top of the bushes moving to indicate someone was steering it at that particular position, now it was of no use both camps moved with stealth, and there was also no way to tell who was who. As the other two guards with the girls ran, the girls were not fast enough to run to safety, their pace was pathetic and discouraging; they were already panting and stumbling, due to loss of energy their legs were becoming rigid and fatigued. It would be better if they stopped, carrying them unconscious would be impossible, after they stumbled and fell repeatedly each time standing more slowly and more slowly, the guards ordered them to stop.

"We will go and help, if we continue at this pace, they will catch up with us and kill us all, if we go back we will help our brothers withstand much longer, so you can get back into Otimbu," they said gasping lightly, "Move on into Otimbu, delaying them is our best option now," they said.

"It is a good plan, I will take over from here," Adanna said.

And the men left, running towards their demise with courage and faith, for the life of another, simply because they were born to die. Seeing they were already facing Otimbu, they ran faster for their lives, Adanna was sure that for herself she would have been on the return journey, if it were for her, but now, all she hoped was that they stayed strong enough to continue running at any pace. Adanna ordered them to leave the path and move into the bush for cover, they have never done it before, but they didn't hesitate they ran into the bush, with the tall grasses slashing across their pampered skins, skins which had seen many years of oiling and perfuming, nothing would be too great a sacrifice for their lives now. They ran and Adanna was solidly behind them, she had attempted to lead, and found out they lagged behind, all she could do now was stay behind and encourage them, to her surprise the girls continued to run. They ran a great distance, just when she was getting surprised and wanted to praise; Gbetu slumped with a heavy thud. That was bad news, great bad news, Adanna got to her. Others who got to her did not stop to attend to her but to gain breath themselves, they too slumped to the ground, the only difference was that they sat up. Gbetu was unconscious, Adanna looked around perplexed, she couldn't carry Gbetu, run, look around, guard, guide and still fight, the girls with her looked so uncertain they could carry themselves now let alone carry someone else, she roused them up from the ground.

"Carry her, the Odemili brook is not far away we can revive her there and don't forget we must make haste, there are deadly people after us, our delay will amount to us not seeing tomorrow, or attending the future marriage ceremony, we planned."

Fima hearing that quickly got up, not her own marriage. The two girls carried Gbetu, each wimping and exhaling, they would walk a little while and would drop Gbetu like a log of wood, they were actually walking now.

"She is human and I hope you people know that" Adanna said, whenever they dropped her like wood. They ignored her calculating how long they could continue before they too collapsed. The two girls did a good job carrying Gbetu, when they sighted the brook they dropped her on the ground again.

"We will drop her into the brook" Adanna said pointing at the brook "And here is not the brook." She said.

The two girls acting like they just regained consciousness and realized indeed there was not a brook took up Gbetu again this time almost dragging her, and finally with the last ounce of their strength dropped her into the brook. Like magic, it worked and Gbetu was revived, they too revived themselves by sprinkling and splashing water from the brook onto themselves. Adanna stood at the bank looking at them patiently, the three of them were red eyed and faint, she would have to do something, after the brook was Otimbu, but before getting to the residential area, a little distance of about 2 miles would have to be made, Adanna roused them up and encouraged them to save their lives. Gbetu resuscitated and aware of the situation now, shook her head in negation, resigning to fate. "Today is my last day on earth" she said, "I can't believe I died this way, tell my family I am sorry. I can't move," she was weeping bitterly now, "so please you all can go without me, I am terribly sorry but there is nothing I can do, life is vain, please go on without me, I will see you in the afterlife" she said sobbing, they could even distinguish the tears from the water on her face. With her crying, Rimma and Fima joined and started weeping too, they were all fatigued and had resigned to fate.

"Very touching and heartwarming," Adanna said, still standing at the bank and looking at them "I will save the attackers the trouble and kill you three myself, no need to wait for them, and after I am done killing the three of you I will kill your family members also."

They had stopped crying now and were looking at Adanna with confusion.

"Are you sure you want to die with the rest of your families?" Adanna asked, they were uncertain of the answer but said "No" because Adanna was approaching with her machete raised.

"Very good, then get up and move, that is Otimbu I am looking at not anywhere else, don't let me repeat myself," Adanna said, still approaching with her machete in hand, the three girls scampered, they stood and walked straight towards Otimbu, without looking at Adanna or each other. When they got close to the forest, Adanna ordered them to stop, before they could enter she scouted the forest.

"The forest is where the danger is," she said "Not the bush, here they can be on tree tops, they can be behind the trees, they can be behind shrubs with broad leaves, and they can attack easily, so here is the greater danger, because they can out number us and even lay traps everywhere, our men are not here so we must protect ourselves now," Adanna said.

She took her spear and gave it to Gbetu she was slightly taller and it would be more useful to her, to Fima she took out all her daggers, both of them actually, and then she gave her something from her pouch, another dagger, Fima inserted two to her waist, to Rimma, Adanna smiled and gave her, her machete. Rimma at first thought it was honour but she was wrong, she just did not know Adanna. Adanna looking at her as she had vehemently and vociferously argued about the importance of being a woman, and maintaining her place, had given her the machete, and the machete was too heavy for Rimma. She had collected it seeing the ease with which Adanna had held it and felt it would be the same with her, when she took the machete it almost fell from her and chopped off her toes, aware now she carried it with two hands.

"I can't carry this" she said in a whisper to Adanna, "How do I carry this?" she asked Adanna, trying to hold the machete up.

"Maybe you should carry it on your head," Adanna answered.

Rimma felt hurt with the answer and started sobbing again, Adanna seeing her shed tears couldn't believe it.

"Ubiakwa!" she grunted under her breath silently, and rolled her eyes, she was a bit frustrated at the condition the man had put her into, babysitting grown-ups in the face of danger, she got to Rimma who was still sobbing.

"This is the one time you act like a man, just this one time, you act like a man, carry the machete like a man, we will all make it," Adanna said.

Feeling encouraged Rimma rebalanced the machete in her palm, this time she held the sharp side in her left palm while holding the handle with her right, she carried the machete with two hands. Adanna wanted to scream at her and ask her, where she had ever seen a man holding the sharp point of a machete, but she didn't, she was not the only one not holding a weapon properly, everyone held their peace. The last thing she needed was a rift in the group. She knew with experience, a rift in a group was a very difficult thing to overcome, especially to a leader, everyone took sides and the opposition became the most dangerous enemy, an enemy that most times only their death in Adanna's thinking could guarantee peace.

Adanna looked at all three of them, Rimma was still almost carrying the machete with the sharp edge buried deep in her left palm, Gbetu held the spear like a holy stick. Priests in the shrine holding calabashes full of potent medicine, or poison or the most sacred objects, have never been so careful, what's more she was looking at the spear and walking, rather than her environment. Fima held the daggers, in such an awkward way that you would think she was trying to kill the great god, living in the sky, at least she was looking at where she was going even though her weapons faced another direction. Adanna was certain she was all alone in this one, she drew her bow ready to fire at any enemy and making sure it was only an enemy. She looked toward the four cardinal points, slowly they moved through the forest and it seemed like forever to the four ladies. Fima dropped a dagger to the ground from her hand anytime she heard a sound, Gbetu was still holding the spear, now her hands were shaking terribly, to her she was holding a venomous snake and must not make many movements, lest it struck her. More than thrice Adanna had noticed Rimma almost dropping the machete at the slightest sound of anything and running away, what was worse Adanna was certain she would run backwards, facing Akom she had argued against earlier on, instead of forward towards her village, she concentrated some more and ignored them. If only the forest would be quiet, the sun was disappearing, meaning when returning home it would be too dark, she was not going to spend the night in anyone's home, not her Adanna.

*****

The four guards did their best against the attackers they had been able to delay them longer than they anticipated, the wits had favoured both sides and there was still a lot to do. They were certain Adanna and her group had not made it into Otimbu now, rather than engage the men in fight, they concentrated more on fighting and running away just to delay some more, it was a tactics of playing nuisance.

*****

Ubiakwa got home and was certain Adanna was back too and also there would be a change in her. The primary motive was to get Adanna associate with girls and feel like a girl. He believed as he was advised, if she got to be with lovely girls she would fancy being like them. She had all it took, and he was certain, he was going to send her away for some time to be with the girls.

Gbetu, Rimma and Fima were lauded as extremely virtuous ladies. Unknown to the four of them, their parents wanted them to mingle with each other and be influenced in a good way. Maybe Adanna would soften, after seeing them and being with them. Women did not go the path she had chosen and there must be a change in Adanna. When he got home and asked about her, he was told she was not back yet. That was unlike her, she couldn't have changed so easily and readily something must be wrong, he called on his servant and asked them to run and call Akom warriors. Ubiakwa could summon Akom warriors whenever the need arose, after all he fed them. They didn't converge but ran out immediately from their various positions, towards Otimbu. When the servants returned to Ubiakwa and told him they had sent off warriors but couldn't find 'Obiagu', Ubiakwa was livid and frustrated, he would have been relieved if Obiagu was with them, Obiagu not going with them was a terrible bad news. They assured him they sent enough well trained and strong and they were also informed it was on Ubiakwa's errand. Ubiakwa felt unhappy at the news Obiagu couldn't be found to be sent along with them, Obiagu assured certainty.

*****

When the warriors got to the spot swiftly, they saw the dead bodies, immediately they knew who did it, and they too delved into the bush. To catch them you must play their pattern, the guards had succeeded in delaying but two of the attackers had followed deeper parts of the bush to escape and head towards the girls, which was unknown to the guards.

*****

When the two attackers saw Adanna they succumbed to that which killed many, they looked down upon the girls. Immediately they entered the forest Adanna with her uncanny ability to detect things, noticed they had company, she told the girls to stop, she looked around more frantically and disorderly now, not knowing where the attack was going to come from. Gbetu looked at the tip of the spear, as she held it up high, still shivering, only Rimma wore courage on her face, but she held the machete all wrong, the machete would do more damage to her than her victim. Fima's eyes were popping out, the way the eyes popped out you would think she was trying to see the invisible world inhabited by spirits, fear was written all over her face, soon she would start crying, her heart pounded so fast it would give up soon too. Finally Adanna detected the attackers, the attackers had to move swiftly, darkness didn't favour them, and they were in a distance from which they could catch the girls should they attempt to run. Stop moving Adanna ordered the girls, Gbetu took the order too far, she stopped blinking and was trying to stop her heart from beating using her mind, it was making too much noise. Rimma was bent low, looking at the wrong direction, since the attackers could be anywhere in the forest, maybe she should look down. Fima's palm was so sweaty the daggers were slipping from her grips. Adanna swiftly turning, caught a shadow run behind a tree, she fixed her gaze towards that direction, the men had the time against them, darkness was approaching, then they emerged from behind the tree. Adanna released her arrow, but it missed them, the men exchanged a look, which meant to them, she was a good shooter. They had to be careful, when the other girls saw the two men, running towards them in a hap hazard manner, crisscrossing each other, trying to dodge Adanna's arrows and also make her targeting one of them extremely difficult. As expected the ladies dropped their weapons and held each other, forming a circle, they closed their eyes tightly with shoulders puffed up, like a child who saw an adult raise his hand to hit them, they were anxiously waiting for a deadly blow to descend upon them. The men continued running in the confusing pattern, and were gaining ground, closing up the space between them. Adanna knew what they were doing and knew it was a smart plan, but they did not know her, she had hunted the swiftest of the animals, the fastest, the most dangerous, those with extreme surviving instincts, and she had killed them all, what was more she killed majority of them in the night.

Adanna picked a particular spot in front of her, since her third shot she fired and missed, she had not fired again. She had monitored the men and just like most animals that were on the run, when she killed them, she guessed their movement, she imagined where they stepped next and she fired towards that direction, so that when they stepped at that exact position, her already released arrow would catch them, it was a good training the animals gave her, now she would use it for humans. She picked a spot, the two men this time were behind a tree. They ran haphazardly and interchanged position all the while moving closer, just as if Adanna could read their minds, she took a target, anticipated they were about to leave the tree, immediately they left the tree she fired at the middle point where they would interchange, the arrow went through the neck of one of the attackers.

Adanna was a bit relieved, the arrow was meant for the two of them, if they had come a bit closer, it would have pierced the two of them joining them together. The remaining one knew going back was not an option, he was however confused when arrows began to fly from impossible directions from Adanna's position towards him, he looked to his right from behind the huge tree he was hiding and noticed there were more than ten people firing now, he grew hot with anger, the mission was futile and over. But he wouldn't run to escape, if he was caught it had had a terrible consequence, in all ways he would still die in no distant time, he decided he would die together with Adanna, it would be a revenge for his colleague. More arrows flew at his direction, each time getting to his front which meant, the people were coming from Adanna's direction, and were trying to encircle him, he left the tree and ran towards Adanna with the intent to kill her. Adanna noticed but rather than run backwards, Adanna stood her ground, seeing him, she fired an arrow and caught his thigh, that stopped him momentarily, he stood again, more angry and determined, his veins popping out, and lining all his body, with blood shot eyes he continued running towards her. Adanna released another arrow and pierced his abdomen the next shot was for his heart, those that have been firing kept firing, piercing the attacker's body with arrows. With him still facing Adanna she changed her mind and pierced his Adam's apple. Certain of death the man screeched and raised his machete to strike lurching forward, covering a distance of 20 feet with two steps, swift with 8 feet remaining Adanna with the speed of a cheetah grabbed the spear from the ground where Gbetu had dropped it and without looking at the attacker thrust the man through the mouth. Adanna had one knee on the ground and one up. The spear protruded and came out through the skull, his grey matter splashed out, the machete dropped to the ground from his hand, then he fell rigidly first forward and then sideway with the spear piercing further. Adanna took her bow again and was ready to fire when some men appeared from the trees, those that had been firing, they were hunters, from Otimbu. The girls were still waiting for death, when they heard Adanna's voice telling them to stand up, Gbetu looked up first opening one eye slightly then the second eye, she saw the men and noticed they were friendly, then she saw Adanna, looking at them with drops of blood on her, the three girls were up now. Rimma looked on the ground and saw the attacker beside Adanna, a spear through his mouth to his skull his eyes blood shot, and wide open she screamed and ran backwards. Gbetu sighting it began to vomit, Fima was stoned seeing it, she had never seen a dead body. Adanna was sad for her, now she was going to have countless nightmares.

The men approached and introduced themselves as hunters, they knew the girls but didn't know Adanna, as they discussed offering their help to escort them. Adanna decided to follow them and also fancied returning alone, she was not going to sleep over. As they prepared to leave with Adanna picking up all her weapons, she would abandon the spear and would get a new one, she got to Fima and asked for her daggers, instead of Fima giving them to Adanna, she raised her hands up as if surrendering to be arrested by a village militia, she also closed her eyes, the sight was pathetic. Adanna shook her head, and took the daggers from the sides of her waist, she actually inserted the two into one place. Certain

Adanna had taken the forbidden objects from her, she opened her eyes and turned towards home, with no one leading or guarding her. They all took it as queue and followed, they heard steps behind each man turned and was ready to release an arrow. Adanna stopped them when she saw it was Akom warriors, she motioned for them to come up, they ran towards her and lighted their torches. In drove they escorted the girls home to their various homes, with a crowd that had gathered from the village, anyone seeing them followed to know what was happening. The girls were quiet and subdued, ready to rush into the arms of their parents and definitely sleep there for months. The nightmares would be endless and disturbing. When they escorted them to their homes, none of them said a word, Adanna was certain, those that wanted to abscond and join a blacksmith would find it hard to even dream or think again of such things, and to Adanna's relieve none of them promised to make an attempt to see or visit each other again, no promises to meet again at all.

Adanna was certain she wouldn't be visiting any of them for any reason, at least now she had an excuse, the girls could only manage to hug, and bow their heads like a disgraced woman. Adanna bid farewell, and turned to return to Akom with Akom warriors. When she asked who the attackers were she was simply told they were mercenaries for a chief priest and it could be any chief priest, all they were looking for was to use them for sacrifice, use their organs to prepare different potion for different people.

"People are hunted not only for slavery and such alike, but now also for sacrifice by a Chief Priest," one said as they marched home to Akom.

CHAPTER 16

It had been days now and the Chief Priest had not been able to ascertain who murdered Amadi. The wife of Amadi and daughter had been pestering him to find out who killed their beloved. Obirika and Nne still mourning went to the house of Ubiakwa again, this time Adanna was not around, she had gone to her uncle's village, all that the family of Ubiakwa could do was to assure them that they had nothing to do with the death of Amadi. Meanwhile Adanna in her uncle's village went to meet Okanoka the 'brave' she was looking for someone to join her in completing the plan she had for the family of Amadi.

The sun was yet not visible and dew was still in the atmosphere; everywhere was damp even the trees were looking sleepy in the compound of Onucha, Adanna's uncle. Servants abound and wives also abound, Onucha was not as rich as her father but he married more wives than her father and yes he had a large barn.

Adanna couldn't wait to meet Okanoka it was rumoured that his back had never seen the ground in any wrestling competition, he had proved to be beyond limit for everyone who challenged him, he was the perfect person to work with. Though Adanna had never met him, his fame was wildly known, as her uncles children couldn't stop talking about him and his accomplishments. They also happened to have attended all the fight that Okanoka had participated in. Now was the perfect time to meet him, Adanna reasoned she would catch him fresh and in the mood to face any challenge, the compound was still silent no one was awake yet. Adanna stepped out of the hut where she had been staying into the footpath outside, in the compound Onucha had 11 huts which he shared accordingly. The place of Okanoka had been described to her the night before. She found her way being an excellent tracker, a skill she picked up from hunting, she found the compound with a perfect description. She was told huts with the drawing of cobras all over. Okanoka had just married and his wife was in one of the huts behind, Adanna stepped into the compound and tried making her presence known. At the first hut that she saw she clapped to awaken anyone who could be inside, but no one answered she tried again a head peeped out from the hut.

"Yes can I help you?" the voice asked.

"Yes I'm looking for Okanoka." Adanna replied.

"Yes who are you?"

I'm Adanna and I'm from…" she wanted to tell him where she was from but paused; she had already told him her real name something she shouldn't have done but she would need him to know her, believing her name was enough.

"Where can I find him?"

"This is Okanoka. What may I do for you?" as he spoke he gradually emerged from the hut. Now Adanna could see the whole of him. She couldn't believe how tall he was, looking at the size of his arm it was almost five times the size of her own.

"I'm here with a proposition, I need someone who would take me to the slave market for a reward."

"Such a thing at this time of the day, why not come back?"

"Are you Okanoka?" she asked again.

"Yes, I am, indeed I am, I just think you should come back later besides the journey is not something for a woman, my dear go home the journey is not something for a woman." He repeated.

"What do you mean it's not a journey for a woman? I will head the journey, all I need is someone who will take me to the slave market and I will pay the person, whatever his price may be."

"And what are you willing to pay? If I may ask."

"Whatever your price is, my father has barns much bigger than yours and own lands, and cowries, I can give a lot of things."

Okanoka was beginning to get excited about the proposition he just married and he liked the fact that the man had a large barn. He agreed to take her for a certain amount of yams to fill his barn and she agreed but still he was still skeptical about her ability, he reminded her.

"Look, I must tell you one thing, the journey is for the strong," he said.

"What will I do to tell you that I'm equal to the task?"

Adanna had taken her bow and arrows, upon sighting a boy coming out from one of the hut, the boy was yawning and robbing his eyes, seeing the mark of a slave on his arms she drew her arrow and shot the young boy on the leg. The arrow piercing his front leg and coming out from behind. The boy screamed in pain and fell down. Okanoka let out a shout.

"What are you doing?"

"He is only a slave," she replied.

"You must be crazy," he said.

"What is the matter, he can't do anything."

Okanoka was alarmed he never hurt his slaves, though they were not considered much but he still valued his slaves.

"Who are you?"

He was now at the side of the boy who was screaming in pain. Adanna smiled at the question which she didn't answer. Okanoka didn't need an answer, Okanoka carried the boy, everyone was outside their hut now, the boy's superior ran towards Okanoka. The boy was not moving anymore he had fainted as a result of the pain, Okanoka was frightened wishing he was not dead, with blood on his body he took the boy into one of the huts. Adanna continued to stare in disbelief, seeing that she had done nothing but shoot a slave. The boy's superior, a woman who had been a slave to Okanoka for many years, knew exactly what to do, she ran to call the native doctor in the village. He was the one that would be able to attend to the boy, Okanoka laid the boy down as others attended to him he rushed back to Adanna who was still standing in front of his hut.

"Who are you and what kind of a person are you?" he asked.

"You asked me what I can do, well I can shoot with a bow and also happen to be a hunter who is good at tracking. I usually come to this village only for visit. I never walk around but I was only told of your compound and I found it myself without anyone helping. So are you still asking me what I can do?"

"So you decided to shoot a little boy?"

"What is wrong? He is only a slave." Adanna asked.

"And so you shot him. Why would you shoot him?" Okanoka still demanded as he spoke his eyes were almost bulging out of their sockets, he was almost screaming.

"You could have killed him, do you know you could have killed him?"

"I know how to handle a weapon."

At these last words he couldn't find a word to say.

Adanna was becoming irritated at his behaviour, she couldn't believe that Okanoka the 'brave' had such a soft heart to the point of almost screaming in tears for a slave boy. Okanoka was still speaking when the servant he sent to call the native doctor was returning and he rushed to meet him.

"Where is the native doctor?" he was clearly shouting now. Adanna couldn't bear to continue beholding the pathetic scene. She called to him.

"Okanoka I don't know why you are fretting, when you consider my proposition, I will be at the compound of Onucha."

Saying this she turned and left. On getting back to her uncles compound Adanna heard the rumour that Akom indeed had finalized plans to go to war with Akuta. Nothing would give her more joy than participating in this war, immediately she heard this she went to meet her uncle who was now standing in front of his hut washing his face.

"Uncle has Akom finally decided to go to war?" Adanna asked.

"Who told you?" Her uncle asked.

"I overheard it on my way coming home."

"Really? By the way where have you been my dear you went out very early?"

"I went to visit someone, I have pressing matters that I went to discuss."

While still talking her uncle shouted to one of his children to bring him his morning food, he ate very early.

"Well my dear since there is going to be war I suggest you stay here with us till things are better, no one can predict these wars and this problem with Akuta and Akom can only bring nothing but death, anything that brings death is something we should not toy with." Onucha said.

"No uncle, I must return at once to help my people I can't stay away because there is war, what will my people think of me? I must return at once."

She went into her hut while her uncle busied himself with food, a head peeped into her hut.

"Can I bring you something to eat?" A young girl asked.

Adanna turned to see who was speaking.

"No, I don't want anything there is no time for food I must make haste, there are other pressing matters at hand, besides food."

The young girl returned to the compound where everything was now lively. Everyone was awake, Adanna continued to pack her things, she came with few clothings she had planned to spend 3 days at her uncles place now an urgent matter was calling for her to return at home. As she prepared to leave she had not gotten word from Okanoka he must not be ready to aid her in this mission of hers, though it was a short time she didn't expect him to run after her, but then she could not wait for him. She stepped into the compound, she called to the girl that had asked her if she wanted food the young girl was now standing beside her mother, the girl answered and she left a message with her.

"If Okanoka comes here to look for me you must keep the message for me, for I shall return once things are settled in Akom, do you understand?"

"Yes," the girl replied.

Leaving the girl, she turned into her uncle's hut who had been eating up till now and informed him that she was leaving.

"War is supposed to be for men I have told you, it is better that you stay here nobody is pursuing you, this is also your home your father won't be happy with me that I heard of war in Akom and still allowed you to go back, he will be infuriated, you can stay here when things are settled you can return home."

"No uncle you have done well for me but I must return home, my people will need me I can't stay here. Where I will do nothing while my people are at war I must go home to assist them at once."

"Okay if you insist, you have always had a mind of your own just like your father. I cannot stop you if it is leaving you want you are free to. But about the person you went to meet, have you concluded your business with the fellow?"

"No uncle but I have left a message for him, the girl I don't know her name, the one that has been attending to me, has a message for him when he comes."

"Her name is Olaoma. No problem then, Olaoma is an intelligent girl, you did well."

"Thank you uncle I must go now."

"Alright my daughter may the gods go with you and be careful when you go so you don't have any problem."

"Okay uncle thank you very much."

Adanna stepped into the footpath the sun was now rising from the east, people in the village had begun to move about and things were radiant as she moved along on her way she saw girls of her age going to the stream to fetch water while the men brandished machete clearly going to the farm. One who didn't know Adanna merely looking at her would think she was a warrior from a far village, but indeed she had only dressed like a hunter and not someone embarking on a journey. She had passed the village boundary and stepped into the land of Akom when she heard the sounds of drums, the people were preparing for war. It was custom to beat drums around the village in times of war.

*****

Oja had gathered all the information he could, he had attended the marriage ceremony of one of the sons of the wealthiest man in Akom and he had seen that men of Akom were revellers and not warriors. He had not seen anyone who could challenge the people of Akuta who were born and bred and prepared for war, the people of Akuta that were famed for their ability in war. The warriors that fought alongside Oja who had heard the news from the Chief Priest were already having a faint heart.

How could they fight when the gods had predicted that it would not go well with them? Oja had called some of the warriors to his place and he was telling them how it was possible for them to defeat the people of Akom.

"We defeated the people of Akuri, and carried their women and men as captives, we did not summon the gods, when we needed slaves for selling and none was available we attacked the people of Ibuto we did not consult our god, we just came back from war against Ogi people and we were victorious. Have I not always led you people well, my dear people of Akuta? Why is it now that those feeble men of Akom that I even see our women as stronger than, going to be the problem that we Akuta will have? I can assure you my brave warriors that we will be victorious, that is why I have called you today to have a drink in my home." He motioned to his slaves to bring out the palm wine that he bought and ordered them to serve it, he also brought out the wines he had bartered for slaves at the seacoast.

"My brothers let us drink and enjoy for I am confident of victory, is it not our strength that will bring us victory? There is no truth to what they are saying, we didn't kidnap their people neither did we kill their people, they want war and they shall have it, and have it to the fullest."

He filled his wine horn and ordered others to do the same. Now they were in celebration mood as the others followed suit and filled their horns to drink to the victory that they would have against the people of Akom. Nothing could harm them as long as they believed in themselves, it had been a long time since Akuta tasted defeat and it was not going to come from the hands of Akom people, those revellers as Oja liked to call them.

The men in his compound each drank to his full before dragging their feets away to go their separate ways. The day was almost over as the sun was setting, lying on the horizon and the clouds had cleared revealing a scanty sky with stars able to be numbered, after the men all parted it remained Anuku in the compound of Oja. He was older than Oja and many who had seen their relationship called him the brain while Oja was the strength. They both complemented each other. When Oja was but a little boy they went to the stream, Anuku and Oja were inseparable, a boy picked a fight with Oja after Oja had defeated his junior brother at a children fighting competition, the boy had wanted to avenge his brother, so he picked a fight with Oja. As they fought in the stream the boy was considerably stronger and bigger than Oja. Anuku picked up a stone and threw it right at the base of the back of the skull of the boy leaving him severely wounded. That had ended the fight and rescued Oja who needed the help desperately, since that day Oja had always felt he owed Anuku something, yet so many years later Anuku was still trying his best protecting Oja. This time it laid heavy in his heart to have something to say to Oja before he went in for a night's rest.

"Oja," he called, "I have something to tell you," Anuku said.

"Speak I'm listening," Oja replied.

"It's about the war I think we should seek peace, I don't think it is proper we seeking war things might go wrong, and the priest has already warned that things might go wrong, so if you ask me I think we should seek peace with the people of Akom try to solve this matter amicably instead of engaging in war."

"Ah! My friend Anuku what can I say, you are always trying to worry about things when you shouldn't, it's unnecessary. Don't worry it's too late now, Akom wants war and they will get it, the gods have spoken but Oja also have spoken and he will back it up with actions when he returns victorious, they are simply right for the picking. It is high time we sold them all into slavery to the white man because that is what they all deserve both men, women and children all of them they are all slaves but they don't know it and I think they should be treated as such, they will learn a hard lesson this time around, enough of us pitying them it is time we sold them off."

"Hmmm, I still think we should seek peace," Anuku replied.

Oja's compound was bubbling with activity as his servants both slaves and free alike went about doing their job of serving those still coming. A little girl was pounding yam while her mother made the soup. Anuku who still remained, now discussed other important matters since Oja was determined to go to war at least then they must decide on what strategy to apply or use for the war. But Oja was full of food and wine he had had enough, as they discussed a messenger from the village elders came to inform them, that the people of Akom were indeed coming to do battle with Akuta, not knowing what it was, his heart was joyful. This was what he liked, a time to show his strength, the people of Akom would know who Oja was, the name they had heard so much they would know the force behind the name.

CHAPTER 17

In Mkpunki the Herbalist was in the forest gathering herbs when a young boy called to him, the boy was running, he must have an urgent message. He ran to him and told him that Mary needed him at once. He dropped all he was doing and ran back together with the boy, he had come to enjoy and reverence Mary enjoying his time with her. When he got to the compound Mary was standing at the entrance of the compound and John was standing just behind her with their bags, Okri and his wife were standing beside Mary. The Herbalist almost out of breath.

"What is it white woman?"

"I have to go back to the seacoast, I just wanted to appreciate you for your help and treating my cut I don't know what to do to appreciate you."

"You don't have to do anything I was simply doing my job and helping out as I'm supposed to do." The Herbalist said.

"Besides it's nothing, indeed I count it a privilege, what else could I have done, Okri here is a family friend, he was my father's good friend I can still remember, all you can do for me is to be healthy and stay safe. Since you are going I will escort you a little, I know a shorter route to the one you people took while coming."

"You are too kind." Mary said.

"Please it's all I can do." The Herbalist humbly answered.

The Herbalist picked one of their bags that was on the ground, it belonged to John but it didn't bother him and John didn't know how to tell him. They all stepped out Olaedo was almost shedding tears but she was not showing it, she was still trying to keep it in. So they set out from the life of Okri, who had never been more blessed than the visit he got from this strange woman. Since she and John got into their lives, they were experiencing things anew. Though he had lost a lot in life now he was content that he was not cursed. Ojani was told to stay in his hut whether he understood or not no one knew, his condition was still a concern but they would live through it. Okri believed that good things could also happen to him. His wife had also experienced peace and was more lively at home now, he was convinced that more good things would happen to him in this life before he went to join his ancestors.

"Maybe one day you will come to visit." Mary said as they walked and held few conversations. It was only John who was chewing the kola nut Okri gave him that was making a sound, it was as if everyone was observing a quiet time. He liked the prospect of it.

"I would really love that white woman or even visit you at the shore." The Herbalist said.

He didn't give up hope maybe one day he would go to this strange woman's place to see how they live or visit her at the shore like he had pointed out. They made their way into the forest path, Mary could still remember the path, it was where she had the first accident now it seemed like years ago, after this path they took another turn in the forest, now it was the Herbalist that was showing them the way, he had assured them it was a shorter route. John was still chewing the nuts as if he had not eaten for months. The Herbalist seeing the effort that he was putting in chewing the nuts offered him water to wash down the bitter taste but he declined preferring to keep a dry mouth and a bitter mouth. Mary wondered what it was that he was chewing as Olaedo asked if Mary would consider visiting again but it was very unlikely.

"I don't know I would have to prepare better and not come alone but till then I will wait."

CHAPTER 18

Akom was still beating the war drum as they could hear the chant from the people of Akuta, Akuta was chanting their war song and they both clashed at the border between Akom and Akuta. Obiagu the greatest warrior of Akom was on ground to do what he did best. Akuta had Oja dike and Akom had Obiagu. There was much bloodshed on that day, the men of Akom had promised to wipe out the people of Akuta as Akuta did likewise. All the able-bodied men felt pain as the battle was a titanic tussle. Both parties each in the early periods of the fight suffered loses heavily, both sides were losing men who were dropping to the ground like dry leaves from a tree during dry season. As was expected Oja was leading the fight, when it became heavy on him, he looked around for Anuku. Anuku had always fought alongside him, but this time they were scattered, he looked to call his men to himself, he saw Anuku but was dealt a crushing blow when a man of Akom thrust through Anuku with his sword. As he did so, Oja felt the world running round him, Anuku had fallen to the ground he rushed to the side of his friend to help him, but there was no response. He couldn't cry now, he was still in the battlefield as he stood up he looked around, it was as if the men of Akuta were blinded. The people of Akom was slaying them, they were all falling through the sword of the people of Akom. Oja much enraged sought to find the man who had killed Anuku, but couldn't. He wanted revenge but he couldn't have it as the battle proved to be against the people of Akuta, their mighty men were falling and there was nothing Oja could do, another thing was he had misjudged Akom, how could this be? His own arm was failing him as he looked around trying to focus five men of Akom were round about him he fought off one, another came, he couldn't fight them all. The men of Akuta were supposed to be stronger but then it was not showing so, had he made a mistake surely the people of Akom must have played a trick on him, because when he went to Akom he couldn't find men strong enough for war, now they were in numbers more than he could count. He was certain that they had played a trick on him, they must have known that he entered their village but that was impossible. He couldn't remember being so confused as he was at that moment, he tried to run back to make a new formation as he saw that he couldn't win the war, he shouted for the men of Akuta to run back, but it was too late just like him they had all been surrounded by the men of Akom. The battle was lost, there was nothing he could do anymore. So much of the blood of men of Akuta had been spilled as he shouted, more Akom men surrounded him, he dropped his sword and raised his two hands in the air, there was nothing more that he could do, the battle was over, the men that surrounded him bound him together with a rope, that he couldn't untie and they led him away. He was now a captive of war, how had the mighty fallen the great Oja had been captured in war, as he turned to look around he saw so few remaining men of Akuta, being also captured while some tried to run away, and the men of Akom pursued.

"Kill them all!" The leader of the men of Akom shouted.

"Kill them all!" the battle was over as Oja was being led away the leader of the men of Akom came towards Oja.

"Oja the great today you shall meet your end," he said smiling.

"You are a coward I do not fear that." Oja replied.

"Indeed you don't, but you shall meet something worse than death, take him away."

They took him away, they were planning to blind him and lead him away into the evil forest. Oja couldn't believe what was going on, the great Oja had fallen. How would the story be told that Oja whom women sang songs about had fallen, the one whom children told stories about, how would the story be told. The men of Akom resumed their drumming as they led their captives to the village square others went to ransack the village of Akuta and pillage it. They killed most that they saw on their way the men of Akom showed no pity to the people of Akuta as they killed their men, the elders who tried to escape were caught and killed and the women, young men and children were tied to be sold as slaves to the white man at the shore. The people of Akom usually kept the slaves they caught in war but this time they were going to sell them all at the shore, they didn't want to keep the people of Akuta as slaves. However they wanted to make sure that no one inhabited the village of Akuta again, they led Oja to the village square, including all the people of Akuta they caught. Shame and sorrow filled Oja, he couldn't believe he had failed his people. He used to bring them victory which with it came laughter but now he had brought nothing but cries, pain and disappointment, how was he going to appease them. He would never make it alright for them. The end for Akuta had come, it was beginning to go dark as the sun went down the people of Akom began to chant, he had never heard them chant before but this evening they were going to celebrate the joy that they have received, as victory given to them by the god 'Utte'. Oja tried to shake away his bonds but he couldn't, the bond was made from a strong material, he felt pain as they were put in a cage made with bamboo stick, they were all tied hands and feet. Oja knew the route to the slave shore far too well, he had often led slaves to it but right now he couldn't believe he was about to be led to it himself. He should have taken the warning from the Chief Priest, who knew what the Chief Priest was doing now and where he was, maybe he had been killed. Oja would never know now it was too late, the village square was crowded with people who came to inspect them and rejoice at the victory. Oja bowed his head between his knees as he couldn't lift up his face to look at the faces of the people of Akom who regarded them as unfortunate. In the night the warriors of Akom came back to the village square to separate them into groups for transporting through the hinterland to the shore for sale, as they separated them and tied restricting cords on their necks and hands trying to bind them together, they would bring the chains and cuff them later so that they would move in straight line when they were moving, it was not going to be easy but it could be done, and it would be done. Oja when it got to his turn was moved to another cage which contained only him and he had learnt earlier they had a special plan for him, he used to be a warrior so a thing befitting a warrior would be meted out to him. He wasn't about to cower at the sight of these men, he would hold his strength through and through and he would continue to be a man no matter what happened. But they had a plan for him, they planned to gouge out his eyes and let him live blind till his death came. He had constantly berated the people of Akom and now was their time for retribution, the night would be cold as the men that came to sort them out had all gone. And each of them was put in a cage awaiting the day they would be moved to the shore. Oja tried to close his eyes and sleep but the scene kept playing, the scene where

Anuku was thrust with a sword, how could he undo this, now the pain was clearly aching his heart. His heart felt dull and heavy and his stomach was boiling as if he was going to throw up, he calmed himself tried to shot his eyes again. After a while the scene where Anuku was bringing him a game began to play, he woke up again, he was going to have to become accustomed to nightmares. He couldn't still believe that Anuku his best friend was gone, how could he change this, he was thinking such when he dozed off, and Anuku playing with him in the stream started playing out. He tried to run Anuku caught him by the ankle and pulled him back into the stream. They both laughed and played as he was about to lift Anuku up he woke again and realized for the third time he had dreamt about Anuku in one night. With that he gave up and decided to be awake throughout the night yet his thought couldn't stop going back to the scene where Anuku was killed, then he knew he was in deep trouble. Maybe Anuku was trying to tell him something, but it couldn't be, it was just that he was in pain. Anuku his best friend was gone forever.

CHAPTER 19

Earlier in the day Mary and her band continued their journey with the Herbalist leading them, they came out to the inlet from where they would take a canoe to get to the shore and certainly it was time to say goodbye. The Herbalist got a canoe for them and he had in truth led them a shorter route to the inlet, they saw the men that gave ride to the seacoast they paid them and Mary hugged each of them as she and John made their way back to the seacoast. John showed no expression as if he had no feelings or maybe he was feeling indifferent. The Herbalist was having mixed feelings he was smiling but had sadness in his heart, Okri and Olaedo who was crying now as she couldn't hold it in any longer walked back to Mkpunki with the Herbalist. Hopefully they wouldn't be any more accidents this time Mary wished as the canoe paddled away into the horizon the water was calm as they travelled on it and things were looking good for the both of them, they were going back to base, in her heart she had had enough adventure. She didn't wish to have another one like the one she had just had, hopefully when she would meet her father they would be able to iron things out, and would have a better way of settling disputes.

*****

In the compound of Ubiakwa things were looking lively. It had been just a day since the war with the people of Akuta ended. All his sons who went to the war returned, none was hurt, he had gone to the village Chief Priest to give thanks to the god 'Utte' and his ancestors for watching over his sons, keeping and bringing them back from war safely. He went with Adanna, the village Chief Priest took his offerings but ordered him to tread carefully as the killer of Amadi had not been ascertained but Ubikwa swore his clean hands and conscience.

"Wise one if I'm the one responsible for the death of Amadi let the gods strike me down."

When he returned to his compound his sons were in high spirit as they celebrated their victory, Ubiakwa had 27 sons and 31 daughters from 17 wives, they didn't all live with him as they all lived in separate places managing their father's wealth. But his fourth wife who happened to be Adanna's mother had stayed with him with her children, today all of them with their friends and well-wishers were all in the compound of Ubiakwa, the war had brought them all home. They were all eating and drinking when Ubiakwa stepped into the compound, they all stood and greeted him, he marched in with Adanna right beside him.

"Father welcome." One of the sons said.

"Thank you my son." Ubiawka responded.

He motioned for a chair which was brought and he sat and began to ask them how they were doing one after the other.

They all answered well, and made him know they were in high spirit.

"By tomorrow Oja's eyes will be gouged out, he has been in Akom since yesterday I think he has seen enough," said the oldest son from his 6th wife.

They all erupted into laughter.

"Indeed Ribelu he has seen enough."

"I don't know why they are wasting time I think they should start moving them to the seacoast as soon as possible." Another said.

"Indeed they should. Why should we speculate? Are we not the men of Akom? let us go and find out for ourselves why they are still in 'Akom' " they all shouted in agreement and unison, those still eating or drinking abandoned it. Ubiakwa was silent now but his face was all smiles as they all marched out of the compound and he wished them well, advising them to be careful and not come to harm. Whether they heard no one knew, they had a mission. As they stomped their way out of the compound, the friends and well-wishers stayed back. Brandishing their weapons as if set for another war, they made their way to the village square to inquire from those watching the captives why they still remained on Akom soil. When they got there, the place was busy as the slave holders inspected the slaves, they met Kadika the man in charge of the slaves, Kadika never had it easy. It was his idea to make war, indeed he was amongst the people who agitated for war with Akuta, he had lost his son who was only 15 years old to the kidnappers. As he never saw his son again, when it occurred he had no other idea but for war against the people of Akuta. When the sons of Ubiakwa approached they called to Kadika to enquire as to what was going on. He took time as he was inspecting a female war captive who looked frail and he wondered if she would make a good sale.

"Kadika," they called out again to him, he turned. This time instead of speaking in unison, Onajide spoke up for he was the Eldest.

"Kadika the great what is going on?"

"We are inspecting the captives, especially those that were brought in today, some are still coming they all will be moved to the seacoast, but we will keep the children who cannot walk the distance." Kadika answered.

"What is to become of Oja?" Onajide asked.

"It seems we will be following the original plan." Kadika answered.

"Indeed that is fair, but don't you think we should keep him perhaps he may serve other purposes?" Onajide asked.

"You speak the truth, but we shall see. He is a dangerous man and keeping him might not be such a good idea."

"You speak well," they all said to Kadika.

Satisfied with what they had seen that the captives were being sorted, they went back to their compound and resumed merry making as they narrated all that had transpired to those in the compound. Adanna taking in every word like a little baby being taught.

CHAPTER 20

The moon had risen to the zenith and its light illuminated the ground, the light was so bright that one could move around freely without additional light in the form of torch, it must be the end of the month. Though the people of Akom didn't count by months but weeks. Adanna came out from her hut and inspected the whole compound, everyone had gone to sleep and only those who had an appointment with the forces of darkness were still up, stealthily she moved out of the compound to the village square making sure not to arouse or make noise. She looked around, no one in sight, she moved on but behind her, following closely was Obeli her brother the last son from their mother. Obeli had gone to urinate and had seen Adanna moving out of the compound at an ungodly hour and in a queer manner so he followed her. As Adanna walked she looked back to see if anyone was following her, Obeli was smart and clever as he aptly kept dodging her and escaping her gaze. Adanna quickening her steps made her way to the village square and Obeli followed closely. Obeli was beginning to get scared he had never left home by this time of the day and what if he witnessed some horrific event, it was not something that he could bear. Adanna went straight to the cage where Oja was and began to call him, by this time Oja was the only captive left at the village square others had been moved out waiting for the day they would start the journey to the seacoast. He opened his eyes towards the direction where the voice was coming from.

"Who are you and what do you want?" he asked, he was tired of people coming to look at him and make fun of him.

"I brought a proposition for you," Adanna said firmly with assurance in her voice.

"What proposition?"

"I can set you free but you must swear to do what I ask you to do."

Oja hearing this, sat up and was now in the mood to talk.

"You are a woman of Akom."

"I know."

"So what is it I must do?" he said trying not to sound happy but he couldn't believe his luck.

"You will swear by the gods to lead me to the seacoast where the slaves are sold, I will release you from the cage."

"Okay I will swear."

"You must take an oath that you will follow the terms that I lay down."

"I agree. What are the terms?" Oja asked.

"I will not untie your hands but the bonds on your legs I will cut, you will escort me and a woman with her daughter to the slave market, I want to sell them off then after that you can have your freedom. Because of the hatred between Akom and Akuta they didn't keep a guard to watch you because the people of Akom believes no one will come to free you but I will free you and you will do this for me." Adanna said.

"What makes you think I know the way? Besides I don't agree if you want me to help you must untie my hands also."

"Then have a good rest, I hope you know what plan they have for you, my brothers say they plan to gouge out your eyes I hope their plans come to fruition." Adanna said.

Oja couldn't believe his ears, his own eyes, a fate worse than death, he had prayed to the gods for help and they did this. It was his chance and he would take it, after all what other choice did he have? As they conversed, Obeli was nearby in the bush close to the market square listening to their conversation. Oja's cage had a bush close to it and it proved resourceful to Obeli.

"What woman and daughter are you talking about?" Oja asked.

"Leave that to me it is none of your concern, by tomorrow I shall come back." Adanna said.

"No! no! no! don't go please let it be today for tomorrow they may carry out their plan you know the one about gouging out my eyes." Oja pleaded.

"It won't be tomorrow, I thought you weren't interested?" Adanna asked.

"I am indeed I am, I will like to help you."

"Then don't worry I will come back tomorrow."

Obeli had heard enough, silently he dropped out from the bush and started towards home he of course knew what woman and daughter Adanna was talking about. It was the family of Amadi. In his thought he wondered what the family must have done to Adanna, now she was planning to sell them into slavery. She clearly didn't like the family, as he left immediately Adanna glanced back but she didn't see him for he was swift in movement, he ran all the way home. He got into his hut that he was sharing with his brother Odika, Odika was still fast asleep and had not suspected that he had not been around, he laid down but couldn't sleep. He forced himself to sleep but couldn't, he went outside once again for him to step out of the hut, Adanna was coming in quietly, he hid himself and allowed her to pass, but he must tell someone, he felt like waking Odika to tell him about it. Then Odika would tell someone again and from there Adanna would be in trouble or he could keep quiet and the family of Amadi would suffer. He had to tell someone dominated his thought. He didn't know what had transpired when he left but how could it be of all the people in Akom it was Oja an enemy. He went back into his hut by now it was almost dawn, if he told someone and Adanna's plans became known, she would be severely punished and he couldn't bear that. What he must do was to tell Amadi's wife and her daughter the evil that was about to befall them as he thought about this silently he slipped into sleep.

*****

When he awoke the day had gone far, people were moving about he couldn't believe that of all days it was this day that he overslept, his heart was judging him. Unfortunately he had a weak conscience, he got up quickly knowing what he must do, it was as if as he slept the idea on how to resolve the matter was solved in his mind. But how he had overslept of all days, Odika didn't even bother to wake him, he rushed out of the compound without washing his face, body or mouth, he was in a hurry. As he got to the compound of Amadi he saw no one, the compound was empty. He had heard that Amadi's wife Obirika had asked all living in her husband's compound to leave, but she stayed there with her daughter Nne, he couldn't see anyone. To make the matter worse he stepped into the main hut which had its closing ajar, he discovered that things had been searched roughly. He then realized his fear, Adanna had acted on her objective. He rushed back to his compound as he entered he searched for Adanna but couldn't find her. Where has she gone? he asked but no one could give an answer as they all seemed confused, Adanna never told anyone where she was going. She laughed with no one, how possible was it then that she conversed with someone. Obeli could do nothing, he waited and searched, Adanna was nowhere to be found, he decided to go to the village square, Oja was still there, he sat pretending as if nothing was going on, but something was going on and Obeli knew it.

No matter what they did he wouldn't sit back and allow evil to flourish not while he could stop it, he must do something to stop it. He ran back to his compound only to see everybody going about their business without the cares of the world upon them, everyone seemed happy and contented, wanting nothing more. Obeli wished he could be in that world for it was the world he used to be in. A world that gave him peace and made him care for nothing else, now he had seen and heard things that had changed his reality, he was not the man he used to be. He wished to be the man he used to be but it was not going to happen he rushed back to Amadi's compound and he saw no one. What else could he do, he decided against telling any of his family members instead he went to tell his best friend Iwobo. Iwobo did nothing but to give him a best friend's advice and also agreed to follow him find Amadi's family. Iwobo knew about loss, he had lost his mother to sickness and subsequently death, while he was very young so his stepmothers raised him and they had not been treating him well in any way instead. Iwobo had been experiencing hardship, to this very moment only the times he came to Obeli did he have peace of mind. Nothing in this world made him want to keep living on, except his friendship with Obeli. His father was also a wealthy man, but he had married too many wives, and so had no time to take care of Iwobo or give him the attentions that he needed, everything about his upkeep had been conducted by his stepmothers. Meeting with Iwobo at his place they both went to the village square they found Oja still seated in his cage, the crowd that did come to look at Oja as a public spectacle had continued to reduce. They were both confused they decided to go home while Obeli waited for Adanna and monitored her, to tell Iwobo the outcome the following day.

*****

In the night Obeli refused to sleep as he hid himself beside his hut waiting for Adanna to pass, he hadn't seen her all through that day not even in the night. When he had learnt she was back it seemed as she came back she stayed in her hut all through. He should have gone to meet her, just to see her, he thought, but it was too late now, as he waited just as the moon was shining so brightly that one didn't need light to see, Adanna passed his hut but this time it was almost dawn. He followed her again this time he already knew where she was going as she entered the path that led to the village square, he also knew what purpose she had, he crept behind the bush where he had hid the first time as they arrived the village square. He was surprised as he saw two more men already waiting at the village square he had not expected to see anyone more over he couldn't see the faces of the men, this time he knew something was not right. Were they the men of Akom or not? Then Adanna who was now standing beside Oja spoke.

"Are you ready?" she asked.

"I'm always ready, I am Oja, well let's get on with it release me so that I can help you."

Adanna motioned to one of the men and he broke the cage with as little noise as he could. Oja's hands and feet were bound by the wrist and ankle, the bond holding his ankles were broken but his hands remained bound. He couldn't believe he was experiencing freedom, he was now anxious wanting to move away as quickly as possible before someone with another agenda saw them and decided to gouge out his eyes.

"Well where are the people we are supposed to take along, how do we get them?" Oja asked.

"That's none of your business," Adanna replied.

"Well I thought that was the essence of the whole thing for me to show you the slave market at the shore where you will sell two people while I gain my freedom."

"We were only able to find the mother we can't find the daughter and the mother is in the forest, we caught her and caged her there, so we will go to the forest and pick her and then we will be on our way to the shore, which you will show us. Understood?"

"Yes, well understood," Oja replied smiling.

He couldn't believe his luck, while Obeli couldn't believe his ears, he should have known, how could he have made such a mistake, he should have sought for Adanna to find out what she was up to all day long, now it was too late. As Obeli hid in the bush a hand fell on his shoulder, before he could turn the hand lifted him up and slammed him on the ground, he shouted in pain but the hands soon covered his mouth so he couldn't shout, now he was facing the ground. When he opened his eyes they were all standing round him while he was in the centre, indeed he had been caught.

"What shall we do with him?" the man who had caught him asked.

"Bring him along." Adanna said, "On second thought" she turned "Who knows you are here?"

Obeli shook his head in negation indicating no, and she took his word for it.

She was clearly angry but didn't show it, as they all went Obeli was dragged along. They went into the forest Obeli couldn't shout, for he was gagged, an idea that came from Oja. When they got to the forest Obeli saw Obirika she was panting and breathing heavily, with tears flowing freely from her eyes she was clearly in pain, she was in a cage and bound hands and feet. When Oja saw her, he reflected how not long ago he was in the same position. Obeli was dumbfounded and was still trying to recollect where he was, he had never been to this part of the forest.

"As you couldn't mind your business you will take her place till we return, I can't have anyone ruining my plans." Adanna said.

As she was speaking Obeli was bound hand and feet and put into the cage while Obirika was dragged out, hunger and pain were her companions now but her captors didn't mind. Obeli struggled all to no avail as he was strongly bound, he couldn't believe what was going on, in muffled shouts he was screaming the name of Adanna and telling her how he was her brother but they couldn't hear. He kept struggling in the cage, but if he had known better he would have reserved the energy because he would need it. As things had turned out plans had changed Adanna ordered them to wait for her as she must run an errand to salvage the predicament which Obeli had caused. It was now morning.

The people of Akom woke up to the sounds of the village messengers with their gong they had been carrying the news about the escape of Oja. No one knew what had happened, the village had ordered a search to find him, he must have been released by someone they all reasoned. But who could that someone be? Oja was nowhere to be found. In the compound of Ubiakwa he woke up to the news that Adanna had dropped a message that she was travelling to her uncle's village with Obeli and he wondered why he was not told in person, he would have told her not to go.

Iwobo didn't know what to do, for Obeli had warned him not to tell anyone, so that Adanna wouldn't enter into trouble but now what was he expected to do for he had not seen Obeli as he promised to show up after learning about Adanna's plans. He went to Obeli's compound and was told the news that he travelled with Adanna. He knew something was wrong for it couldn't be. Being a master tracker he went to the village square and sought to search for footprints, but it was all scattered as many people since the disappearance had gathered at the village square to know what was going on. Iwobo was becoming desperate he would be devastated if Obeli was not found. What would he do now surely he had to find Obeli before dusk, as he stood around and sought for anything that may give him a clue, an Akom warrior was in the scene observing him.

"What are you doing?" The man asked.

"Ahhhhh, nothing really just looking for something." Iwobo replied.

"And what could that be?"

"I'm looking for my bag." He lied.

"And your bag is in the village square, there is no bag here go look elsewhere."

Iwobo pretended not to have heard. The man pushed him as he fell, he fell backwards into the bush that was beside the main path of the village square. Other warriors began to stare at them, the altercation had drawn attention which was the last thing Iwobo needed. As more warriors began to gather to ask what was going on, Iwobo tried to raise up his hand, he touched something he looked down to see what it was, it was Obeli's wrist beads it was cut. He would recognize it anywhere for he had one like it too, he made them and gave Obeli one as a sign of friendship. Then it was Obeli who was supplying him food, he looked at where he had fallen he saw that there were footprints, thank the god 'Utte' he picked up the wrist beads and followed the tracks. Both the man that had pushed him and those that gathered were looking at him in amazement as he didn't bother to answer the man or anyone else for that matter. He followed the foot tracks, the trees beside him on both sides began to grow taller and bigger, he was now leaving the part well known by the people of Akom, he was moving into an unknown world but he had to do something. He must find his friend Obeli, as he moved following the tracks the forest began to be a treacherous place, no one usually came to this part of the forest. Who dared enter this part of the forest? But Iwobo pushed on making his way through this perilous place seeking for his friend. As he moved his heart began to question him if he was sure of what he was doing, the track he was following still showed a lot of footprints but he didn't and couldn't decide which one that belonged to Obeli, as fear began to overwhelm him he picked up the pace because the sun was past mid-day, the sun began to go west he didn't want to be caught by a wild animal. Just as the thought was in his mind a poisonous snake slid passed by him, he jumped and escaped the snake, it would have bit him, he took this as a bad omen. Would he find Obeli, he was wishing nothing happened to him because it was not very often that one entered the forest and left with happy tales. He picked up the pace again, he passed a large tree he couldn't have known the name of the tree, then the footprints that he had been following scattered to many directions. The path he was following now seemed confusing, he searched further and saw that a slender footprint turned back and headed the way he came. He had missed this initially, then the footprints now all seemed hap – hazard, he gave up and turned back to leave. As he looked around once more the footprints were still confusing, satisfied he had tried and ready to quit totally. He heard a muffled cry, in any world he would know the voice of Obeli, nothing could confuse him about it, and he was certain the muffled cry he heard was the voice of Obeli. He shouted Obeli's name and the muffled cry increased and seemed louder, he frantically began to search the forest looking for where the voice was emanating from, indeed it was the voice of Obeli and he was in pain. Running to and fro, Iwobo saw a bush that looked out of place, such bush could not grow in the forest for they seemed to be without root, Iwobo rushed to it touching the leaves it fell down on its own. For the second time in one day a snake was in between the leaves Iwobo could have touched it and it would have bit him, had he not been fortunate to see it before hand, he used a stick and flung it away. He now uncovered the remaining only to see his friend in a cage, he couldn't tell the joy he was feeling there were tears in Obeli's eyes, quickly he opened the cage and carrying him, he helped him out from the cage made with bamboo sticks. For how long the person who made the bamboo cage had taken, no one knew, but the person did a meticulous work, the cage looked similar to the one Oja was put in at the village square. Iwobo very relieved, helped his friend up to his feet as they hugged, he tried ungagging his mouth and untying the hands and ankles he had brought out a knife and began to cut the bounds it took him time to do this.

Both of them were clearly happy now Obeli sat on the ground for a moment, then he got up and hugged his friend for the second time and thanked him for rescuing him. They both made their way back to the village, the time was clearly against them the sun was beginning to set. It had taken Iwobo almost all day to search for Obeli, Obeli still feeling the pain being tied down for almost a day, was famished and thirsty, his ankles and wrist were hurting him, luckily Iwobo had a water pouch he emptied it almost at one gulp, Iwobo encouraged him and took him to his place for his place was closer than going to Obeli's place. Obeli in Iwobo's place refreshed himself, he didn't know about the lie Adanna had told. Obeli instead of going home decided to find Amadi's daughter, he couldn't help but wonder where in the world she was.

Now he was clearly involved in their life, and he felt it was his responsibility to help them, he must help them. Besides going home would make him to start explaining where he had been all day, he didn't want that, also it would mean exposing Adanna. But if he did, he would be putting her in danger, but of course he should report her after all she kept him in a cage. Obeli was now in a dilemma for he didn't know what to do, tell the whole village so that Adanna would be stopped, but if he did so, Adanna's punishment along with her friends would be death. For he had learnt from Iwobo that the village had decided that if they found out that whoever it was, that rescued Oja was a person from Akom the persons penalty would be death. He didn't want to be the reason Adanna would be killed, going back to his father's compound might mean certain death for Adanna. Unless he lied and that was what he was going to do, lie. Iwobo brought him food he devoured it not minding the hotness, after eating he now had strength to speak.

"I've decided on what to do." Obeli said.

"What is it?"

"I will follow Adanna to the shore and rescue the wife of Amadi, Obirika but first I must find her daughter."

"How do you intend to do that if I may ask, you are not a warrior how do you intend to overpower them?"

"I believe my ancestors will protect me, how I'm going to do it I don't know but I must do something and I know there will be a way. First let's find her daughter, we will check their compound again, and I think we should leave now."

"Don't you think we should tell someone?"

"We can't, if we do we will be condemning Adanna and her band to death, I can't have her blood on my hands except you want it on yours."

"The gods forbid. Not me," as Iwobo rejected it he moved his hand over his head. A gesture that indicated he rejected the wish.

As Obeli rose up he felt like a new being his strength had returned and now he must act. Iwobo gave him a bag and they each filled them both with provisions that would last them for a two days journey. They had dried meat in it and a pouch of water before setting out. But they wouldn't be needing it, not today, they went to Amadi's compound only to find Nne in her hut and people gathered about her, she was crying and women around her were consoling her.

"What is going on?" Obeli asked.

A woman stood up from the ground where she was seated and led him outside.

"My brother Nne is looking for her mother Obirika we have been looking for her for almost 2 days now, since she disappeared no one can find her or know where she is."

Of course Obeli knew where she was but he couldn't tell anyone if not his sister would be killed. They both decided to go home and come back the following day for there was no way they could help her without arousing suspicion from the sympathizers around Nne. So they went into her hut again and told her sorry and promised to come back again the following day. Nne was shocked when she saw them, for she knew Obeli, and she pointed out that it was his family that had killed her father now her mother was gone.

"What do you want from me?" She shouted in pain, as tears flowed freely from her eyes down her cheeks.

Obeli assured her he came for good and not for evil they both stepped out of the hut and went home. What had happened to her father he knew nothing about, but her mother he knew something about and he was going to help her, no matter what. He was not going to have her pain on his conscience, for there was no way he could live with himself. So he made up his mind to help her in whatever way he could and first would be by getting back her mother to her.

*****

In the night Obeli couldn't sleep so he decided to go back to his own place, he told Iwobo, after disagreeing initially he later gave up the argument and wished him well. They arranged to meet in the morning as early as possible to go to Nne's place, they had not decided whether they would tell her about her mother or not. Obeli left, as he got home everyone had gone into their huts, he could hear some snoring while others chatted away the night hoping for sleep to come and take them. Obeli entered his hut and Odika saw him, there was surprise on Odika's face. Obeli didn't know what to do he had decided not to tell anyone the truth about Adanna, he loved her as a brother despite what she had done to him, but whatever her reason was he would find out.

"Where is Adanna?" Odika asked.

Obeli's heart began pumping more blood than was needed as his head felt heavy. Was it because of the question or something else how could Odika be asking him about Adanna, what does he know that he Obeli didn't?

"I don't know." He responded.

"But she said that both of you were going to Uncle Onucha's place?"

Obeli now knew what Adanna had done that early morning when she turned back and then also he knew what to do with his own lie, he had already prepared a lie but Adanna's own was better, all he had to do now was tell a little one if there was anything like a little lie.

"Well we forgot something so I came back to pick it, by morning I will go back to meet her."

"Hmmm!" Odika said nothing again but went and laid down closing his eyes it wasn't long before he slipped into a good night rest. Obeli now knowing what he must do also went to sleep but before he could sleep he made up his mind to wake up early and not over sleep like he had done a day before.

CHAPTER 21

Adanna was feeling a bit contented, her plans were not going perfectly well, she would have wished for Nne to be amongst the persons for the slave market but since she was not around and her mother was. All was not lost after she learnt the route to the seacoast Nne wouldn't have anywhere to hide, she would personally take her to the shore, just like she was doing her mother. They had to make a few more days journey to the seacoast from her village but every step of the way Adanna questioned their movement. How it was that they were trusting a total stranger in the person of Oja. He had not spoken much, he spoke only when he wanted to give direction or request for something. Adanna had never seen such a man before, from what she had heard only war talk loosened Oja's tongue, as a warrior he prided himself on how he was a man of character, but all that flew away once he was talking about war and Adanna had no plans to start a chat about wars with him. He was a hero but that was his business for now he was a captive. On their journey they had crossed so many villages then they got to Akumi, after a few days. Akumi people were said to be peaceful and fun loving but there they saw other people who were bound for the slave market at the seacoast they decided to spend time there, top their supplies and refresh before moving on. When they got to the village square, people were not paying attention to the slaves it was a sight they beheld every day, nothing new to it as they made their way. Adanna had enough cowries and soon where they were going, her cowries wouldn't count much but was still useful those people had another money, copper bars. They would be buying food only and try to get water from other slavers, the slavers had their own places they had built, that they would stay when they were travelling with slaves, and they had their ways of getting supply. When they got to the people where their money was different they would barter what they had. Adanna was prepared as she had items she could barter, an advice she had picked from Oja, though she didn't know her cowries were accepted everywhere. The food they would be getting was not for her but the men with her, she had had enough food in her life. As her father made sure she lacked nothing. When they got to the village square the slaves were bound and they placed Obirika with them, but the other slavers rejected this as they began to argue, a man asked them to calm down and take it easy with them, he promised to take charge of Obirika himself Adanna thanked him. Meanwhile Obirika was still in tears.

"Adanna my daughter please, what have I done to deserve this, don't do this thing you are planning to do remember I also have a daughter like you."

"Woman shut up your mouth, do you think you can change our mind after we have walked this far" Adanna's aide said, with Adanna silent and acting like she couldn't hear Obirika's plea.

Obirika cried even louder.

"What is making her cry, woman shut up!"

A voice loomed from behind Adanna and her men who were standing around her.

"She is crying to her god to come and help her." Adanna retorted.

"Well she is getting what she deserves."

Adanna now turned to see who was speaking it was the man who had assisted them before, he was the village slave handler, that was his work, looking after slaves at least that was what he said. He was fully into the trading of slaves and he knew everything about it. Adanna was pleased to see someone who believed Amadi's family was getting what they deserved. Obirika was still crying when Adanna asked him where she could get supplies and she was told that he would in fact escort her to the village market to get supplies because the market that sold for that particular day was still open. Men who had been interested in Adanna always got scared when she revealed herself. Akintu didn't know what he was getting into, Adanna accepted his offer, the men with Adanna decided to wait for her at the village square while she went to get the supplies including Oja whose hands were still bound so he couldn't move freely about. They moved away and Akintu led the way then he asked Adanna.

"Is the man also for sale?"

"No he is our guide, he is not for sale." Adanna answered.

"So what is your name?" Akintu asked.

"Mmerika." Adanna lied.

She would never tell a stranger her real name, she was too smart, besides her mission was supposed to be a secret.

"Mmerika what a beautiful name, so what brought a beautiful girl like yourself into slave trading?" Akintu continued.

"I'm doing it for my father." She lied again. Though if you look at it from her point of view she was indirectly telling the truth, though her father was unaware of what she was doing, neither did he send her.

"Hmmm, that's interesting, so what do you intend to do after selling them?"

"Return to my village and marry my fiancé."

This crushed Akintu he had fancied his chances with her. Adanna was good at lying and she was doing it perfectly.

Akintu was trying to get his head straight whether he was to continue with her or leave her and run away, and let her wander about a little bit before finding her way but he thought against it.

If she was about to get married maybe there was still a chance for him, after all she was not married yet, maybe she was not happy with who she was with and wouldn't mind a change, so he determined to continue with her. She was beautiful and he believed he stood a chance, he had abandoned everything he was doing just to escort her to the market, she was a chance worth fighting for.

"So how is your husband to be?" Akintu asked.

"I don't know, maybe he is fine maybe he is not I don't know." Adanna was enjoying the fact she was toying with him, she could tell him whatever she wanted to and he would believe it, after all he was a stranger.

"Well I, myself I'm not married but my parents are looking for a wife for me, from our village."

"Well that is nice I hope you find a good match." Adanna said looking at him.

"Indeed I hope too." But he heard her loud and clear when she said she didn't know about her fiancé, it meant she didn't care, Akintu couldn't believe his luck.

As they walked along the footpath people were becoming less and less seen, Akintu urged her to walk faster as the market was about to close, the sun was moving down the west and soon it wouldn't be visible in the sky then the moon would take over. Adanna with the urge walked faster but Akintu was not content he still had questions that he wanted to ask her and Adanna would be okay to avoid them. When they got to the market Adanna bought the supplies as she was about to pay Akintu obliged to.

"Don't worry about paying let me pay please, allow me to."

"Don't bother you have done enough good already besides I can afford this."

"Don't worry I know but still let me." Akintu persisted.

He paid with the money he had made as a slave handler. They both made their way back this time not much was said as Akintu didn't know what else to ask, he had never been with women and talking to them was hard work for him, he was even surprised with his earlier accomplishment of asking Adanna those questions. Of course he knew her as Mmerika, when they got to the village square he discovered he had made a lot of effort and got little result because it was still little that he knew about Adanna. When they got to where Adanna's men were, Oja was asking for the bonds on his hands to be removed.

"Over my dead body we should remove them so that you will kill us." Adanna said with certainty.

"I won't, I have made you a promise and I intend carrying it out, I intend fulfilling my promise, you have to believe me Oja always keeps his words, I swear by the gods that I will not harm any of you."

"The final answer is no, no one is releasing you from those bonds and the matter is settled."

By the time they had something to eat it was twilight and they all agreed they should get a nights rest at the place but Akintu who was still around forbade them to do thus, he instead offered his place to Adanna reminding her that he intended to take care of her. After a little deliberation they all agreed to go to Akintu's place and spend the night, but Obirika would spend the rest of the night at the village square with other slaves for sale, they had provided a place for them. It wasn't an ideal condition but again their situation demanded little comfort that could be granted. They were not in a position to ask for anything because currently they were merchandise and little was spared to take care of them, Adanna and her company went to Akintu's place to spend the night.

*****

Obeli was still sleeping when Iwobo came to their compound, Iwobo woke him up.

"Did I oversleep?"

"No you didn't but it is about time, I think we should get going," they both prepared and left the compound of Ubiakwa.

"What are we going to tell Nne?" Iwobo asked. "We can't tell her that it is Adanna that took her mother she would go and tell the village heads and the warriors will be after her and that won't be good for us or her."

"When we get there the gods will direct our lips because we don't wish to get anyone into trouble or even ourselves."

As they got to Nne's compound there was no one around, they searched all the huts, then they decided it was another wasted effort. When they were about to turn back they decided to check the back of the huts, at the back, the grave of Amadi was there. As they approached they heard sobbing at the back of the huts, when they looked they saw Nne sobbing besides her father's grave. She was looking so unkempt, it had been days since she bathed or ate she had been mourning the loss of father and now mother. In the compound of Amadi there were several huts but now all was deserted, only Nne inhabited the compound, the worst part being that no one knew where her mother's corpse was. If indeed she had been killed. On the other hand her body not being found still gave her hope that her mother was alive, she thought as she sobbed. All she had to do was search for her instead of wallowing in pain and doing nothing, she was about to stand when she saw Iwobo and Obeli. She was startled she didn't expect consolers by this time of the day. Iwobo and Obeli greeted her she greeted wearily in reply as she didn't know what to expect from them.

"We have come because of your mother." Obeli said.

Nne's heart almost popped out from her body.

"My mother, what about my mother?" she said slowly with a lot of expectations in form of explanation from them.

"She is not dead at least not yet we know where she is being taken to." Obeli said.

It was good news to Nne who was now shivering, as she couldn't control herself and what she was hearing made certain of it. When they calmed her down Obeli spoke.

"Your mother is still alive but we have to go and find her we have an idea where she might be taken to."

"Who are the people that took her?" Nne asked still surprised and confused.

"Some men." Iwobo answered.

"Nne look at what we want you to do just stay here don't tell anybody about this, we will go and find your mother, it is a perilous journey but we believe in the gods that we would make it, so all we are asking from you is stop crying and stay here. We shall surely return with her." Iwobo said.

"I lost my father and no one knows who killed him, now my mother, I have lost almost everyone who I care about."

As she narrated her ordeal Obeli and Iwobo were moved to tears, she had lost everyone she cherished in her life. It must be tough for her, there and then they got determined the more to help her and bring back her mother. As they still discussed Nne ran out of the compound.

"My mother who would help me?!" she screamed.

Of course no one heard her to help her, Obeli and Iwobo ran to her and caught hold of her, they brought her back to the compound. Her sympathizers were gone, when they calmed her down yet again she became still again, as they waited for the next thing to do.

She sat on the ground, later laid on it and started crying again. Iwobo and Obeli both heartbroken too, began to console her. When they had done the much they could they began to tell her their plans on how to rescue her mother from these mysterious people, and how she was supposed to be silent about it. Iwobo and Obeli gave her an assurance and decided they would leave immediately as they were already prepared. Nne asked them to wait for her as she went and bathed, when she was through she told them she would like to join them. They refused at this notion, but she persisted and started packing her things, Iwobo and Obeli still refused they had no second thought about it, they asked her to remain while they went to search for her. As it was not a journey for women, it was a hard and difficult journey, she knew she couldn't win them in the argument, so she let it slide. Iwobo and Obeli rose up to go, assuring her one more time it was the best thing to do, and making her know the more secret their mission, the better for everyone. After saying this they left, they had to go back to the place where Obeli was kept, from there, they would pick up their trail and follow them. Iwobo knew the route to the slave market at the shore he had been there before. His half-brother caught for borrowing and not returning and threatened with being sold off into slavery. When he learnt that his creditors were planning to sell him he ran away. Iwobo and his late father searched for him up till the slave market at the shore but couldn't find him, he had in fact ran away and never had been seen or heard from again. No one knew the fate that had befallen him he didn't even return when his father passed away. They got to the cage and to be given some help from the gods they saw their foot marks and followed the track, nothing or anyone had been to that side of the forest and what a relief for Iwobo and Obeli. They left since yesterday morning and it was important that they make haste in chasing after them, as they made their way through the forest, the track led into a footpath they followed the footpath. When they had walked a considerable distance, they decided to rest just then they noticed that someone had been following them. When they walked they heard sounds of footsteps behind, when they stopped, the footsteps stopped, now as they were about to sit down and have rest a form in the shape of a human being crept behind them and hid itself. After a while they stood up and continued walking the footsteps behind started again now they were certain they were being followed.

"Show yourself!" Iwobo shouted they both unsheathed their swords, "Who is there? Show yourself" they said with fear creeping into their hearts and manifesting in their voices. Obeli made the courageous move towards the spot the footsteps was last heard, he was showing he was the brave one, as he moved closer he cut away the bushes that were blocking his path, and finally got to the place where the shadow was last seen.

"Who is there show yourself or I will cut you into pieces." Slowly Nne emerged from the bushes. Obeli heaved and Iwobo was certainly relieved.

"You, you have been following us, we told you to stay back, Nne what do you think you are doing this is dangerous, you could have been harmed!"

"What did you expect? That I would stay at home and do nothing while my mother is in danger, I have to do something to help her and that is what I am doing I'm helping find my mother."

"Nne we have not even concluded on our plan on how to get your mother from the men who are holding her," Iwobo said faintly.

"When we get to that point we will find a way to handle it, but I'm coming with you and you can't chase me back, I'm coming with you."

"Hmm, making you go back alone would be dangerous, but you must keep up." Obeli said.

The sun was setting down, they had to find a place for rest, but if they were to meet up with Adanna and her band they had to move even in the night, as they moved Nne asked Obeli.

"Can you help me describe the men you said are with my mother? What do they look like and what are they looking for from her?"

They knew they had to lie to her again.

"They are just like men Nne, we can't describe them to you, it is not possible let's just focus on the journey, besides even though we are with swords we are not going to fight them, like I said we would just be as discreet as possible. 5 in total as we saw." At least Obeli said the truth now.

"Five? How do we intend to overpower them?" Nne asked.

"I don't know when we get there we will figure it out." Obeli said.

As they talked and walked, Iwobo began to search for a place where they would rest for the night, the sun had gone down and they needed rest. It was only the first day of their journey and the second of Adanna's how would they ever catch up. Unless something befell them and delayed them.

*****

As Adanna rested in Akintu's place her mind raced back to Obeli in the cage, she worried, but she believed days wouldn't kill him. It was his inquisitiveness and busy body that got him into the trouble that he was in, and nothing could be done for him. She thought about this and she drifted into sleep.

*****

While Iwobo, Obeli and Nne on the other hand told each other stories and sleep also caught up with them. It would be a long day ahead tomorrow because they would have to start asking questions on if Obirika had been seen.

*****

In Akintu's place as they slept Oja who was kept guarded by two men thought of how he might escape, if only he could get a hold to their knife or sword he would be a free man. But he wouldn't move without arousing

Adanna for she laid before him, from now on he had decided that the least chance he got he must use it to escape. He also thought he made a mistake by leading true, he should have led them to another place where they didn't know, maybe there he would have escaped, he didn't trust Adanna and her group and he was also sure they didn't trust him. Something must be done by him, through the help of the gods before the plans of his enemies materialized, definitely he still saw them as his enemy even though they helped him escape they were still his enemies. With the thought of revenge in his mind he decided to go to sleep. He would try another time there was still time for him to escape and also take his revenge on the people of Akom.

CHAPTER 22

A messenger with his gong had gone out announcing for the people to meet at the village square. The disappearing of people of Akom still persisted, despite the war with Akuta. Could it be that the disappearances were an act of the gods? Ubiakwa was not concerned about the disappearance of people in Akom, his farmlands, plantations were doing very well and he was getting wealthier by the day, sometimes he got a strange feeling that something may be wrong with Adanna and Obeli, but his worry only lasted a minuscule moment and then his mind told him they were okay at his brother's place and no harm would come to them. The gods had been protecting them and would continue to protect them, the call for people was so that they would discuss the issue of disappearance, they had heard news of what befell this people that were kidnapped and Ubiakwa didn't think it should be so. Only those caught in war should be sold into slavery, when the messenger had finished. This was the thought in the mind of Ubiakwa he solidly supported the notion that if anyone should be caught going against the law such a person should be taken to the slave market, the call was made in the morning for the people to gather in the evening. When the evening came people of Akom gathered at the village square and the main things they discussed were the issues already in the mind of Ubiakwa, when they had finished the meeting the resolve they came to startled everyone. The village heads had decided that everyone should use self-help if anything came against them, could it be that the village god couldn't protect them anymore everyone wondered. It was a challenging task as this was no solution at all but the village heads had assured them it was for the time being and later on things would be sorted out better.

*****

When Adanna awoke, everyone was still asleep including Akintu who had promised to protect her. She had complete dislike for lazy people and to her for the people she was with to still be sleeping they must be lazy. She thought of waking them but decided against it, instead she left the hut, and decided to take in the morning air, and use the time to refresh herself. She went to the bathroom and had her bath, before taking a walk to the forest before they awake she would be back. The sun had not risen, but one could still see about, it was dawn. She wanted to go and pick fruits which had fallen in the woods, with no one watching she took her sword, her bow and quiver and went into the forest, as she went the deserted footpath didn't bother her or make her feel lonely or scared she marched on. Fear was for cowards and she was no coward. After she had gone a while her companions awoke when they searched for her and couldn't find her they went to Akintu's hut and woke him. What had happened to Adanna? Where could she have gone? She didn't tell anyone she was leaving, they continued to search for her in all the places they could after a while they gave up, each man returned and sat down all around Oja who was also awake now and was assuring them nothing had happened to her.

"She probably went to get something I don't suppose anything had happened to her, I think everyone should calm down she is big girl that can take care of herself." Akintu said.

Oja concurred with him.

Still not relieved but perturbed they wanted to search again, Oja brought up an idea which none of them had thought of before. He asked if they had followed her footprints by then it was too late for other footprints had followed hers and it was hopeless, they sat dejected.

"There she is" Akintu whose heart was beginning to fail him sighted her first. When he saw her he smiled with joy pointing to her, then the others saw her. She was carrying two full bags of fruit on each shoulder a fit only possible for men and Adanna alone. When she had entered the compound questions began to rise as to why she had given them such a hard time.

"Why are all your faces like that?" she asked because they were all smiling.

"We were worried that something had happened to you, we woke up and couldn't find you." Akintu replied.

"Well I'm here now, I went to the forest to kill time."

"Truly we are relieved," one of her companions said.

"It's all okay I couldn't tell anyone since you all were asleep, let us get ready to move out I don't have much to do anymore. Oja I hope you are ready, everyone should prepare lets be going."

Akintu was expecting a special thank you from her at the moment none was coming but still he must make this strong woman to love him. How he was going to do it, he did not know. In a little time they were ready and they went to the village square where slaves were kept and took Obirika. The men with Adanna thanked Akintu and promised to repay him when they would meet again, still waiting for his special thank you from Adanna, she went to him and asked which way they would take to the shore he told her the directions they were to take. She didn't trust Oja even at that, she needed to have her own direction, then what Akintu has been waiting for.

"Thank you for helping us, all of them, I really do appreciate," she said formally like a warrior giving orders.

Still Akintu's heart elated, a thank you coming from Adanna or Mmerika as he knew her. He didn't know what it meant, he wished for more chat or a promise of returning the favour but he didn't get any. The thank you from her was even too much, she turned and with her band she followed the direction that had been given. When Oja was asked for direction he chose the same path then Adanna knew they were following the right path.

As they moved they got to Mkpunki after passing many villages for many days. On the path they followed they kept meeting people who stared at them like they were meeting strange beings or people from another world. Adanna and her group didn't understand why they were being stared at, was it a strange thing to have people for sale? The village of Mkpunki was close to the shore. The people of Mkpunki had heard about the war between Akom and Akuta, they were expecting that soon the people of Akom would begin to sell the war captives from Akuta. Those that saw Adanna and her company wondered why they were so few and why only one woman was bound, and only the hands of one man tied. As they marched some ladies who were not people of Akom neither were they from Mkpunki but understood the language of Akom met them and told them what was going on. When they got into Mkpunki they needed rest for they had marched all day from their last stop, when they went to ask for where they could spend the night, Oja had to speak, for the language of the people of Mkpunki was a bit different. But the people could still understand each other when the people of Mkpunki spoke Adanna could hear the words which resembled that of her people, Adanna was no novice to the language for she had learned it a long time ago. No one was willing to help, the people of Mkpunki didn't like the people of Akom that much, they had never trodden the same path, also they saw and reasoned things differently. The people of Mkpunki were observing the week of sacrifice, it was a week where everyone brought the fruit of their occupation a token of it, and it was presented to the gods. During the week of sacrifice no one went out, or did anything. Everyone was in a solemn mood, the people of Mkpunki had high regard for their god, they had observed the ritual for 6 days and Adanna and her company came in on the 6th day they would have to wait for another day before they could move again or do anything. Concerning their slave they would have to pass through Mkpunki before they could reach the shore where the slave dealers were. Adanna perplexed needed a solution, she couldn't be stuck in Mkpunki, she needed a solution which did not entail spending the rest of the day or 2 days in Mkpunki. As she was deliberating with her men, Oja came up with a plan.

"I have a friend here we can go to his place he will accept us, he is very hospitable and he is my very good friend."

Adanna not in the mood to put her life or lives of her men in the hand of Oja refused, but she didn't have any option she either stayed with Oja's friend or spent the night at the village square with other slavers, which she didn't want. Their ways of life didn't suit her, she was running out of ideas. She needed help desperately and she also needed ideas on how best they were to survive.

"Any other ideas on what we should do?" Adanna asked.

No one said a word it meant they would be trusting their lives into the hands of Oja but Adanna wouldn't have it, she would rather battle the cold in the slaver's quarter than spend the night not only once but two nights in the hut of a man, who was ready to be and may even be an adversary of the people of Akom. As they were contemplating, the Herbalist came along, Adanna and her band had been standing at the entrance of the village everyone who wished to enter the village must follow the foot path. When the Herbalist saw them he recognized there were strangers. He had never seen their like before in Mkpunki especially Adanna was remarkably different, both in dressing and demeanour.

"May the gods be with you." The Herbalist said.

"And with you too." They replied. Adanna recognized he was a herbalist for he was carrying the bag that those who gather herbs carry in Akom, she was surprised that all herbalists had the same culture when it came to their animal skin bag. It was the Chief Priest that was also a herbalist and he carried the same kind of bag in Akom.

"Why are you all standing here what may you be looking for?" the Herbalist asked.

"Ah, we are travellers, we just need a place to stay." Adanna answered.

"What is your name?" the Herbalist asked Adanna aware she looked different.

"Odabi" Adanna answered lying about her name again to the shock of her men, who must hold up the new name.

"You people do know we are in the week of solemn assembly, it is a week where we sacrifice to our god." The Herbalist said.

"So we have heard, some ladies passing by made mention of it to us, so it appears that we are stranded. We did not know that it was the week of sacrifice in

Mkpunki, please can you help us we just need a place to stay for two nights." Adanna pleaded.

"I think I might be of help to you, follow me."

As they walked the Herbalist led the way followed by Adanna who had been conversing with him, then came Oja and finally the three men that followed Adanna and had Obirika.

"If I'm to guess you people are going to the slave market for I see the woman and man that are bound." The Herbalist said.

"Oh! yes it's only the woman that is for sale, the man is our guide, he is only showing us the way after which we would release him, I must thank you for accepting to help us we have been standing there for a long time, and no one seemed to care, only the ladies who spoke with us and none offered to help you are far too kind."

"You are welcome. If I'm not mistaken you people are from Akom?"

"Indeed, we are from Akom" Adanna answered filled with pride.

"How come you can understand my language? Any way my maternal grandmother is from Akom besides the language doesn't differ that much, it is not very often that we get visitors from your part, I mean from behind the forest, you should have sent scouts ahead to find out what the journey would look like, but never mind you are here now and it won't hurt me to assist you." The Herbalist said.

"Thank you once again." Adanna said.

"So what abomination did the woman commit?"

"She is a debtor who is disliked." Adanna said.

"These days are treacherous one must be careful slave dealing is not something one should take easily; you people must be careful as your journey still lies ahead."

As they spoke, they passed a compound and the Herbalist pointed out that the compound belonged to Kubu, the strongest fighter in the whole of Mkpunki. Adanna was impressed for he had wealth and it showed in his compound immediately she saw it, it reminded her of her own father who was also one of the wealthiest men in Akom, the 'one of the' is for humility's sake. She knew her father was the wealthiest and the most influential in Akom, my darling father she thought to herself, she began to miss home for it had been days. But her task must be completed before she returned, her father had a special place in her heart and no one would know about it, they passed another compound and the Herbalist pointed out it belonged to Okri one of his friends and a dear family friend. The Herbalist began to tell them stories about the woman from the shore who came to visit. They had never seen a white woman before except she, Adanna could not recall seeing such a woman anywhere.

She kept mute maybe one day she would, the Herbalist told them all the white woman had told him, he was very lively when he talked about the white woman, his voice got more excited and his strides changed to a dancing mood. She must have given him so much joy Adanna thought to herself. Adanna couldn't believe all she heard, Oja was impressed especially about the story of how the Herbalist had used local herbs to heal her cut and cure her, and also making sure that she went back in good health. When he talked about her return to the seacoast his spirit came down and he sounded depressed and down cast. As they continued on the path, the Herbalist kept pointing to places and discussing who was who in the village, Herbalist thought it necessary to tell them all, since they would be spending two nights. Spending two nights annoyed Adanna immensely. Finally they got to the compound of the Herbalist, he introduced them to his mother, and also to his servants he was the first and only son of his mother who was the first and only wife of his late father, he took them to the huts at the back of the compound and gave Adanna a hut all to herself for she was the only lady, while Obirika was taken to where other slaves (but for the Herbalist 'servants') were. Oja stayed with the men who never let him out of their sight, though he had done enough to gain their trust, but they still refused loosening his bond even when he wanted to do the necessary things for himself. Adanna was very pleased on how lucky they had been to get a person like the Herbalist, it meant luck was on their side, the only unfortunate thing being the delay caused by the festivities.

The sun had disappeared from the sky, and only the light which ushered in darkness was available. Soon it would be dark and they would count it as a day gone. They were given food to eat and water to bathe with and once they were done they prepared to sleep. As Adanna laid alone in her hut her mind went back to Obeli, though she was not disturbed he shouldn't have meddled with what was none of his business, a part of her wished that someone had rescued him and before he said anything they would be done with what they wanted to do. Another part of her ached for not finding Nne, she wished it were the two of them that were bound for the slave market. Her plans must go accordingly as she wished it she drifted into a pleasant sleep, she had told her men to watch Oja more carefully now since he had a friend in Mkpunki, he would be planning a means of escape. With that her men watched Oja like they had never done before. The Herbalist walked around the compound to make sure everyone was well and safe, as was his custom, even so now, he had strangers as visitors he went round and even observed Obirika. Who it seemed had accepted her fate and was fast asleep. Done watching everyone the Herbalist went back to his hut and called it a night.

*****

Making their way through the forest as they had abandoned the tracks, gladdened Iwobo knew the way. Nne had proven to be more than meets the eye. Since the journey began she had shown inexhaustible strength putting up courage where the men didn't. With her determination they marched on, they had been moving for a day. It was time they took a rest. Nne was not showing she needed rest, she couldn't be resting while her mother was in anguish. Iwobo brought up the suggestion that they should rest, she wanted to refuse it at first but later obliged. When they sat Nne brought the idea that they should also march in the night and for that they would need to make lights. Obeli rejected the idea of moving in the night.

"But if we don't move, we won't be able to meet up with them we have to double our efforts." Nne said.

"Whether we double our efforts or not we will still meet them." Obeli answered.

"I know where we can find them when we get to the slave market," Iwobo added.

"But we should still move and meet them on the way, it would be better for us." Nne said.

With that resolve, they decided to move in the night just to keep Nne happy. But it was not in the mind of both Iwobo and Obeli, as long as she was happy, if it was possible. As they marched that night silence reigned amongst them, Iwobo tried desperately to think of something that would make their moods lively as they marched on.

"I have a story to tell," he said.

"Really? Now?" Nne asked sarcastically.

Iwobo only meant well. Then Nne thought for a while she needed to keep the people with her happy, she needed them.

"I'm just joking Iwobo, please do tell us your story." Nne said finally.

Much relieved he smiled too, he had thought she was angry with him, after she had mentioned several times she couldn't be happy in anyway while her mother was not. She had a soft heart they had come to notice. All the while Obeli had said nothing his mind had been preoccupied with how the events that await them in the future would unravel, whether it would go well or not.

"My story is about how tortoise became wealthy."

"Obeli what did you learn?" Iwobo asked when he ended his story and everyone was commenting.

By the time they had finished with the story the night was long spent and they were weary, they decided to spend the night under the sky which they had all agreed, when they prepared to sleep Nne began to sing.

My good mother I want to dance and you said I shouldn't hurt my feet,

My good mother I want to sing and you said I shouldn't hurt my throat

My good mother I wanted to run and you said I shouldn't hurt my legs

You have always taken good care of me my good mother

My good mother my friends and I want to play and you said I shouldn't hurt myself

My good mother I'm going to the stream and you said I shouldn't hurt my head

You are too good my good mother

As she sang and thought of her mother tears rolled down her cheeks.

Iwobo and Obeli each wanted to perform a magic and take Nne's hurt away, to do something so she could stop crying, they could do nothing but remain silent and hope she drifted into sleep, not long their prayer was answered and she slept off.

*****

The people of Akom had waited long enough. In their meeting they decided to start moving the captives the following day even without Oja. They had searched for him. All the elders had refused to take a slave. They wished that all of Akuta should be moved to the seacoast. Emmrika spoke, he was the most jovial as his friends regarded him to be. He was always playing his flute and singing for the children, with the resolve the meeting ended.

CHAPTER 23

When Adanna woke up the compound was still empty and the cocks were crowing, she passed the Herbalist's hut and noticed he was awake, she knocked but he was not in, he had gone to pick herbs and didn't tell anyone. Adanna herself didn't know the village so she couldn't go anywhere, but as her usual self she opted to go to the forest. After a while she made her way back to the compound of the Herbalist, as she entered the compound he was already standing in front of her hut.

"Where did you go? Everyone was looking for you, only your men said we shouldn't worry that it was your custom." The Herbalist said.

"I went to the forest."

"The forest is a dangerous place, there are dangerous animals and evil things in the forest." He sounded concerned but Adanna didn't notice.

"Don't worry about me, I can take care of myself so don't worry" with that she went into her hut, not long the Herbalist mother called out to her to come and bath as her water was ready. Adanna who was now accustomed to people serving her happily obliged. Once she was through she decided to go see Obirika, when she got to the hut where she was kept, she didn't look dejected anymore as she had accepted her fate and washed herself. Adanna looked at her with disgust when she saw Adanna she began to plea and beg for her freedom.

"My daughter, please forgive me if I have ever wronged you. Don't sell me as a slave, don't forget I have a daughter just like you." Obirika pleaded.

"May the gods strike your mouth." Adanna replied.

As she said it she walked away while Obirika began to weep. She went back to her hut, the compound of the Herbalist was bubbling with life people came in and went out. Children were running around playing both the free born and the slaves. The Herbalist was hardly around as he was always called to come and attend to those sick, while also people waited for him in his compound. Indeed he was a busy man. Oja sat in the compound wishing that the men watching him would walk away a little as he planned to call one of the children and send him to the place of his friend and ask him to come and rescue him, he was patiently waiting for the opportunity at the moment all he had to do was sit down and look around with them, doing nothing and just watching the day pass by. Adanna felt sick because of boredom, what she would do was to follow the Herbalist next time he was going out.

CHAPTER 24

Erika began to feel the excruciating pain she used to feel at the base of her skull, and her friends helped her to go lie inside, so not to aggravate the pain she felt, the pain was getting worse. Gemeri told another of the girls to run and call the Herbalist. When she got to the compound of the Herbalist he was not around. She dropped a message with his mother. The sun was going down, it was just on the horizon, as if it was about to sink into a deep sea. When she left, the Herbalist came back to attend to the people who waited for him in his compound, he would have to discharge some and ask them to come back some time later. When Adanna learnt he was back she went to meet him as she was going, his mother also went to tell him about the girl that came for the daughter of Lebachu. When they both stood before his hut, out of respect which was rare with Adanna she decided to let his mother speak first. She told him that a girl came to call him for the daughter of Lebachu was sick again, immediately he heard it was Erika. He quickly moved into his hut, discharged the people waiting for him, telling them he would visit them, some only wanted potions and he gave it to them then hurriedly took his bag and staff and stepped out to help Erika. She was a constant worry for him, with that Adanna followed him for he had not given her audience, as they both left the compound she made the request of following him around as she had nothing to do. The Herbalist accepted, why not walk with her for a change who knows what may come out of it?

*****

It was the 3rd day of their journey and 4th of the people they were after. If the gods were on their side they could still catch up with them but not at the pace they were going. They needed to walk faster and put more speed to their march. Nne knew this and she made her thought known to the two gentlemen with her.

"We will walk at this pace and still meet up with them don't worry." Obeli answered.

They were not in the mood to walk faster the journey was already taking its toll on them, they were weary and wondered if Nne was too. But how could she be it was her mother that they were looking for, if they didn't find her what would she do? With this resolve, they began their march in a short while they would be in Umi village and would refresh and top their supplies, they hoped that no evil awaited them in their journey. They got to Umi village, and also saw the slaves bound for the seacoast, Nne rushed to them, this was the umpteenth time she was seeing slaves bound for the seacoast She remembered her encounter with Akintu the village slave handler of Akumi she had ran to the slaves in Akumi in hope of seeing her mother but she was not amongst them. As she watched them she had asked a man who was attending the slaves, if he had seen her mother then she gave a detailed description of her mother.

"Really?" Akintu was shocked, "That is your mother? I'm not sure if I'm correct but it may be the woman I saw with Mmerika and her company."

"Who is Mmerika?" Nne asked.

"The most beautiful woman I have ever seen." With that he had shrugged, as if he had just come back to his senses. As he had said the name Mmerika he was lost in thought, he was thinking about Mmerika and he was smiling to himself, he realized himself and slowly walked away, Nne went after him.

"Please can you tell me where they went?" Nne had asked.

"To the shore of course, I am Akintu by the way, lovely lady what is your name."

"Nne!"

"What a beautiful name, you know I'm looking for a wife, maybe you are the lucky one, I'm sure you are from Akom your village seems to produce beautiful women."

"I don't think so sir thank you very much for your help." Nne said. Obeli and Iwobo were still looking around for Obirika. Maybe Adanna had changed her mind but Obeli knew his sister she was the most determined he knew.

Since Akintu conquered the fear of talking to women it seemed to him that he could marry every and any woman that crossed his path, days ago it was Adanna now he thought it was Nne.

He moved away again, this time Nne didn't follow him, she moved back to where Iwobo and Obeli were standing and related what has transpired between her and the slave handler.

"That man over there," she pointed "Said my mother is with a woman named Mmerika and some other people."

When she passed the news Iwobo and Obeli both glanced at each other surely they knew who Mmerika was.

"What else did he say?" Iwobo asked.

"Nothing" Nne answered.

"Did you ask him when they passed here?" Obeli had asked.

With the question she turned to find Akintu and ask him but he was gone, he wasn't in the village square any more.

Back to the present Nne felt peace at least her mother was still alive, on the other hand she felt pain because she didn't know when they passed the village of Akumi and in what condition she was in, with the information they had gathered they got supplies and on the way from the market square in Umi village they asked some ladies who were selling jar where the stream was, they needed a bath badly. Iwobo and Obeli had suggested believing Nne would appreciate it.

"We will bathe when we get back." Nne said to them.

"We can't continue like this, let's go and bathe and then continue the journey" Obeli pleaded.

Nne refused, "Then I will continue the journey without you both," saying this she passed them, for they were leading the way before, they couldn't let her march on, on her own, so they followed her, succumbing to her decision. Gradually Obeli was beginning to feel what she felt, he couldn't get her image out of his head and he wished for nothing else than that Nne had her mother with her. So he could see what smile looked like on her face. Nne was very pretty, and an envy of other girls, the gods had richly blessed her. She was the desire of every man that laid his eyes upon her, her hair was full and long unlike the hairs of her mates, her height was perfect and her ebony complexion bloomed, in the heart of Obeli he had seen a woman he would like to call his wife, but how to tell her might be an issue from now on he would fully support her and make her happy as much as he could do, he would be the reason why she smiled. He must see a smile upon her face before their journey ended he now knew what his destiny was. They moved on with Nne leading the way, but when they got to the village square Iwobo resumed leading the way.

*****

The captives had been sorted and everyone had gathered to see them as they were marched off. It was the warriors of Akom that would march them off. The children in front, followed by the women, then the men, all the captives from Akuta were tied as they marched out. Ubiakwa with other elders were in happy mood, soon they would have the items the warriors would return. He remembered the gun he had gotten when they led slaves to the seacoast and they were also expecting wines and lots of them, he had assorted wines all which he had bartered for slaves at the seacoast. As they passed people cheered and all considered it a day for revelry. The Chief Priest came and gave a speech, imploring the people to rejoice for their god was still alive, they increased their shouting and the women began to sing. As they sang the warriors who were taking the captives to the shore began to whip those that refused to move or stand. For these ones, the sun had set in their time. These ones wouldn't see their fatherland again, their brothers were selling them to a faraway land where they didn't know the custom or tradition. Their future generation wouldn't know where they were from or what had befallen their ancestors.

*****

It was almost dark when Adanna left with the Herbalist, she had a long stick which she had sharpened the end point to be pin pointed.

"What are you going to do with that?" the Herbalist asked feeling a bit frightened.

"It's for protection."

"Protection against what," he said, almost laughing at Adanna's edginess.

"Against whatever that may attack."

As if she knew danger would be on the way as the words were coming out from her mouth two young men jumped out from the bush beside the Herbalist, the pathway was deserted. The Herbalist was rattled and surprised.

"Drop everything you have on the ground." One of the men commanded.

"Come and take them, if you want to die." Adanna sternly replied, now pointing her weapon at them.

The other of the men who had not spoken began to laugh and his friend joined him, now they were both laughing.

"My lady won't you drop that thing before you hurt yourself we only want to have fun with you two." He said laughing louder.

He approached Adanna by now the Herbalist had dropped all he was with on the ground.

"Just be obedient and nothing will happen to you," the assailant cautioned.

"Over my dead body." Adanna said and spat out violently on the ground.

"Okay let us have it your way," he said frowning, he came forward to drag the weapon from Adanna, but she was quick, she avoided that and with the pinpointed part pierced him by the side of the belly, after making a 360 degree turn. He quickly moved back as his friend caught him, he held his hand to the side that had been pierced, he was bleeding, his companion saw it and was confused. Should he attempt his own and try grabbing the weapon from Adanna or should he help his friend who was bleeding or should he just flee. He chose the last one, he fled. His friend seeing that he had been abandoned, managed to get up, and limped away, with the Herbalist surprised at Adanna's bravery.

"You better run!" she shouted to them, "That is what you get for attacking an Akom girl."

"An Akom girl indeed, so are all of you this strong and brave or is it just only you?" The Herbalist said, picking up his possessions that he had dropped on the ground.

"I don't have an answer to that question." Adanna said looking at the Herbalist in a way that, suggested such questions annoy her.

"Well then, at least now I know what an Akom girl is capable of, remind me to be careful next time when I meet an Akom girl," he rose to his feet for he had been kneeling since and dusted himself, "The girl we are going to meet is very dear to me, but with this danger we have encountered I think we should go back."

"Let's continue the journey." Adanna ordered.

"They may have gone to re-group and come back with a larger number," the Herbalist said pointing to the direction the robbers had ran to.

"Those were hooligans, scoundrels that is what they are they are gone for good, let's continue on our journey." Adanna assured.

"I must thank you," he said as they marched on. "You definitely have saved my life back there thank you very much."

"I saved both of us."

"Indeed you are right."

"Such is the problem we are facing here in Mkpunki. Our leaders don't care about any of these."

"It is everywhere even in Akom." Adanna said looking forward and sounding unconcerned.

"Every man to himself, no one cares about the other," the Herbalist deeply concerned, "Akom we have heard from travelers how you people defeated the people of Akuta and would soon sell them all into slavery."

"That is what they deserve."

"I don't think that any man deserves slavery. Nobody knows what they are going through, we sell our brothers to the white man and we never see them again, no one knows what they pass through. Whether they survive or die or what is done to them we know not, slavery I tell you is an evil. We black men, we all now start wars just so we can have slaves for the slave market, people are disappearing every day, why? because kidnapping is now the order of the day, I tell you slavery will kill us all, no man should be a slave not even in our villages." The Herbalist was raising his voice now having lost the fear of the men that just accosted them.

"But you have slaves in your compound."

"They are servants, they were bought by my father when he was alive now they serve his family, if anything they are treated better than some free born. So you see slavery is not good."

"You can say all you want there will always be slaves and Obirika is one of them."

"Really you don't even want to see reason, Oh! here we are this is where we are going." The Herbalist pointed.

"You don't want to see reason," he repeated as he opened the wooden barrier that served as gate he stepped into the compound, a young girl met them and led them to where Erika was lying, immediately he held some herbs to her nostril for her to inhale, she was always having problems breathing. He also gave her some potions to drink and she drank. Lebachu stepped in and was pleased to see the Herbalist already at work, gradually she began to regain her strength.

"I will be back in the morning." The Herbalist said.

"Thank you great one, you are too kind." Lebachu said.

"Yes, she will be fine but I will come a little late in the morning for I don't want to encounter what we encountered tonight," he was proud of Adanna who was waiting outside. He narrated the story of the two men who had accosted and harassed them earlier, all was terrified and at the same time proud of Adanna who was still standing outside with blood stained weapon in her hand.

"Indeed it is a perilous time we are living in." Lebachu added.

"Indeed it is," answered the Herbalist. "We must start going, Peace be with you all." With that the Herbalist left and motioned to Adanna for them to start going, like an ever ready gun, she responded and they marched home. This time with a quick pace and saying little, when they got home the Herbalist narrated the story all over again to his household. The act of Adanna had left a lasting impression upon him. Adanna went to the hut Obirika was and observed her then she went and checked her men who were guarding Oja, everything was in perfect condition.

*****

Nne had increased her pace, in a day's time they would be in Mkpunki. Iwobo and Obeli were still marching on they couldn't have it said that a woman surpassed them in strength. On their journey they had seen many strangers who made them feel they were on a lost course, because they were all in unity not reflecting the want and pain of Nne, most if not all the strangers, all seemed happy and content as if nothing was wrong with the world but with Nne everything was wrong. Nne had been wondering what she would do if a fight was required to free her mother, she would tear apart anything that stood in her way. She had resolved to be merciless, but the task was more than meets the eye. Iwobo had been diligent leading them stupendously and had not faltered even now he didn't want to stop not now that they were close to Mkpunki. Obeli was marching behind the two feeling agitated and at peace at the same time for now he wished nothing but what would make Nne happy. Again he wished they were in Akom where he had plenty and could give to her and also make her happy and contented but such a time would come, he assured himself, very soon he would be everything Nne wished he was, now they must do the necessary by finding her mother.

*****

Adanna knew by noon she would be gone. She would complete her business at the shore and go back to Akom. The return journey wouldn't be this slow they had been slow because they had to drag Obirika along but when going there wouldn't be much burden only her and her new gun. Yes her gun the one that would look just like her father's, it would be a thing of joy, when she would be holding it, and it would be very useful for her hunting, she would fear nothing.

*****

Adanna again went out with the Herbalist, as she had nothing to do. It was time to move on, it was the 8th day of the week of sacrifice and they were free to leave. She had to tell him, outside her hut the women were seated weaving baskets, clothes and gossiping, she reasoned that she would always have better things to do with her time than to sit down and weave baskets, tell old wives tales to children and make them believe in whatever you wished them to believe in. Neither was it washing, she would always have slaves for that. Sometimes she wondered why it was only the women that cooked why couldn't the men cook also, was there a law forbidding them. And again only at a young age did men go to stream once they were grown they realized how it is a woman's job to go to the stream, she would have none of that, what she wanted to do was what she would do. She took her weapons with her, after meeting the Herbalist she and her gang would be going. The Herbalist had come to cherish his times with her. She didn't talk much but was a good listener and always ready to show forth manly characters. This time they went into the forest as the Herbalist went to pick herbs, a thing his father had taught him, and now he had discovered so many for himself. He was quite good at what he did, he wouldn't dream of doing anything else. What a fine thing it was for him, as they marched along, he showed he felt certain he wasn't wasting his time. For the first time someone was joining him to pick herbs since his father passed away.

"When my father used to bring me to this forest, he would teach me the herbs that do good and the ones that brought harm. My father always regarded everything as meaningless. Most times he would ask me what I thought of life as a young boy. I would tell him that I believed life was a gift, the god 'oda' had given us life to cherish it. But he would tell me that's not all, my father never believed in gods but he believed that man should love his neighbour. It always did rent his heart when someone he was tending died. He would call me and tell me that life was meaningless, all you have to do was love your neighbour. When the white woman came and I conversed with her she told me the same thing from her strange religion. My father never collected money from those he gave herbs, and we used to welcome so many strangers into our home then. It is unfortunate others don't see my father, the way I saw him, now no one cares about anyone. Look at this plant it is bitterleaf, it can be applied to a wound and it would heal, we can also use it for food, nothing else. My father believed the plant gave and took nothing back, he reasoned that if only we could give and expect nothing back, there won't be so much hardship."

"Your father must have been a wise man." Adanna said.

"He was the wisest I have ever known. My grandfather was a hunter but my father didn't want to follow his path instead he decided to be a herbalist to be able to help people, and I've chosen to be like him, see the world the way he saw the world there is nothing like it." The Herbalist said.

"And how do you see it?" Adanna asked.

"Like he saw it, it is meaningless, a man is born today he toils all his life to put food in his stomach, at the end of the day he dies. No one knows what will happen when we die, of course the Chief Priest say we are reborn but that is not what the white woman said. For me I have never seen a man die and then get reborn. So the same for me, life is also meaningless, we come into the world, we grow old and we die and another generation continues from where we stopped. Everything changes nothing ever remains the same yet nothing is new, it's all the same things existing in nature, the humans none has ever reincarnated that I know."

"I have never thought of all these before."

"It is important that we ask ourselves some questions some times. People believe the gods have the answer I don't always believe so, there are so many things that have not been answered. Would you follow me to the places where I'm to give the herbs after mixing them?"

"I actually came to tell you that we are leaving once the sun is at the highest point and it would soon be so." Adanna said subdued.

"Indeed you are right, I thought you people wanted to spend some time, but it is okay, all is well I will follow you home then."

Adanna never fully understood all he said but she didn't care. It was none of her business what life was all about there are so many things she had not thought about. The Herbalist made some more picks and they went home.

*****

Nne was almost running, fear began to grip Iwobo and Obeli as to where she was getting the energy from. They were almost in Mkpunki, things had been favourable to them and they had not encountered any problem except when they stopped and Obeli helped an old woman to carry her firewoods on her head. Nothing more had happened, Iwobo had stopped telling jokes, stories and singing. He was conserving the whole energy for the journey now. As it appeared that even a woman had strength more than him. They were now entering Mkpunki, Nne could feel her mother close by, she could tell that she was not far away as the bonds between them meant that she felt what her mother felt. Her mother that had been too kind to her, consoling her since the death of her father. Everyone knew she had no one else, if she lost her mother, she would be alone in the world. Now she reasoned what made her even leave her mother, why was she not there to protect her when they came to kidnap her? She would have fought back no matter how many they were, because it was a matter of life and death, now she was about to lose her to fiends. Callous people who didn't consider she was the only one she had in the whole wide world.

*****

Adanna returned with the Herbalist and he wished her well, soon they would resume their journey. Adanna was excited to move on, when she went into her hut she called her men she should have taken Okanka, Uja and Aroro, but the men she had taken have proved resourceful. They had kept the business going but they were doing it for a reward that they would get and she couldn't confide in them not like she would have done to Aroro, Uja or Okanka. She never considered her crusader group for such purpose, Nini had always wondered why. When two of the men came, only one was remaining to watch Oja. He was the same one that had caught Obeli, nothing escaped his gaze and he did his job like a veteran. Adanna tried to trust them, they were men of Akom who would do anything for a fee. When Oja noticed that he was alone with only one man, as he was seated in front of the hut they had been sharing while the man watching him was standing behind him, he thought of how he would trick him to come to his front, there was a stone as big as a coconut in front of him.

"Please help me with water." Oja said.

"I will when they return." Eke said. The names of the other two men were, Neti and Buni.

"But I'm really thirsty, you can trust me, have I done anything that would make you not to trust me?" Oja couldn't believe himself, Oja the great whom they sang songs about begging for water, and the person he was making the plea to, refusing, how the times have changed.

He didn't need the water he wanted an opportunity where he would get the stone closer to himself, and put it to the task that he wished to put it to, as he continued his plea, a child came along crying. Oja called him and brought him closer to himself, the man watching him looked away after he took the child upon his laps he began to console him, the man stepped back further from Oja. Oja took the opportunity to whisper into the boy's hears, he told him to go to his friend, he gave the direction and description of his friend's place asking him to come to his rescue, he set the boy down and the boy ran out as Oja ended with a promise of a reward for the boy. The boy instead of going on the errand went and told his mother all that Oja had said. The enterprise failed Oja. The mother of the boy troubled, went to the Herbalist.

"The people you brought here are asking for trouble. How can he send my little boy on such a dangerous errand?" she asked sadly.

"It's okay I will handle it." The Herbalist replied.

The Herbalist went and narrated all to Adanna, who thanked him and apologized, and she said nothing to Oja who didn't know his plan failed both getting stone to smash his guards head to run away and asking his friend to come to his aid.

*****

The Herbalist was waiting for them at the entrance of the compound, as they made their way from the back of the compound. Adanna walking hastily, they said their goodbyes, secured Obirika and left. Thanking the Herbalist for his kindness, the shore was no longer far away, they could make it that same day, as they marched along Oja began plotting his move as to how to escape. All his plans had failed, his friend had not gotten back to him and now they were leaving. He wouldn't know where they were. They moved and he considered his position, if he took the man by his right he wouldn't have enough time to take the man by his left and another was at his back with Adanna and he wouldn't do much with his hands bound. How would he survive? He kept his pace while still calculating his chances of escaping. Something must happen, he should have escaped when they were in the forest but if only he had the chance then, but they were ready for him then, watching him very closely, he supposed that by now they would be less vigilant. One of the men that had been watching him, he didn't know what his problem was, he was taking his job too serious, he really needed a break. They were getting close to the shore Adanna sighted the canoes. The canoes would take them to the white man's barracoon, where the white men were, she didn't want to stop at the riverbank. If possible she wanted to be there when Obirika was hauled into the ship and watch the ship set sail. They got to the riverbank, they met slave dealers at the riverbank who were also putting the captives in the canoe ready and set for the port where the white men were. Adanna motioned to one and called him to herself she told him they wanted to sell slaves.

"You can do that anywhere here, unless you want to meet the white man, the white men would be more than happy to buy." The stranger said.

"Can you add them to your own we will follow suit." Adanna said.

"Who and who if I may ask?"

"The man and the woman, the man is Oja he is a renowned warrior from Akuta, the woman is......" before she could finish he cut her speech off.

"I don't really care to know their names all I want to know is, if they are for sale."

"They are for sale, what can I get for them? I want a gun."

As she was talking he shouted a command to his second who was doing something he looked like he shouldn't be doing.

"You want a gun, when you get to the barracoon you can also tell them that, they will be more than happy to give you a gun, since you are selling them. Let me tell my men to tie them down." The slaver said.

"Please do." Adanna was feeling anxious now.

As Oja kept looking around he was still planning for his escape. Adanna gave her men a sign and they pushed him down, both him and Obirika. Obirika was already tied, they began to tie Oja,

"What are you doing? Hey! will you stop that, what do you think you are doing?" Oja shouted.

"Keep your mouth shut." The man replied.

"Adanna what are you doing, why are they tying me, we had an agreement. You promised to let me go?" Oja shouted louder.

"You really didn't think I was going to set you free did you, if you did you must be a big fool Oja and delusional, honestly I thought that you were wiser."

"You serpent, you are betraying me, after all I have done for you?"

"Consider it a good thing, my village men would have mutilated you, I'm doing you a favour, I'm setting you free, go to where they will take you and have peace there."

"Adanna it is me Oja that you are betraying, Oja will have his revenge I will haunt you forever you and your generations to come."

As he spoke he was being tied, after tying him he was still shouting "I'm Oja Adanna."

"Oja dike the mighty one, I will haunt you forever."

As if stirred Obirika began to sob.

"Adanna my daughter please have pity, I'm old enough to be your mother."

"Indeed you are but where you are going it will not matter, take them away."

They both were hauled away Oja was still struggling showing the man he was, it took four men to take him to the canoe and bind him with chains, which he could never break, both of them were bound on the neck, which joined others and their ankles were shackled and their hands bound.

Oja desperately wished his friend would show up, but he was nowhere to be found, he pleaded to the gods to save him, for the first time in his life he was genuinely scared nothing could explain what he was feeling and thought. He felt like grabbing Adanna and squeezing her neck till there was no life left in her. He couldn't do it, not now, now he was bound, he had brought people to the seacoast to be sold and now he was being sold. He couldn't see any familiar face, this couldn't be happening to him, Oja dike with numerous slaves now to be a slave. He had been betrayed, how could he have been so stupid? Adanna touched her bag and felt the supplies the Herbalist had given her, her plans were going well, soon she would have all she desired. She had planned it well, she would have to come through this path again, with Nne and all those who have wronged her. She observed as Oja and Obirika were placed in a canoe, then her new acquaintance which she had met at the riverbank, informed her of the canoe they were going to use. She entered and sat down as her men followed, she really meant it, that she would watch them set sail, she wouldn't have her endeavour truncated, she must follow it to the latter, she sat down comfortably.

"I want you people to be careful now, very careful this is now a critical point, and we must be vigilant, this people are not to be trusted, none of them," as she spoke her new ally joined them, he had been in slave business for as long as he could remember nothing surprised him anymore and nothing touched his heart. He had heard so many cries and pleas and he had learnt to ignore it all. They made their way to the shore from the bight Adanna very much pleased soon they were at the shore. Adanna's new acquaintance introduced her to Mr. Cowe who was a slaver, quickly they exchanged pleasantries with the help of interpreters. The environment was nothing like Adanna imagined, there were quarters for the white man which was looking beautiful and neat like nothing Adanna had ever seen before, it pleased her immeasurably. Soon they presented their slaves who were inspected for fitness and usefulness especially the dentition. Those that were into catching slaves knew by now what the white man wanted, so they didn't bring maimed, old or unfit people, the people they brought were strong men and women who were capable of doing hard labour. Where these people were shipped to, none of them knew and they never bothered to find out. Oja dike now certain aid wouldn't come couldn't hide his anger as he kept struggling.

Obirika had given up hope. Soon it would be dark, she had looked around, Adanna with her group had gone into the office of the white man to discuss terms of transaction. As she was looking around she fell into despair, then she saw a young woman, very beautiful, the lady couldn't behold them, from the way she looked at them something was troubling her but she didn't know what. She came and looked at them with a young black man by her side they both looked distraught. Obirika had never seen a white woman before and this one looked kindly on her. She also inspected them and moved away. Obirika continued staring in despair. Mary had gone back to where she was staying alone away from the slaves just so she could clear her head when she noticed three people behind her they were crouching behind her shade. She had come to know the locals and these ones didn't look dangerous, but wanted something she couldn't tell what it is they wanted. Nne had seen her look at her mother when no one else was looking. She decided to try her luck.

What could it cost her. If she tried and got into trouble, so be it. What her mind was telling her was what she would do. Iwobo urged her to wait till night so they could try and break the chain, but it was an idea that would end in futility for they didn't know how to open the locks. Nne re–assured them and got more confident when she saw John.

"Let me do it." Obeli pleaded.

"No I will," Nne responded humbly, and it soothed Obeli. She went to John bending her back not wanting to be seen. She explained to John that she wanted to talk to Mary. John agreed and proved an ample interpreter as Nne spoke to Mary after hearing her ordeal she was moved, almost to tears. It was a sad story indeed, how could it be that such a fair lady have suffered much and the worst watch her mother taken away. Quickly Mary ran to the slave handlers and ordered that Obirika be loosed and unchained. Obirika couldn't hide her surprise and apprehension; does the white woman want to eat here and now?

"But madam why set free?" The slaver asked.

"I'm buying her, when her owner comes tell the owner I bought her." Mary said.

Obirika whose shackles were being removed didn't understand a word they were saying but she couldn't still hide her apprehension. Mary took her to her shade, as they walked towards the shade, Obirika saw Nne she couldn't believe her eyes, she burst into a sprint towards Nne and embraced her tightly almost cutting her air supply.

"Nne is it you?"

"Yes mother it is me." She turned to Mary, "How can we thank you?"

John interpreted.

"Just go, it's all fine." Mary said smiling and pleased that she had caused some people to have joy.

"Really?" both Nne and Obirika surprised.

"Yes indeed you are free."

"Mother she said we are free." Nne said. They continued embracing.

Oja didn't know what was happening he was expecting his shackles to be loosed too, but they were not.

When Adanna came out from the office of the slave dealers, where she had gone to make the exchange of humans for a gun, she inquired as to where about of Obirika, by the man who was watching her but was told she had been bought.

"By who?" she demanded.

"By our Master Lady Mary."

"And who is the Mary that be?"

"A captain's daughter."

With her new gun hanging on her shoulder Adanna couldn't hide her anger, she writhed in pain.

"No, no, no this can't be happening, which way did they follow?"

He pointed to the direction, immediately she motioned to her men and they followed in hot pursuit. She couldn't let Obirika have her freedom, this time she would end the matter, she had been too lenient. This time she wouldn't show any kindness she would end Obirika and whoever it was that was helping her. As they ran after them, Iwobo, Obeli, Nne and Obirika who were now exhausted withheld their joy as they walked hastily back to their canoe. They had started moving when they looked back and saw people running towards them, they looked closely and saw who it was, Nne was bewildered.

"What is she doing here?" Nne asked pointing towards Adanna.

"She is my slaver." Obirika answered.

Obeli felt like entering the ground, he was speechless, Iwobo shouted to the man paddling.

"Please paddle faster" Adanna and her group mounted their own canoe and began to chase. Obirika couldn't believe her luck she wished for help. As they made their way to land they began to run with all the strength they could muster, they were supposed to be weary but with their pace it was not showing. None of them wanted to be a slave. Obirika was leading the pack, Iwobo and Obeli couldn't believe her speed, as she ran past them all. Nne was the last, Obeli ran like a cat in pursuit of a rat. None of them wanted to get caught. Not going the way they came instead of entering the village of Mkpunki they followed the forest path. As they ran Adanna and her group made it to shore and followed in hot pursuit running as fast as possible in the forest. Adanna could see Nne not thinking twice she fired her gun, aiming it at Nne but she missed as the bullet hit a tree before Nne. Instantly Nne knew she had just escaped death, she increased her pace and was now together with Obeli, Iwobo wondered how long it was, that they would have to run, they kept running still, nothing could make them stop. A pit was dug as a trap for forest pigs, others passed it Adanna didn't see it as it was properly covered with leaves. As Adanna chased after them she fell into the pit and was badly hurt. Her men stopped abruptly to help her, she was slipping into unconsciousness but still managed to say "Go after them" in pain as she was lifted out of the pit.

"Adanna I have to take you to the Herbalist," as Neti spoke he didn't observe she had become unconscious. He lifted her up and decided to take her to the Herbalist, the remaining two men chased after Obirika and co. a little while and then turned back. It wasn't their job to chase after people, Adanna wasn't paying them for that. They made their way back to the place where they left her. In their mind they had done the job that she paid them half for, and was to complete payment for. They took half payment and when the job was done to collect the remaining half. Now the job was done and they needed their pay. When they got to the point, their colleague was making a bed to carry her on from the woods lying around. They joined him and made the bed, when it was ready they carried her on it to the Herbalist. They took time in making their way, by asking directions from people they got the way they even made gestures for the people of Mkpunki to understand them. As they approached the Herbalist's compound he saw them, for he was sitting in front of his hut, he ran towards them. He saw that it was Adanna, his heart ached he had hoped that no evil would befall her, people had gathered to watch what was unfolding.

"Quickly, take her to my hut," he said to them as they moved he watched Adanna to ascertain the level of harm she had suffered, but that could wait he ran into the hut before them and started clearing spaces where she would be laid. Adanna was still unconscious, the men brought her into the Herbalist's hut and placed her where he pointed, immediately he started to fan her and asked for water to sprinkle on her all in a bid to resuscitate her. As he diligently continued to work on her, the men moved out of the hut to deliberate amongst themselves on what their next point of call would be. Whether to wait for Adanna in Mkpunki, or go back to Akom to wait for her but by now those people and Obirika were heading to Akom, and would definitely tell people who the captors of Obirika was, so they decided against it. They would wait for Adanna to re-gain consciousness and from there know what to do. In the hut of the Herbalist he was still checking Adanna for signs of life and she needed cleaning her body was all muddy which must have happened when she fell into the pit and her garments were all soiled but that too would have to wait. The Herbalist tried to make sure that none of her bones were broken, so far it had turned out well but the ankle of her left leg looked somewhat out of place. He closely examined it and strongly believed that it had a problem he got some calico materials and two sticks with smoothened surfaces placing them side by side he began to tie her ankle after applying the necessary herbs and doing what needed to be done on the leg. All day long the Herbalist did nothing else but attend to Adanna, he couldn't entertain the thoughts of having her hurt. By the side of Adanna was lying all her belongings the Herbalist picked all of them up to put it in a better place for her and also to keep it safe until she woke up, and now also she still needed cleaning.

CHAPTER 25

Obeli and Iwobo had long stopped running including Nne and her mother since they noticed that no one was pursuing them anymore. They had been walking though and they were walking as fast as possible to get away from their enemies, before they changed their minds and decided to resume pursuing them again. They all walked fast and tried to take different route when possible. None of them was talking, all that each of them had in mind was to get to a safe place. Darkness was approaching and they were weary, but sleep was far from their eyes especially Obirika who believed she had escaped death and needed to be thankful to the god "Utte" for keeping her and her daughter. When they had moved a considerable distance without anyone following them they became assured that their chasers had gone back. It was almost dark and they had been walking all day, they ran half of the day and walked the remaining of the day. Exhaustion was beginning to set in and the fact you couldn't cheat nature was bare, they couldn't move any longer. Obirika feeling tired but not wanting to risk her life until she got to a safe place urged them to move on even if for a little longer they made fire and also marched in the night, their legs was now almost sore, Obeli who couldn't take it anymore spoke up.

"I think we should stop here for rest, we are quite exhausted," he said.

"Let's move a little more, then we can be rest assured that our pursuers won't find us easily." Obirika reasoned.

"But they are gone?"

"We can't be too sure let us just keep moving at least move out from the normal route." Obirika said almost pleading.

"That is what we should do the remaining distance, we will walk, let us move out of the main footpath." Nne said.

"I think that it is a good plan," Iwobo added "We can still find our way even though we are not following the normal route."

"All I can say is let us move out of the main route and then rest." Obeli said.

"Alright, agreed." Obirika said.

With the resolution they moved from the path they had been following into another path that would make it hard to track them, if anyone decided to follow them. Obirika had not said much she had been considering what to do. Now Nne was walking beside her, and held her hand she couldn't believe that after so long she would see her daughter again, or even regain her freedom, it was a thing of joy for her and for now she must ensure that she didn't lose it again.

*****

Since the warriors of Akom took the captives of Akuta out of Akom to the seacoast, Akom had remained calm. Nothing in the form of strange happening was occurring only the fact that people were still disappearing occasionally, everyone had gone back to attend their barn or farm, or all the activity that people of Akom were known for.

Ubiakwa was somewhat bothered, he had not seen Obeli or Adanna, and his mind told him something was wrong but how could he find out, they went to his brother's place.

CHAPTER 26

The Herbalist had slept in another hut as Adanna occupied his hut, but occasionally either his mother or him would go to check on her. This was the first day since she passed out, she was breathing fine, but had not moved an inch. The Herbalist had done all he knew and now his mind was telling him to do nothing but wait. Hopefully she would wake up and when she did she would be fine, he arranged for her to be cleaned and still waited till she woke up for other things. She breathed fine and looked fresh, unlike the day before where she was looking pale. After a while the men that she came with, who were now once more guest of the Herbalist came to check on her and felt downcast when they learnt she had not woken up. The Herbalist assured them she would be fine, but in his heart prayed for it to be so.

"But how are you sure?" Buni asked him.

"I have checked her and done all I know how to, she will come around, in a matter of days."

"Days!" They screamed.

"It could be less, but let us hope for the best." The Herbalist said.

"Is there nothing else you can do, she can't remain like this?" Buni said gesturing towards Adanna.

"I have done my best she will be fine I can assure you." The Herbalist once again assured.

As they spoke one of the servants of the Herbalist came into the hut and dropped her garments that has been washed, and left as she was about to leave the Herbalist beckoned on her.

"Nnadi bring my food, it is funny that I should ask before my food is served." He turned to the men, "Gentlemen have you eaten this morning?"

"No we haven't." They answered in unison.

Nnadi was still standing patiently waiting and listening to their orders.

"Bring food for my friends here. Who is to cook food this morning and why have you people not served anyone?" The Herbalist asked.

"Master we are still cooking." She responded.

"At this time you people are still cooking?"

"We are sorry master."

"Please call my mother for me and bring me food once it is ready."

"I don't know why I'm feeling particularly hungry this morning." Said Buni.

"It is normal my brother you should feel such." The Herbalist answered.

"Well I ate last night." Buni continued still surprised.

"It happens sometimes and when it happens you should satisfy the hunger," Eke said, the strongest one amongst them his biceps was almost the size of a boy's thigh.

"That is exactly what I plan to do and nothing more." Buni said.

The Herbalist had said nothing more, even though he had ordered for food, he didn't feel like feasting not when Adanna was in the state that she was in. As they all sat together in the hut waiting for their meal, the Herbalist gazed at Adanna and wondered what he was not doing right, maybe there was something that he needed to do that he was not doing. If only the gods would answer and bring her up, he would consider it a great act of the gods if she would open her eyes. But none was happening as she laid there motionless one of the men the shortest amongst them feeling like something was missing in the Herbalist life asked him a question.

"If I may be so bold sir, why is it that you are not married? I can't help but notice that there is no woman that you have ever identified as wife since we have been staying here." It was Neti speaking.

The Herbalist smiled, it was a question he got asked so often. 'Why he was not married.'

"Marriage is not something to be taken so lightly." He said.

"Sir there is nothing to it, just see a woman and pay her bride price and she will be yours." Eke said joining the conversation.

"What if she doesn't want to be yours?" the Herbalist asked.

"Well she has no option but to accept, a woman is not supposed to have such rights." Eke said.

"My brother we are all equals and she should have such rights." The Herbalist said, correcting.

"If you think so my father married 6 women and I don't think any of them had the right to tell him they didn't want to marry him, as far as I'm concerned they are all happy." Neti said.

"You can't speak for them whether they are happy or not." The Herbalist said.

The others remained silent and only waited to talk when their food was brought, the discussion of marriage did not in any way disturb them. Buni continued pestering the Herbalist who only made him to understand that marriage should be more than paying bride price. As they continued their argument, Nnadi brought their food and served them, they all ate and the Herbalist whether consciously or unconsciously made sure not to enjoy his food as long as Adanna was in the condition that she was in. In the night of that day, he kept checking on her and she didn't move, all day they ate and discussed other matters including the weather and farmlands. The Herbalist was not a farmer, though there was a farm that was not that big at the back of his compound where he usually did little farming, and also planted some herbs, farming was not his thing. Instead his mother was the farmer and the remaining servants who farmed with her, his cousins were also farmers and fishermen, but stayed far away leaving only him and his mother and the slaves. In the compound the Herbalist preferred calling them servants instead of slaves as they ate and discussed one of the men the heavily built one (Eke) who talked little brought up the idea of them returning home.

"I'm sure it's a good thing for you people to want to return but I urge you to remain a little longer, at least wait for (Odabi) Adanna, are we not treating you well here?" The Herbalist asked weary.

"No no no," Buni said in quick succession "Indeed you have been too kind, you are treating us well, it's just we need to get our life back, now that our journey or should I say mission, has ended." He said.

"My brothers," the Herbalist said, "let us please wait for (Odabi) Adanna to come around she will recover soon and we will know what to do from there." The Herbalist said.

"It's like you read our minds, that is what we are actually doing but it is good that you are okay that we should wait for her."

As they spoke the girl Nnadi came to the Herbalist's hut, and told him some men were looking for him, and they were in front of the compound.

"What do they want?" he asked.

"They only said they wanted to see you master." She courteously answered.

"Bring them in let them wait, let me finish my meal, tell them I'm eating." The Herbalist said.

"I have already done that master."

"Good."

The Herbalist hurried his food and went to meet the men while Adanna's men continued with their food and their plans.

*****

Obirika was the first to wake up in the forest and when she awoke she called Nne her daughter, who was also just waking up, and took a little distance away from Obeli and Iwobo, she had told her she wanted to discuss something very important with her.

"My daughter," Obirika said "I'm scared, what are we going to do?"

"About what Mama?"

"Don't you want to talk about who kidnapped me?"

"I do Mama, but I thought it would be better if we don't talk about it. At least not now, when we are settled and fine then we can talk about it."

"It can't wait seeing that is it Adanna the daughter of Ubiakwa that is responsible for all the hardship we are going through."

"What exactly did we do to her, what harm has the family of Amadi, ever done to her?" Nne was almost screaming now and perplexed, tears rolled down her cheeks. Obeli heard her voice and woke up, he heard people talking but couldn't see anyone a tree was blocking his view but he was certain he was hearing voices.

"Calm down my daughter bring down your voice." Her mother pleaded.

"But mummy what did we ever do to her?" Nne was still in tears, crouching and holding her stomach to pacify her hurting abdomen.

"I don't know what we did to the family of Ubiakwa so now my daughter I don't think we should be going back to Akom, instead let us go to my village we will never set foot in Akom again."

Now Obeli was up, and felt concerned when he heard Nne sobbing, he went to the tree closest to them to know why she was sobbing. He had sworn to protect her and that was what he was going to do but first he needed to know what they were talking about. Eavesdropping was not good but he couldn't barge into where they were talking and expect them to fill him in, he needed to know what they were talking about. Nne and Obirika didn't notice anybody was eavesdropping. Obeli had hidden behind a tree and he didn't even wake Iwobo, he was surreptitiously doing what he was doing.

"And do you know who these men with you are?" Obirika continued.

"Mummy I know it is Ubiakwa's son and his friend." Nne said, still sobbing.

"We can't trust them, they are dangerous."

"But they have been helpful mama without them I wouldn't have found you."

"My dear there is nothing we can do about it they are from Ubiakwa, I wonder what they are planning all I can say is that they are dangerous and we can't trust them we must make a decision."

Obeli still eavesdropping was heartbroken he had wanted to tell Nne about Adanna but there was no way he could do it without hurting his sister. Now she got to find out this way but he had proven to her that he was not evil.

"Mother I think right now whatever you decided is what we will do, but we still need them, Iwobo is the one who knows the way, I think we should still be with them till we get to where we can find our way on our own."

Obeli weakened took a decision, he must tell Nne how she made him feel, he must tell her that her pleasure was his pleasure, he must tell her that she made the world a happier place for him, he must tell her that ever since he came to know her he could hardly think about anything else. He would do it and no matter what she was the one he would like to spend the rest of his life with. He moved away from the tree where he had been eavesdropping and went to lie down again, but the thought that Nne may not like him because of Adanna kept playing in his head, he had already proven himself and was ready to do more for her. He tried to pretend that he was sleeping then Iwobo woke up, since Iwobo was up there was no reason for him to pretend that he was sleeping. When he awoke the forest was calm, the birds though had started to chirp it must have been their noise that woke Iwobo up.

"Where are Nne and Obirika?" Iwobo asked.

"Over there behind the tree." Obeli answered.

"Hope all is well?" Iwobo asked.

"Indeed all is well hope you had a good night rest?"

Iwobo laughed, "good night rest on the ground in the forest, I hope to have it better when I get back to Akom."

"Me too, let's get going, let me call them." Obeli said.

As he was about to move Nne and her mother emerged from behind the Iroko tree.

"I was about to come call you two, let's get going we still have a far distance to cover." Obeli said this with what he heard, he had to pretend he didn't hear.

"It is a good idea." Nne said.

"I hope everyone is alright?" Obeli asked,

"Indeed we are." They answered in unison as if they were all expecting the question.

Obeli packed all his belongings as the others did likewise and they set out. They waited till they got to the next village before they thought of breakfast as they all moved out, Obeli looked back to make sure, they were not forgetting anything. When he did indeed they were forgetting something. Obirika had forgotten her water pouch he went back and picked it and ran to meet them.

"Obirika, here" handing it to her "Your water pouch." Obeli said.

She looked at him indeed it was hers, the pouch Nne had given her not long ago.

"Oh! Thank you." Obirika said.

"Hope nobody else is forgetting anything?" Obeli asked.

They all took a careful look of their belongings and responded in unison.

"No"

"Okay good."

They continued marching, it would be noon before they get to the next place where they could see humans it was not even a major village, when they got there they should consider their next move.

Iwobo had been marching alongside Nne, and he had nothing but smiles on his face. Nne looked at him and wondered what could be making him smile in their condition. She didn't bother to ask, he had been helpful to her indeed without him their journey would have been futile and she remained forever grateful. It didn't take them long till they got to the next relieve point where the slavers had built. The places were usually well stocked with food and they had their mouthful, and satisfied stomachs when they got there, they took a while to rest.

Feeling refreshed they had decided not to stay too long in a particular place, not long then they would leave the main path again, so that anybody tracking them would have found it difficult to do so. Nne was pleased with the idea since it came from Obeli and Iwobo agreeing. Iwobo seemed to know the whole place, his tale about knowing all the places because of his lost half-brother was heart breaking. Nne felt for him it would be a nice thing for him to one day see his brother just like she had found her mother.

"I know a stream down this path we can go there to bath." Iwobo said.

"Very good but ladies first, so you people will have to wait." Obirika said.

"We agree totally, just be quick so we don't spend too much time here." Obeli added.

Nne and her mother moved with them, they got to a point and stopped then Iwobo pointed to the path. The two of them set out Nne carrying all her belongings as well as her mother carrying also all her belongings. The few Nne had given her with hope she indeed would rescue her mother and her mother would need them.

"Aha!, before I forget." Obirika said pointing to the heavens she brought out her water pouch and poured out the water in it, while asking the gods and her ancestors to protect her. Nne bewildered.

"Mama what are you doing?"

"Nne you can't trust this Ubiakwa's son that is with us."

"Mama he is harmless."

"That is easy for you to say, you don't know what I have seen. This people, Nne this people," she repeated. "They can't be trusted, I think I should even throw away the pouch entirely who knows what he put inside."

"Mama he is not the problem, Adanna is the problem."

"They are all the same every single one of them, the same."

"He didn't put anything in the pouch, he was just being nice when he brought it to you, besides they risked their lives to help me get you."

"My dear will you be shocked if you find out they have other agendas?"

"Okay Mama let's just go and bath." Nne said as they walked along.

"I'm not saying I'm not grateful, I have all reasons to be grateful and the gods knows that without you my story would have ended in misery. We were two that was bound to be sold but I believe I'm the only one who escaped."

As they spoke they marched through the path, the path was deserted. There were tall bushes by either side of the path, tall grasses and trees. It was impossible to look inside or see anything in the forest, the path though deserted still showed footprints, Nne and her mother wondered who it was that would be coming to such far away stream, when they got there they were relieved to find it empty they quickly entered and had a good wash, they had to be quick before someone approached and also to give Obeli and Iwobo time to have their own bath.

"Mama what do we tell them that is the reason why we can't return to Akom?"

"We don't have to give them any reason, it is our own decision to make, they can't decide where we go besides there is nothing in Akom for us. I just believe it will be only anguish that we would meet there should we decide to continue to stay, dear my parents village is the best option for us."

On the other side Obeli and Iwobo were standing at the entrance of the path that led to the stream like two warriors protecting royalty, they had come thus far in helping Nne and her mother, when they started the journey they didn't know it would pay off in the way it had. They never knew they would succeed now that they had almost succeeded. They felt nothing but pride in themselves. Despite the pride they also felt apprehension, hoping that no evil again would befall them as they stood Obeli hoped that Obirika's feeling towards him would change. He wanted nothing but peace for them and happiness in abundance for Nne the woman that he had for the first time ever come to have a feeling for, and he knew the feeling was a good one and not an evil one. The feeling that wished good for another person and hoped that no evil befell them and came to the point where what made the person happy made him to also be happy. As they stood and held the handle of their swords which since the journey they had never been presented an opportunity to use. Obeli looked at Iwobo, who was standing to his right he noticed that he was having a smile on his face. His face all through the morning had been that of a happy face and he wondered what could be making him so happy.

"Why are you smiling Iwobo," Obeli asked skeptical of the answer, "What could possibly be making you so happy?"

Iwobo quickly caught himself he didn't know he was in fact smiling "I'm not smiling. What makes you think I'm smiling?" Iwobo asked with a feigned frown.

"Because I can see, all morning even to the slavers point you have been smiling so don't tell me you were not smiling I know what I saw."

"I'm not smiling." He just couldn't lie to deny it at this moment.

As he spoke he straightened his face and made it look stern to prove the point that he was not smiling. But deep in his heart he knew he was smiling and he couldn't hide it but to others he had to lie about it. Trying to change the topic.

"What are we going to do about Adanna?" Iwobo asked.

"What do you want us to do about her?" Obeli asked.

"I don't know, but questions will be asked. Especially if we all return are we going to fight her or what? Because the way she pursued us I don't think she is going to give up that easy."

"I will tell my brother Odika about it. He would know what to do, I don't want Nne or Obirika in slavery that is certain, so she is going to have to give up her quest." Obeli said.

"But what if she refuses and what if Obirika reports her to the village heads that she is the one that kidnapped her, what are we going to do?"

"Iwobo I don't know and to be honest with you I don't want anything evil to happen to Adanna she is my sister my only sister from my mother and my father loves her very dearly."

"You know the penalty for kidnapping, besides the village heads and the peer groups all agreed to make anyone from Akom who kidnaps another Akom person to be banished and be made an outcast in Akom village, so if Obirika returns and reports to the village heads Adanna would be banished and be made an outcast."

"That won't happen my father is influential and he is also a member of the village heads, he won't abandon his daughter to such fate."

"Don't forget your father was amongst the men that made the law."

Obeli became silent of course he had thought about what will happen to Adanna. But he had not really given it much time he believed that Adanna one way or another would be exonerated and now he was faced with the fact that he was helping someone survive, to the detriment of his sister. By helping Obirika, Adanna would be at the receiving end of the wrath of the people of Akom.

"But what is making her do the things she does?" Iwobo asked still mesmerized about Adanna and her choice of actions, ever since he had known her, not once had a story of how she was feminine been told rather it was about her trying to rob shoulders with men in the village.

"I don't know Iwobo, I'm not in her mind." Obeli answered "And for your information my father likes her just the way she is."

"You know with the way she is acting, men will find it difficult to marry her."

"I believe one day she will marry." As they both spoke about marriage their hearts pumped more blood than usual each suspected it must be because of the thing they had discovered for themselves. As they discussed Nne and her mother emerged from the path right of Obeli and Iwobo, they had never looked so beautiful, Iwobo caught himself salivating as he stared at Nne, and Obeli couldn't help but to feel his heart pound more, the women were looking renewed.

"Boys I think it is time you had yours, we feel good." Nne said smiling.

"Indeed you do." Said Obeli.

Wanting to look the same Iwobo rushed off pushing Obeli aside, Obeli seeing that Iwobo had a head start ahead of him began to run also, playfully they wanted to know who would be the first to get to the stream. Seeing how they playfully rushed out Nne brought it to her mother's attention.

"Mama see how playful they are you can be now assured that they mean no harm."

"Nne we will leave that to the gods to decide I bear no ill towards any man, if anything I'm grateful."

They were not going to keep watch they looked around the path they were standing on led straight to a village and they didn't wonder why no one was in sight they have actually prayed to the gods to make it happen that no one would be in sight till they got to where they were going. Not long Obeli and Iwobo appeared now that everyone looked calm they started their journey once more with Iwobo leading the way. They were going to the village ahead but they would not be entering the paths that they followed while coming neither would they visit where they were groups. Obeli had brought the idea.

"We shouldn't enter any village or go to where we were before so that people will not recognize or see us and tell anybody. Who may be looking for us" he had said.

When he brought the idea it was a brilliant idea none of them had thought about it. In case Obirika's captors tried to locate them they wanted to make it as difficult as possible. There should be no eyewitnesses. As they marched a bird flying up above pooped and the poo dropped on Nne, when it touched her she was startled. Immediately they all gazed to see what had caused it, it was a bird none like they had seen before. Obirika smiled, it was a sign of good luck. Iwobo quickly went to Nne, as if Nne was in grave danger without hesitation he began to remove the poo. It had fallen on her shoulder as Iwobo carefully removed it out of nowhere Obeli felt anger that Iwobo was touching Nne. There and then he knew he was jealous but he couldn't do anything what Iwobo was doing was harmless. As Iwobo cleaned Nne with a leave he had plucked from a plant nearby he brought out his water pouch and dabbed a cloth and cleaned her shoulder thoroughly. As he tenderly cared for Nne their eyes met and for a moment something stirred in someone's heart.

"Thank you very much," Nne said with a smile.

Iwobo smiled stupidly, "Ah! It is nothing just doing what I'm supposed to."

They marched on, Iwobo's smile had returned and he didn't know it. He was leading the way so this time no one saw it. Nne was behind him, followed by Obirika and Obeli was the guard from the rear, they marched in a single file, as they moved Obeli hoped that nothing again would happen to warrant Iwobo touching Nne. Just then as he thought about, how it had made him feel they heard voices behind immediately their hearts felt like thunder just struck it. Fear gripped them and they were not sure of what action to take next, Iwobo had heard the voices, instinctively he dove into the bush at his left others immediately seeing that it was a better idea than running followed suit. They all hid themselves in the bush that was to their left, hopefully they would not encounter a dangerous animal as they hid in the bush. They waited for the people to pass Iwobo and Obeli were holding the tip of their swords ready to fight and protect Nne and her mother. When Obirika saw them, her heart felt light towards them but she still had to believe what she believed about them. The bush they were hiding in was nothing but tall grasses and few trees scattered here and there but moving farther down inward was tall trees all in the area. They bent down and eagerly watched the path, as they waited a woman with her family they guessed she was with 5 young people the oldest male amongst the youngsters could not be above 20 years and they were carrying loads which looked like their belongings. Nne and her company, kept wondering why these people were taking a deserted route, their demeanour looked frustrated as it was only the woman who looked dejected that occasionally spoke as they passed. Iwobo in his heart thought, that they were nothing but outcast from a village, before one can become an outcast he must have committed a very bad act. Nne wondered what it could be that they sought for but however their fear had died down, as they became assured that the people could cause no harm. They were not the people they feared. As the people passed and moved a considerable distance Iwobo emerged from where he had been hiding he looked and couldn't see them anymore. They would have to wait a little bit for them to go farther before they move out from the bush and that they did. The people moved a considerable distance and he motioned to others to come out, they came out and resumed their journey.

*****

In Mkpunki the Herbalist returned with bush meat in his hand, his hunter friends had made a kill and wanted who they would sell it to. The Herbalist made a good option so they brought it to him and he bought. When he returned, his visitors were still in his hut they were through eating. They had no other thing to do so they waited beside Adanna who had not moved or even blinked her eyes since she fell. What could be the problem they didn't know. Nnadi was beckoned and she came and cleared the locally made plates, they had used to eat, they felt refreshed. They had eaten, pounded yam with fish pepper soup, also adding roasted bush meat. The visitors wiped their plates clean, the meal must have been very delicious. The Herbalist came into the hut he checked on Adanna and picked up his herbs bag he left and assured them he would be back soon. He also implored them to keep an eye on Adanna, he would not be long.

"If she stirs please call my mother, if you need anything please also call my mother." The Herbalist said.

"It's alright we will do as you have just said, no problem at all" Eke said.

"Thank you very much I have a lot of things to do today, but I wouldn't mind watching her. Since you gentlemen are here, I trust she is in safe hands." The Herbalist said and left.

Eke still in confusion spoke up "What exactly are we doing we should search her bag if there is enough money we take the portion that she has promised us. If it is not enough we wait for her in Akom, when she returns she gives us the remaining balance. It's not as if she treated us well when she was with us, we can't just sit here like women nursing babies and wait for her we have to make our move now."

"You speak truth," Neti said, the men were all well built with one slightly bigger. They have been doing manual labour for a very long time and when Adanna approached them with her proposal, they jumped at it; it was an offer to be great. A golden opportunity, they believed it was time that their luck would shine and Adanna gave them a perfect reason to abandon their jobs of only clearing farmlands for people. Now if things would turn out well with Adanna's proposal, they could have their own farmlands. But as it was going they only received part payment and now they sat beside an unconscious Adanna who had promised the other half when the job was completed. The job was completed, though they doubted Adanna was doing this for the gain in it, probably for the fun of it as it suited her personality and daily life endeavours. The woman that escaped was not their fault, neither was it their fault that Adanna injured herself, as far as they were concerned they had done the job they were asked to do.

"I don't think that is a nice plan" Buni said, he was now known amongst the group as also the outspoken one, he had a very strong conviction that they should wait for Adanna as they discussed they looked at her.

"Is she even breathing?" Buni asked.

Eke checked her nostrils, she was breathing, "Indeed she is breathing."

Eke continued to speak, agreeing with Neti that had spoken.

"I agree with you both but I still think that she is an Akom woman and it is important that we as a clan should take care of each other," Buni said.

"The Herbalist must have gotten to you, because he is one that sounds the way you just did." Neti said.

"And so if he had gotten to me what about it am I speaking lies?" Buni asked.

"If by this time tomorrow she doesn't wake up, I will take from her anything I find, I will not be called a thief after all she owes me. We have done what she wanted and if there is anybody owing anyone it is her owing us," Eke said.

While they spoke they never stopped gazing at Adanna whose beauty had not left her as she laid on the bamboo bed covered with calico material, she looked as lovely as always. Not even the condition that she was in could change anything about her beauty. As they watched it still donned on them that they should be doing something aside waiting for Adanna. Still, thinking of their next move.

"What do you people say we do have her bags here, and we are the only ones here, I think we should take an action," Eke said determined to seize his opportunity "I had a lot to do in Akom, I can't imagine wasting my time here."

"Let's still wait, you people can do what you want or say what you want, but all I can say is that we should wait for her and not only wait for her but wait on her we can't leave her without the Herbalist coming back." Buni said.

Neti chuckled and left, he went back to their hut and laid down. On his way he had met Nnadi who was sitting in front of the Herbalist's mother's hut, she greeted him but he didn't answer, he was frustrated. Amongst the three he was the only one with a family and his son should be about the age of Nnadi. He didn't like the way things were going, he had wanted to use the money Adanna would give him to buy head oil lamp for his hunting and also a nice machete for himself and his wife at least they would not have to be borrowing equipment to clear other people's farms, they could own their own equipment. It seemed Adanna had picked poor hardworking men for the journey, the three were hard working but didn't have much to show for it, for they had been living from hand to mouth. And now it seemed that Adanna and the god "Utte" was toying with them in this strange place. As he laid on his belly he thought about how it was that he had never crossed the boundary of Akom, not to talk of coming to the seacoast. He had never seen such a large body of water, indeed it was his first time, within him he had promised himself he would never make such a journey again. At first when they started out he was nervous now he had gained a little confidence. He laid in the hut and stared at the thatched roof of the hut where he had been occupying since the night before, he never wished to see the place again, even though the Herbalist had been very hospitable to them. He longed to be with his wife and son. If he got more money he would maybe think of marrying another woman. Now he was content but also wished that the gods stopped mocking him with their false hope that they always gave him. Making him think that one day he would catch a break. Still looking up, a lizard scurried by, he thought of standing to kill it but decided against it the lizard would help eat the ants that disturb in the hut so why bother to kill it, no need. As he laid, still feeling every bit dejected, the Herbalist returned this time he called out to them his two companions in the Herbalist's hut came out, he showed them what he had brought home.

"Do you know what this is?" he asked.

It was a bunch of leaves that he was holding, the leaves were looking different. Eke looked and thinking a little while.

"It is a herb for (Odabi) Adanna." He said.

The Herbalist smiled "Maybe, maybe not, I didn't think you men would know what it is actually, it is not for (Odabi) Adanna," as he spoke Neti who had been lying down in the hut came out and looking at the leaves didn't know what they were either. The Herbalist though not in the mood to laugh felt he should but he didn't, he simply smiled and shook his head.

"I knew you men wouldn't know what it is. It is for the bush meat that I bought this morning it is (nchawu and uziza leaves) I will use them to prepare the bush meat. Don't you men eat bush meat in Akom?"

They chuckled "We do but we leave that to the women to do, going to the kitchen is not actually a thing we admire doing." Buni said.

"Welcome to Mkpunki, because here we men also cook, I can speak for a very few though, I myself don't cook but I'm sure few cook definitely in Akom too, but since these are leaves I know what they are for, 'Nnadi!" he called out, the little girl ran to him she took the herbs from him and went towards the kitchen. "Anyway brothers my mother will be doing the cooking not me."

"Aha! But you just suggested that maybe you cook." Buni said.

The Herbalist smiled "Maybe I do cook but it won't be today I have other things to do, you men should relax my mother will prepare it and serve us. Hope all is well with you people?"

"What can we say (Odabi) Adanna's pain is our pain." Eke said, the one who had suggested they take her things. Buni who had been supporting Adanna turned in shock, such hypocrisy, he looked at Eke and Neti who had been canvassing to carry away Adanna's belongings and leave her, was now also claiming to have her pain.

He shook his head and stared in disbelief he couldn't believe his ears. The Herbalist now approaching them moved into the hut and felt sadness overwhelm him, he had prayed that Adanna awake before he got back but now his prayers had gone to deaf gods. Adanna had not moved from her position, she was still lying in the same position he had left her, now she was going to make him do what he had never done before and that would be to go to the Chief Priest to ask him for help. After all the Chief Priest was also, a medicine man though he had a feeling that the Chief Priest didn't like him, maybe he was harbouring an ill feeling towards him. As he had heard people claim, since someone told him that the Chief Priest had said he was the only medicine man in the village. People acknowledged the Herbalist, and all agreed that he was gifted and talented and knew what he was doing. That his trade had brought rivalry with the Chief Priest was a consequence he had no control over.

The Chief Priest had never come to him for help and he likewise had never gone to the Chief Priest. The Chief Priest was unarguably older than him and should possess a far greater knowledge. He knew also that if there was anything, he could do to bring Adanna back, and he did it Adanna would appreciate it. Only he could bring her back, and lift the sullen feeling he had which was now spreading to everyone in his compound. Everyone looked gloomy on the account that he too whom they considered the head of the family also looked gloomy and downcast. Of course hopefully, the Chief Priest would not consider the rivalry between them. Amongst all the neighbouring villages the Chief Priest had always remained the one to attend to the sick and not an unknown herbalist, or the son of a herbalist 'who knew nothing about herbs' as the Chief Priest had been reported to have once said.

When the Herbalist heard it he didn't give it much thought, if indeed he didn't know what he was doing people would not patronize him, he must put his pride aside and work together with the Chief Priest for the betterment of Adanna.

The Chief Priest had not considered maybe it was his mysteriousness, heavy fees, the fact he believed in unseen powers for help which very often did not happen, the shrine was hidden and so far, that had made the people of Mkpunki to patronize him less often and instead opt for the Herbalist to relate their health issues to. He was not sure the Chief Priest could help, but had to try anything now. One biting issue being that Adanna's stomach had not witnessed any food, which could be causing a serious problem. If Adanna didn't wake by nightfall, he must seek a way to feed her and how to do that was one of the reasons he must check the Chief Priest. He could not also, discover any visibly showing broken bone, except the ankle which he didn't know if it was broken, maybe the men with her didn't see what had happened. According to them they were running in the forest path pursuing some people in the forest and unknown to them there was a pit covered. Adanna didn't see it and she fell into it while trying to aim her gun at the escapee and her helpers. The story worried the Herbalist he wished Adanna was not so bent on her path but then he felt he should help her. He didn't know why. Now the only trouble in his mind was getting the Chief Priest to offer help. He was not sure that the Chief Priest was going to do anything he had not done himself but then it was said that one man does not possess all the knowledge, and two heads were better than one, if anything it would be useful for another herbalist to help him in what had become now a quest, to save Adanna. The Herbalist sat down in his hut that Adanna now occupied, sitting he carefully scrutinized his method of handling Adanna's problem, whether he was at fault or was missing something but it couldn't be he had done everything he was supposed to do, and he knew he did it well. The Chief Priest would request for some things and he didn't know what, for him all he required most times was money, if the individual did not have money he would barter with him or her, there was no knowing of what the Chief Priest may require in order to help a stranger who was not from Mkpunki. Just not to lose much time he decided to take a hen and some money in case he desired either. That he reasoned would be a better thing to do, not known for his pride he called the men accompanying Adanna, they all came out. Eke and Buni, who had been watching Adanna had gone to be with Neti in the hut that was assigned to them. The three of them entered the hut where the herbalist and Adanna were.

Wondering what it was that could be the matter, what could the Herbalist want to say now, every time they got summoned their stomach tightened in fear that they may have overstayed their welcome. Obviously the Herbalist and his family members had been far too kind.

"You summoned us." Eke said.

"Yes indeed I did," the Herbalist was backing them while facing Adanna, the bamboo bed she was lying on was close to the mud wall, anyone entering the hut would see the person lying on the bamboo bed, as it was directly facing the wall and the entrance and anyone facing the bed would be backing anyone coming into the hut. "I want to discuss an issue bothering me that I have not discussed with anybody and it concerns (Odabi) Adanna and her health."

The men's attention peaked "Speak we are listening." They all said.

"I have never claimed to know it all in this trade, sometimes it is good to get advice from other people so that you don't become lost in your world and go to your grave before your time." The Herbalist said.

"You speak well we totally agree with you." Eke said.

"I have decided to go consult the Chief Priest on behalf of (Odabi) Adanna, he is also a medicine man just as well as a spiritual leader, you see in Mkpunki the Chief Priest also attend to sick people, but here also I happen to be a herbalist who also attends to sick people, I don't know but I have never harboured any ill feeling towards the Chief Priest, though people claim they are not sure if he does the same, I have never heard directly from him either, neither have I ever approached him before for anything. (Odabi) Adanna's situation is pushing my hands to do this."

"We think it is a good thing you are doing, if the Chief Priest can help (Odabi) Adanna I don't see how it is wrong for us to help her through him, please all I can say is let us march ahead without hesitation let us get the Chief Priest involved as soon as possible, with the look of things, she is not getting better and I believe all we are trying to do is first of all awake her it has been since yesterday that she became still, time is running out we really need to help." Eke said.

"So you agree with me that I should consult the Chief Priest?" The Herbalist asked.

"Indeed we do please anything possible for her, anything at all," Eke said.

"Yes, because I have considered the fact that she has not eaten to be a crucial point. Alright then you men will accompany me to the Chief Priest's shrine, I shan't walk alone the sun is moving down west it must be the afternoon now, so we should hurry so that we can make it back before sun down I have to cancel all my appointments today," the men were happy at this "Will do them tomorrow, please you people should go and get prepared in a few moments we will start going."

As they moved out the Herbalist turned to Adanna who he had been backing all this while as he had turned to speak to the men, who stood at the entrance of the hut, as he sat he gently spoke towards Adanna bending over and shifting his seat, he sat on a log of wood which served as seat, whispering to her.

"(Odabi) Adanna if you can hear me, please wake up, please I beg you, wake up," he sat upright and spoke to no one in particular, but hoped Adanna would hear, just the moment he lifted up his head, his mother came into the hut.

"The bush meat is ready," she said.

"Thank you but we will eat when we return," the Herbalist said.

"Why? Where are you going?"

"To meet the Chief Priest."

"Dear you have never done such a thing before."

"I know but I will swim across the Abiam river just to help her."

Etiti worried at her son's dedication to this strange woman, now she was deeply worried her son was taking the case of the woman too personally.

"Is there anything I can do for you?"

"No Mama you have done well."

As he spoke he began to pack all the necessary things he would need for the journey. If they march like men they would be at the Chief Priest's before dark and return before morning. He went outside brought the hen he would use and tied it up he then kept the hen in front of his hut went to Adanna's men's hut to check for them and hurry them.

"Gentlemen are you all ready?" he asked.

"Just a moment more please," Buni pleaded.

"Okay no problem." He answered. He marched back to his hut. In his compound everyone looked as if the condition of Adanna had affected them as the compound lacked enough sign of the living, most of his people were in their hut even Atimbi the gregarious. She was always in front of her hut telling stories to children in the compound now no one was in sight. Were they all in their hut? The Herbalist was certain they had not gone to the farm he had told them to rest today, if it was the situation of Adanna that was making his family look dejected he must do something to remedy the situation. He looked around the compound only the fowls and goats were visible he thought of going to their huts to check everyone but decided against it he would some other time. He had to go check for Adanna's men and do nothing but help her, he marched to his hut and prayed to his personal god for the first time in many years, he looked around in his hut, looked at her belongings, as he stood with one hand on the wooden 'door' post of his hut he stared at her and wondered what to do next, a little bit lost in thought a hand gently touched his shoulder he turned and it was one of Adanna's men Eke, they were ready. He bent down picked his bag, usually it was herbs that would be in his bag but this time around it was not. The bag was now occupied with different things he had his water and dried meat should in case they get hungry. Looking at Adanna one last time they marched out of the compound on his way out he called to his mother and informed her they were leaving.

"Go well my son, the gods be with you all and grant you your heart desires".

"So shall it be, thank you Mama." The Herbalist answered.

With that they marched out. It would soon be dark, the sun had moved and was on the verge of going down and they knew they had to hurry to be able to make it. The Herbalist touched his bag and felt the palm oil head lamp in his bag it was his father's while the hunters used the head lamp to hunt his father used it to find herbs in the night, this time around, the head lamp would be solving a different kind of problem, the Herbalist marched in front, for he was the one that knew the path while the men followed behind. As they walked the Herbalist tried his possible best to return the greetings that were coming his way. It was not out of the ordinary for people to greet him for they knew him well, at this time most people that he saw were those returning from farm. It was not yet planting season it had not been up to four weeks since the people of Akom celebrated their new yam festival. Those that were hardworking went to make sure that their farm didn't over grow with weeds, making it difficult to weed when the planting season commenced, or tend other plants in the farm. Others went to hunt.

As they walked the Herbalist with his group met the men that had come to sell bush meat to him earlier, they were two, one was holding the other in fact was helping him as the other leaned on him and tried to walk but he had problem doing so. The path they were on intersected with the path the Herbalist was walking on but the path faced the other way, from the position of Herbalist his path was perpendicular to the path. The men were Nanni and Adike, in the whole village they were known as the mischief makers, the proper mischievous ones. They were always in one trouble or the other if they didn't cause the trouble they knew who started the trouble. They were always together in their dark endeavours, through all the troubles they caused. Also they were very good friends with the Herbalist who seemed to be affiliated to all and sundry. Nanni saw the Herbalist, with the pain he shouted his name.

"Herbalist!" The Herbalist who had noticed them stopped.

"Oh! Herbalist thank the gods we saw you," he said and closed his eyes to muster enough strength and courage to drag himself forward again as he was aware the pain would increase with every movement he made. Adike whom he had been leaning on who was also helping drag him along and providing support now looked up to see the herbalist. He was just as relieved as his friend was. Seeing the Herbalist meant he would not have to drag his friend any further. Truth be told he was already exhausted. The

Herbalist came back from his path and turned into theirs seeing they needed his help, one of them had a cut and the Herbalist attended to it.

"How are you feeling now?" The Herbalist asked after applying leaves he found in the bush on the cut.

"A lot better." He said and began dusting his body of sands for he had been sitting on the ground.

Adike held him up.

"Take him home I will come and visit you people once I get back, I have an important place I am going." The Herbalist and his men went back on their path and marched away, as they did so Adike, shouted.

"Herbalist bring us something!" he was smiling now and the Herbalist laughed at his request 'if only he knew where we are going.'

"Are they brothers?" Buni asked.

"If only it is that," the Herbalist replied, smiling now and proffering an answer "They are not brothers but their bond is more than that of brothers; there is no one in Mpkunki who doesn't know them and how they have come to cling to each other. Naani is the only son of his mother but his father had many children than he could care for, Naani's mother had given birth to twins twice and they were all killed Naani is the only son of his mother to come alone. She didn't have any daughter before she died since then Naani had taken to different ways to survive funny enough Adike has the same story but his mother gave birth to only one set of twins and she is still alive but his father is late no one actually knows how they met, right from their teenage days they have been together and causing trouble every now and then. Today must be an unusual day for them normally they are the ones that cause other people to have injuries."

"Hmmm, I believe they have a sad story." Buni said.

"We all have sad stories my brother just that some people have learnt to live with theirs and make peace with the gods. No man can claim to have it better, even the rich have reasons why they won't close their eyes in peace." The Herbalist said.

"You speak the truth." Buni said.

Now as they walked, they were flanked on either side by farmlands they had crossed the bushes, the sun was still shining but its heat was not hot anymore, its rays were indeed bearable and the Herbalist and his men considered this a good thing. They had not gone far but with their current pace they would get to the Chief Priest soon enough. With the problem of Naani and Adike behind them they sought to move faster but after a considerable distance they had marched on without meeting people anymore. Not far from their right, they encountered a woman on the ground in what should be her farm, half of the farm was weeded while the other half was not, the woman was on the part that was weeded and she was crying out. The Herbalist was the first to hear her cry, he stopped walking to listen more intently.

"Do you hear anything?" he asked the men with him.

"Yes a faint cry." Eke said.

"Over there," Neti was pointing, "Is that not a woman?" They all turned to the place he was pointing to, they saw that it was a woman and they rushed to her.

"She must be in trouble." Eke said.

"Indeed, she is." The Herbalist said.

As they ran towards her the Herbalist was leading the pack.

"Please help me." She cried.

She didn't actually need the help.

"What is it?" the Herbalist said, he could see her now she was heavily pregnant and it seemed she was in labour.

"I think she is in labour." The Herbalist said "We can't take you back to the village you have to deliver here."

"I know oooooooo!!" She said with gritted teeth.

"Alright alright just relax yourself and be calm everything will be just fine." The Herbalist said also trying to relax himself the men with him had moved away since seeing it was a woman in labour. Men have no dealings with such, no matter what.

"I can't relax, that is the problem the pain is too much," before she could finish pronouncing the word too much she let a shout of pain, there was no garment, staying beside her and also as far away as possible the Herbalist ordered her to push. The woman herself had ordered him to move away, as she tried to handle the business on her own. It was a usual occurrence for women to deliver wherever and whenever on their own, without any help, only those fortunate to be at home when labour came had the luxury of older wives or good will women attending to them. The woman with loud screams pushed, as they would be fortunate, it didn't take long, took her an effort of three times before the cry of a baby was heard, it was a bouncing baby boy, she took the child and cut off the umbilical cord, wrapping him with a part of her garment, she rested a bit, but not too long then she got up. The Herbalist and his men approached her and congratulated her. She thanked them took her baskets and her farming tools, looked around and decided to call it a day.

"You have to be strong now, just head back to the village and do the necessary things you are supposed to do, for the baby, and yourself you will be fine," the

Herbalist said, as they all left the farm together. She would feed the baby at home.

"Wow what a day we are having." Eke said.

"It is not always like this I can assure you." The Herbalist said.

"What could her story be?" Buni asked rhetorically "I can imagine."

"She just didn't know it will be today, that is why she came to the farm when due, women make that mistake sometimes and she is lucky."

"What if we didn't come along?" Neti asked.

"She is very lucky, anyway, she actually didn't need or use our help, I believe she was just fine and would have done it whether we were here or were not , women often give birth while farming, some continue with the farming, one was going to the stream when she went into labour, she went into the bush delivered, she didn't return to her home but continued to the stream, a lot while travelling or going to other villages market do still deliver on their own I'm sure you men know all this, our women are indeed strong."

"Surely they are."

"In my place the women are strong, but do not mind being pampered." Neti said.

"They all like being pampered." The Herbalist said.

They had moved a considerable distance when they got to a shallow stream, the men were surprised at the sight of the water, they would have to cross the stream, the Herbalist without hesitation stepped into the stream. "Do not worry it is only knee deep, you can cross."

With his assurance they followed him and crossed the stream, the chilling water cooled their body that had been under the sun, they would not be having a bath though one of them desperately wanted to, maybe another time, they crossed the stream. Looking down intently you could see tadpoles and little fish that never get too develop peacefully. When they crossed the stream they were flanked by tall trees and tall grasses, they had moved into the deeper part of the forest, the birds were making their last flight, and trying to return to their abode, all the animals that walk by day began to move to their abode while the nocturnal ones were getting ready to move out for the night, look for food and basically survive. The Herbalist and his men plowed forward he had prayed to not have anything that would delay him any longer, Adanna's life was depending on their mission. If the gods decided not to answer his prayer, of bringing her up, she had lain in her condition for far too long, as they marched, and the fact that he would not know what to do should the Chief Priest fail, kept playing in his head, but there should be a solution somewhere. All he had to do was find it, the sun was now gone but the days light was still visible without long darkness would emerge, it was twilight. The Herbalist increased his pace and the men with him followed suit.

"Why is your Chief Priest's shrine this far?" Eke asked.

"He likes to retain his mysteriousness and all that has to be done to get an image, the image of 'I'm not an ordinary person, I hear from the gods and I belong to the gods, without me men will not know the gods and all that."

"All chief priests are like that ours is not this far from the people because he is also the native doctor, in case anything happened it is him we call." Buni said.

"This one too is a native doctor, but when my father proved he knew what he was doing with good visible results, the people patronized him, just as well as they patronize the Chief Priest, but considering the distance and the fact you have to cross a stream, they don't fancy it very much. He claims to be closer to the gods where he is, but don't get confused he has agents who reside close to the village and help around. When the matter is too much they bring the case to him."

"But you are taking a risk doing this, what will people say if they find out, you go to the chief for help when you are supposed to be the one helping them, don't you think they may then decide to go to the chief priest instead of you?" Neti asked.

"I don't really care, my ego has nothing to do with saving (Odabi) Adanna's life, I will still remain the Herbalist, and I'm sure I will always produce result, right now all I care about is helping (Odabi) Adanna."

The Herbalist and his men were now approaching the shrine, they drew out their swords the Herbalist advised them to put them back as no occasion warranted it.

"This place is eerie," Eke protested.

"Even at that it is not dangerous I assure you, just put back the swords we are now close to his shrine nothing is going to happen." The Herbalist assured.

"It is just in in case." Eke said.

"I know but no problem will materialize."

With that the men put back their swords and marched slowly looking behind and sideways and forward in apprehension, all in a bid to welcome this strange environment, it was not every day that one went to the shrine.

CHAPTER 27

Since Iwobo and his crew resumed their marching they had not seen anything out of the ordinary on the path. They still maintained their resolution to walk out of sight. For their own day, they had been marching since morning sharing their stories about life. Iwobo's story seemed to be one of the saddest, apparently Obeli had not lived at all, rather had survived in the comfort his father had provided, all his woes were about how he was not pampered well enough. But then they all agreed Obirika had the saddest followed by Nne, Obirika had recounted her ordeal in the hands of her captors. As they approached Akuma they made a decision, this time it was Iwobo's idea.

"We will go to the market and get supplies, let's not all go into the village so that people will not recount stories of seeing us four, we have to be discreet about our movements now, should they be asked if they saw four people they will say no but rather two or three, which should be to our advantage."

"So who and who is going?" Nne asked.

"I will go with Obeli," Iwobo answered, "Nne you and your mum should stay here and stay out of sight when we return we will let you know."

"This place is open." Obirika said.

They had followed another path that led to the village and the path they stood on was less travelled upon. There was no shade in sight, it was just short grasses and a path cut out because it has been treaded upon, "If you move down a little, there used to be a slavers lodge down there don't go to it but stay around there, it should be deserted by now, I don't think they still use it, because of the new path, you will be safe there and we would meet you people there." Iwobo said.

"Okay that sounds better." Nne said.

"I'm not going to a slavers lodge or anywhere near it. Please any other alternative?" Obirika asked.

"Ma'am I can assure you nothing will happen to you, the place should be deserted now, the slavers used it as a resting place but they don't anymore." Iwobo said.

Trying to persuade her mother Nne placed her two hands on her mother's shoulders as she was standing behind her, she placed her hands on her shoulders as assurance that nothing would happen to her and also for agreement that they should go there. They gave a list of what they wanted, basically food, roasted yam, fruits and dried meat, that seemed like what the men would also be getting for themselves, with the list inserted into memory, the boys moved out into the village. Iwobo still had enough money with him as they marched along the market path, it was what every market was like, women were mostly the traders with some men who had come to barter what they had. They passed a woman who was selling snails, she had put her snails in portions and Iwobo wondered together with Obeli if she would be making any gains because children also took it as a past time to gather snails from farm. The woman in question was giving suck to her baby. After her they passed a woman who was selling weaved materials she had mats and baskets and hand fans all made from palm fronds. The people of the village were aesthetic to a certain level in desire, as the weaved mats and baskets and hand fans were adorned with different colours. Seeing the wares Obeli's mind riveted back to his brother who loved nothing more than to stay in his hut or sometimes in the compound to weave baskets, and mats and hand fans. He would seem so engrossed that nothing else that happened distracted him. Obeli had not found anything in doing that made him so engaged that he thought of nothing else. Just no handiwork, for now thinking about Nne gave him happiness and made him lose appetite. Sometimes he even wished that every moment he spent it with her. He was glad that Nne had come to occupy his heart. As they marched along they took their time looking around before finding what they were looking for. They bought the items and began their march back to Nne and Obirika. They had tried their best to be quick and stay out of sight but that was impossible, they made known little of their intention to others. As they marched Iwobo saw a woman selling jewelries and women wares not wanting Obeli to know his purpose he urged him to move on, with a promise to meet up.

"Obeli there is something I want to get, please move on I would join you shortly." He had said.

"Let us go together then." Obeli said.

"I don't want to delay you."

"I will not take long just go please."

"Okay but be quick."

Iwobo knew he shouldn't lie to his friend, and he didn't lie just did not want his friend knowing his business this time. Obeli went on and he went ahead to buy an armband, and a waist bead, for Nne to beautify herself with. He had thought that Obeli would be furious should he find out that he was using money that they could have spent on something necessary for their survival on the journey on Nne. To him Nne was valuable more valuable than anything he could think of, this he also thought would make it easier for him when he told her what he wanted to tell her though he didn't know if it was the right time to discuss such things. There can't be a better time than this, now that she had recovered her mother and everything was seemingly okay with her. Buying the armband and waist bead he put it in his bag, and ran to meet up with Obeli who had gone a considerable distance. The distance he had covered surprised him, as he didn't spend much time buying the gifts, he met up with him and they marched on getting to Nne and her mother. They had passed no one on their way when they entered the path and they had seen nothing out of the ordinary, they brought out things they had bought and shared it. Iwobo kept the gifts he bought, he sought an opportunity where he would be alone then he would give the gifts to Nne. They looked back to make sure no one was following them then they moved on. They would soon need rest Obirika was relieved to be out of the slavers lodge she wondered why they had a lodge on a path that was supposed to be known by few but then again most paths were made by them. Obirika had her mind calm now, she also began to feel a little at ease with the boys.

"Mother do you still fear them and their motives?" Nne had asked, because she asked if they could trust them with what they would eat.

"Nne do you think we should have sent them to buy what we will eat?" she had asked and her daughter assured her that they should.

"Mother if they wanted to kill us, they would have done so besides I have been thinking of it, I can't see why they would do the things they have done if they wanted to kill us, initially they had wanted to come alone without me, they in fact started the journey without me, I followed them, lurking behind until they caught me, they asked me to go back but later reconsidered seeing it will be more dangerous, so I forced them into allowing me come along. They were willing to take the risk alone, and again Obeli wouldn't be working against his sister if he wanted us dead, they have done enough to prove that they deserve our trust. For me I trust them completely and I can sleep with both my eyes closed in sleep when together with them. It is you that have to come to peace with them so that you can have a rest from your troubles."

"My daughter you don't know what I have seen."

"Mother you have been through a lot, I don't imagine to comprehend what it must have been like for you. But with them have no fear, I can assure you that, trust me on this one."

"Let us still be cautious."

"Okay mother I will always agree with you on that one as for me to be honest I can't trust anyone easily anymore."

"My daughter it is the best."

With them all marching, Obeli's stomach made a growling noise.

They all laughed at the noise, "hunger it is," he said.

"Indeed hunger it is." Iwobo supported.

Left for him he would have suggested they stopped for food, seeing that it had been a while since they ate, but he said nothing preferring Nne and her mother to make the decision, so that it would not seem like he was imposing anything on them. They continued moving and they heard Iwobo's stomach make the same noise, his was even louder, that caused a reason to laugh again in their circumstance.

"Obeli you have infected me with your noisy stomach."

"Or it is you that infected him." Nne goaded.

"Never! It is him, he is the one that infected me, my stomach just does not make noise."

"Be kidding yourself," Obeli did retort.

"What do you mean I can go days without food." Iwobo bragged.

"Liar, if I didn't know you I would have believed you." Obeli said. Nne was smiling now while Obirika seemed amused. "Please pay no heed to him, Iwobo here eats at least five times a day."

"My great ancestors o!, Obeli you are such a lousy liar."

"Please deny yourself." Obeli said.

"I can go days without food, and my stomach will not make a single noise." Iwobo bragged on.

"So why is it making noise now you have not even gone a full day?" Obeli asked.

"You infected me, that is why, you have given me your bad lazy spirit." Iwobo said.

"Don't even go there, see who is talking."

"Boys please you people should relax we will soon eat." Nne said.

"Nne like I said I can go days without even water you can ask anybody, they know what I speak is the truth." Iwobo said.

"Please don't mind him the man you see before you can eat like a labourer in fact his portions, is that of if not five labourers combined, he is well known for his achievements in overeating." Obeli said.

"You both seem like men who eat well." Obirika added.

They laughed at her comment, "Please look at us well who eats more?" Obeli asked.

"I cannot really tell." Obirika said.

"At least try." Obeli pressured.

"You will not force me to take sides."

"Ah! Believe it or not Obeli eats more than I do."

"You are kidding yourself." Obeli responded.

Marching a little farther with no one in sight Obirika brought their argument to an abrupt end.

"Gentlemen and lady I think we should stay here and eat." She said.

"Ah! Finally." Iwobo said and rushed to the spot.

"Now you all have seen who likes food more, take it easy, don't rush." Obeli said.

"As if you don't feel like rushing yours likewise." Iwobo said bringing out what he was going to eat.

"No I don't." Obeli said.

"Are you both not going to drop this argument?" Nne asked.

"He is claiming who he is not or should I say he is denying himself." Obeli said.

Nne, clearly amused was laughing as she brought out what she wanted to eat too.

"Obeli I know you pray before eating," Nne said.

He laughed "gods of my ancestors come and eat," he said and threw a piece on the ground, he made more libations and called more spirits, "My ancestors have yours" he did it some more and began eating. They rushed their food as they were all famished. Obeli and Iwobo ate like they had never eaten before, indeed the meal was a far cry from what they used to have but they managed it. After eating, every attempt by Nne to get them to move was falling on deaf ears. "Nne, relax we just ate let us just relax nobody is after us." Iwobo protested, "Because I don't think I can move, I even think I have over fed."

"What if someone is trailing us from the last village?" Nne asked.

"We would have seen them." Obeli said. As they spoke Obirika was already fast asleep on the ground where she had eaten, and now Iwobo and Obeli's eyelids felt heavy, it was just natural that after such a heavy meal that the body will elect to fall into sleep, a fact Nne couldn't comprehend, she was weary of feeling comfortable as long as they were still within reach of their enemies, but tonight they had to make an exception and sleep at that spot.

"Just relax," Iwobo pleaded, "be at ease nothing will happen." Where they were the sun had also disappeared and night will soon be present.

"If we rest by this time it means we must wake up as early as possible to march on." Nne said.

"That is a good point, but believe me it would be hard for anyone to trace us. So as the body has elected to fall weak, I think we should just let it." Iwobo said and with that he dozed off.

Obeli still lingered a little but was certain that it was sleep that was calling. How the body was treacherous, a moment ago they were feeling strong, now just after a meal the body had given up its strength.

*****

The Herbalist was calm and relaxed but the men with him were not, they had never been to such a shrine before. Before they came together and started working together long before they met Adanna and she presented her proposal to them they had been to the shrine in Akom, to ask the Chief Priest why they were having a miserable life, nothing they did seemed to prosper. The Chief Priest had told them to make a sacrifice to their ancestors with a he-goat each in their ancestral shrine, they had gone home disheartened if they could afford a he-goat why then did they have to consult him. To them it seemed the Chief Priest didn't comprehend their problem. The Herbalist didn't see the Chief Priest of Mkpunki as someone with all the answers. For what he knew only his mother made prayers to the gods and ancestors as for him, he would rather be pragmatic than believe in what he knew nothing about. The fact of the Chief Priest also being the medicine man he believed there was a chance he could help Adanna. The path clearly now showed that a shrine was close by, the area was surrounded by large tall trees, with dead leaves scattered on the ground from all corners, chirping of insects could be heard and the songs by birds could also be heard the left and right of the shrine was covered by small trees and grasses that hung under the large trees. They got to the shrine, surprisingly the shrine looked quite big the entrance of the shrine was covered with leaves, on the ground were dead leaves forming a carpet, the shrine was covered round with tendrils and palm fronds which were green in colour they still looked fresh, the palm fronds served as a wall to the shrine, a palm frond was delicately inter woven to form door space but there was no door the palm fronds serving as a wall were all laced with red calico cloths.

"The walls are made every three market days," the Herbalist informed them.

Filled with awe now they moved into the shrine, the shrine was built around two large trees, the trees were tied together with a red calico cloth which looked like a screen. On the red calico cloth were drawn the head of the god, on the floor directly beneath the tree was the god itself, the god was a carved sculpture of a well designed head, the god didn't have hands but had the facial human parts and it had eyes, a long calved nose, a mouth with no ears. On the left of the god was another smaller god, also the same on the right the shrine had a seat for visitors and a seat for the Chief Priest, the seats were tied with red and white calico cloths, on the floor of the shrine was a mat and on the mat there was a calabash which contained what looked like water. Also on the floor was a long-decorated item which looked like a designed stick, there were red and white chalks, a skull of what seemed like the skull of a human being and from the skull was coming out smokes, the shrine contained other things which the Herbalist did not recognize. Entering the shrine there were shrine messengers standing at the entrance, the Herbalist met them.

"Say your name so you may enter."

The Herbalist said his name, and the men with him also said their names and they were allowed to enter. Now looking up, the roof of the shrine was made of the same palm fronds but there was no design of red calico cloths on it, only some items were hung which looked like eggs these items were hung with red or white calico cloths. As they entered a young boy dashed out to call the chief priest, he was not present when they entered after a little while they began to hear the sounds made by the Chief Priest walking staff, the staff was made of iron and the staff had beads attached to it which made noise when the Chief Priest stomped it on the ground. As the sounds got closer, they could hear chanting of a voice it must belong to the Chief Priest; what the voice was saying they couldn't decipher, he must be making incantations one of them reasoned. The eerie strange voice was to strike fear into anyone close or in it, again the Herbalist made a silent prayer as he sat together with the men, he crossed his fingers as a sign to bring good luck, not satisfied he rubbed his elbows with his palm, literally and associated himself with anything good, then he crossed his fingers again. The Chief Priest's entrance continued to be nothing short of dramatic, one of them wondered if he was so always dramatic when entering the shrine. They all sat together quiet and gazing at the direction where the boy had run into and where they were also hearing sounds from, the seat they sat on was directly facing another opening where the sound was coming from. In the shrine there were two entrances the one they had come in through which was now on their left-hand side and the one which they were facing where the young boy had ran into, they were obviously expecting the Chief Priest to emerge from the second entrance. As they would have it he made his entrance, while coming in he closed his eyes, instead of marching forward he spun himself three times and then opened it and this time no noise was coming from him, the men wondered if they should have done the same, it was not every day that you come to a shrine. They made the journey once in a while in Akom. The Chief Priest entered and went straight to his mat and sat he obviously did not have a seat. He was still making incantations and singing unknown songs he would shake his head and sing some more, after settling down he finally spoke.

"What can I do for you gentlemen?"

The Herbalist with the question knew it was time for him to speak up, and say his intention.

"Good day, ancient one, and the god's servant, my name is..." about to pronounce the name the chief priest cut in abruptly.

"I didn't ask for your name, just say why you came." He said with his voice undulating from low to high pitch.

"There is a girl in my hut she is badly hurt I happen to be taking care of her as I am a Herbalist, and I have done everything possible to help her. She fell into a trap pit yesterday, and has not awoken since then, I don't know what else to do. I felt that you as a follow medicine man may know what else to do."

"Your problem is not with the gods." The Chief Priest said.

"Ancient one but we cannot really know for sure, it may be the gods are causing her sleep so." The Herbalist said doubting it.

"It is not the gods, she has a bad omen but I will not pretend to be who I am not," the Chief Priest went ahead to list a lot of things that the Herbalist should do.

"If you have done all these things, they are the things I should have done myself, I am afraid there is nothing more I can do to help you, you have done everything I would have done."

The Herbalist felt his world crash including the men that were with him, he had so much expected a solution from the Chief Priest, now all he got was nothing. If she didn't wake then there was a real problem, with a dejected heart they turned to leave one of the men trying to find hope asked again.

"Ancient one, there is nothing you can do?" Buni asked.

"I'm afraid nothing, I wish I could have been of more help to you, but the Herbalist is quite capable besides I have heard of him before and I really do think that he is capable. It is only the gods that can help her up now, no man wakes a person called to the other world, she has been called to the other world where no man goes and for her to come back it is the gods that will release her and she may return, if she doesn't then she joins them there permanently. Not even I can look into that realm, no man can, so take heart and wait for her to return but I doubt it, cases I have had myself they never return none of them ever does, an ordinary man cannot see the gods and return to tell of it, I will say go. If she doesn't wake I shall be in the village in no distant time then I shall visit and perform her passing right. We must pity such a one, who knows what her past deeds must have been like for her to meet such a fate."

With that they turned and left. The journey home would even be sadder than the one they had made to the place all 'there is hope' they had told themselves silently meant nothing now, there was nothing they knew they were going to do anymore.

*****

In the Herbalist's compound the women had just finished cooking dinner when the Herbalist's mother heard a loud sneeze, everyone was out from their hut, the mood was still solemn but also everyone was trying to be normal, and live happily. Then Etiti heard the sneeze again she was picking corn when she heard the sneeze. She gently put down the sieve and left her seat she edged closer to her son's hut, suspecting it was Adanna, the sound of the sneezing voice was strange, she had looked around and to the direction the sound of the sneeze was coming from and saw no one she knew, she couldn't tell the joy she felt when another sneeze was heard from the direction of the room. It was indeed Adanna, she rushed into the hut, only to see Adanna rubbing the back of her neck, and trying to clear her eyes, everything seemed fuzzy and unclear, she couldn't remember how she got to the room. She had been trying desperately to stand up, but felt great pain on her left ankle and right knee. When Etiti came into the hut she saw Adanna trying to get up, smile shorn on her face. She was elated, she quickly ran to her and holding her back helped her to sit down, sitting down she felt pain sitting too, but her back ached more than her waist, the place looked like no place she could remember.

"Etiti, is this you?" Adanna said in a low voice.

"My dear it is me." Etiti answered.

"What happened how did I get here?" She said dizzily.

"Dear it is a long story, just try to relax everything will be clear to you okay, let us not rush anything."

"But I was going to the seacoast?"

"Yes you were, like I said don't worry at all everything will be clear to you just rest."

Adanna felt all her muscles ache as she tried to sit up, the bamboo bed felt stronger than usual.

"Ah!" She wimped "My back ache so much."

"Sorry but you have been lying down for so long, sorry." Etiti said, "My son will soon be back they went to get help for you the gods be praised that you are well, we didn't know what we would have done should you not have recovered, it is great indeed that you are awake. Nnadi," Etiti shouted from the hut, the little girl ran in "Bring water, quickly, quickly" Adanna was now rubbing her temple as Etiti rubbed the back of her neck, and her entire back massaging it.

"You will feel better" she said re-assuring Adanna, "We thought you would not wake in time we were already thinking of ways to feed you if you didn't wake but now that you are awake, we will rush it without hesitation, so drink water first and I will bring you something to eat."

"Okay I will appreciate that" Adanna said.

Reluctant to leave, she decided and left, Etiti left hoping to bring her food as Etiti left Adanna's head felt heavy, she quietly dropped it on the bamboo bed and tried to doze off again, she held herself, the whining noise in her head was getting lower and she could hear the chatter outside, obviously Etiti had broken the news to them about her recovery, she wished to know what was going on outside as the chatter grew louder, but she couldn't as she felt the continued pain on her legs. She couldn't recall being in this hut everything about it looked strange to her. She was not even certain she was in Mkpunki. As she laid on her back staring into the thatched roof, people began to trickle in, they would come in look at her and greet her like she was returning from far distance journey. As the people from the Herbalist's household kept coming in, many were feigning a smile unfortunately Adanna did not know how to smile. It was not a part of her, Etiti came back with the food, Nnadi had brought water. Adanna gulped the water, which made her feel like a part of her consciousness was brought back into her and the reality seemed a bit realer, as she drank again she coughed out violently, Etiti patted her back offered her the food and she began to eat with haste. The good thing was maybe by chance or forethought Etiti had prepared pounded yam a delicacy of Akom, with vegetable soup and a big fresh fish.

"Eat slowly, do not rush it, try to savour each mouthful if possible." Etiti suggested.

"It is just like I have not eaten in ten market days." Adanna replied.

"I know, just eat my dear you will get better and my son will soon be back he will take care of you more, there is nothing more that I can do, for now I think after eating you should sit up, let the food go down then you can lie down again."

"It's like all my bones are crushed, and all my muscles ache."

"Sorry my dear" Etiti said and patted Adanna once more. "It must have been terrible for you, your men told us what happened it is even an act of the gods that you are alive such a fall could have killed someone, but such, didn't happen to you we must be grateful."

"I guess I should." She said, took a bite of the fish, all her jaws ached, she ate with the pain, this was about survival, she was not enjoying the food.

"Etiti" she called out "I need to wash my mouth before I can enjoy this food."

"Can you stand up?" Etiti asked.

"I don't think I can, but I will try," believing to be as ever strong, Adanna tried in vain to get up, and stand on her own two feet. Nnadi was called to support her and Etiti was also at hand with the both of them she couldn't manage to get up, finally giving up.

"I don't think I can." She said.

"It's alright we will find a way, you will have to improvise, we will bring you a bowl and you can use it." Etiti suggested.

"That is better." Adanna said.

With the resolution Nnadi ran off, to bring a bowl when she came back Adanna was able to wash her mouth, Adanna took another attempt at the food, this time it tasted better, just as she began to eat people began to come see her again.

"Sorry about your health. Hope you are feeling better now?" one of them asked.

"Yes I'm feeling better, thank you very much for your concern," in her heart Adanna didn't feel like seeing people. She was not used to been pampered like this though her father had tried to pamper her, she hated it. She believed in doing things her own way.

*****

"Are you sure it is not because you are a herbalist that made the Chief Priest not to help us?" Buni asked.

"I doubt it is because of it, I did what any medicine man would have done to revive someone you heard him yourselves, there is nothing more he could have done and then he added her spirit has gone to other world, making it impossible to call her back." The Herbalist answered.

"So what now, what are we going to do, we can't give up just like that or is she going to remain like that or worse never come back to the land of the living?" Eke asked.

"All we have to do now is pray to the gods for help, I am not much of a prayer-oriented person myself, my mother does that for me, but I feel we should." The Herbalist said.

"I have to get back to Akom, my family is waiting for me." Neti said.

"Let's just hope that something good will happen." The Herbalist said.

"You people here know what we planned, I think we should carry it out." Eke said to the others.

"What plan is that?" The Herbalist asked.

"It's something we decided, you don't know about, you don't need to anyway." Eke answered.

"Alright if you say so, I hope it is a good plan?"

"Indeed it is you can trust us, we wouldn't plan any harm." Eke said.

"So you people are finally going through with your plan." Buni said.

"Indeed we are." Neti said.

"Alright the gods be with you two." Buni said.

"You know you are always invited, you can join us if you want." Eke said.

"I don't want to." Buni said.

"Gentlemen, what are you really talking about?" the Herbalist asked sounding frustrated, with their shrewd talk. "What are you people talking about?"

"We are just deciding our future, and the next thing to do considering the recent development." Neti said.

"Okay but don't plan any evil." The Herbalist suggested.

"Do we look like evil men?" the Herbalist didn't bother to answer he knew they didn't think being a slaver was an evil thing. They didn't see it that way.

"No you don't but be careful what you are planning." With that they closed the topic.

Marching home was not as tedious as when they were going, the men observed that with all journeys it always happened that going seemed farther than returning. Anytime one made a journey, while going it took like forever, "Is this not the farm where we saw the pregnant woman," Buni asked.

"It is, I wonder why it is so with journey." Eke remarked.

"Well no one can tell I guess it is the apprehension, and anxiety that makes it look that way but the good thing is we are almost home not far from here is also the point where we met Naani and Adike." The Herbalist added.

"Indeed it is, wow!" Eke exclaimed.

"Soon we will be home." Buni added, as he said the words melancholy set in on them all. Again they had gone to what they believed to be their last hope and their prayers were not answered, now all they could do was stare into the approaching night in despair having failed Adanna. They went home expecting to see no one on the paths all must have gone to their homes by now and were telling bedtime stories, as the men recounted their day's stories how they had fared, the women with their children entertained each other eating laughing and playing. The Herbalist was once again leading the pack he got to his compound and from the far could see beyond the red mud walls that everyone seemed lively, they got to the bamboo gate he could see people coming out from his hut where Adanna was lying his heart sank in within him as the acids in his stomach churned. He quickly went into the compound as the men followed suit, one of the servants in the compound greeted him, he answered paying little attention as his gaze was fixed at the entrance of his hut, walking faster now he hoped that no evil had occurred as he marched his mother appeared at the entrance there were smiles on her face. The men with him perplexed had hoped the worst had not happened, they didn't understand Etiti's smile.

"Welcome my son." Etiti said.

"Mother what is going on?" The Herbalist asked.

"She is awake."

"What!" smiles broadened on his face he couldn't hide his delight. "How, what happened, how did she ...." as he had these words in his mouth, he rushed into the hut only to meet Adanna's eyes towards his direction, his heart had never known such joy before and for the first time for Adanna she smiled girlishly at him. When her men came in her smile widened they all couldn't tell how relieved they were it was indeed a happy moment for them all. The Herbalist had reasoned out a lot of things which he was happy he was not going to carry out anymore, their worries were over.

"Welcome back," the Herbalist said kneeling beside Adanna's bamboo bed.

"Thank you, just that all my body aches though." Adanna said.

"They will stop in due time I will mix herbs for you right away once you take them it would help you relax more."

"I would appreciate that" she said in a low voice, she tried to adjust herself and did so with whimpering, adjusting herself came with a great pain, as she moved the bamboo bed remained steady. The Herbalist had gotten a seat, he sat beside her and seemed to stare right into her eyes, not having any options this made her uncomfortable, but she couldn't protest, the fact that one was trying to show her pampering emotions weakened her and she found it a great distaste. After staring a little more the Herbalist went out and Adanna's men took over.

"We can't tell how relieved we are Adanna, thank the gods you are okay." Eke said.

"I didn't know you all were still around." She said, like they would leave without their money. "I will pay you off in the morning so you can go your ways, you have tried enough for me, besides our job is done, I have been doing a lot of thinking for the brief moment I have been awake, and I think it is the right thing to do."

"No, no, no" they protested in unison, "You can take your time," they said.

Buni who had protested at their idea of taking her money was surprised at their response, were these not the men claiming a moment ago to carry out their plans, now claiming to not be in a hurry. They continued to ask her questions, that even the Herbalist had not bothered to ask.

"Is your body paining you?" Eke and Neti were asking with Buni silent and just watching.

"Yes like I said before it aches, every inch." Adanna answered.

"What can we get for you?" they both asked again.

"Nothing, I am fine thank you."

"Do you want water?" they persisted, through the questions they were trying to show affections and perhaps also hoping to make her add more money in the morning out of gratitude for their caring.

"Look I appreciate your help, but I need rest so stop asking me these questions." Adanna said coldly as her usual self. Then they knew indeed it was still Adanna and it was her speaking. With little to do they called out to Nnadi and she brought seats for them, they sat in the hut and waited for the Herbalist to return while watching Adanna who had closed her eyes with the hope that it would keep out more visitors. 'I wonder what they are coming to see' she had said in her mind, 'Did I give birth.' As her eyes were shot the call of her fake name opened them, "Odabi," it was the Herbalist calling.

"Take this herb that I have prepared."

"Really this fast." She said.

"I prepared them since really hoping you will wake, so why delay now that you are finally awake?"

"Thank you." Adanna said.

"You are welcome" The Herbalist answered.

The night would be a happy one for the Herbalist he went to his mother and enquired as to how the good thing happened.

"We were all outside when I heard a sneeze," Etiti said beaming with joy, "She sneezed three times and when I went into your hut I saw her with her eyes open and I was overjoyed."

"Ah! I feel very happy, that is a good thing indeed. Now I can sleep well."

The Herbalist's mother had decided to help Adanna in whatever way she could. She had never seen her son get so emotional with a patient for a long while, since she figured he had matured in his trade, it was now unlike when he was just starting and wished to cure and help everyone. She had every mother's dream of witnessing their children get married to someone they cherish, and she wouldn't mind if it was this strange woman that would finally make her son consider marriage. She wondered if he ever thought of it, he behaved like marriage was a strange notion, which should not be talked about, unfortunately for her, he was her only offspring and the only hope for grandchildren. After the barrage of questions her son went back to the hut to look at Adanna once more before returning to his own bed in another hut. Everyone had gone to bed and everywhere looked deserted, lying on his bamboo bed the Herbalist thought about the issues of the day. He wondered how Adike and Naani had fared. The pregnant woman was she okay what could have become of her? Then finally his thought went to Adanna. Moments ago he had thought he would lose her not knowing what to do to revive her. Now everything seemed perfect, he thought about all these and how life changed so easily with it he dozed off.

CHAPTER 28

Nne was the first to wake up, she felt guilt this time, or pricking of the conscience and then was angry at herself, believing she had slept too much, yet with the feeling she didn't want to wake Obirika. She stepped on a twig and it snapped, this awoke Iwobo. The four of them had been sleeping on the ground, the fire they made Iwobo and Obeli had woken intermittently to stoke the fire and it had kept them warm till morning, not even the morning dew quenched the fire. The morning was a bit foggy as mist hung around in the atmosphere with much contemplation Nne thought of waking her mother but didn't. Iwobo stood up and looked at her, her hair was scattered but she still looked beautiful, the two greeted. Iwobo sat and thought of what to do, whether to wake them or wait for them to awake.

"Please rouse Obeli up." Nne said, "We should be going."

Iwobo obeyed, Nne did likewise by waking her mother, Obirika stretched her left arm and yawned with sleep still in her eyes, immediately she gathered where she was, she knew they must move. In about a moment all four were ready to move, when they got to a well-known area they would take another bath but for now they must move on since they had spent a lot of time in one position. The fear of being pursued was still with them and the fact that they had easily escaped death, was also still with them they moved along wishing the day to be like the previous day where they had little incidence.

They all moved having each called their gods and their ancestors in their heart to protect them. Iwobo was leading the way while Obirika and Nne followed, Obeli was the last in line. The path all seemed the same if one had not been to these parts before he would certainly be lost the path only allowed for one person trekking at a time as they were tall bushes and trees scattered about; moving deeper into any of the sides the person would move into where only the trees formed a canopy for the ground and these parts were not easy to go to except with a machete for clearing the way. Obeli had advised that they still keep out of the main slave route as the men of Akom who would be leading their captives to the seacoast may follow the route. Nne had wanted to follow the route so as to meet them but Iwobo and Obeli decided againt this, Obirika had claimed she didn't want to see any slave dealers anymore, however Obeli had suggested this to protect his sister Adanna.

"The good thing is that it is not only one way that led to and fro to the seacoast, we can follow another route." Iwobo had said and that route was the route they would follow, "The only thing is that we will meet a lot of villages and clans on this route, the slavers do not like following it, the villages and its occupants are not known for their hospitality, especially to slavers as they are always raided for slaves, these villages prefer to sell their slaves themselves."

"So what do we do?" Nne asked.

"They are friendly so I guess we will just put up with them." Iwobo said.

"How do you even know so much?" Nne asked.

"Like I have said we searched for my half-brother a very long time and believe me, we are still searching for him at least I am still searching for him even now that my father is no more."

"Hmmm." Nne hummed.

"The thing is once you come to these parts, it is hard to forget them." Iwobo said.

Obeli was still mute to this point, not having said a word since they started out in the morning occasionally he glanced back to make sure no one was following them. With the words still in Iwobo's mouth they met a group of girls going out to the stream from the path they had come from, they didn't bother to hide from them, the girls were six in number and they all seemed happy with their water pots held by one hand under the shoulder they went about their business. They met Iwobo and his group and they greeted them and passed. Iwobo and his group knew that the village wouldn't be far ahead they increased their steps. They were in dire need of refreshments and bathing wouldn't be so bad.

"What is the first thing we should do when we get to this village?" Iwobo asked.

"Bath, eat..." they all said simultaneously.

"Bathing I think" Obeli finally said, "Let us move faster."

They got into the village and everyone seemed happy to meet them as strangers. Contrary to Iwobo's words the people had learnt to accept things as they were. They sought for who would help them, they went to the market square and saw men armed and these sort of men they had been seeing right from the entrance of the village. Every corner they went to men were standing there armed and having a look out, the village was just like the rest of the villages they had seen, clean compounds with huts scattered inside of them, they went on, marching on the path that they had entered. On one finally they met a woman with her son who was clearly going to the farm.

"Are you strangers?" she asked as she was walking past them.

"Yes we are and we are in need of some things." Iwobo said.

The woman smiled, "Because of the two women with you who are like myself, I will help."

She took them to her husband's compound then to her hut, where they refreshed, she also brought out new clothes for the women and some surprisingly for the men, where she had gotten them they knew not, she didn't look rich, but seemed comfortable. She ordered her slaves who brought food for them. Surprised at her hospitality Iwobo couldn't believe their luck, the first time he had come to this village in search of his half-brother the man they met refused to help them saying he would only help them if they gave him money, they gave him money and he turned out to be a fraud. All they had asked him was, "Did you see a man who is tall, dark, broad shoulders, he also has a birth mark on his shoulders?"

"I may have seen him." The man had said.

"Please can you tell us where?"

"I shan't answer your questions unless you give me some money," the two of them were surprised, Iwobo's father brought out ten cowries, and gave to the man he took it and his reply to them, simply shocked them "I don't think I have seen the man you are talking about try some place else."

They thought of seizing him and collecting their money but he was with others who were ready to fight, since that day Iwobo concluded that you couldn't get help from this sort of people now this woman was showing him the other side of the villagers.

"When you are done eating I think you should rest a while but stay indoors, don't come out as security in our village had been tightened." The woman said.

"What is really going on?" Obirika asked.

"Exactly last six market days we were raided by slavers they came and took our young children, every now and then this evil men would come to our village in the afternoon when everyone had gone to work, or when everyone had gone to sleep, they would kidnap our children and go sell them off at the seacoast. We have been trying to put a stop to it, that is why we have our warriors all keeping watch for them I really wish we would kill them every time they come. That is why every time I go to the farm I go with my little boy, my husband's second wife lost three of her sons to these raiders they just came and wreaked havoc without any warning, unfortunately we have not been able to capture one alive and ask them where they are coming from." With these words Obirika felt her food unsettle in her stomach, she just did not wish to remain in this place anymore, before the raiders would come, "You seem agitated?" the woman asked looking at Obirika whose hands were visibly shaking. "Don't worry you are safe." These words did little to settle Obirika's mind, "By the way where are you people coming from?"

"We are coming from Mkpunki," Iwobo answered.

"Wow! That is a far place. Indeed it is, well you can stay for as long as you want my husband has gone to the farm. I'm sure he would be expecting me and my son, we will leave you in the hands of our slaves, as for me I must leave now."

"We appreciate it all, all we just need is a bath and we will be on our way, we still have a long distance to go." Iwobo said.

"Where are you going?" the woman asked.

"Akom" Iwobo answered, believing the slavers after them would find it difficult to search for them here, seeing they were not welcomed here, besides the woman deserved to know, for her kind hospitality, it would be evil to repay such a one with lies, people should be trusted including her type, but now they just had to trust blindly.

"My servants will give you water for bath then," as they spoke she called out and a girl approached, she gave the orders and she ran off, a moment later she came back to inform them that their water was ready. The women went to bath first then followed by the men, they would have to manage, to bath at the stream was still the best, but would have to wait till they got to their destination before they could afford the luxury of bathing in the stream, they had asked the woman her name before she left them.

"Enule." She had said smiling at them.

From her looks Obeli figured she wouldn't be too old, she had a very beautiful round face and a dimple formed on two of her checks whenever she smiled, her height was good for a woman, and her son looked every bit like her. After they finished bathing they donned their new garments, thanked the people in the compound before leaving. Looking lost Iwobo seemed uncertain which way to take, whether the left or the right.

"You don't now remember the path anymore." Obeli asked.

"No not that at all, just thinking which way will be faster."

"Let's take the left," they followed blindly, what options did they have they had to follow the only person who knew the way. As they moved they passed a large tree that had the area around it cleared the ground was well covered with fine sand, and there they saw some soldiers loitering about, they greeted to show they had no ill intent to the soldiers who had not seen them at first, when the soldiers saw them they halted them.

"Stop!" One of the warriors called out.

They stopped, "Where are you coming from?" he asked.

"From Enule's compound. Any problem?" Iwobo asked.

"Yes the problem is with you people." The soldier said.

"Which village are you from and where are you going?"

"Hope there is no problem with all these questions?" Iwobo asked.

"Just answer my questions."

This was a good time for a lie, but may proof costly, truth was better here, "We are from Akom, and we are headed towards that direction." Obeli said.

"You lie, you are spies and it is you people that send these slave raiders after us, you are the informants." The soldier said.

"We are no such things." Obirika protested.

"Shut your mouth when men speak," the warrior shouted and stared at Obirika malevolently, "We will soon find out." By now more of the warriors comrades had gathered and they were now three in number, he quickly sent one to Enule's compound to confirm that they were from there. The soldier ran off towards Enule's compound, meanwhile Nne and her crew were ordered to stand by the side of the path, as of now two more warriors had come making them four in number, minus the one that ran-off to Enule's compound, who would have made them five. When he returned he mentioned that Enule had gone to the farm with her son, but the people in the compound had corroborated that they came from the compound.

The warriors were dressed in their normal war wears, with charms for protection tied on their arms. They had always claimed that with the charms 'You can't get hurt,' they also tied snake skin on their heads, no one knew if this was also a protection ploy. The men looked fearful, as their muscles stood out, they were indeed men of war trained for that purpose. Generally everyone was a warrior so long as you belonged to the youth age grade, brandishing their swords they looked ready to kill. Obirika was now standing behind Iwobo, while Nne stood bravely beside Obeli the four of them were facing the warriors as their backs were facing the path, making it possible for only the warriors to see who was passing by, while they couldn't.

"I don't trust your stories, I will have to take you to the village heads before anything is done. I strongly suspect you people are spies, giving out information, and always causing us to be raided by those savages."

"Like we said we are not spies we are travellers." Obeli responded.

The man that had spoken who seemed like the leader, for he was the one that always spoke and ordered others, maybe it was because of his age, he looked older than them all.

Iwobo protested, "You can't take us anywhere, we have a place very important that we are going to, and we can't be delayed so do whatever you want to we won't follow you."

"Then you will go by force." As they approached to grab Iwobo, he unsheathed his sword, Obeli did likewise.

"No, no, no." Obirika started screaming like one possessed by the forest spirits, they all turned and started looking at her.

She fell down on the ground and started weeping.

"Please we are innocent." She said with tears rolling down her cheeks. "We are innocent please, we are innocent," she continued crying.

The soldier now apparently moved turned to her, "We are not arresting you people, just want to show you to the village heads you will do the things necessary and will be on your way." He said, "Since you say you are from Akom, Akom is still far from here, the faster you make your decisions the better it is for you."

Nne now standing behind her mother, who was on the ground, "Take us to your leaders then," she said indifferently, the warriors looked at her to show their displeasure that a woman would talk to them like that.

Iwobo and Obeli sheathed their swords.

"We will be taking all your weapons." The soldier said, reluctantly and after much arguing, they both handed over their weapons which consisted of swords, daggers, and a stick spear, they handed it all over. The warriors formed a circle around them while the leader moved before them Iwobo, was finally having a déjà vu. Maybe the clan of Umuti was not to be visited, he always had a negative story to tell whenever he visited Umuti. He wouldn't let this men's action spoil what Enule had done for them. The leader Gamki he had learnt to be his name made it certain for them to know that he felt pride in what he was doing. As he took them past the main village, past other people's compound, if Iwobo, and his crew were planning to be discreet and have no one notice that they visited, such hope was gone now. Those around in their compounds came to the front of their compound to witness what was going on, they all stared at them, like caught criminals, the spectators, ran to view. "Gamki who are they?" One woman asked who was obviously Gamki's friend.

"They are strangers." He said.

They have now passed her compound not going far from her hut, "Gamki" she still shouted, "Are they spies?" shaking his head in disbelief. "We will find out." He shouted in response.

As they marched through the compounds people kept running out to view them, the situation confused Iwobo, who didn't know if they were surprised to see their warriors walk strangers or that it was untold to be caught by the warriors. Nne wondered what they were going to do with them, Obeli felt uncertain also. If only they knew who he was, one thing was certain though, they wouldn't be mentioning slavery to this people. They passed several compounds few were uniquely designed with different patterns, while the rest bore the usual doomed appearance showcasing poverty, if any one was present in them the person ran out, to see who was passing. They went on this path for a considerable time before passing a place that seemed deserted then the path formed a T-junction walking straight would be walking into the bush they turned left walking past nothing but bushes now after a while a compound appeared on their left. It was a considerable large compound with about ten huts, the leader Gamki smiled and pushed the logs of wood made gate in. Obeli wasn't impressed he had seen better, his father's compound was bigger and looked better with more servants, they all passed the wooden gate and moved into the compound. They all marched to the biggest hut that was at the centre, Gamki, knocked by clapping his hands.

"Elder Machi!" he shouted.

"Who is it?"

"It is me Gamki, we have come for your counsel on a pressing matter."

"Give me a moment." Machi said.

His voice sounded shrill, like a high-pitched woman, when he emerged from the hut those that saw him, for the first time weren't surprised. He was a very old man and he marched out with a walking stick, which took him forever to do. As he came out Gamki and his men bowed to greet him, Machi was the oldest in the village but his faculties were still intact, they brought such decisions to him to decide on. He had married many wives, had many sons and daughters, he had lived his life in full. He was also one of the wealthiest men in Umuti. When he saw them, he called Gamki to himself as he sat on a chair in front of his hut. Gamki whispered some things to him, and he whispered back, when Gamki, returned he whispered to one of his men the same one he had sent to Enule's compound, the young man once again ran off. Machi was a frail man, his veins and wrinkles couldn't be differentiated he took time before he spoke as if searching for words.

"You are welcome." He finally said.

"Thank you Elder." Iwobo responded.

"Well you must know that our people are a peace loving people, we love prosperity, but every now and then," he cleared his throat and continued, then as if receiving revelation, he inhaled sharply and opened his mouth, "Where are my manners? Please give them seat to sit on," he called for a slave, who came and he ordered her to bring kola nuts and its pepper for their visitors, when the seats were brought he asked them to sit, they sat but the warriors remained standing, he continued.

"Like I said, my people are a peace loving people, and from the raids that have been going on, we can't seem to be extra careful these days. For example Nwakidilo, my good friend lost one of his wives and her entire family to these raiders, they almost wiped out his family." Iwobo and his group, almost sympathized with them, but they couldn't forget their own predicament. What are they doing there? What had he whispered to the man who ran off? And what makes them think they are the spies they are looking for?

"Eat your kola, none of you have touched his or her's." Machi said.

"We appreciate the kola, but we are not hungry and we won't pretend we are happy," Obeli said. "We are sorry for your problems. In Akom, we are having the same problems too. We are not spies neither are we the raiders."

"Ah! So I was told. You are truly from Akom?"

"Yes we are." Obeli continued.

Nne and Obirika who has stopped weeping and was now moping, sat together, not saying a word. When men are talking a woman should be careful to speak, Iwobo and Obeli were representing them.

"We demand to be set free at once." Obeli said.

"You will be, sorry about the way you were treated, but you are not apprehended, I can assure you that." They strained a little to hear Machi, and were relieved when they heard they were not under arrest, by anyone.

"We would like to be on our way then, since we are not under arrest." Iwobo said.

"You will soon, very soon but there is something we must do before you leave, I would very much like it that you eat your kola it's a sign of goodwill between us, the people of Akom and Umuti. The people of Akom are not our enemies, so please eat your kola." Machi said pointing to the kolas.

"We will take them, we just ate in the hut of Enule and we are satisfied, so we won't be demanding our stomach to make accommodation, indeed we are fine." Obeli said and as a sign of respect they all took the kolas, it was great evil to disobey an elder of the village.

"If you say so."

As Machi spoke they kept looking around in the compound, as people went about doing one thing or the other. Two little girls were playing a game in front of one hut, while others played a game which involved dancing they were all little girls. Nne looked at them and wondered how it had not been long ago she played the same dancing game. She would dance with her friends and her mother would tell her if she could dance well, maybe one day she would join the girls who danced at the village ceremonies. Nne had cherished such moments, there were no signs of Machi's wives, his first wife had died a few market days before and all wondered how Machi had come to out-live his wife, his other wives, remained but she was the wife of his youth. He called the young girl that had brought seats to him and his visitors before. She came bent down in front of him and a moment later disappeared into his hut, a while later she came out with a small wooden box. They knew what the box contained immediately they saw it, it was a snuff box, Machi slapped it on his left hand with his right hand, and proceeded to open it he took a pinch and inserted it into his left nostril, when he inserted it he inhaled hardly and then exhaled while rolling his eyes and violently shaking his head sideways, he repeated the same procedure with his right nostril each time exhaling in what could be termed a sense of pleasure. This sight infuriated Obeli and Iwobo, it couldn't be told about the ladies, the man was obviously delaying them, and he had his pleasures while doing so, ignoring their pain.

"Sir do you think it is possible that we should be going?" Iwobo asked to break the silence.

"Just a moment please, you must bear with us, we wouldn't want to have our visitors treated ill every time they visited, but since our guards have seen you and thought it necessary to follow this process, we must follow the process." As Machi, answered them the young man who had been sent on an errand returned, following him was the Chief Priest of Umuti. There was no way for the people of Akom to know who he was but they suspected him to be so, only the medicine men dressed like he did, they all turned to look at them, as they approached they came straight to the centre of the compound where they were and the warriors seemed satisfied. Only Iwobo, and his crew were in suspense as they imagined what this could mean, the Chief Priest walked with a simple staff, adorned with a lot of charm, he was looking every inch a medicine man, as he carried his animal skin bag, he was paunchy and plump, everyone knew in his shrine he fined heavily, in a moment he approached. Nne couldn't help but notice, that at the sight of the man all the children had disappeared into their huts, it was not a thing to wonder for when they were young they used to tell stories of how powerful medicine men were, they would be told stories of how medicine men had turned someone into an animal, or how it was possible, for medicine men or the Chief Priest to disappear. Nne's favourite story of their power of course it was terrifying to her as a kid, but now, not so much was how the Chief Priest of Akom had turned a man into a toad. Nne didn't see how it was possible but had believed it as a kid and a part of her still does, other children too now also believe such stories, the Chief Priest approached, laid his mat on the ground, brought out his small medicine staff, made incantations to the staff which was a sculpted head of wood with human facial features, he spoke into the sculpted head and then gave a menacing glance at Iwobo, then Obeli and finally to Nne and her mother Obirika, he laughed still holding the sculpted head, without looking at them. Machi, now putting his snuff box away, said "It is time."

"Time for what?" Obeli wanted to scream out.

"Have them come to the front," the Chief Priest commanded. All the while Gamki had been standing beside them, he was facing Machi, and was on the same line with them. Machi with his finger directed them to stand in front of the Chief Priest, with a red cloth on the ground serving as barrier between anyone who stood and the Chief Priest.

"You must take an oath, that you are not an enemy of Umuti, and that you, would never harm anybody from Umuti also that you have not brought harm to Umuti, or thought evil about Umuti," the last one confused Iwobo, he was very certain he hated Umuti and its people, if anything he wished them ill in his heart except maybe Enule, and some of the Umuti children. "If you ever do so the god of Umuti will strike you dead now and here."

Another confusion, their faces wore uncertainty and their minds did thorough scanning if they had committed any of the offences mentioned. Unfortunately they couldn't remember much and that was a source of anxiety, Machi mentioned all these with his weak voice. The warriors seemed satisfied with what they were witnessing. Nne and her crew were dumbstruck as they couldn't believe their ears.

"Is this how you treat all visitors who come to Umuti?" Obeli asked.

"No, but since you people looked suspicious we have no choice." Gamki said.

Two men and two women suspicious, Nne found it hard to fathom, but in this situation, they had no options.

"Young man you should be the first," Machi said pointing to Iwobo.

"I will go first." Obeli said, with a mean look he stepped forward, he couldn't have Iwobo going first, he started this journey and dragged everyone else in, he should take responsibility of any issue that arose, he made his way and stood before the Chief Priest.

"Step onto the red cloth." The Chief Priest said.

He obeyed looking angered and agitated, he wouldn't do what he was doing had it not been in a strange land, Obeli's countenance remained the same, "Is 'not liking' Umuti people amongst the offences," he kept asking himself.

"Repeat after me I," the Chief Priest said and he obeyed.

"I."

"Call your full name." The Chief Priest said.

"I Obeli Ubiakwa."

"Very good." Machi muttered, all were staring at Obeli, and the Chief Priest.

"I swear to the god 'Nufika'," the Chief Priest said, and he repeated,

"I shall not harm any person from Umuti, and I shall never think of doing so, on the very day that I do such, may 'Nufika,' strike me down with his thunder," all was said and repeated Iwobo came and stood on the red cloth and said the same things including Nne and Obirika, when they were done the Chief Priest, packed up without saying a word he turned started his incantations and left.

"So what now?" Obeli asked.

"Nothing you are free, you even can go to any part of Umuti that you want. Do you want anything I have provisions for travellers?" Machi asked.

"No we are okay thank you," Nne said with as much respect as she knew, women didn't talk amongst men she knew.

"Since you want nothing else follow me so I can show you the way out." Gamki said.

"Have a peaceful journey." Machi said still seating on his chair. They were given what was collected from them, they turned and left. The path didn't confuse them as Gamki had imagined, Iwobo only needed to visit a path or place once and the whole thing was in his head. Gamki, led them past the path that led to Machi's compound, and Iwobo sensing that he would want to make them a public spectacle again, to show the inhabitants of Umuti that their warriors were working hard to safeguard them, declined his offer to follow the path they came through to Machi's.

"We would go straight this way," he said to Gamki.

"But that will make you go round the village, it's far the path we are taking is better." Gamki said.

"I know but we don't want to go through the path, we used while coming, we have our reasons."

Gamki couldn't understand their reason, neither could the men with him, but Iwobo's company did. They didn't want people to see them, that was also the reason they didn't also want to follow the other path that the slavers followed, they would have met Akom warriors marching Akuta slaves to the seacoast, now even Nne did not want to behold such sight to remind her mother of her own misery. Iwobo with his crew parted from Gamki without saying goodbye or smiling. Their faces were frowned and stoned after what he had made them pass through, they weren't in the mood to share pleasantries with him or pretend to be in good spirit. The day was still young, Gamki and Machi couldn't have chosen a better time to delay them. They marched on, they saw nothing but small farmlands interspaced with compounds, and huts, definitely for those who wanted to be secluded, mind their own business and stay alone in Umuti.

"They are still looking at us." Nne said.

"Let them look who cares." Obirika said finding her voice again.

Gamki and his men still stood at the T-junction, they were facing the path they had come through while Iwobo was leading his crew to their left. They stood transfixed, as if what they had done was not enough, they still harbored some feelings that these strangers may be up to something, maybe they had a hidden agenda.

"Let us just get away from here as soon as possible," Nne said.

"I don't feel good anymore, this place makes me feel more dejected than ever." Obirika added.

"I don't know what we are going to do, we need to march undetected and now we have five or so more villages to meet, can we still cut corners and march with no one knowing who we are?" Obeli asked. "We need to be discreet" he finally said. Like it could solve the problem they were facing. "I really don't know but I think we are right by following this path, we will cut off people we don't want to be seen by, and we will march through strangers but the problem still remains that people will see us and worst still, remember seeing us and telling anybody who asked about us, that they have in truth seen us," Obeli said.

"That shouldn't bother you Obeli, what we will do is march round the clans and when we need anything we won't go in all at once. We will share ourselves, they would be looking for four people two men, and two women, when we go in at least only in pairs they might not find it so easy identifying us, but unfortunately as we march on there is nothing we can do about it." Iwobo said.

"Should we disguise ourselves?" Nne asked Iwobo and Obeli, both seemed to be a pot of good ideas.

"How do we do that?" Iwobo asked.

"I don't know" trying to think a bit, "Don't you have any ideas?" Nne asked.

"Hey! Iwobo with ideas," Obeli mocked smiling.

Obirika had a smile now, "Obeli don't start." She said.

"Leave him let him fool himself I'm impervious to his jokes." Iwobo said.

"Please idea man, continue." Obeli said.

"Well that is all I have, we cannot get costumes here and I don't really think any will make us inconspicuous. I think we should keep moving and moving faster. How about we move in pairs from now on, two in front two behind," pausing to think about it, on his own he rejected the idea, "It would do little to help, let's just march on, hopefully all that see us will be those that mind their business and say little about others. How do we even know that those we pass by, will be found and made to recount all they had seen in a day including the people they passed by?" Iwobo said.

"You don't know people they could be busy bodies. Iwobo you speak as if you have forgotten Mama Dibia, she seems to know everyone and everything that happens in Akom." Obeli said.

Iwobo remembering her laughed. "You speak the truth, she never goes out always in her compound, but seems to know everyone and everything that happens. There would never be a time that you visit her without her telling tales of all that has happened."

"Who is she? I have never heard of her." Nne joined the conversation.

"If you do not know her you have missed a lot, and you are from Akom. How is it you don't know her?" Iwobo asked.

"I try to mind my business." Nne said.

"Really?" Obeli asked.

"Yes." Nne said.

"What can I say Mama Dibia is fun that is all, and by the way she is Obeli's aunt, so be careful how you talk about her in his presence." Iwobo said.

"Please don't mind him, feel free to talk about her however you want, but it is uncanny you have never heard of her in Akom."

"She always knows the trend, I'm sure she knows everything about you." Iwobo said.

"Really!" Nne now trying to be sarcastic.

"I'm serious, she will." Iwobo persisted.

Obirika had said little, she knew Mama Dibia but was also surprised her daughter didn't know her, with their discussion they seemed to have forgotten about their just concluded ordeal, they hoped to not find further hindrances on the way, the path they were walking on was just as Iwobo had described it, tall bushes with grasses, farmlands and sometimes huts in compounds. They would march through these paths with the aim of not being seen.

"So what you are saying is that these people might have their own Mama Dibia?" Nne asked.

"It is possible but how that woman gets her information nobody seems to know. It is as if the birds and the trees whisper to her, that is why one must be very careful how he or she speaks, you will never know who is listening, anyway that woman has always been a mystery and she will always remain so." Iwobo said.

"Watch your mouth." Obeli retorted.

Iwobo raised his hands as a sign of surrendering and kept mute.

Walking past some huts in a compound Iwobo saw girls in a compound playing, they wore armbands and trinkets like the one he had bought for Nne, he reached into his animal skin bag and felt the gifts. Touching the gifts fear gripped him, what if Nne did not reciprocate his affection? Would she feel bad that he thought of such a thing despite their situation? But there was nothing more that he wanted except seeing her happy, what he was doing he would have done for free which was his original intention, but for what he felt, it happened on its own, without the control of man, and no evil would be committed should it work out. Her happiness would mean his happiness, he wished that the journey would last forever but to have it better he wished they were safe and together. Women like gifts he had heard a man say one certain time. He couldn't remember the rest of what he had said, but he had heard such comment and he believed his gifts would say a lot for him where his words were deficient; it would make it sufficient and reasonable. He didn't know how he was going to say all he wanted to say, but the gift would help along. It was just to find a perfect time to give the gift. Obeli must not know he would see it as a waste of resources, he wouldn't understand, how Nne made him feel, it went beyond what words could say. Iwobo led the pack and marched gingerly, his smile had come back again and he didn't know.

CHAPTER 29

Adanna in Mkpunki woke up with a headache, she slept on her bamboo bed, she was still getting familiar to the Herbalist's hut. The cocks were crowing while he-goats bleated, sounds of pestle and mortar could be heard, it was as if the sounds were in her dream as she slept. As she opened her eyes, she saw the Herbalist staring at her with a smile on his face, he was sitting on a log of wood beside her bamboo bed, at first she didn't have words.

"Good morning" the Herbalist greeted staring at her with smiles still on his face.

"Good morning," she responded trying to rise a bit but she had to lean on her right elbow, with her left elbow on the bed, she tried to raise herself, then she felt the pounding in her head.

"My head hurts so bad, it is like a pounding is going on in it." Adanna said.

"Sorry it is expected, it will soon stop, I should have herbs for that," saying these words the smiles on his face were gone and a face lost in thought took over.

"Try to relax, I will be right back," he went to his hut, and prepared herbs with water and ran back to Adanna, she was lying on her back, still gazing at the thatched roof, when he entered she was surprised at how quick he had come back.

"Take this it should help." The Herbalist said.

Because of the feeling of inadequacy, Adanna would do anything to see that she got back to her old self, she couldn't live like this, like a quadriplegic, who needed help to do everything. Very soon the people helping would get tired and she would need to find a new way to find anyone happy and eager to help her. She wished for no such thing, she wanted to get better and she would. Without flinching she gulped the medicine, it was bitter and had an obnoxious smell. She had anticipated that the taste would be worse. She handed the small calabash back to the Herbalist, who took it back gently as he continued to gaze at Adanna. He had been gazing at her but this time with a renewed interest, as if by looking at her he would make her heal faster. Adanna was a strong woman and she had proven to be so, he needed no one to tell him about it. The herbs should start working any moment from now, "How do you feel?" He asked.

Adanna a bit relaxed but uneasy, with the Herbalist still staring at her.

"A bit better now. What was the medicine I drank?"

"Don't worry about it, it is a mixture we have found to work on anymore with a pounding head as you described."

"I must say it is good." She said.

"Try to move your toes let me see," the Herbalist said.

Adanna obeyed and moved her toes, the Herbalist was happy, "Some many market days ago Nwadi, one of the village palm wine tappers went to the farm to tap wine, he went alone, it was when the sun had gone down, he checked his climbing robe, it seemed intact he climbed up to the tree, few moments later his robe snapped and he fell from the tree, he had not been able to move his toes, and since then he had not been able to stand let alone walk. Okidi went to his farm, he climbed a mango tree to pluck some mangoes, unfortunately for him, the tree branch he was standing on snapped, and he fell he was able to move his toes and after a while he started walking," the Herbalist said. The fact that Adanna could move her toes meant very soon she would walk too. The Herbalist starting from the toes began pressing them, getting to her knees, "Do you know I'm touching you?" he asked.

"Yes I can feel it," Adanna replied.

"Good, very good, all will be well in just a short time all will be well okay. Just be patient, can you raise your knee?" Adanna felt she could do it, before she could attempt it her men came in looking refreshed, the Herbalist was obviously taking good care of them, they seemed to lack nothing.

"I wish we would have it this plenty always" Buni had said, when they came into the hut obviously they had been having the discussion walking into the hut.

"Me too, in Akom we struggle to eat but here we even have slaves."

"Servants!" the Herbalist corrected and kept quiet.

"Okay servants to add to the delicious meals, but most importantly the peace that seems to reign here, shielding its occupants from the harsh reality in the outside world."

Adanna seeing them as if she had read their minds hesitated a little before asking Buni to bring her bag. She didn't know which one to trust. Her animal skin bag was with her all the time before the accident and since then she didn't know what had become of it. She hoped all she had was still in it, and no one had pried to the bag. Buni took the bag which was lying on her feet area, together with her other belongings which included, her weapons he brought it to her. Showing the strong woman she was, she took the bag and forcing herself up, the Herbalist quickly went to her and helped her raise her back. She turned left and rested it on the mud wall, looking into the bag she was delighted to have found all in her bag. She quickly took out cowries and handed it to them. They too were delighted with the payment they simply knew that their partnership had just been terminated.

"Thank you Adanna, we will find our way back to Akom immediately. What do you intend to do now?" Neti asked.

"Don't worry about me just go." Adanna said and momentarily felt the fear of being alone.

With their money in their hands and the gifts received prior, they went into their hut and packed their things to move back to Akom, still concerned. "Now that we have collected our money, and we are going back to Akom, do you people remember that there is a young man we put in a cage back home, what are we going to do about it, this surely means we have committed murder." Neti said.

"When we planned this journey we knew we won't stay in Akom again just go and take your wife and child and find another village, start anew, they also will be looking for Oja so we can't really return to Akom, as for me right from the moment we set out I knew I won't be staying in Akom anymore, I have no one there." Eke said.

"Since you have no one there that is why it is easy for you, I have a family there." Neti said.

"You should have thought all these things before you embarked on this journey." Eke said.

"All I'm saying is are we murderers now?" Neti asked.

"No we are not and to be sincere I don't care." Eke said.

"You should care, let us stop this discussion, for me I think we should focus on the journey we are about to embark on." Buni said.

"That's fine with me." The two echoed back.

"Please before we go I think we should give a special thank you to the Herbalist he has been more than kind." Buni said.

"That's definite." All concurred.

Adanna looking at the Herbalist who was sitting beside her speechless wondered what his own fee would be.

"I have only few cowries remaining, I think you should take it, I will think of what to do next, but it would definitely be me owing you to pay back when I return from Akom. Do you agree?"

The Herbalist smiled, "I don't want your money."

"Then what do you want, all these you are doing must have a price," Adanna said.

"Why not relax first and stop troubling your mind about money?" The Herbalist said.

Adanna found the Herbalist confusing.

"Can I ask you a very strange question?" Adanna said looking at the Herbalist.

"Why not, ask right away."

She didn't know how to proceed, tilting her head.

"How did I get into these garments?" she asked tugging the garment.

"My mother did, she also cleaned the mud all over your body, didn't even allow the servants to do it," the Herbalist answered.

Adanna nodded, and seemed lost in thought; she owed the family big favour.

"What can I do for your family?" she asked.

The Herbalist smiled again, "You will soon find out but for now all you can do for me is to get well."

"How long did you say I was out again?"

"Almost two days, your men brought you here."

Her back began to ache, she ignored it, and allowed the pain to continue when she could have easily relaxed on the bamboo bed.

"The sight of you was awful that day but my heart is glad now that I see you, it is really heart-warming." The Herbalist said.

"The problem is, I can't remember much about it but I remember sketchily the events that led to it but not so vividly." Adanna said robbing her head.

"It happens that way sometimes give it a little time it will all come back."

As they both sat, one of the men, Buni clapped his hands at the entrance as a sign of knocking before entering the hut, he called the Herbalist to himself as the Herbalist got out the other two were standing there with their bags ready, and ready to resume their journey that had been cut short.

"Gentlemen I can see that you are ready." The Herbalist said.

"Indeed we are." Buni said.

"Travel safely, if you ever need anything when next in Mkpunki, feel free to let your legs lead you here." The Herbalist advised.

"We can't help but notice the ones you have done already," Buni said, "here." He tried to give the Herbalist few cowries out of the cowries he had been given, he wanted to be generous, or prove he had the heart of a giver, but lacked the means to give. His friends smiled and mused at his attempt. Eke felt tempted to say "At least give more cowries." But couldn't, he was not even planning to give any at all himself, his compatriot at least made an attempt.

"Why would you want to do that, no my brother, money is not the issue here, please take your money I believe she gave it to you people, so you can help yourselves." The Herbalist said.

Buni thanked the Herbalist and quickly withdrew the money, no need to persist, so that the Herbalist may not succumb to the pressure and decide to take the money, "thank you" he said once again relieved, "Utte knows I need the money," he said in his mind.

"Take care of yourselves, it is nothing huge that I assisted you people, so please don't worry."

Astonished the men couldn't believe their ears, "You are too kind, is this how all Mkpunki people are?" Buni asked.

"I really don't know," the Herbalist said smiling.

"Thank you very much," with the grateful hearts, and showing much appreciation, the men set out. Buni promising himself to make something out of his life, and try to be as nice as the Herbalist, he had certainly touched their lives, Buni had considered becoming a herbalist himself, though he thought it too cumbersome and onerous. Looking at them as they marched on the Herbalist kept waving at them, they greeted his household, on their way out they went to his mother's hut greeted her.

"My sons it shall be well with you." Etiti said to them.

"Thank you mother." They responded like teenage boys. They also greeted the servants, those they had made friends with, promising some to come again, they took care not to invite anyone to Akom, certain they wouldn't be staying in Akom. And they didn't want to lie to this new people that had been so nice to them, with everyone out now and waving at them they opened the wooden gate, and let themselves out taking the right they moved out of sight.

With them gone the Herbalist went back to the hut to wait on Adanna. His mother also prepared herself and made her way to the hut to check on Adanna for the day before she went to the farm to weed and tend other crops, while also preparing for the next planting season. The Herbalist was in the hut when she came in.

"How are you?" she asked looking at no one in particular, Adanna and the Herbalist both answered fine at the same time, there was no how they could have known who the question was for, his mother smiled.

"(Odabi) Adanna how are you?" she finally said. She called her Odabi because that was the name Adanna had given them all.

"Fine thank you. And you how are you doing?" Adanna asked.

"We are up and about to begin the day's work." Etiti said.

"Sounds like fun." Adanna said.

"It is work my dear," Etiti said smiling "Work that is all it is, anyway I just came to check on you, I will see you again in the night."

The Herbalist had not said a word, as he watched the two women chat, he was now sitting at the head of the bamboo bed resting his back on the wall, while his mother stood at the entrance covering it. Etiti was a sight, her plumpness gave a very young look which hid her true age.

"Nnadi will bring you people food. (Odabi) Adanna, how will you manage?" Etiti asked looking at her.

"I can feed myself thank you," she said re-assuring Etiti, "I will try to eat light."

"Mother do not worry I will be here for her, if she needs anything I will let you people know, or better still let them know since you would be going out."

"Okay then my work here is done, I will leave you two, please stay well." Etiti said.

"You too stay well, and have a safe day." The Herbalist said.

"I always do, there is no problem to that. Alright," she heaved and left.

"What exactly would you like to eat?" the Herbalist asked.

"Anything that doesn't involve me chewing hard."

"Thank the gods it is swallow we have, don't know really but I'm sure it is what they are preparing they always do."

"It is great then."

"Indeed it is."

A moment of awkward silence fell in, with both not knowing the next words to use. Adanna was having it tough with the attitude of the Herbalist. It was not like she was a baby but he had decided all on his own to baby sit her, in a short while the usual for the Herbalist began to set in. People started coming to him with their so many health problems. Nnadi came into the hut to call on him, he was initially reluctant to go but then, he had to help whenever his help was needed. Adanna felt certain it would be okay, a moment without him staring at her or in his presence would be a welcomed development.

"Who and who is actually there?"

"I don't know them sir, they said they wanted to see you when they came in, and I've never seen them before, but I'm sure they are patients."

"Okay let them wait, I'll be with them in a short while." The Herbalist said.

No need sending Nnadi to go ask for their names, new people came every day.

He stood from his seat walked to the side of Adanna's bed, gave her a quick glance and went out. Coming out his visitors had already arranged themselves in order, with those that came first sitting at the end to the entrance, while others sat further down on the bamboo bench, the Herbalist came out and the first person he saw was Mama Adubi, then a lady he had never seen then finally Elder Ebiki, and five other strange faces. The Herbalist went back into the hut he now occupied. He took his herb bag, breathed in heavily and exhaled then went to his visitors, as he sat, mama Adubi was the first.

"My son I don't know what else to do, my stomach has been aching me for a very long time now, for almost three market days, I have not been able to rest, the trouble is much." As she spoke her voice became soft as if she was about to cry. "I don't know what to do." She said faintly.

The Herbalist looked into his bag he didn't have a herb that would have helped with the pain.

"Is that all?" he asked.

"Yesssss" she said stressing the 's' in the yes and gave a wimp, "It is all." Mama Adubi said.

"Don't worry, I will mix you something but you will have to wait." The Herbalist said.

"Hope you won't take much time?"

"No not at all, if you want you can go home when I mix it, I will bring it to your place." The Herbalist said.

A visit to her sounded good, Mama Adubi would cherish nothing more but to be visited. The Herbalist used to visit before, not knowing what prompted him, he stopped visiting, promising her he would visit, reminded her of his 'used to be mission' of visiting her. With the offer well accepted, Mama Adubi stood up and gently tapping her walking stick on the ground marched away.

"Go well Mama," he called out after her.

"Thank you my son." She responded.

"Yes my lady what can I do for you?" the Herbalist turned to the second person on the bench.

"Orife sent me." She said.

"Oh! Really, how is he?"

"He is fine but his son is ill he asked me to tell to come visit as soon as possible, he would have come by himself but has to watch his son as his wife is not around, and the little boy doesn't let us get close to him."

"He is still young where did his mother go?" the Herbalist asked surprised.

"She travelled to their village for her sister's burial."

"Okay, I will see what I can do. Is that all?"

"Yes, well no," recollecting herself, "He also said you should come with his medicine."

"Okay I will do just that, and my regards to him and his son."

"Thank you sir," she said and walked away.

"Ebiki, how is it going?" the Herbalist asked turning to the next person.

"Well what can we say, things are not so good when it comes to health, that notwithstanding we should still remain grateful." Ebiki said.

"If you say so, so what is the problem this time?"

"It is the same old recurring problem, still the knee ache that has refused to heal, like I always ask is it a crime for one to seek what to eat? Others go to the farm and come back unscathed, mine turns out to be a sad story."

"Ah Ebiki, we all have sad stories, so don't let it bother you, I will give you something right away, I hope the medicine I give you helps at least."

"Yes it does, it does that is why I keep coming back."

The Herbalist got up, went to his new hut and in a short while came out with a drug in a calabash and handed it over to the man.

"When you get home turn it into the cooking calabash and heat it, and then drink, this one is new let's see how it helps with the problem, I'm sure you still have the balm, keep using it too." The Herbalist said.

"Very nice I appreciate, this is nice" he repeated, "Thank you very much," he picked up his walking stick, and went home.

The Herbalist attended to the rest in the same manner when he was done, relieved that no one else was around. The Herbalist went into his old hut that Adanna was now occupying, when he went in, he was surprised she was sitting up, she had risen without anyone's help, as she rested her back on the mud wall, the Herbalist entering smiled at her and she reciprocated. He took his log of wood that he was carrying with him putting it down, he faced her, searching for words to say to her, he thought of starting with how surprised he was that she was sitting up, but decided to save it.

"Who were those people?" Adanna asked, somebody had to do something and the self-regarded proactive did.

"Those were my patients; they came for herbs and treatment." He said nodding, "I'm sure you must have witnessed them before," he said still nodding. "Will you be okay on your own? I have to go out for a while, I need to go give two amongst them drugs," saying the words he sighed, "But my first point of call would be Mama Adubi."

"Why? Who is she?"

He shook his head sideways, not knowing how to proceed on answering the question.

"What can I say she is the sweetest woman you can ever come across, I have known her since I was a kid, then she would allow us to pluck mangoes in her compound when it is ripe, and also play around. The only thing is she never had male children, she had about six girls and they are almost all married, should be one or two remaining to get married, so she is the only one living in the compound now. The other wives of her husband all moved out when her husband died mysteriously." The Herbalist re-adjusted himself, "She is a very nice woman, and I used to visit her to stay and chat, I believe she enjoys it."

"So what happened to her daughters don't they visit?" with the question the Herbalist was surprised as Adanna or Odabi as he knew her was not known to have shown interest in what he did, or who he met, for the very brief moment he had known her, it was a good thing he didn't conclude to know everything about her, with her new found interest, he would cherish their moment together.

"Her daughters do come but I guess not as often as she would like, people would wonder why she won't go to stay with her daughters, but she loved her husband dearly, and wouldn't want his name to vanish from the face of the earth, forever, or have people say that her husband's compound is deserted like a cursed place, I wish you had met her, she is truly kind."

"Really?"

"Yes."

"What exactly happened to her husband?" Adanna asked.

"My dear no one knows, I don't do well with gossip, but from what I heard he just died, others say the gods, others say it was an untimely death, no one knows, before I and my father could reach him, because he struggled with death on his bed, he was gone, such things you can never know much about, she is not so unfortunate."

"How do you mean?" Adanna asked.

"She had children not like she didn't have them, just that she didn't have males."

"A lot of people consider it a great tragedy they don't have male children to carry on the name of the family, but her husband's other wives had sons, so it is not bad for him, but I'm sure she would have loved to have a male child." The Herbalist said.

"Okay I believe you."

"Alright I have to go now, there are two people I'm going to meet."

"Who is the second person?"

"That would be Orife, and his son, you have not seen any of the people I've mentioned but once in a while I go to give them medicine."

"I wish them well." Adanna said, she herself couldn't believe the words coming out from her mouth, she had never bothered herself with the affairs of other men.

"Hope you are good?" he asked.

"Yes I am okay."

"I will only be gone for a moment, Nnadi is out there if you need anything, beckon on her."

With the words and him still speaking he went out, and it seemed to Adanna he continued to speak as he went along. Now all alone, Adanna checked her toes again they moved, she desperately needed to get back on her feet. With her hands she pushed her two legs off the bamboo bed, touching them on the ground the cold earth sent a cool feeling through her feet, connecting to her nerves to the rest of her body, fixing it firmly on the ground, she tried, standing up pushing all her weight up, she tried using the bed as a support for her hands. But with all she tried she couldn't get any feeling on her waist, at that moment she knew she was trying in vain. She sat on the bed with her legs on the ground thinking of what next to do. How was she going to get up? She tried standing again but her legs felt wobbly and weak, she couldn't. Exhausted, she felt like crying, her eyes watered, for a moment she began to feel how inadequate she really was. Such a thing had never happened to her before, she had never been in such a position where she would need help to do the necessary things of life. She thought of what the Herbalist would do, but nothing came to mind. How was she going to get up?

She needed to start walking, as she sat alone on the bamboo bed she felt lonely for the first time, she just wanted someone, to do exactly what her mother used to do. A feeling she had always fought against when she was in Akom, now she wished she was in Akom with her family. She remembered the time she would go to the stream to have a bath, and all times she went hunting. Her life had evaporated right before her very eyes. What could have brought her to this position? She didn't have any regrets, she looked to her left in a corner was her bag and her newest acquisition, a long Dane gun, she didn't desire the gun anymore all she wished was for an act of the gods to help her and make her walk again. She hated the feeling of hopelessness that she was having, it was not a nice feeling to know you have a problem and there was nothing you could do to stop the problem. Adanna was having pains and she couldn't stop it, the headache was back, and now she would have to wait for the Herbalist to come back. Anyone who told her she would one day need help to raise her back from the bed she wouldn't believe it. All her life she had laughed in front of danger and fear, but now facing the fact that she may never walk again, in a strange land made her heart pound very fast, her hands tremble, and her throat very dry.

"No!" she said looking round in her desperation for something to help her stand, there was none, no one was around so no one had to know, she placed her hands on her head gently brought it down onto her face, tears wanted to come out again and she fought it, she inhaled sharply as if she had made her peace, she laid back on the bamboo bed, as she closed her eyes she drifted off into a deep sleep, her body must have had enough, or it was the drug she was taking.

CHAPTER 30

The Herbalist first went to Orife's compound because it was closer to him, before Mama Adubi's compound. On getting to the compound he saw nothing out of the ordinary on his way just people going about their business, without the care of the world on their faces. Entering the compound, the young lady that had come to relay the message earlier on ran to him to welcome him, she asked to carry his bag but he didn't oblige. He went to the hut where Orife was known to stay, he clapped his hands as a sign of knocking. From inside the hut Orife recognised the voice of the Herbalist, and his knocking.

"Herbalist please come in, we have been waiting for you," Orife's voice loomed from inside the hut.

"Thank you Orife. How is the boy?" the Herbalist asked.

"He is getting better but, I think what he has is fever."

"Don't worry at all, for children it is normal, he is growing so expect such sickness once in a while."

"Are you saying it is because he is growing that he is sick?"

"Yes that is what I mean, such fever set in when a boy is growing."

"Is there anything you can do for him?" Orife asked.

"I have herbs for fever for him," he proceeded to give it to the boy, "As you have said, it is fever, but he would come around, here take this." The Herbalist handed him a pouch, the man puzzled as to what to do with the pouch before he could ask why. The Herbalist guessing his confusion, "It is for you, drink it, for your body aches."

"Ah! Thank you, as if you know what I want, all my joints are aching."

"Well I think such also comes with age."

"Hmm, so our sicknesses are now being attributed to age?" Orife asked not caring for the answer.

"Sometimes it is." The Herbalist answered.

"Thank you very much, you are kind." Orife said.

"Learnt your wife travelled?"

"Yes she did, she went to her sister's burial, the sister was a lovely woman while alive but it is okay such things happen. Besides it is her elder sister, her mother's first daughter, she was quite aged."

"Really?"

"Yes she lived a fulfilled life"

"It is all good then. When will she be returning?"

"We are expecting her today, before the sun goes down."

"Okay I will come again in the morning there is another dose that he is supposed to take."

"We would be expecting you."

"Are your visitors from Akom gone?" Orife asked.

The Herbalist felt dumb at the question, who told him that he had visitors, tongues must be working in Mkpunki, how did he know? Feigning seriousness, "They are gone now."

"Okay, including the woman? How is her health?"

Who told him about the woman?!

"She is getting better."

"I was surprised when, I learnt they were from Akom."

"Yes they are," the Herbalist answered, surprised at how much Orife already knew about them, that meant the news must have gone round the whole of Mkpunki, "I will be going now." The Herbalist finally said.

"Thank you," Orife said. Orife wanted to talk to him about getting married, he considered himself to be the Herbalist's friend, and as a friend they should talk about such things but he would wait and have them discuss it another day. Without words the Herbalist patted the boy on the head, hopefully the boy would get well soon, as he looked every bit like his father, they both had an open teeth, which accentuated when they smiled or laughed. Orife was a tall man and no doubt his son would be just as tall, like the boy's siblings, their ebony skin radiated when they oiled it, their hairs were full like the one the Herbalist had seen on the white woman. He wondered where she was now, and pushed the thought away, she was definitely fine wherever she was. From the Orife's he went to Mama Adubi's compound, again strangers were greeting him on the way. He got to her compound, it wasn't as usual, people were in the compound the Herbalist started wondering how long it had been since he last visited, not asking questions he went to her hut.

"I think she is sleeping." A voice said from behind. The Herbalist turned, it was a sight he would never forget Mama Adubi's granddaughter was beautiful, but she was just a kid when he saw her last, her beauty caused the Herbalist to smile.

"I will go and wake her." She said.

"Do you remember or in any way recognize me?" he asked still smiling.

"You used to bring us medicine as kids." She said.

"Very correct and I still do, however it is granny that I do so for nowadays. Please tell her I'm here."

She went into the hut and the next voice the Herbalist heard was that of Mama Adubi from inside the hut.

"Herbalist please come in." She was awake, from the sound of her voice, she had really been sleeping, it was a good thing then that she could sleep. She had maintained her hut in the compound, the compound almost had 15 huts, and most were not occupied, the compound had always been kept clean even at her age, Mama Adubi still swept. The Herbalist smiled and went into the hut, the beautiful girl was now sitting on the edge of her grandmother's bed, the two of them sat on the bed.

"How is the stomach?" he asked in the most polite way that he could.

"The good thing is that it allowed me to sleep off about a moment ago" Mama Adubi said smiling.

"That is a good sign," the Herbalist said.

"Yes it is, but sometimes it would ache me terribly."

"Sorry, it will stop," the Herbalist re-assured.

"When? that is the question."

"I believe these herbs will help," he said reaching into his animal bag and bringing out some leaves, he gave it to the girl and told her to cook it, and give to her grandmother the liquid from the boiled leaves to drink.

"Dear hope you heard him?" Mama Adubi said as the girl walked away.

"Yes grandmother."

Paying attention to the Herbalist once again, "My son it has been long since you visited, is it because of your visitors that you no longer visit, the Herbalist could only open his mouth and gawk, has just about everyone in Mkpunki heard.

"Well mama," he laughed awkwardly, "I don't think it is because of them," he fought back every urge to ask her who told her about them.

"All I'm saying is that you be careful with those Akom people, we don't speak the same language you know, despite they almost sound the same, and we don't have the same customs, so be very careful, with them especially their fighter woman."

What! Who told her about Adanna, now certain he was living an open show life, he changed the topic of discussion from himself to her.

"How are your daughters Mama?"

"They are fine, what can I say," as she spoke she raised her legs and placed them on her bed, the Herbalist got a feeling that the chat was coming to an end and she was prepared to go back to sleep, hopefully, she would wait to take the drugs.

"Mama the drugs will have to be taken twice a day, you will drink a mouthful now and in the evening another mouthful, tomorrow I will bring more, you need them fresh so I will be bringing them daily, if I have the chance, if I don't I will send somebody," the Herbalist packed up his materials.

"Are you leaving?" Mama Adubi asked.

"Yes I have a lot to do and I think I should give you time to have rest."

"Okay my son you have done well, greet your mother for me, tell her it won't be so bad if she visited, when I came I was told she was not around."

"Yes, she went to the farm early."

"Very well, just tell her it would be nice if she visited."

The girl came in with the herbs as it was steaming hot, "Just drop it at the corner and let it get warm." The Herbalist said, pointing to a corner. "Mama drink it when it is warm."

"I will."

"I will be going now, he waved at the damsel." Greeted again and left.

He had only one thought now as he raced the paths of Mkpunki, how Adanna was doing. He believed now that she needed his constant supervision, again he wondered how it was that all of Mkpunki knew about his affairs. It did not used to be this way, the sun was at its zenith, and was shining fiercely, his skin felt the heat from the sun as he went home, the heat made him quicken his steps, the hat was not helping much. All he needed now was a cold drink from his clay pot, everyone on the path seemed to know him and he held up his head high. Nothing wrong with what he was doing, when he got home his household greeted him, he couldn't pinpoint who exactly it was that was selling him out. He went straight to Adanna's hut, he found her sleeping, he smiled to himself and began to arrange some of his own possessions still in the hut to make more space for her, he would have it sparkling clean by the time she woke up. All he had to do was arrange, the floor looked clean, Nnadi must have swept it, but he wouldn't have it so, he would do his own cleaning. Nnadi came in to inform him more people were looking for him, he ignored her and continued doing what he was doing. He would finish it before attending to anybody, and that was what he did. When he came out, it wasn't what he expected, it was Mama Adubi again, he was surprised. Had he forgotten anything or done something to Mama Adubi, when she saw him come out from the hut she smiled.

"Mama, hope all is well?" he asked.

Setting his seat before her and facing her directly.

"All is well my son, is there anywhere where we can discuss secretly."

The word secret made the Herbalist uneasy. Was there anything secret about him?

"Let us go into my hut." He took her to the hut he was now staying, she walked slowly leaning on her walking stick, which was in front of her and she tapped it delicately on the ground. Finally they made it into the hut, which was at the right-hand side of the hut where

Adanna was staying. The hut itself was sparsely decorated, it only had coloured designed outside, but the inside was a scrubbed mud wall, shining beautifully he went along with his seat, which he gave to Mama Adubi to sit on, but she didn't sit on it, instead she opted to sit on the bamboo bed.

"Don't worry my son let me sit on the bamboo bed it is higher." As she sat the Herbalist went to the huts entrance, he looked sideways to make sure no one was around, satisfied they were alone at least the people around were huts away, he sat on the log wood seat he had offered to her.

"So Mama you wanted to tell me something."

"Yes my son, I do not know how to begin but as you know my husband is late and for a while I have been living alone, in my compound except my slaves, and occasionally some of my daughters who visit, you know that almost all my daughters are married."

"Yes I know."

"Before I even proceed, can I ask you why you haven't married?" Mama Adubi asked.

"Well," the Herbalist said unsure as to how to answer the question, "I plan to but the thing is I haven't really seen anyone."

"And there is no one you can think of, you are really certain of this?" Mama Adubi asked.

"I may have but I have not given it a serious thought." The Herbalist said.

"I won't pry more, or try to place on you a burden difficult but it is a burden every man must carry. In simple words, I want you to marry my last daughter Irima. It is not good for a man to remain alone, your life will be more fruitful and sensible if you marry and start having children then you can witness joy in full, there is nothing as sweet as marriage. You are unarguably one of the most respected men in Mkpunki and I think it would be nice of you marrying someone who would make you complete and to the little I know used to make you look perfect." The Herbalist amazed and trying to imagine what people saw when they see him, looked at Mama Adubi and was certain she knew what she was talking about and was confident about it.

"I have thought of Irima, but I can assure you, I don't even know what she looks like now. Do you think it is possible for me to meet her?"

"Sure, why not, it is possible, but I need to know what you think about my proposition." Mama Adubi said.

Marrying Irima was something the Herbalist had not thought about much, but perceived a while ago as possible, it would take him a long time to process the information. His fear now, was that he didn't want to turn down Mama Adubi, in a strange way he was not sure of what to do.

"Mama, you will give me time to think about this, it is not a decision one can make in haste."

"You take your time, but remember she is a woman and can't wait forever, once you agree I will let her know, also you must know there are a lot of suitors coming for her already, so I also think you should hurry in your thinking."

"I appreciate this Mama, thank you for actually considering me worthy."

"Oh! nonsense you are as good as any man in Mkpunki, and finer than most. I will just let her know when you are ready."

"Thank you very much Mama."

"You are welcome my son, the drugs are working, you are doing a good job, so keep it up, my stomach feels much better, you are almost like a magician." Mama Adubi said smiling.

The Herbalist shy now, "Thank you." He said smiling. It was good to know that people thought good of him, if Mama Adubi could say so many nice things to him it meant a lot to him and he wouldn't deny it. He was going to make sure it stayed that way, it wouldn't be strange if he got married after all his age group were getting married, one he knew that he was far older than, just married his third wife and he went to his marriage ceremony as the only son of his mother. He was certain that she would be expecting a child from him, Etiti was longsuffering he knew, but one day she would request a child from him. As a child what else could he do? He had often taught others, that one of our duties to a parent was to make that parent happy, no matter what the sacrifice was, so long it was good. Whether a wife was found for him or he found himself, he remembered promising himself he would never get married, his mother would indirectly remind him that he needed a wife especially when he demanded for food.

"You know a wife's food always taste better," she would say and he would know that she was telling him to get married. Has Mama Adubi, already discussed it with his mother? He would never know. As if called by an unknown voice Mama Adubi, with much strength lifted herself up from the bamboo bed and smiling at the Herbalist, headed for the door.

"My son hope to hear from you soon, and I mean very soon."

"You will Mama."

"But don't feel pressured, I know I have asked questions, like I said she has a lot of suitors just felt you should be the one."

"Thank you Mama," he said scratching his head.

She went out, without turning back she left, Herbalist still dazed couldn't do much but seat and stare at his feet and the ground all of a sudden the urge to marry was building up in him, he sat for more moments to figure out what to do, without much progress he stood up and went to his former hut where Adanna was still lying. He looked at her and he felt happiness inside, whether she was awake or sleeping her presence alone made him happy and the fact she was recovering well was also another good news. Checking up on her, nothing was out of the ordinary, with no more people to attend to, he went out to pick herbs till before she woke up, hopefully before he returned she would be awake.

*****

Their stomachs felt satisfied and their feet were not weary, neither was any part of their body demanding for rest. They were alert and ready for the journey, they had been marching through Umuti, without much problem but the sun was taking its toll on them. They were used to it, during wet season when the sun became this hot, they would expect rain to fall afterwards. It was not the wet season yet, Iwobo with his fingers swiped sweat away from his brows and cheeks, they have all been swiping sweat away. Looking ahead, they saw an Umuti warrior, when they got to him, they looked away hoping not to be stopped for the second time, when they had gone a considerable distance they all sighed a sigh of relief.

"With the way the warriors are standing and not moving is the sun not disturbing them, like it is disturbing us." Iwobo remarked.

"Who knows?" Nne added.

"I guess they are doing their job and they are doing it well." Obirika joined in answering. Something she did rarely.

"I don't care what they are doing they shouldn't just stop us anymore, because I won't take it lightly with them, I don't care if they are warriors." Obeli added bitterly.

"That is just it my brother, no matter what they do, they should not just try to stop us, and make me do things I don't wish to do." Iwobo said.

"I doubt if they will stop us again." Nne calmly added.

"Let us not get our hopes high just yet, there is still some distance for us to march before we pass the great and mighty Umuti." Iwobo said sarcastically.

"Great and mighty my foot." Obirika said angrily.

"I'm just saying I believe that is why they are uptight." Iwobo continued.

"If they are so organised and mighty why are they getting raided." Nne reminded them once again.

"I believe it is everywhere nowadays," Obeli said, calmly recalling that, that was what he had heard to be the happening for a very long time. People getting abducted forcibly.

"You think someone will dare to raid Akom and carry off its inhabitants." Nne asked.

"Gentlemen and lady it is everywhere and everyone is doing it, I'm a victim remember, it is so much into us that we don't know what it is to be humans anymore." Obirika said with a cracked voice.

Any time a talk about slavery started she got very emotional, not wanting to remember the ordeals she had passed through, with hands tied and sometimes legs tied and forcefully marching, it was indeed a dark time she would never forget and she prayed for those she saw in the same condition with her to get hope and have a better life.

"It is everywhere just not the same magnitude in Akom, Umuti people are over doing theirs." Nne said.

"You can't blame them for trying Nne, you just can't blame them." Obirika said.

They have gone a considerable distance since seeing the last warrior of Umuti.

"But Obeli speaking tough, are you ready to fight?" Iwobo goaded.

"Why won't I be?" Obeli responded with confidence.

"You people shouldn't bother much because after we pass that tree." Iwobo pointed to a tree that was standing ahead, they were tall grasses all about the path, even to the path leading to the tree that appeared to be an Iroko tree.

"Why should we be happy because of a tree?" Obeli asked.

"After that point we pass over to Dubiri, the second village on our way, that spot marks the end of Umuti." Iwobo said.

Getting closer to the tree they now saw human figures standing after the tree, under the tree was a well cleared area without any sort of grass under it but just sand, the men were standing beside the enormous trunk of the tree which concealed them. Iwobo sighting them as they approached the tree cautioned his followers to be careful, the men standing there seemed ominous, they had not anticipated to see anyone there. Obeli and Iwobo drew out their clean swords never before used, as the tree continued to conceal the men standing beside it, the tree was standing on the right side of the path with the path going beneath its shades, the men were also standing on the right-hand side after the tree with the tree concealing them but the foot point of their spear could be seen. Moving cautiously Iwobo came closer first, already Obirika was clutching the arm of Nne, who was marching behind Iwobo, with Obeli coming last. Nne was putting up a strong face and making bold steps, slowly Iwobo passed the tree and was relieved to see it was no one else than the warriors of Umuti. Again they also were surprised, two of the men there they could remember was amongst the men who had detained them earlier on, after walking past them, they all felt uneasy, all at once.

"We are being followed." Iwobo said.

Nne looked back as if she would see the person following them. "Where?" she asked when she didn't see anybody.

"The men we saw I know you all recognized one person, they are 6, in total and I have seen 2 before." Iwobo said.

In apprehension, "What do we do now?" Obirika asked scared.

"Let us keep going maybe they just wanted to make sure we are not spies." Iwobo said, also panicking a bit, "That tree marked the last piece of land belonging to Umuti, we are out of their domain now," Iwobo added carefully trying to assuage fellow panicking Obirika who had Nne by her side almost picking up on the panicking too.

"Let us just hope nothing more happens, I wonder what makes them think that four people, two men and two women could be spies, or raiders." Nne said.

"Funny enough they can't even consider my innocent face." Obeli said smiling and the words elevated the agitation.

"What makes you think you have an innocent face?" Nne asked.

"People always say so." Obeli replied proudly.

"Amazing, I have never said so, never noticed it or even thought about it, but now that you are saying it, Obeli my dear friend, your face is scary, it can give a child nightmare, and I'm serious." Iwobo said.

"I do not blame you Iwobo, your problem is jealousy" Obeli was swinging his sword as he spoke, which went too close to Obirika, and Nne saw it.

"Master innocent face, sheath your sword before you hurt someone." Nne said.

"So what are you saying, you don't need my protection?" Obeli asked as if hurt by her words.

"We need it plenty, but no danger for now sir." Obirika said supporting her daughter.

"Since you put it that way, let me obey my lady." Obeli said.

"Since when did you become obedient, stubborn goat." Iwobo continued with his cutting remarks.

"Since I was born my boy, since I was born."

"Me your boy?"

"You are my boy, I have been your big daddy for a very long time," Obeli said.

Nne and her mother couldn't hide their amusement, "Please you two shouldn't start again," Nne pleaded.

"No, leave him let him be calling me his boy, if I'm your boy how come I'm the one leading?" Iwobo asked.

"As my boy I have put you in charge to lead, so that I can defend from the rear which is a man's job."

Nne shook her head and sighed attempting to hide her pleasure at their baseless quarrel.

"I know I mentioned it but I'm saying it again, we are now in Dubiri, and you people should know that the people of Dubiri, are not as hostile as the people of Umuti."

Obeli courteously interrupted, "Don't be offended, but do you think we are still being followed?" Obeli asked.

"I don't think so, they should probably know when to quit," Iwobo said.

"I hope so, what do we do now with what we have been trying to avoid, we didn't want anyone to know our whereabouts, now the people of Umuti and its warriors will happily describe us." Obeli said.

"By then we will be far gone, it doesn't really matter anymore, it will take them at least 2 days to know we followed the old path that leads through Umuti." Iwobo said.

"We went undetected earlier so…"

Before he could finish explaining, Obeli understood him.

"Yes yes, I now understand if the earlier people didn't see us it would be hard for them to know we followed this path, had it been they saw us that is where there would have been trouble, it's all good then." Obeli said.

"But I still think we should be discreet and vigilant." Nne added as Obirika skipped, jumping over a passing agama lizard, it had horrified her as it scurried past them.

"You speak well Nne, of course we will still try to keep out of peoples gaze, but if we can't do it, we shouldn't feel worried as for this Dubiri we will just keep to the path that takes us out of it, going round it and passing through are almost the same thing so we won't be losing time." Iwobo said.

"Hopefully we don't get any harassment here," Obeli said.

"That is if we mind our business, but I was about to say that the people of Dubiri are friendly unlike their twin brother Umuti, so we shouldn't be surprised of an occasional act of hospitality." Iwobo said marching on,

"Hopefully we will get it, is there anything we need?" Iwobo asked.

"I don't think so, I think we should just march on without hesitation." Nne said.

The path they were on looked deserted, but they could see footprints on the ground to show people had passed that very path.

"Do you think we will see anybody on this path?" Obirika asked.

"Sure people have passed here." Iwobo said.

The sun was moving to start descending to the west, where it could face them, burning their faces better.

Iwobo, walked like he had this at the back of his mind, sometimes he walked forgetting that people were following him, when they called him or spoke to him he remembered to slow down. As they passed through Dubiri, nothing seemed to be out of the ordinary, the path they would soon enter had people's farmland both on the left and on the right-hand side. They marched a little further and Iwobo could see the path that went in two directions, to the left would be going to Dubiri main stream, to go right would be their direction. When they got to the end of the path they were on, they followed right. Up till now they had not seen a single soul on the path. Obirika didn't know whether to be relieved or worried, 'Hopefully, we will pass through Dubiri, without being seen,' Iwobo had said, 'Let us just hope so' Obeli answered.

The ladies kept mute, and continued staring both left and right, and forward, the scenery was pleasant to them, surprisingly they passed the farmlands without seeing anyone. Through the farmlands the path was a long one stretching almost 2000 feet, they saw nothing but birds in the sky, scattered palm trees, weeded but not cultivated farms. Soon they passed the farmlands and got to thick bushes which covered the path's sides, these were definitely uncultivated lands. They passed the area with thick bushes, they got to another part with half weeded farmlands, just entering this part an antelope ran pass the path, it came out from their right-hand side and quickly ran into the left. Iwobo and Obeli spontaneously lurched after it, not minding the thickness of the bush they galloped into it, following the antelope they ran clearing the remaining path the antelope made with their hands just as they ran at a great pace. Obirika and Nne perplexed could do nothing but wait for them at the entrance of the bush. Nne attempted entering but her mother advised her not to, and she retreated, clapping her hands as if sliding one on another in disbelief, she held the top of her head in amazement still staring into the bush. Her mother placed her hands on her waist as the both of them laughed with mixed feelings, they were sore afraid, terribly frightened to be left alone, yet they knew there was little they could do to stop the two males with them on their new quest. They laughed quietly but haughtily with perplexity and distress.

"Boys will always will boys." Obirika said.

"Hey! Mama what are we going to do now?" Nne said stressing the exclamatory word hey! and clapping her hands in utter amazement.

"See the way they ran in, as if they know where they are, what exactly are we going to do?" Nne asked.

"Just let them be, they want to catch a game," Obirika answered.

Nne was still trying to peep into the bush to see them, but it was impossible, the bushes had covered the part they entered in through.

"Mother what do we do?"

"We have to wait for them." Obirika said.

"This is unbelievable, what exactly do they want to do with an antelope, eat the meat or what?"

"It is to eat the meat definitely." Obirika answered with a surrendering voice, just as helpless as her daughter.

The bush was at the left side of the path and a further step forward was a cleared farm, but the bushes had not been cleared, notwithstanding one could move freely in it, Nne and her mother had seen it, but didn't bother to go check it. Waiting a long while they still had not come out.

"Mother you say we should wait, what if something had happened to them?"

"Nne nothing will happen to them, they are men. You can never know which will hurt them more to tell them to do something or not to do it, they all fancy themselves to be brave men who can hunt."

"And it is an antelope they are pursuing, what runs faster than an antelope?"

"If you tell them not to chase it they will simply ignore you so my daughter, most times it is just better to let them do what they want to do, if you interfere they will see it not as caring but insult on their manhood."

Nne and her mother spoke a while, Iwobo and Obeli, still had not come out.

"What exactly is going on? I don't like this anymore mother." Nne said now getting frustrated.

"My dear we are almost home exercise some patience, they will be out soon." As if she sensed them, just with the words in her mouth, Obeli was the first to be seen, they had followed the cleared path in the farm which was ahead, he came out to the path and called on them, Nne looked up to her right and saw Obeli beckoning on them.

"Thank the gods they are out mother let us go." Just then Obirika saw him too, they both marched forward, now facing front they met only Obeli.

"Where is Iwobo?" Obirika asked.

Obeli who was gasping for breath had both hands on his knees as he tried to catch his breath, when he heard the question, he pointed to his right, which was the left of Nne and Obirika but they couldn't see anyone where he was pointing to, the bush still covered their sides. Nne and Obirika quickened their steps and looked to their left again, now they had gotten to the cleared farmland, where they saw Iwobo still looking around in the bush.

"What happened?" Nne asked.

Obeli clutched his stomach and then stood erect still breathing from both mouth and nose furiously, he opened his mouth, words were not coming out only heaves, finally he spoke bending down again with his hands on his kneecaps.

"We couldn't catch it, it was too fast."

Nne wanted to ask him how they expected to catch an antelope but refrained from asking the question. Without saying more, Obeli shouted Iwobo's name and motioned for him to come out.

Iwobo was still clearing bushes and peeping into them, obviously still searching for the antelope, without much words anymore he finally gave up and started walking towards them. Nne and her mother were standing on the edge of the farm now, before he could reach them he voiced his surprise and frustration.

"Obeli I do not know why we didn't catch this antelope, it would have made a good market sale or we could have just exchanged it with just anything, we would have been richer." Iwobo said, while also gasping for breath.

Nne and Obirika gave each other a concerned look because of his plans for the antelope. The women had their mind on them wanting to eat the antelope.

"Where did you people even run to with the way you are panting?"

"Can you see that tall palm tree, he pointed to a tree almost 900 feets away, we ran after it, to that palm tree."

"Good gods that far?"

"Yes" Iwobo said proudly.

"We really wanted to catch it." Obeli added.

"So what happened?" Nne asked.

"Dear as you can see, it escaped, and we didn't catch it, today is a lucky day for it, next time, it won't be so lucky." Iwobo bragged.

"Hopefully there won't be a next time." Nne peacefully added.

"I think we should be going just give us a moment."

Obeli took his water pouch, he took a gulp, others could hear the sounds of the water go down his throat feet away. Iwobo did the same, they looked ready to go.

"Let us go."

"Wow!" Obeli exhaled, "My sister once caught an antelope, I don't know how she does it, but she is good." Obeli said as if anyone needed the information.

"So your sister is a better hunter, what a shame." Iwobo said.

"I don't blame you, is it not the two of us that went after it, why didn't you catch it?" Obeli asked.

"I would have caught it, it is because of you that it escaped." Iwobo said confidently.

"I don't blame you." Obeli said.

Surely Obirika knew the sister he was talking about, why was it that she was the only one seeing Adanna for the evil she was, she was a woman but didn't feel like such. Passing through unknown villages bound and in great distress, she didn't show an iota of pity, causing her pains unbearable. She couldn't remember crying so much in her life for days she ate little and cried more. Now Obeli, was praising her for being a good hunter, she had thought in the inner recesses of her mind that she would forget about her past. But just remembering that Adanna was a woman made the painful memory fresh, because it was also a woman like her that had caused her great anguish. As her mind went back to those days, she felt weakened, her muscles lost strength, it made her tremble, uncontrollably her stomach suddenly felt heavy and her mouth watered, light headedness was setting in. Only Nne noticed it as Iwobo and Obeli chatted away, insulting each other in a friendly way or playfully to others, but of course serious to them. Looking at her mother who was ahead of her, Obirika's steps lagged.

"Mother are you okay?" Nne asked. Getting close to her and looking into her eyes, she held her stomach with her left hand her right hand was now at the back of her mother's neck, staring into her eyes, "Mother what is it?" Nne asked.

Obirika shook her head, there was no way she could tell her it was the fact that she remembered the horror she passed through and that the thought of it made her sick.

"It is nothing, it is nothing," she repeated, Obirika took her water pouch, and drank from it, the water didn't taste good in her mouth, but it was water nonetheless, she had to persevere and be strong for her daughter's sake she knew.

"My dear let us move on, I'm fine." Obirika said. The sign of worry was all over Nne's face.

"If you are tired you let us know mother." Nne said.
"I know, I know."

Obeli who now had noticed them talking and Nne holding her mother turned his attention to them.

"What is wrong?" He asked facing the two women in front of him, Iwobo turned back to look.

"What is it?" Iwobo asked. They were both concerned now.

"My children, it is nothing, don't worry, let us move on." Obirika said.

Saying the words she believed it and increased her pace, Obeli and Iwobo, believed her and remained silent for a while, before resuming their argument once again. Nne and her mother still found it amusing, they have been in Dubiri for a reasonable time now, walking through it, yet they had not seen a single person, not even in the farms they ran into or bushes around, not a single person was seen.

"What could be happening, why are we not seeing anybody?" Iwobo asked.

"So you want to see someone, well I prefer it this way not seeing anybody helps our course." Obeli said.

"It is just eerie, that's all." Iwobo said.

"Let it be whatever it wants to be I don't care." Obeli said.

No single soul would be seen by them in Dubiri. The village had called a meeting for all persons to gather at the village square for an important deliberation. The village had been thrown into turmoil as a family had brought their problem to the elders, who in turn invited the whole village to deliberate on the matter. A man had died when he went to tap wine, now a stranger wanted to claim his compound and throw his new wife out.

This was the event that occurred in Dubiri on this particular day, causing Nne and her group not to see anyone. When they were passing the meeting was still going on.

Iwobo and co. had expected to meet a lot of people on the path they were on but met none. They were oblivious of the happening at the village square due to Iwobo's later report of partial lack of hospitality from the people of Dubiri, they had decided not to stop for anything in Dubiri. If they walked faster they would be out of the place before they knew they were there, and the plan worked perfect for them.

"I wonder why we are not seeing a single soul here yet, do you think everything is alright, I'm scared, it is almost out of the normal." Obirika said.

"Indeed it is." Nne added in support.

"I really don't know what is happening, but my guess is after our previous ordeal in Umuti, the gods have finally smiled down on us." Obeli said.

"Trust me, you don't know this people they may even treat us more harshly than Umuti people." Iwobo said sad.

"Let us not forget Enula and her assistance, surely they are not so bad, at least not all of them." Nne said.

"How do we know she had no part to play in it?" Iwobo said as if the anger of whatever they might have done to him had been rekindled. All three felt flabbergasted. "Iwobo don't say that." Was coming out from the three of them simultaneously.

"Why shouldn't I, you do not know those people." He responded.

"Iwobo we have seen them, they are not so bad." Nne said. "Just trying to defend themselves is what they are doing, in their condition I would do the same thing."

"Do we look like spies or raiders, do we look like men and women who would hurt other souls? No I doubt we do." Iwobo said.

"Looks can be deceiving sometimes, it really could." Obeli said.

As he shifted his sword tied to his waist, and waited for Iwobo's reply.

Which was all the more surprising, "Why are you all trying to correct me, when I'm sure of what I know, in fact too sure, this people are not kind people, not hospitable is that not all I said and I mean it."

In Obeli's mind he noticed his friend had actually added not kind to the adjectives for describing the Umuti people, when they were trying to make him remove others.

"They are not nice people." Iwobo continued vehemently, "Whether it is because of my experience or not they are just not nice people."

"Very fine, and all we are saying is that you can't take the actions of a few people to judge a whole village because whether you accept it or not, there are still good people there, like in Umuti; Enule was one of them, so that is all we are saying." Nne said.

"I will never accept that thought, no matter what you say." Iwobo said bitterly.

"So you hate them?" Nne asked.

"I don't hate them, I hate the things they do, they are not just good people, that's all, I won't say anything again."

They marched the paths taking in the scenery. They wouldn't deny they were enjoying it. Only Iwobo must be finding it disquieting, he walked with his head down, glancing back occasionally to look on those following him and beyond them. No one was following them, Nne and her mother marched behind him, with Obeli still maintaining his position of being the last man. The position gave him purpose, he was protecting the rest of the group, it took a man's heart to do such. Something he never knew he had, Iwobo may be leading but he was the one protecting. If there was any attack it would come from the back and he would be called upon to use his sword. He had prayed not to use the sword and so far no condition had warranted the use of it. Anyway, when danger came that they should have fought they ran. Their enemies' weapon was far more superior; it moved a million times faster than sword and had a more devastating result. He had seen the Dane gun used before and it was used by his father on those rare occasions where he accompanied him into the bush to hunt. Thinking about hunting and his father brought a longing for Akom in him, he missed the place. It was where he had known all his life now he had embarked on a journey almost against his own wishes. He had done the right thing, all he wanted to do was do the right thing no matter the fact that he went up against his sister. At least now there was a genuine happiness in Nne, she had lost a lot and having her mother back was indeed a good thing. Obeli looked forward to the people before him and he appreciated that life had brought them to him, they were all cherished and loved now, and for sure he had them in a special place in his heart. Looking at them a tree branch which was small in size, was lying carelessly on the ground, Iwobo got to it he took it and flung it into the bush on his right-hand side. Their walk was beginning to be a happy walk soon it would be noon, the sun had been taking its toll on them and they would need rest, he wouldn't want to make the decision alone.

"Iwobo when do you think we should rest?" Obeli asked.

"Anywhere but here." Iwobo said. "Let us walk and get into the next village before we think of resting."

"Will we see stream on our way because we need to refill our pouch." Obeli said.

Nne and her mother remained mute listening to the conversation for a reason unknown Obeli was speaking their mind.

"We will rest there, I wouldn't want us to rest in open space again that is why I'm thinking we should head into the village and find a place." Iwobo said.

"How are we going to do that?" Nne asked, finally breaking her silence.

"There is a family I know there." Iwobo answered.

"And they will welcome us all?" Obirika asked.

"Sure I know they would be more than happy to help us, the people of Fujiri are nice unlike the two we passed."

"Well let us just hope so." Obeli said.

"We will get out from Dubiri then get to Fujiri by nightfall, it won't be wise for us to continue marching, so I think it is better we stay there." They marched considerable distance passing nothing but bushes and sometimes weeded farms, and farms that were not weeded. They continued on this path as they marched through Dubiri, until a bit past noon, as they went their legs grew weary. Iwobo spotted a tree on the path it had full leaves, it would be a good shade they went under it and rested for a while, they almost emptied their pouch to quench their thirst. Iwobo had assured them a stream was not far away, so there won't be any harm gulping almost all of it. Still with supplies that Enule gave them they proceeded to chew something and get a little strength back, while the sun continued to heat the earth. The clouds were scarce only a tree could provide shelter from the sun's rays, as they sat under the tree and chewed their dried bush meat a gentle breeze was swooshing under the tree trying its best to remedy the harm done by the sun that they had been under. As they chewed they drank.

"Iwobo how did you get to know, the people we are going to meet at Fujiri?" Obeli asked.

"Just how I got to know about these ones too," he said pointing towards the direction of Umuti and Dubiri. "The family is just a nice family they saw us and welcomed us just like that, without asking much from us, that was when we were looking for my half-brother with my father, we stayed with them and they asked us to come back anytime we pass this way again, so that is it. And I should add it is a large family but the owner of the compound is really a nice man, he has about 6 wives and a lot of children that we couldn't count neither could we ask how many they were, but all seemed to be welcoming, and we enjoyed our time in Fujiri despite our circumstance and reason for being there not something to have a merry countenance."

Nne smiled, just like the rest.

Obeli was grinning, "So because they were nice to you, you now think we would enjoy our time there, well good to know."

"Of course you will enjoy your time there, I can assure you that, not only the family but everyone else was nice, they co-operated with us and directed us to places where we could go to search for him, others even volunteered and went with us, it was just a good time because we did the things we should have done all along. Had it been the others helped like them I won't have the opinion I have about them. Trust me Fujiri people are good people, even their stream is good because the water is so very clean, until we left there every quarter we went to, we found people willing to help, even our host had a slave come with us to assist us, so when we get there I'm sure you will find it pleasant too." Iwobo said.

None of them said a word as they had their mouth stuffed with meat, this time they would have to concur with him without arguing with him, they nodded their heads in agreement, their feet would be rested before they moved out again, they were almost out of Dubiri where they were was the boundary and soon they would enter Fujiri.

CHAPTER 31

She hadn't slept much in the afternoon, bad dreams kept re-occurring to her. She laid on her back and it ached, she would need to change position but none suited her, all over her body was beginning to ache. Again it seemed when she slept no matter how little, the pain would be gone. When she was awake it started all over again, with no one around she placed her two hands on the bamboo bed and lifted herself. Seating up now through gritting of teeth, she placed her legs on the floor, once again she tried in vain to get up. She thought of crying as tears swelled up in her eyes, but she fought it back again. She couldn't stand, she tried again mustering all her strength, the thought of being a cripple hit her and she knew that she would rather die than be handicapped. She was sitting upright with her two legs on the ground, she tried again lifting herself up by placing her two hands on the bamboo bed, she first stood on her legs but still had her hands on the bamboo bed, her back was now facing the entrance, she was not sitting anymore all she needed to do now was remove her hands from the bed and stand erect, she waited a while and then did it.

Immediately she removed her hands from the bed her legs gave in, and she crashed to the floor heavily, she fell with all her weight, her legs were wobbly. Adanna still did not cry but felt like screaming, that, she held back also, people were in the compound but no one was close to her hut she could call. After letting the pain pass round her body and slowly subsiding, she tried getting up on her own from the ground, it was futile. After much struggling, she couldn't reach the bed to grab it and help herself up. Thoughts of regrets began to swell up in her, she thought of how it would have been that she was in her father's compound, having her own kind of a good time. Then she thought of her father, who knew what he was like now, maybe he had learnt the truth of her mission, if he had, he should have sent people to come and find her. She thought of her brothers and Obeli especially, he would be dead by now. Finally she believed that tears were going to flow down her cheeks but none did.

She shook her head furiously and brought her consciousness back to her present situation, she was sitting on the ground. She shifted herself till her back was resting on the mud wall of the hut. She was inches away from the entrance as the entrance was to her right, she sat facing the bed and wondering how she was going to get to it, it was a few feet away. She closed her eyes, and thought of the day it happened. Who were those people that rescued Obirika? She never got to see their faces, all she remembered was chasing after some people who had taken her slave, her desire of seeing Obirika sold as a slave had been thwarted and now she was in suffering. She didn't even know what next to do with herself, she had paid off the men with her, now what ...? As she sat on the ground nothing was making sense to her anymore. The Herbalist came in and was startled to see the bed empty, he quickly dropped all he was with on the ground, he turned to his left and saw Adanna or Odabi as he knew her on the ground, she just sat without moving her head to even acknowledge the presence of the Herbalist, he looked at her and felt sorry for her.

"Why are you on the ground Odabi? he asked bending down and touching her shoulder with his left hand. She didn't still turn she was just gazing at the direction of the bamboo bed, "Odabi" the Herbalist called again, each time, with a very soft voice, he called her three times and she didn't turn. Then she finally spoke.

"I tried to stand up but I couldn't, instead I fell." With the words the Herbalist looked around in the hut as if to see evidence that she really fell, he said nothing, he didn't know what to say, Adanna smiled and repeated the words absent mindedly, "I" she said now hitting her chest, "I tried to get on my own two feet and couldn't," she was repeating and laughing in derision now, self loathe was everywhere in her, she repeated the words.

"I tried to stand up but couldn't. What does this mean?" she asked the Herbalist, who was still searching for words.

"Does this mean I am handicapped? Why can't I stand on my own, I am asking you, why can't I stand?" she was still just speaking and laughing. The Herbalist who had sat with her on the ground looking at her managed to speak.

"It will take time but you would walk and stand I can assure you that, it will happen very soon, just don't give up, you will be alright, Okay, you will be alright, we can't explain why things happen but one thing is certain you will be alright, trust me on that one." The Herbalist said.

Hearing the words Adanna heaved, and stirred her body trying to rise again, the Herbalist caught hold of her intention and proceeded to help her up, gently supporting her from the back now, she made steps towards the bamboo bed, where she was once again laid, she rested on her back. "Thank you." She said, as the Herbalist dusted himself. "Anytime" he answered. They both stayed again with moments of awkward silence. None knowing what to say, yet with so much to say. The Herbalist sat beside her bamboo bed, and just stared at her with his piercing gaze. Adanna just closed her eyes not wanting to meet his, the Herbalist sat for a while, then stood up and went to the hut entrance, where he picked up his herbs bag and staff which he acquired new. He looked at Adanna or Odabi again, she was obviously lost in deep thought, as her eyes remained closed but she was not sleeping. He left the hut, and went to his new hut where he began to prepare herbs, first he started with Adanna's herbs, and mixed the ones he thought would give her strength, she really needed strength and the herbs that would be good for her bones and muscles, he would do nothing but prepare herbs for the remainder of the day. Hopefully no one would interfere. Sensing he was gone Adanna opened her eyes, with the free time she began checking her muscles by trying to find movement in each one. She did what the herbalist had told her to do before and that was moving all her muscles. She started doing it gently moving all her muscles, having in mind the new pain from the fall a little while ago. All her muscles were responding, the Herbalist had told her this was a good thing. But why couldn't she stand? She ignored this thought and continued moving the muscles. A head popped in, it was Nnadi the servant girl that had been so hardworking and caring to her, she wondered what it could be.

"Can I come in?" she said, somewhat scared.

"Yes you may." Adanna said.

She stepped into the hut as if someone would reprimand her if she was caught doing what she was doing, she looked back several times, and then made her way to Adanna's side, she knelt on the floor beside her.

"Ma'am how are you doing?" Nnadi asked.

"I am fine dear, getting better."

"Can you stand now?" Nnadi asked softly.

"No I can't but it will happen with time."

"I am very sorry I have been wanting to come and say that it would get better, but I've not had the chance." Adanna searching for words didn't know what to say. She couldn't remember being in such situation before. In her father's compound in Akom, she had never been asked such questions by her father's slaves before. None would dare to, it was a very uncommon situation for her, she never knew relationship existed between slaves and their owners to the point where they would seem concerned for their owner's affairs.

"What is your name again?" Adanna asked.

The girl smiled. "Nnadi."

"Okay, Nnadi thank you for your concern I really appreciate it." Nnadi smiled at her. Adanna looked at her and could see the purity of her soul.

"Well Ma'am, just get better." She said smiling at Adanna, she said goodbye and left the hut. Adanna bewildered didn't know what to do, she resumed her exercise, twisting and turning all her muscles, if people had been in her condition and walked, she too would certainly walk regardless of what it looked like. The Herbalist had promised himself that he would concentrate on mixing and preparing the herbs, but he had to check on Adanna, he left the herbs and went to check on Adanna, this time he met her with her eyes open, he had also noticed she was trying to move her muscles, he came in and Adanna turned to meet his gaze.

"Just checking up on you." He said smiling like he was the happiest man on earth and had no problems.

"Thank you" Adanna said.

"I am preparing herbs, it should help, I gave them to a friend once and he recovered well."

"Let us hope it works on me too."

"Trust me it will, I will give them to you in the morning, have to allow it settle, it works well in the morning, though…" he started rambling.

"Okay, you know the best." Adanna said.

"Do you need anything?" the Herbalist asked.

"Trust me what I need now you cannot give it."

"Try me."

"You can't, you just can't, I think you should go back to preparing your herbs."

"Why, you do not like my keeping you company?" the Herbalist asked.

"I do, just do not want to be the reason why you are distracted."

"I would rather have it that you distract me than anything else in the world." The herbalist blurted out, he didn't know when he said the words, and it startled Adanna, who widened her eyes in surprise. Trying to retrace his words, seeing that the words used earlier seemed pregnant.

"What I meant was that I enjoy your company." He said, clearing his throat, as he said the words but it was already too late, there was no way to take back his words, he stood at the entrance of the door not knowing whether to bolt out or enter the hut, he desperately waited for Adanna to redeem him by saying something that would show whether she was pleased or disturbed.

"Thanks for considering me so." She said.

It didn't give him what he wanted but it was okay, he came to her side and sat down looking at her. Once again he lost words to say, again he thought in his mind he had a lot to tell her, but did not know where to begin. But then again at the present moment he didn't have words for her. Adanna broke the silence.

"Which one do you think is better to die or to live and be handicapped?"

The question surprised the Herbalist, he had not expected it, he looked at her and fear filled his heart, why would she mention death? It was not a good word to mention, but then again he weighed the question, he had heard her loud and clear, but couldn't tell exactly why she had asked the question, what could she be thinking?

"I don't know which one is to be had. I have seen people that are handicapped I do not know how they feel inside but what is certain is that they move on with their lives, and live happily not considering their situation. In life one must decide on what part to play, not necessarily the part given to us by the gods. In Mkpunki we have handicapped people who do their parts well like Atombili the flute player he was dropped by his mother's slave when he was a baby, he survived and has found joy playing the flute, no one has ever come to report that Atombili begged him or her for anything, he plays flute and people pay him for it, he just married his 4th wife recently, believe me he is doing well for himself. Atombili is a symbol of power here in Mkpunki, such a man like him staying with him takes away your sadness, because he knows how to laugh and his laughter is infectious, he is always cheerful and boldly declares that he does not miss his legs, you have to look at him once in a while and discover that life is more than it presents."

Adanna was just staring at the thatched roof, while the Herbalist continued with his speech. Talking to her while also praying to the gods that she saw hope.

"I am not saying that you should be Atombili, but you can have a cheerful disposition to your situation.

"Very good." The Herbalist said as he remembered something, "What about the late Ekumiki, he was deaf from birth but lived to have one of the largest farmlands in Mpkunki, he was also a great fisherman, he married 9 wives. What about," he stretched the about while pronouncing it as if to remember the next person, "What about Akituki he was blind but was a revered drummer, he went on to marry more women that I can care to remember, even Obitudi the dwarf though he does not consider himself a handicap he is a respected warrior in Mkpunki, leading men twice his size and height, also he is a hunter who marched boldly, I can't seem to call all of them but the list is endless." Adanna was still patiently listening to him as he continued with his speech, "Your condition is not worst, besides I know I didn't mention a female trust me one of our queen was once crippled and she still ruled, things can obviously get better, there are men who are handicapped but consider themselves favoured by the gods, it is not the end of the world."

Adanna was still lying still saying nothing but taking all the words in.

The Herbalist continued, "All I am saying is that you have to see beyond the now, and consider the tomorrow."

"What if things don't get well in the tomorrow you are talking about, what if things become worse?" Adanna asked.

"They will not, even if they do, one thing that is certain is that nothing is permanent, nothing at all in the affairs of man, and we must believe it is changing for the better, bad things will happen, no doubt about that. We all must have trouble one day or another."

"Very good, now you are speaking the truth." Adanna said.

"Those bad things make us stronger." The Herbalist said.

"It doesn't make me stronger only more hard-hearted." Adanna said.

"You really have to see the bright side, you could have died."

"Which would have been better for me, I would rather die than stay alive and be in this condition."

"I know you don't mean that, what about your loved ones those that are happy because you are alive and care so much about you, because I know you care too, and you are not hard-hearted, hard-hearted people are afraid of death, they will give anything to remain alive but you are not."

"Listen you have done so much for me that the last thing I want to do is ask you for another thing or make any request in any way, but if I remain in this condition, I wouldn't mind you mixing poison for me, then you would have done your greatest service to me."

The Herbalist was startled with the words, he didn't know from which angle to approach the discussion anymore. He just sat quiet and stared at her in disbelief.

Adanna observing he was silent now, "Are you angry with me?" she asked.

"No, I'm not." He answered looking away absent mindedly.

"Okay good, my back is aching please help me sit up."

"I will in a moment. But I have to ask, do you really mean what you just said?"

She turned and faced the Herbalist who was at her right-hand side, looking at his face then into his eyes, "I mean every word of it, now please help me to sit up."

"No, wait a moment you are asking me to be a murderer is that how much you think of me."

"No I am asking you to be a helper which is what you are good at, I have seen you and I think no one else can help, but you, now help me up." She stretched out her hands, with no words coming to mind the Herbalist stood up, holding her hands he raised her up, adjusting herself she rested her back on the mud wall, now she was facing the Herbalist who sat back on his seat, still looking at her.

"You know, I think the problem is not my back, but my knees, that is where I feel a lot of pain and weakness, I noticed it when I stood." She said nonchalantly.

"That is a good news, I will give you balm, or better still I will do it myself, plus the herbs you are taking it shouldn't be a problem. Can I check the knee?"

"Sure."

He proceeded to check her, pressing around her kneecap, he pressed round the kneecap asking each time if it hurts, the kneecaps weren't broken but she felt tremendous pain when they were touched, and it was not swollen.

"This is indeed good news, I was praying for it not to be your back, people I have seen having problem with it like I have told you, have problems walking, but it is good news indeed, I will massage it for you with the balm till it gets better."

"I appreciate, it is obviously getting better."

"Any other area that you have noticed, or is it just the knee?"

"Knees actually, and yes it is only them."

"It is all good then."

As she spoke about her knees the Herbalist felt relieved his worst fears were gone, and her words about dying wouldn't be carried out. With the knees being the problem they would certainly heal and she would walk again.

"I can't wait to stand again, I am virtually in the dark nowadays not seeing the sun or moon when I want to, but its light, or knowing what is happening." Adanna said.

"Speaking of what is happening travellers passing Mkpunki mentioned that Akom men are on their way with prisoners for the slave market, they are actually leading them to the seacoast. In a few market days they should be in Mkpunki." Adanna's heart raced at the news, but she maintained her calm and returned to normal in no time. She could suppress fear. "Hope it is not a bad news, just thought you should know, do you think you know anybody amongst the warriors?" the Herbalist asked.

"So that what will happen?" she asked.

"I don't know. Don't you want to meet them?" the Herbalist asked.

"I don't, you must not tell anyone I am here."

"Why?" the Herbalist asked in bewilderment.

"Have you told anyone I am here?" he asked, the Herbalist strongly believed it was not a secret especially in Mkpunki.

"No I haven't, but thought you would have loved to meet them."

"Please I don't want to, and you must not tell anyone I am here, nobody should know."

"Okay, sure if you want it that way."

The Herbalist surprised at her request once again. Maybe it was her mysteriousness that was making her interesting to him, Nnadi came to the hut and clapped as a way of knocking.

"Yes Nnadi what is it?" the Herbalist asked. She came in.

"Master I wanted to ask you and madam if I should bring your food."

"That would be very good. I am sure that you are hungry?" he asked looking at Adanna.

"Yes I am." She answered.

"You have heard, go and bring the food." The girl went out with the order.

"Nnadi is a good cook," the Herbalist said smiling at her, "She is good but not better than my mother." He laughed.

Adanna managed to smile, by just moving her left cheek backwards.

"Anyway I am going to leave you for a moment I need to go back to preparing the herbs," with the words he stood to go, when at the entrance, "I will be back soon, try to enjoy your food." He said.

"I will." Adanna replied and he left.

*****

At Dubiri's border they rested a good while. It would soon get dark as the day was no longer young.

"I think we should start moving." Iwobo said.

"Indeed we should." Obeli concurred. The two men stood up, dusting themselves they held out hand for Nne and Obirika. Iwobo helped Obirika. While Obeli helped Nne, picking up all their items they set out.

"Are we still going to the stream?" Nne asked.

"That is if you people want to, but I don't think you should be thirsty by now." Iwobo answered, keeping his face towards the direction he was marching to.

"I am not, just that we discussed it." Nne said.

"The people we are going to should have water, shouldn't they?" Obirika added.

"Indeed you are right, so it is settled then, we move straight to the home of our host no stopping." Iwobo said, moving a considerable distance. "There you have it, we have passed Dubiri, without seeing a soul, maybe they have been raided just like Umuti, their case being it is the total raiding not selection." Iwobo said.

Obeli smiled "Just maybe."

Iwobo continued "We are now in Fujiri village."

The footpaths were narrow and could only allow them walk in single file, it was not strange they had been marching on such paths since their journey, Iwobo took out his sword to clear the path which was partially overgrown with grass, they could barely see the ground but was sure there was a path there.

"Is it that people do not take this part or what? That has made it to be so overgrown with grass?" Obirika asked.

"I doubt the people of Fujiri ever go into Dubiri, I've told you they have little in common though they are brothers, because from what I was told they never war with each other, they live in peace and they inter marry, which is very rare but still happens once in a while, aside those they hardly intermingle. The people of Fujiri are quite industrious and self-sufficient, yes they still deal with other villages for goods they do not have, still they are self-sufficient, there is nothing you are used to that you cannot find in Fujiri, they are talented."

Obeli looked away, he was getting weary with the Fujiri praise already.

"Hope we find it just the way you have described, no need for surprises." Nne said.

Obeli had also brought out his sword, clearing the path remained by Iwobo, he still retained his positioned of last man on the line.

"If the raiders are here what do we do?" Obirika asked out of fear, she just did not want to be caught in anything slavery again.

"Obirika they won't be here, though Fujiri has their own slave market, but slave raiders will find it hard to operate here." Iwobo said.

"So you think Fujiri is perfect?" Obeli asked still clearing grasses.

"It is not but a good place all the same."

"It is better than Akom?" Obeli asked. Iwobo laughed at the question "There is no place better than home."

Nne smiling now "At least you know that." She said.

Walking the paths they got to an area that was a sight never before seen by them, this part of Fujiri the ground was clean, with large trees forming a canopy, you could walk under the trees with the sun only able to pierce through spots left by the tree's leaves, this path stretched a considerable distance of almost 900 feet. They walked this path, and still saw nobody.

"Iwobo I hope there is nothing wrong? By this time of the day people are supposed to be walking around, how come we don't see anyone?" Obeli asked.

"I really do not know." As Iwobo had the words in his mouth, from a path they couldn't have seen, three damsels emerged from it "There is your answer," Iwobo pointed to them.

"Okay" Obeli said.

The three girls came out and not noticing them faced front with their wood logs on their head, they went chatting as they moved ahead. With their minds relaxed Iwobo led his group. When they got to the point the girls had emerged from they didn't see a path there but bush, surprised at the girls bravery they moved on, people actually follow unknown paths now, just to hide from kidnappers but also the method has its own disadvantages.

"Iwobo you failed to mention they also have brave girls." Obeli goaded.

"Now, you know, they really do, the place we are going to they have nothing but brave women." He said, while laughing. Nne caught the laughter from him and joined in laughing, they made progress after leaving the trees' canopy, they took their left and turned to another path which was also clean but had no canopy, though trees still bordered it at both sides, this time they met people coming from their farms, who greeted them warmly. Following this path they went straight ahead and got to the village square which had a large cleared area the village used for several gatherings: Wrestling matches, village meetings and deliberations, dancing competitions, any gathering at all. This time around as Iwobo and his crew passed, it was used for slave gatherings, they had assembled slaves for sale, the sight terrified Obirika, as they passed them. About a 200 hundred men, women and children would be there and they were all chained and tied together, all were crying and pleading. The place was with an acrid smell of all manner of waste. As they passed they heard the swooshing sound of whips and the sharp sounds of it landing on human flesh, and of course the resultant sound of crying, everyone was crying except their black slavers, those that wanted to buy still stood around making their picks.

"Most are going to the shore." Obeli said.

"Definitely" Iwobo agreed. Obirika said no word, she knew exactly what those people were feeling. No one answered or said another word till they got to their host compound. People greeted them and moved on with their affairs, with the happenings at the village square not disturbing them. It was now a sight very familiar. They went on passing compounds and single huts. After walking a straight path they turned left and meeting no one on the path they walked a little while.

"There is where we are going." Iwobo said pointing to a compound that seemed somewhat deserted, strange considering that at this time of the day there should be people in the compound. They marched to the compound, Iwobo entered, passed the tree that was in the compound.

The compound of the Atibi's was indeed a large one, they went round the first hut which belonged to the father of the compound, the entrances were all closed, moving to the main compound they saw no one and it surprised the new visitors. Such a large compound should always have people in it, now in the large compound with huts surrounding them, Iwobo asked his friends to wait while he scout the compound. He went about knocking at each hut entrance with no response, perplexed he went back to them. As they stood in the centre of the compound, there were signs that the compound was still in daily use. They could see logs of wood for seating in front of the huts, and cloths spread on the roof of the mud houses to dry, at their extreme left was a log of fresh cut cassava stems on the ground. Iwobo now with them had no explanation for them, they didn't expect this sort of welcome, the day was gradually coming to an end. The heat of the sun was no longer as hot as it had been earlier. Evening was moments away, not knowing what else to do they sat under the sun after waiting a while no one came.

"Do you think we should leave?" Obirika asked.

"And go where?" Iwobo asked in return politely. With fear of disappointment, "I do not know anywhere else welcoming, let us just wait awhile more."

"I am not sleeping under open space again, I have imagined sleeping under a shade." Obeli said.

"What choice do we have, let us just wait." Iwobo said.

"Iwobo you mean it, that you do not know another place?" Obeli asked not expecting an answer. The goats tied behind were bleating, including the chicken which chirped away, making all sorts of noise.

"Those are animal sounds I am hearing, I am sure you do too, they are certainly around, let us just wait for someone to come back. We really do not have any choice and no I do not know any other place or who would be ready to help?"

Almost dejected, they were staring at the floor, thinking of what to do next, they didn't see when Iriki emerged from behind them. She had come in through the entrance they used.

"Good day my people." She greeted surprised at the strangers in her master Atibi's compound. They turned in unison to look at her as she had stems of cassava on her head. Iwobo didn't recognise her.

"Good sister how are you?" Iwobo said.

"I am fine." Iriki answered.

"Please do you know me?" The others were disappointed when Iwobo asked if she knew him.

"I have never seen you before. Who may you be?"

"I am Iwobo, I was here not long ago with my father. The Atibi's welcomed us and gave us shelter here. In fact it was that hut." Iwobo pointed to a hut at his left, and all looked at it all at once, "We were hoping that they would be here because we really need lodging once again."

"They are not around none of them is, I am the only person around." When she said the words they felt their world crumble, as all their hopes evaporated. From Iriki's markings they could see she was a slave. Obirika was glad she didn't receive such markings. They didn't know how to ask her for permission to stay there and her words surprised them.

"You say you know the Atibi's?" Iriki asked.

"Yes, actually only me, because I have been here before, but my friends here are new." Iwobo said.

"Can you describe them."

"Can I describe them?"

"Yes you said you know them." Iwobo looked at his company in confusion who urged him to go on with the answer.

"Well they may have changed but I know the father of the compound the great Atibi, is a slim man with good facial features a slim nose, a well packed teeth, he is slightly taller than me, he has 6 wives, I wasn't opportune to count his children when I was here but his third wife has twin daughters."

"You could have heard all these from someone and come here to pretend, you could be an impostor." Iriki said.

"What! No no, not at all, well the Atibi's are a lovely people, they do everything together and they deeply love each other."

"So?" Iriki asked.

Iwobo was noticing the disdain feeling in her words but could care less, as far as he was concerned he needed to say something about the Atibi's that would make him and his company stay there for the night and he couldn't.

"I can't let you stay here please you have to leave." Iriki said.

"Okay in that hut," Iwobo pointed to the hut he had stayed in again, "In that hut there is an old water pot in it, the father of the compound Atibi designed it himself and made it himself."

"Even if you are correct, I don't know about it, please leave."

"When will they be back?" Iwobo asked.

"I can't tell you that." She had her load on her head all the while as she asked them to leave she went and threw down the load in one corner where the others were. She acted as if she could push them out all by herself if they resisted. The thought of it amused Obeli, she wasn't plump, and not very tall, but had a very beautiful, face, and sparkling white teeth, she had no decorations or trinkets, as she was a slave, with the mark clearly on her biceps. She dropped the stems and turned towards them getting closer.

"Please you have to leave." She said.

Iwobo had to obey, he was not going to refuse. They picked their bags and pleaded one more time.

"We are coming from a very far place, we need a place to pass the night, and the Atibi's are our last hope, just tell us when they will come back." Iwobo pleaded.

"I can't, just leave." She was more than serious now, giving up hope, they turned to leave. Obeli couldn't wait to say. "I thought you said they were nice people," he was planning to say it, and say it very loud. When they turned they heard chatters from a group of people and smile overwhelmed Iwobo's face, he knew the voice, they stopped and waited then they appeared from beside the mud house it was Atibi and all his family. Iwobo resisted the urge to laugh out very hard and loud at the woman chasing them out, his friends diligently stayed behind him. Atibi saw him and smiled broadened on his face.

"We have visitors." Atibi said as he emerged into the compound, Iwobo bowed and greeted him and his company followed suit. Atibi entered the compound, with all his family members following him, he marched in followed by his 6 wives in the order of their marriage sequence, followed by his sons, then daughters and finally slaves.

"You look so grown now, help me remember that your name." Atibi said.

"Iwobo, Master."

"Exactly, Iwobo my son, how are you doing? It has been a long time," he approached Iwobo and placed his right hand on his left shoulder with Iwobo, bending low, though Atibi was considerably taller than him. "How is your father?" He couldn't have known.

"My father is late Master."

Atibi's eyes narrowed and furrows formed on his forehead, "What!!" he placed his two hands on Iwobo's shoulder now, "I am very sorry for your loss."

"It is okay Master, thank you."

Atibi's family was still standing behind him none had said a word of course they couldn't speak while the father of the home was speaking, they would simply meet Iwobo later or talk if permitted to.

"My son I am very sorry for your loss, but we must never kill ourselves over dead ones. They are now ancestors watching over us, we are also coming from a burial, my last wife's mother died and we went to felicitate with them."

"Oh, I am so sorry Master."

"It's all right like I said we can't kill ourselves over the dead, go and relax." He called a slave, "Take them to the visitor's quarters and make them welcome. My son we will talk more later."

The woman who had been trying to pursue Iwobo and his friends from the compound was still standing behind them, master Atibi saw her.

"My dear who are you?" Atibi asked her.

Iwobo was shocked at the question, he looked at Atibi then the woman.

"I am Iriki sir, your 4th wife asked me to bring her cassava stem, and I have done so, I will be going now."

Iwobo, wanted to scream "So you don't even live here?"

She looked at them as they were speechless and left.

Atibi went to his hut and everyone dispersed. Iwobo was led to the hut he had used the first time with Obeli, while Nne and Obirika were taken to another one. Making bathing a priority they had their bath, and food was served, pounded yam, and bitter leaf soup, with grasscutter meat. The Atibis had killed it and it served as meat for the night. After the meal Obeli and Iwobo went to greet the father of the home and thank him for the meal.

"Thank you Master for the meal." Both said.

"My dear children you are welcome, what more can we do than to eat to remain alive. Hope it was pleasant?"

"Very pleasant Master, very pleasant." Iwobo said.

"Good to know, I just wish you had come at a better time we would have prepared something more delicious, today is my first wife's turn to cook, considering the visit we made and all that she could have turned out something better."

"Thank you sir, by morning we shall be on our way." Iwobo said.

"So soon?" Atibi asked.

"Yes Master."

"It is all good then, do not forget you are always welcomed in Atibi's compound."

"I appreciate Master." Iwobo said.

Obeli thought about what Atibi had said, and began to prepare his mind to tell Nne what he thought. They both left Atibi's hut still wishing him well, they made their way to their hut. Iwobo took a detour and made Obeli go into the hut alone.

"Obeli you move on there is something I must do." Iwobo said.

"What is that?" Obeli asked.

"It is personal." Iwobo said.

"Since when did you start doing personal stuff?" Obeli asked.

"Okay fine I will tell you later, when the time is right, I promise now please go on." Iwobo said.

"Suit yourself don't even tell me, it is not like I care." Obeli said.

"I know you don't, sacrificial goat."

"Your family sacrificial goats." Obeli said as he went towards the entrance of the hut.

"It is your own family that are sacrificial goats." Iwobo replied.

"You now lack respect is that it?" Obeli asked.

"Goat, which respect?" Iwobo asked.

"Fowl" Obeli said and entered.

Iwobo passed Atibi's sons' huts and went to the ladies area, hoping nobody saw him he went to Nne and Obirika's hut and called for Nne, thankfully without hesitation she came out. Iwobo could see fear in her eyes.

"Hope all is well?" She asked hoping not to hear any bad news.

"None at all. How are you?" he asked not sure where to begin.

"I am fine" Nne said.

He dipped his hand into his animal skin bag and brought out a beautiful anklet and other beautiful jewelries.

"Here" he said "I want you to have this, don't say anything, I just want you to know, I wish for so many things and to give you this and see you happy is one of them, please accept it. I believe it would say a lot that is in my mind that I do not know how to say, I believe I will stop here tonight but there is still plenty that I would do in the future. Nne you hold a special place in my heart." He pushed the jewelries more into her hands. Nne dazzled just stood and watched. Iwobo turned and left. Nne knew what it meant but for now she didn't know what to feel.

The insects chirped away as their sounds were the only sounds that could be heard, passing the huts you could hear snoring coming from some huts. As he walked away he felt the chilling breeze of the night all over him giving him little time to contemplate on what he just did, a mind had told him he would regret doing it, but now all he heard in his head were voices telling him he should have said more, and another saying he should have knelt down while telling her. He fought the urge to look back. He got to his hut that he was sharing with Obeli, went in and found Obeli lying on his stomach still awake. Obeli didn't move when Iwobo came in or even act to show he noticed his entrance.

"Why are you still awake?" Iwobo asked.

"Will soon sleep, just thinking about some things." Obeli said.

"Some things like what?"

"Trust me you don't want to know."

"Oh! I want to." Iwobo said. They heard a loud cough from the hut next to theirs and it reminded them that it was night and they should keep their voice down, they lowered their voices.

"You have to tell me." Iwobo persisted.

"I am not ready yet. Where did you go?" Obeli asked.

"Went to check on them and something else." Iwobo answered.

"How are they?" Obeli asked.

"They have settled in nicely."

"Good, very good."

Obeli was thinking about his position and how to tell Nne he liked her, but had a lot of reasons which would make it almost impossible and it was killing him inside. Obeli turned to see Iwobo lying with his face up and completely lost in thought, he knew he should get rest. It felt nice sleeping under a shade once again, and he was going to cherish the night.

The journey was still up ahead and tonight the gods had been kind to offer them good night rest and with it he dozed off.

CHAPTER 32

Earlier in the same day far away in Mkpunki, Adanna was still trying to push her frustration away as she nibbled at the food Nnadi had served. In her estimate she had had peace as she was quite content to be left alone and not bothered by anyone. She ate the little she could, and had time to think about her next steps, when she did nothing came to mind, the only thing occupying every of her thought was the fact she couldn't walk on her own. She resumed moving her muscles, the only sounds she heard were the sounds of goats bleating, chickens with her chicks and their crow, and little girls playing in the compound. She relaxed for some time and tried to hear any sound from the Herbalist but heard nothing coming from him but then again it was difficult as other noises must have drowned it out. She thought how to move if her legs continued to disappoint her, she could think of nothing besides such thought would really suit the Herbalist. She needed a drink and she was not going to call anyone for help. Through the Herbalist's ingenuity the water pot which was made of clay had been placed directly opposite her and she would reach it without anyone's help. With much energy she sat upright with her two hands, she lifted her right leg first and placed it on the ground. Feeling a little pain, it was a pain she could bear; she lifted her left leg and also placed it on the floor. All that was remaining now was for her to reach out for the clay pot across the floor and in doing so, she would need energy in both her legs, she tried it and her knees quacked. Sending a sharp pain all through her body, such she had never felt before. Also she discovered that there was no strength in her knees as they felt feeble, she quickly sat on the bamboo bed and inwardly congratulated herself for having the power not to scream when the pain hit her. The pain had sent a sensation like she was being slashed with machete all over her body, wincing she let the pain pass, it sent a shaking shock in her body and all her organs felt it, even her teeth trembled. Sitting on the bamboo bed, she placed her hands on her knees and bowed her head, trying to feel normal. The thirst was almost throat crunching now and she knew it was not because she was very dehydrated but it was a way for her body to tell her it wanted what she could not give.

Adanna had noticed, it was when there was no food and you had no means to get it, seeing it as almost impossible to get, that the body would desire for it, more even when you eat and have none left, the body would start demanding for more food, but those that have it plenty, hunger wouldn't pester them like it did those who had it little.

Poor man's children tend to have more appetite for food than the children of the rich who had food plentiful. Now there was water but she couldn't get to it and she believed that was the reason her body was demanding for water. She looked at the water jar and laughed never in her life had she imagined her current situation, it never crossed her mind neither did it ever come to her attention that she would ever be in such condition. She couldn't remember being sick, even as a child, she had searched her mind countless times to remember when she was so incapacitated that everything had to be done for her and nothing came to mind. The seat the Herbalist had used was at the edge of her bed to her left using her hands she raised herself up as she still sat on the bed, adjusting her sitting with her hands providing the power. She got to the log of wood seat and then also using her hands she began to shift it. She would shift it and then adjust herself on the bed, by changing sitting positions she did this until the chair was in between her and the water pot. Seeing that the chair was lower than the bed, she prepared herself, for the pain, with her two hands on the seat in front of her she supported herself and moved from the bed to the seat. The pain was not as much as she had thought it would be, there was still some distance between her and the pot and she had an idea on how to manoeuvre it. She now knew she couldn't rest on her legs, she placed one of her hands on the ground beside the seat and using her left hand she shifted the seat forward, all her weight went to her right hand that was on the ground, all the while she was facing the water pot. Repeating the move one more time, she got to where she wanted, she cleaned her hand and proceeded to drink water, tasting the water it turned out she was not very thirsty after all. Another trick of her body that she had discovered, when it wanted something desperately especially food or water and finally got it, it began to make you feel that maybe it didn't want that thing as badly as it made you think. She felt angry even though she knew her body often behaved in such manner. Satisfied she didn't want water again, she rested a while before resuming her journey back to her bed. She was attempting to do this, when the Herbalist knocked and stepped in, he smiled when he saw her.

"How did you get there?"

She looked up at him, trying to decide where to begin with the question.

"Don't even bother," he said seeing she was struggling with coming up with an answer. "Here let me help you up." He said as he approached her.

Adanna bluntly refused, "Don't worry," she said, "There is a way I did it, it took me time but surely I will get back."

She began struggling to get back, laboriously straining to move herself. The Herbalist watched for a while to see how she was going to do it. It was really going to take her time, and he wondered why she had sharply refused his help. Watching her some more, as she moved she tried talking and explaining how she was going to get back.

"I..." she was saying before adding other words to the sentence the Herbalist got to her, he put his right hand under her thighs and the left at her back he lifted her up and gently placed her on the bed, she didn't finish her explanation. She was caught off guard by his lifting, his actions numbed her, she was speechless, and fear gripped her. The Herbalist looked at her tenderly.

"I just came to check if you had eaten, I guess you are okay, I will check back," he smiled at her, winked and left. She had seen few kind men and she considered them weaklings, but this one was different, he seemed to live in another world. In Akom few were close to her, and even more few try to help her and it was those that knew nothing about her. But here once again the Herbalist simply confused her, both with his actions and his words. She pondered it trying to understand the sort of man the Herbalist was, she did for a considerable time until it was evening and those that went to farm were returning. Etiti returned and she heard her voice from the sound of it she was marching straight to her hut, she could also hear her giving orders to her servants, as expected she heard a knock and a head popped in, it had a cheerful face then the whole body.

"Welcome." Adanna said.

"Thank you my daughter, I was thinking of you all through the day in the farm." She cocked her head, still looking at Adanna.

"Hope you have eaten?" Etiti asked.

"Yes I have, thank you." Adanna answered.

"You will get well, do not worry, you won't remain in this condition my ancestors that protect us are powerful and will always help, and your enemies will weep, you will surely recover, so shall it be."

"Thank you I will recover" Adanna said, "I am glad you are back safely."

"Yeeees…" Etiti said showing her two palms up with smiles, as a sign of gratitude, I am back safely, you don't know what happened today." Looking around she saw what she was looking for it was the seat, she took it and sat down.

"My daughter," Adanna prepared for a lengthy tale, though Etiti didn't not look like one that talked that much, "We were at the farm today, weeding a small portion for the remaining crops in the farm, peacefully, the sun was taking its toll on us, scorching our backs but we didn't mind. We continued with our work, we had been on it till when the sun was very high, all through the morning nothing out of the ordinary happened, when the sun was on the summit we decided to take a break. My late husband's sister came, at first I was startled she was all tears. When she came she was bruised, I was heart wrenched when I saw her. She told me her husband plans to sell her son into slavery." Adanna wondered why it was news, but managed to remain silent and attentive, in Akom and other places she had heard of men marrying so many wives to give birth just so that they can sell them, also no one was against a parent selling the child into slavery to offset a debt. A lot of people did it.

"She also said," Etiti continued, "It is because of the slavers from Akom, who would soon be passing Mkpunki to the seacoast to sell a large number of slaves caught in war, I don't know what to do for her."

"Don't you think it is because of money that he wants to do it?" Adanna asked.

"I believe it is, I will have to go look for money now." Etiti said. "I will tell my son, he should know what to do, he always does."

"Yes I think it is a good idea."

"But I won't give him the money and let him keep the boy, apparently he does not want him, I will take the boy and give him the money he wants for him, my sister-in-law will have to bear but I will take the boy from her." Etiti said assured of her abilities.

"Can I help, I still have some left over money that should help." Adanna said.

"Do not worry at all I can handle it," Etiti said exhaling, "Not only that I brought palm wine. Would you like to have some?"

"No I am okay, thank you." Adanna said.

"The good thing about it is that it is fresh." Etiti said trying to change Adanna's mind.

As she spoke the Herbalist came in, "Mother you are back, hope the farming went well?"

"Indeed it did."

"You are welcome"

"Thank you my son."

He handed over the mixed herb to Adanna, she sat up straight, took the potion with her right hand, using her left hand to pinch the top of her nose, in a bid to close her nostrils she knew how bitter the potion would be, doing this she gulped it at once. The Herbalist took back the calabash from her and waited a moment to watch her.

"How do you feel?" Etiti asked.

"I guess okay."

Adanna adjusted herself so that she could rest her back on the red mud wall of the hut, the Herbalist watched her a moment, satisfied she was okay he left.

"I will soon leave to go and drink my palm wine, it is unfortunate that you do not want some, I only hope I don't become Mgbejunu."

"Who is he?" Adanna asked.

Etiti grinned, "Well he is a nobody, but also a somebody being that he is the village well renowned palm wine drinker, he only drinks palm wine when it is fermented, which causes him to be an embarrassment to some people, though I don't fault him because he really has a sad story, it is just tragic."

"Really, what happened to him?"

"My dear it is like I said a sad story. Okay this is what we have been told. Mbejunu, was one of the most respected men in Mkpunki he was the complete package, and he had it all, he was intelligent, extremely intelligent he was handsome, still is, was once considered the most handsome in his prime, and I can't fail to mention he was well talented, he could do it all. Could dance, sing, wrestle, weave, just name it by only looking at you do what you do, he would copy it and replicate it perfectly. As a kid his parents used to take him everywhere they went, and people adored them for having such a beautiful child. A lot of people gave him presents, just for being beautiful, in the village when he was growing he was simply adored even elders accorded him respect and everyone expected him to be great as his destiny was bright and shining. Because of his characters adult befriended him when he was yet a teenager (young man), and I heard that as a teenager he was well grown, strong as any man could be then he found his love in music. He played the flute and played it better than any man, everything was happening for him, he was well known and became the desire of every woman and an envy of his peers. Every young man wanted to be like him, look like him and act like him. Then what everyone calls Mgbejunu rain of death, began to occur." As Etiti told the tale of deaths in his family.

Adanna interrupted her, "This tale is terrifying." She said. "What was killing them?" she asked.

"I don't know that still remains a mystery."

Once again the Herbalist knocked and came in, seeing that they were both in a discussion.

"Hope I am not interrupting any private discussion?"

"Not at all, was telling her about your friend, Mgbejunu, about his life." Etiti said.

"Ah! That sad tale." The Herbalist said. "Hope it won't disturb her?"

"Disturb me in what way?" Adanna asked.

"I do not know for me it makes me wonder a lot of things, whenever I hear the tale, or see Mgbejunu. Mother you are free to continue I will check back later."

"Are you still mixing herbs?" Adanna asked.

"It is actually preparing and I am done, though I have to watch some before I call it a day."

"You can stay and listen to the story."

"I will rather not it disturbs my thinking I don't think I can do what Mgbejunu is doing." The Herbalist said.

"But you know he is actually not doing anything." His mother said.

"Not at all he still has a little piece of his old self in him. He still loves children. You people should go ahead, let me get back to my hut." The Herbalist said and left.

Etiti turned to Adanna who was still eagerly listening, to every word. Etiti continued, "The sad thing my daughter is that Mgbejunu children when they were still kids, were always sick had pale skin, one had a jaundice, and they were always complaining of pains all over their body, not long after their mother died they were still kids, they all died one after the other, now Mgbejunu has no kids, and he has taken to drinking wine."

"He doesn't want to marry again?" Adanna asked.

"Everyone is advising him to, maybe after mourning his children it is only his second wife that remains now, hopefully he would drop the palm wine and get married, but I believe the grieve is too much for him that is just why." Lost in thought with the words, Etiti recollected herself. "My daughter it is a painful tale, though my son says it is a disease that he has seen it happen other places, and people tell of it, that is what he thinks, if you don't already know he already has his own thinking about everything, for me Etiti I say it is bad spirit." Etiti stood gradually from her seat. "Let me go and bath, I will be back, you don't have to worry, you will get well soon my dear, everything will be fine."

Adanna closed her eyes and opened them, "Thank you Etiti for your kind words I believe I will get well too."

"Alright my dear." Looking around the hut Etiti finally stood and left.

Adanna in her head tried to imagine what Mgbejunu would look like, she remembered a man in her village who was also a drunk but she didn't know his story besides he died while she was a kid. Lately she was beginning to notice a lot of people in her village, then she wondered if all men had sad tales especially those that drank. Would she be able to bear what Mgbejunu did bear, she looked at her legs again and wished they could come back to life, and be the way they were before. She could hear Etiti barking orders outside, the sound of the pestle and mortar, goats bleating which was unusual someone must have disturbed their shed, and children chatting outside. Everyone seemed full of life, and happy. Her situation weighed her down, she was in a hut all day by herself, and could do nothing for herself, the world was moving by and everyone not in her position seemed happy with the world, now it simply meant the world was cruel to her. Fate had abandoned her and reduced her to nothing, how could she regain her mighty old self. She couldn't even walk and now depended on someone else to do the necessary and basic things of life. In this world she had actually lived it alone.

Would someone miss that she was gone? She looked around her hut and everything was just the same just like it was when she first woke up. Today, she wished for a change now her heart burned and her stomach seemed to be on fire, the pounding in her head had begun again. She wished to see her father and brothers though she never told them she ever needed them in her life, if anything her actions had always shown otherwise but now she would like to be in their company she needed to rest her head, with her two hands she moved her legs and gently tried to lie down. Still in the process the Herbalist came in, saw what she was trying to do, he went to her held her head and helped her lay it on the bed.

"Thank you." She said.

He smiled "You are always welcome."

"My head hurts so bad, there is this pounding inside it I don't know just what to do with it." She said as she closed her eyes and placed her two hands on her belly.

"I know it will be just like that but will go down with time."

"I am preparing herbs for you that would do just fine."

She opened her eyes to see the Herbalist on his knees and his eyes on her, she looked at him.

"What would I have done without you?"

"I guess everything." He said still smiling.

"Not at all, I would have been forgotten in that pit, if not for you, I'm still rattling my brain to think of a way to pay you back."

"To be honest you can't thank me for anything just yet, get well and strong enough to be on your two feet and we will think of a thanksgiving together, but for now just focus on getting well."

"Alright, thank you once again." She said.

The Herbalist nodded and left, he went to his mother's hut, she was not there he went to the kitchen and saw her there, sitting in front of the kitchen with her gourd of palm wine and horn in her hand, she smiled when she saw him.

"You know palm wine is for the rich, I mean the rich." The Herbalist said.

Etiti giggled then she laughed, "Do not make this palm wine choke me." She said still grinning, "It is a gift I did not intend to throw away, and I'm going to finish it."

"All alone?" the Herbalist asked as he sat down beside his mother, who was holding a drinking horn, in her hand. He took it from her and had a sip.

"You are free to join me." He said.

"And since when did you start drinking, boy I thought I trained you well?" Etiti asked snatching the drinking horn from him.

"Look at me" he said pointing to himself, "Do I look like a drunk?"

"Not at all dear you look like your father." Etiti said as they both smiled.

"People tell me I look like you that is what they used to say when I was a kid, and some still say it now."

"Really" Etiti said feigning surprise.

"Yes." The Herbalist answered.

"Please give me one amongst the people who say it."

"Daiki still says it, I know she is your friend."

"She says it?" Etiti asked.

"Yes she does and she is not the only one."

"Okay if you say so."

The Herbalist took the drinking horn from his mother's hand and took another sip.

"I won't have that, go and get your own drinking horn."

"That is a good idea, Nnadi" the Herbalist called out, in a short time the girl materialized before him, Etiti gulped the content of her horn and proceeded to take another fill.

"Mother go easy on it."

"I have not had it in a long time so I'm going to enjoy it."

"Get me a horn." He said to Nnadi still smiling.

"Yes Master" she said and left.

"In the meantime," he said and took the horn from Etiti again, took a mouthful. As he drank Etiti exclaimed "Herbalist wait for your horn you are disrupting my enjoyment!"

He laughed, "So my name is now Herbalist?"

"Is that not what people call you," Nnadi came with the horn and handed it over to him.

"Thank you," he said to her, "and you have joined them to call me Herbalist?"

"Yes" Etiti said as she took another gulp, the Herbalist poured for himself from the gourd.

"Have you told Adanna about her people that are approaching Mkpunki?" Etiti asked.

The Herbalist looked wearily at his mother, and was disturbed and agitated, Etiti did not talk about slavery, everybody tried to keep it away from her, only recently did she put up nonchalant attitude towards it, and that was how he was able to take Adanna in, after so many decades of her disassociation from all its related activities. Her apathy for it was too deep and personal. Although she had given up hating anything to it because she discovered it was everywhere, in every corner and life there was the tale of slavery, in all forms.

"Yes I did, and I don't think it pleased her." He said.

"She warmed me not to tell anyone she is here."

"She did?" Etiti asked.

"Yes and she was serious about it."

"Why would she want that" Etiti said slightly raising her voice.

"Mother please bring your voice down."

"I know I'm sorry."

"Well maybe she is not comfortable with it, like I am." He said.

"Everything is wrong with that I will never forget but why to her? Are they not her people? People selling people to other people from unknown destination."

The Herbalist tactfully monitored to get an opportunity to change the topic.

"Son, maybe you have seen, maybe not, but I tell you have you ever imagined to be in the position of the slaves, how they do what they do, they tie their hands like animals, they tie the necks, including children, they are flogged constantly, constantly, and marched through open countries, those that are not strong enough get whipped to become strong, there is death, there is pain, there is suffering, die on the way and you rotten away, children crying, crying, just crying, innocent children. When children cry their mothers run to them to comfort them. When these slave children cry they get whipped from slavers as comfort." Etiti looked at the Herbalist and with all certainty looked into his eyes, "Whips do not comfort." She said to him. "The women suffer just as much as the men do, how can anyone be made to go through such a thing in their own world, it is the worst cruelty of all, every man deserves to be happy."

The Herbalist stared at the ground, and then his drinking horn, "Such things shouldn't be. People now sleep with one eye open and one closed, it shouldn't be. A young man tried to escape, he was shot in the back, and thrown into the forest, he was not even buried. Nobody knows where they are being sold to." Both were now calmer as they discussed, both were weighed down with thought.

"You were with the white woman from the shore, you didn't ask her?" Etiti asked.

The Herbalist shook his head "Can't remember asking her, but I believe it is to their place."

Etiti continued "All I wonder is those men that are driving them to the seacoast like they are animals, I simply wonder what goes through their mind and why the gods can't help the case of such men who have been born by women only to find out their life doesn't matter. Their case is just like death, no one returns to tell stories of their journey if their fate becomes better than ours who claim to be free. Sometimes I wonder what if they meet more pleasant things over there. But then they get pushed out like animals, they simply will be treated like animals."

They took gulp from their gourd, as Etiti remained silent for a while.

"You know I forgot to tell you," she finally said to break the silence, "Your Aunt's husband want to sell their son to the Akom people. They are in want of money and he believes it is the only option."

"Really, his son? Others sell daughters and we cry out his own he wants to sell his son." The Herbalist said shocked.

"It boggles my mind anyway I have decided to buy the boy."

The Herbalist exhaled "If you don't I will, they obviously don't deserve him."

"And here we are talking about those who wish to have children and the gods have offered them none. Those that have throw theirs away," Etiti said.

"It is a confusing world we live in." The Herbalist added. And took a gulp "So when are you brining the boy?" he asked.

"I will see them tomorrow."

"Do you need money?" He asked.

"No I don't, I have some with me, should be okay. I will also take some livestock to them so they can barter, I don't think it is poverty that is making them rather your aunt's husband want to sell their child probably because of something else. Imagine me selling you. No matter the hardship, what kind of survival would that be that I would sell my son, one that I really do love like a piece of merchandise?" All this while none had drunk from his or her gourd, as they both spoke and stared on the ground, "Has it always been like this?" he asked. Etiti made an unsuccessful attempt to laugh, but it just sounded awkward in that situation.

"It has not, it is since we learnt that there are people from another world that our greed increased. You have seen the new things they brought."

The Herbalist nodded and spoke faintly "Yes I have seen the goods they brought."

"I don't know who made the request first to start selling people, who even brought up the idea, it's none of my business, my problem is with our race that commit atrocities against one another just to have people to sell." Etiti said.

"The truth is we don't love each other we only look towards comfort that can be gotten in whatever way and the disturbing thing is that it doesn't prick our conscience. I have seen the thing they come in, I have never seen such a thing before, I have watched it come and go, it is not like the canoes we have it is very big, I wish you would see it someday mother in good terms." The Herbalist continued sensing his throat had dried he took a gulp. "Those people's lives look much better than ours and I think they love themselves that is why they are smart enough not to use their own kind in doing whatever it is they require our kind to do."

"What makes you think so, do you know?" Etiti asked taking another mouthful of the palm wine.

"They must be faring better than us. That is one possibility I strongly believe, it all adds up if we are better than them we would be the ones buying them. You know what those bound for the seacoast go through before boarding the ships." The Herbalist said.

"My son things have not always been like this, I used to think that those that are sold deserved to be but now I am thinking otherwise, it is not a good thing I think my son, it is not." Etiti said patting the Herbalist at the back. "Well" he said as he cracked his knuckles still holding his wine horn, I wish them well."

"Me too."

"It is just that it is disturbing," the Herbalist said and put his wine horn in his right hand he had been holding it with his left, using his now soft palm he ran his left hand across his face, then ran it across his head, moving it back and forth, then brought it back to his face and let it rest on his jaw. Etiti was still drinking from her horn.

"I have something I want to tell you."

Quickly swallowing the wine in her mouth "What is it?" Etiti demanded.

The Herbalist heaved, took off his left hand from his jaw, robbed his left eye and ran the palm across his face once more. "Mama Adubi was here."

"The Adubi that I know."

"Yes that very one," tilting his head jokingly he looked at his mother, "Is there another one?"

She smiled, "Go on, what did she say."

The Herbalist heaved again, and exhaled forcefully, as if caught by a feeling he decided not to tell her about everything "She says you should try to visit her, you know her family and ours are in very good terms." The Herbalist had not forgotten about her marriage talk but he would need a longer time to process it.

Etiti smiled "Well I will visit her soon, it is a thing I should have done. How is she?"

"For her age she is quite strong, but has occasional problem common for her age."

Etiti feeling she had drank enough stood with the words, "I will visit her, let me check on them so that you people can eat." She turned and went straight into the kitchen, the Herbalist took his final gulp from his horn, looked at Adanna's hut but didn't go into it, instead he went into his own hut. He looked around in his hut things were so different now, with darkness approaching, he lit his oil lamp, he took a herb he had mixed for Adanna and went to her hut. Hastening his steps when he heard her cough out loudly, he knocked and entered.

"Are you alright?" he asked.

"Yes I am."

"Heard you coughing."

"I think it is okay now, it's nothing serious."

"Here" he handed over to her a gourd. She didn't ask what it was she knew it must be her herbs, delighted with it she took it and drank. The bitterness didn't deter her. At this point she was willing to do anything to leave her miserable condition.

"Any other one." She asked.

The Herbalist wide eyed, "No" he was stuttering "Just this one" he said.

"How long do you think it would take before my knees regain strength?"

The Herbalist still stuttering "It depends on the level of damage, for all I can see it is not swollen, so I'm guessing in a few days or more you should be okay. Tonight I will apply balm on it and massage more. First you freshen up, eat and that should be the last thing." Saying the words he took the gourd from her, "I will come and see you then." He said. Adanna pleased with the arrangement said nothing but nod her head in agreement. The Herbalist left. Adanna sat upright, with her back on the mud wall, she gently began to massage her knees she felt pain but it was one she could bear. A small price to pay for a reward of walking again, still doing it. Nnadi knocked and brought in her food, dropping her food the girl smiled at her "Ma'am how are you doing? She asked.

"Doing better." Adanna said.

"You will certainly get well I'm sure of it."

"Well thank you very much I believe I will."

Nnadi turned and left, Adanna got to her food, finding out she had appetite she made sure to eat her full, it was yam porridge one of her favourites as she took a mouth full her salivary glands came to live watering her mouth, the vegetable leaf used made it more so endearing. She ate and had much pleasure with each mouthful, whoever that cooked the food was a good cook. Eating slowly and savouring every bit of it, she took a bite of the fish, she had also come to like the fish, the people had fish in abundance, it was not like the dried one they ate in Akom. This one was fresh and sweet, almost through with her food.

Etiti came in with smiles on her face. "I can see you are enjoying it."

"Yes very true I am enjoying it, it is very delicious." Adanna said.

"I'm glad you like it."

"I hope all is well?" Adanna asked Etiti swallowing water.

"Yes it is okay, I came to say good night. Nnadi will draw your water for bath, have a good night rest."

"You too, you must be exhausted from the day's work."

"It is as if you know, truly I am. Good night." Etiti said and left. For another moment, Adanna, looked around her hut, the chirping insects had begun. The fireflies flew into her hut she saw it and was pleased for a short moment. Nnadi came in again to take the plates.

"Nnadi nice timing" Adanna said.

"Thank you ma'am," she took the plates, and the long process of assisting her to bath ensured. She did it and the Herbalist came in to do as he had promised he massaged her knees and was surprised at Adanna's determination not to show forth pain. She had only whimpered a little and grinned her teeth aside that nothing else. She must be in a world of pain the Herbalist thought but she revealed little, he did the best he could and assured her she would get better. With the encouragement, he assisted her to lie down she laid facing up, with her legs stretched, feeling exhausted, she closed her eyes and drifted off, not even remembering to wish the Herbalist good night. He waited a little in her hut, almost everyone had gone to sleep. Using his oil lamp he finally left her hut looking at her one last time. He went round the compound ensuring all was good now. He went into his hut, separated the herbs he would deliver the following day, sensing he had done all that was required, he laid on his bamboo bed, and mama Adubi and her visit came to mind. He thought of what to do, but seemed confused, he let it slide. What to do would become clearer later no need to rush it, with that he slept off.

CHAPTER 33

Adanna was sitting with Etiti as she watched her peel a coconut. Etiti was dexterous with the cutlass on the coconut, she peeled it masterfully. As Adanna watched on, 3 hefty men walked into the compound, she was backing the entrance to the compound while Etiti was facing it. Etiti had been telling her stories and they both found it entertaining. When the men came into the compound Etiti ran. Adanna turned to see the reason she was running before she could do anything, the men caught a hold of her arms and dragged her up. She now looked closely the men were all masked, she couldn't see a face, from nowhere she saw the Herbalist he was also caught by the men. She tried to release herself from their grip, but she couldn't, she looked back Etiti and Nnadi were crying and screaming. The Herbalist was still struggling all of a sudden, they were not holding her anymore, she was free. The men were numbering up to 20 now. She saw the Herbalist as they dragged him to the entrance of the hut, she ran into her hut, she got her gun and took an aim, she was certain she had targeted only the captors, she fired her gun, the bullet left the gun with an untold velocity, then she looked. She saw no one anymore only the Herbalist who was now on the ground, writhing in pain. She ran to him as she ran blood was dripping from his mouth. Adanna couldn't believe she had killed the Herbalist, as she ran to him, she felt a hand on her neck. She quickly opened her eyes. She had been dreaming. The Herbalist was looking into her eyes, as she opened her eyes she gazed in relief, she closed her eyes and opened them again when she realized she had been dreaming. She couldn't tell how happy she was.

"Are you okay?" The Herbalist asked, he was using his back hand to check her body temperature.

"I'm fine it was just a dream." Adanna said panting.

"Yea I figured, but a bad one it was. Do you want to talk about it?"

"No I'm okay, it will pass…"

With the words Etiti marched into the hut with her oil lamp, "Hope all is well?" she asked yawning and robbing her right eye.

"She had a bad dream." The Herbalist answered.

"My dear hope all is well?" she asked now focusing on Adanna who nodded, she came into the hut and stood beside her son to take a proper look at Adanna, they were both staring at her with care that made Adanna know she was loved.

"Do you want us to stay with you?" Etiti asked.

"No, no, not at all, I'm fine, really I am, please go and have your rest, it is really nothing." As she was still speaking, they heard shrieking sounds and hollow sounds, the voices were like they were crying in treble and auto, with an occasional interpretation of a drumbeat. Immediately Etiti and the Herbalist heard the cries, Etiti quickly put off her oil lamp, and the one in Adanna's hut, the Herbalist didn't move as he was still standing beside Adanna's bed, Adanna was forced to ask "What is it?" Etiti quietly shushed her, patting her left arm, the cries and numerous sounds continued as they listened they could detect they were passing their compound. They had heard the cries when it was coming from far, now it sounded near. In a little while as they all kept mute, they could hear the sounds getting away and they could tell whoever they were, were getting away, they stayed in the dark and in silence. Adanna couldn't see a thing, just the awareness that people were with her, none made a move, then they were certain they were gone, they couldn't hear a sound anymore. Etiti felt she could speak now, as the Herbalist took the lamps to go and lit them. Etiti felt her way around till she found a seat to sit on, she had to wait for her son to return. Adanna didn't know what was going on.

Etiti sensing all was okay now. "My dear those are Iripite society, whenever they are mourning one of their own they seem to wail round the village, crying as they marched along, at the end," Etiti was speaking with her voice very low, Adanna had to strain to hear her. "At the end of the march they make sacrifices, it is a secret society so no one knows who is amongst them, and they can't be seen, if you happen to look at them they will kill you, the laws of the land allow them to, they have killed so many people. So that is why we were not to make a sound, as it is rumoured that they are strong medicine men. Who knows who had died amongst them? Anyway my daughter, do not go out whenever you hear such noise." Etiti said.

"With my condition I don't think I am going anywhere."

"Very soon you will be able to move."

The Herbalist came in with the lamps hit.

"My dear these people their tale is a tale of terror you don't even want to know what they do, sleep well." Etiti said. Adanna nodded, Etiti took her lamp from her son and greeted them both good night and left.

"I think you should go and get some sleep, sorry I disturbed you." Adanna said to the Herbalist.

"Not at all you didn't disturb me, since you are confident you will be okay, I will be going back to my hut now. Have a good night rest." The Herbalist said and went to his hut. Adanna knew much about secret societies they were so many in Akom, she knew sleep coming back would take a bit longer but she was wrong, trying to consider her position she drifted off and slept off again.

CHAPTER 34

Iwobo was the first to awake in Fujiri, he woke up feeling on top of the world. It was as if he had no troubles in the world, he was even laughing to himself. His heart was exceedingly glad, nothing seemed to be a problem for him. Giving those gifts to Nne, had unlocked something inside of him. Now nothing mattered, his heart was liberated and now he relished more than anything else to see Nne's face, he sat up. After looking at the thatched roof for some time, Obeli was still sleeping. His friend was not a morning person that he knew, or maybe his father's wealth had gotten him soft. Iwobo now getting ready to leave the hut couldn't just wait to see Nne. It was like he had not seen her for decades and he was certain too that seeing her would make the world perfect for him. He looked behind him, Obeli was still at peace in his sleep, he stepped out of the hut then he looked to his left at the direction of Nne's hut.

Nne had to have a good night rest she didn't allow Iwobo's gestures towards her to hinder her peaceful rest. His actions were something she planned to ponder on but not at that very moment. She had a good night rest and was waiting for the compounds slaves to come and call for them or maybe Iwobo since he knew the host better, she also was awake as well as Obirika, who was beginning to get relaxed and lose some of the tensions she had before. Even her pessimistic forebodings were waning. They both sat on the bed and anxiously waited to have the day going. Not till they were away from Fujiri would they have peace. Obirika sat and looked at her daughter then she went and sat closer to her.

"My senses tell me a lot is going through your mind" Obirika said. As she crossed her left arm on Nne's shoulders and caressed her right arm.

"I still do not know our plans." Nne said smiling at her mother.

"I have been doing a lot of thinking too my daughter and you will agree with me that there is nothing for us in Akom anymore. We can't go back there, in my believe when a place offers you so much evil, it is better you do your best to avoid the place."

Nne looked at her mother trying to interrupt, but she continued speaking, making Nne to hold onto her thought.

"I know what you are going to say, that it is the people and not the place, but my dear it is the people that make the place, so like I was saying there is nothing for us in Akom, we will go to my brother's place I am sure he would help us, plus we need his protection, for us staying alone would be dangerous."

"But my father's house would be deserted is that not a bad thing?" Nne asked. Obirika looked puzzled for a while then she spoke "Your father has brothers I'm sure they would be more than happy to claim his place, it won't be deserted I have always been happy that you are my daughter, people will taunt me for not having a son but you are worth more than ten sons to me. In my next life I wish to have you, and when I re-incarnate I wish to come back to you." Obirika looked at her daughter brushing through her hair with her fingers squeezed her tightly. Nne reciprocated by hugging her mother, "I can't wait to see uncle Ujuru." Nne said.

"He would be thrilled to see us." Obirika said. They both smiled, still in each other's arms, they heard a knock they had been anticipating it, a head popped in and informed them, water for bath was ready and that their food would be delivered to the hut.

"Thank you my daughter." Obirika said to the young woman, who greeted, turned and left. They both arranged the hut making it look neat and comfortable, also making it easy for the slaves, not to give them much work. Obirika went first and then Nne.

Iwobo went to Atibi's hut to greet him, he had waited to see Nne, but she didn't come out. Then Atibi called, Atibi had woken up a long time ago and was already preparing for the day. Iwobo entered his hut.

"Good morning master Atibi." Iwobo greeted.

"Iwobo how are you?"

"Very fine sir."

"Hope you had a food night rest."

"Yes I did."

"I saw you in front of your hut and I just want to make sure you were okay, this is not…" Atibi interrupted himself as Iwobo was still standing at the entrance, "Please come in and sit down."

He pointed to a seat.

"Thank you Sir." Iwobo quickly came and took the seat offered. Atibi resumed his speech, "I just wanted to know, because I didn't get the chance to ask you last night, did you later find your half-brother?"

Iwobo shook his head in response first before saying, "No we didn't."

"Hmm," Atibi exhaled, with a genuine look of care written all over his face, his eyebrows arched as he gazed on Iwobo, "I'm sorry for all your loss, I have lived more years on this earth than you have and as nature will have it, I will be the first to go and meet my ancestors. That is how I suppose it will be, because that is how it is supposed to be, but nobody has control over these things, sometimes everything just goes berserk and we try to make out meaning from all of it. No young man should face such things, we are always better when at the end of the journey a man goes at a full ripe age, when all his members have fought the fight and has gallantly bowed out, then a man should go. But if you have days left, it is supposed to be that you live it out, my son you must be strong. Bad things happen, and good things happen, they both must happen. So when the bad happens let it pass, and when the good happens celebrate, but then again we pray that our good will be more than our bad."

Iwobo nodded with rapt attention and in agreement, "All I can say is, be strong." Atibi said.

"Thank you Master your words mean a lot to me."

Atibi not saying a word to Iwobo's comment, stood up and went to the edge of his bamboo bed, dipped his hand unto the corner and brought out a weaved bag, reaching inside it he brought out six palm frond weaved hats.

"I'm surprised you people didn't have these when you came, I wonder how you have been surviving with the sun." He counted four as the hats were together each placed on top of another pressing them all into one, he picked four from the six, remaining two and handed it over to Iwobo.

"You people will need this."

"Thank you sir." Iwobo had taught of buying hats, but they were being frugal with their money, though that didn't stop him from buying gifts for Nne.

A hand knocked informing Atibi he had visitors, "Thank you I will be with the person soon." He was informed of who they were, Atibi's response meant he didn't know them. Iwobo with the gifts thanked him once again and took excuse to leave.

"Yes you can go, go and prepare yourself and make sure you take enough provisions, I will see you before you leave."

"Okay sir." He left, entering the compound his eyes were on the hats as he inspected them, when he looked up, he saw Nne, emerging from the bathroom and walking towards the hut they were occupying. His heart skipped just by mere sighting of Nne, it started pounding faster, he waved at her with smile on his face. Seeing him she smiled back. Walking closer to him and to the entrance of her hut, "Aren't you preparing?" she asked.

"About to," he was having high blood pressure.

"Okay see you then?" she said and went into the hut. Iwobo smiled at himself, feeling well pleased, it was exactly as he had anticipated, seeing her would give him joy and it did, it just did. Turning to his left his gaze met Obeli, still robbing his eyes. Obeli had seen everything, but was confused, or more so figured it was nothing. They could smile at each other, but his curiosity had a better of him. "What are you smiling about?" he asked. Iwobo who was now close to him as if caught doing a bad thing quickly gave up his smile putting on a stern look.

"I was not smiling." He said.

"You can lie to yourself. Where did you go?"

"Master Atibi called me."

"Hope all is well?" Obeli said still trying to arouse his sleepy eyes.

"Yes it is." Iwobo said.

"Thought someone took you, so I was planning to come rescue you." Obeli joked.

"As if you can," Iwobo retorted.

"Big head, what makes you think I can't?" Obeli said half-awake now.

"We all know how strong you are." Iwobo said.

They were both in the hut now. Obeli continued, "Are you saying you are stronger than me?"

"Is anyone arguing that?" Iwobo answered.

"Look at this lizard." Obeli said.

"You know if we wrestle you don't stand a chance?" Iwobo said.

"I don't blame you." Obeli said.

Both still arranging their belongings.

"Anyways our water is ready, so I will be going to bath. As your master I have to bath first, it means you are respectful." Obeli said.

"Iwobo clapped his hands as if dusting them, gave out a mocking laughter, "Children of nowadays no respect, can you imagine?"

Obeli shaking his head, "It is I your master that you are disrespecting." Still saying the words he was now at the exit of the hut. Iwobo was at the edge of the bamboo bed about 4 feet from the exit where Obeli was standing. Iwobo made an attempt to run to the exit but Obeli was fast to take to his heels running towards the bathroom.

Looking back Iwobo was not in pursuit he stopped and walked the rest of the distance to the bathroom. He walked past two huts that were to his left greeting everyone in the compound he didn't know who was who, but greeted all. He took a turn to his left to the bathroom, glancing to his right at the direction of Nne's hut. He had promised himself to tell her what he felt, damn the consequences. If he got rejected or not it wouldn't bother him, he went into the bathroom with the thought in his head. Trying to focus he decided to sing. Iwobo sat in the hut replaying a moment ago where he saw Nne in his mind and the feeling was the best feeling he had ever had. It made him feel so blessed, soon they would march out and be together, that he also cherished.

Nne and her mum were in their hut preparing, none spoke as they wanted to eat quickly. Clearly the Atibi's knew how to take care of a guest, they were quite happy at their position, as far as they could remember the words of Iwobo had proven to be true for the most part. Nne peeped outside having eaten enough to see slaves hustling about their master's business. They must be getting ready for the day's farming. She walked back inside and sat beside her mother, who was still trying to force feed herself. She just didn't have the appetite something inside was bugging her and she was certain it was her situation.

"Don't you think we should finish this food?" she asked her daughter, "so that the people won't feel bad."

"They won't Mama." Nne said.

"Maybe we will pack it and go with it."

As if set free, Obirika concurred, "That is what we should do." She stood up and washed her hands. They both sat on the bed, waiting for Iwobo and Obeli. Obirika looked at her daughter keenly to notice the new jewelries on her left ankle and right wrist and new beads on her waist. "Someone went to market to make herself look better." Obirika said smiling at her daughter.

Nne smiled, "It is a long story Mama."

"Nobody is rushing us, we have enough time in our hands."

"They are gifts Mama, there is even necklace and earing, but I want to give them to you. You already have these ones I would have asked you to choose before I wore them." She turned as if hit with a new idea, "Is that what I should have done Mama."

"It is okay and you can keep them all, I'm content and I have enough." Obirika said.

"You should still have them Mama, I want you to." She hugged her mother. Who wanted to ask her "Gift from who" but decided not to. She would tell her when she wanted to, she knew and trusted her daughter. Obeli knocked and informed them they were ready.

"Hope you people are ready?" he asked after greeting them both.

"Yes we've been waiting for you both." The ladies said. "Okay let us go."

Quickly they took their belongings and marched into the compound. Iwobo saw Nne and also noticed she had donned the jewelries he had given her, his heart gladdened. They went to Atibi's hut and Iwobo went in to inform him they were leaving. Still standing in the compound, Master Atibi came out to meet them, he called a slave and sent her to call his wives who were not in the compound as those who were in the compound and saw their visitors came to hug them. They brought out gifts, Atibi gave them mats and cloths, while they stuffed their bags with enough food that would last till the next stop. Everyone was hugging them except the slaves who knew their place, after the hugs they were wished a successful journey. Atibi told them to wait, he went to his shrine and brought a small feathery staff, he looked at them intently and proceeded to pray for them.

They all thanked him and his household, his wives, sons and daughters had smiles on their faces as they also wished them well. With that they marched out of the compound, finally out of the compound they took their right turn, to Iwobo the path looked different but he remembered it all the same.

"I will surely miss these people." Obeli said as he took up his position which was at the rear of the group. Obirika and Nne marched together, and interchanged position without thinking about it.

"They are good people," Iwobo said "I wish next time we meet I will be in the position to do something for them. They surely do need help, he has assured us things will get better and I believe it will be so, such a wonderful people, I don't think there is anything that can be done to show appreciation for such kind gestures."

They walked and lost sight of the Atibi's compound, Obeli looked back to see if he could learn the path, should in case he felt like coming back to the Atibi's someday. They marched through Fujiri, without much apprehension they had left the well-treaded path, still with their earlier resolve to stay out of sight.

CHAPTER 35

Adanna awoke in Mkpunki feeling refreshed despite the occurrence of the night. Opening her eyes, life had fully resumed in the compound. Everyone to her observation was fully awake now, quickly her mind went to her knees, she moved them and noticed she could, her heart warmed with joy, the massages must be working, she was still feeling pain a little, but not like it was before. She actually expected it to have healed completely, but it wasn't. She raised her right knees first and noticed she could, then it got to a point and she noticed the pain started. She moved her left and the same but with her left it could go further than her right. For the first time she smiled to herself in her condition. As expected, not long after the observation, she heard a knock at the entrance of her hut. She didn't know if it was the Herbalist or his mother, they both had the same pattern of knocking. Maybe the mother had passed it onto her son as she would have it, it was the Herbalist.

He came in "knew you would be up by now. How are you? And good morning."

"Good morning too and thank you, I am fine." Adanna said.

The Herbalist nodded with smiles. "As usual Nnadi will take care of you my mum will come to see you later. How are the legs?"

"Mmmm the legs? See for yourself." She raised her knees up to the surprise and amazement of the Herbalist.

"Wow!" he exclaimed "I must say you have an amazing body the way you are healing it is quite unprecedented."

"Hmmm thank the gods. I have a good physician." Adanna said.

"It is all you." He said smiling and pointing at her, "This is, this is good, it is really good."

"I can't wait to get back on my feet, on my own." Adanna said.

"You are doing great." He took a seat and sat on it, getting closer to Adanna's knee, he began to press the kneecaps. "Please tell me which side is paining you when I touch it."

He kept pressing round the kneecaps now he was pressing her right knee, no need pressing her whole leg. As Adanna had indicated it was only her knees.

"All the areas you are touching are all paining me, but the pain is not as before." She said.

"Okay, okay, well good then, very good, let me go and get you, your herbs for the pain. I will be back anything else?"

"No nothing at all."

He left with warmth in his heart. Adanna resumed her own check on herself, raising her knee, every time she did so it excited her, the prospect of walking again after so many days kept on a bed. Things wouldn't be so gloomy again. Continuing from where the Herbalist stopped, she pressed her knees, and got the assurance that it was healing. She heard a knock, which she responded to, first came in Etiti and then Nnadi both surprised to see her knees up.

"You can raise them?" Etiti asked with smiles as she approached her. This time sitting beside her on the bamboo bed as if they were mother and daughter. Nnadi greeted Adanna who responded. Etiti sitting beside her began to touch the knees tenderly, with Adanna still wearing her recently acquired smile and it suited her, instead of the frowning face she was accustomed to. Etiti inspected the knees, carefully with smiles.

"I told you it will all be well, you can see now." Etiti said. "And I believed you." Adanna said. Etiti gave orders to Nnadi. "You can see she is awake, now prepare her bathing water and food." Nnadi quickly went out. Nnadi had wanted to congratulate her but would wait for another time.

"It is good to see you are getting okay, Nnadi will take good care of you, I have a women's meeting to attend today."

"So that means no farming?" Adanna asked.

"None my dear, it is all good and I will be going to bring the boy, I have finally decided to, I discussed with my son yesterday and he seems okay with it," Etiti said standing up, "I will see you later" she said reaching the exit, "Take care of yourself."

"I will," Adanna said. Still expecting her medication from the Herbalist, she continued with what she was doing and that was checking her knees, looking at them she wondered what it was she was going to do first when she finally started walking. She would take a walk into the forest to hunt game, the prospect of it excited her. Again she thought about childhood, she couldn't remember to be sick, even as a child she had been strong and always about. The things that did put her peers down never did put her down, and her mother had always been proud of her. Supporting her for being the strong girl that she was.

Then she fought with boys and beat up girls she remembered a fight she had as a kid, she was returning from her maternal home, she had gone to see her grandmother who was now late, she had not been as slim as she was now, and the girl called her a fat cattle, she hated being called names, and calling her fat was one of them. She had a pineapple on her head she quickly dropped it, surprised at her agility. She caught the girl who was making a bold stand, opting not to run. It was a fight like none she had had before, they both punched each other, scratched and bit, she finally managed to push the girl down, and landed on her she took sand and let the girl's eyes have a fill of it, she could have killed the girl that day, before they were separated by passersby. She remembered her mother standing by her and supporting her for defending herself when the girl came with her parents to report her. The parents of the girl had complained of so many injuries sustained by their daughter.

"Look at my daughter her canine tooth is out," the woman pointed to her heavy blood shot eyes and the fact that the girl's left eye was swollen. "Look at my daughter" the woman continued saying "Bruises all over her body, what kind of an animal do you have, and you are calling her a daughter." Adanna confidently stood beside her mother who was shouting on top of her voice. "It is you daughter that is an animal not mine."

"Your daughter is a beast!" the woman said.

The men tried to calm their wives.

"Ask your daughter what she said to my daughter." Adanna's mother continued shouting.

"Is that why she should hurt a fellow being like this" the girl's mother had said. Shouting even louder than Adanna's mother and pointing to her daughter's battered body.

"Take your daughter and get out of here before death will strike you down." Adanna's mother said before taking her daughter and walking into their hut. With Adanna and her mother leaving, Ubiakwa had tried to calm the enraged visitors. That was a long time ago, she was no longer fat but still fought to preserve herself, she had been strong then and still was, her teenage years have been filled with similar stories, she had always fought. She would never allow anyone take advantage of her. The day she went into the forest to hunt she felt like she was flying, the cool forest, with so many stories of evil and unforeseen ghost in it, she enjoyed it. Her mind was firmly in the past when the Herbalist knocked again, he came in and handed her a gourd, she didn't ask questions but took it and drank it all, the drug were becoming more bitter and more bitter every time.

"You know others I will beg them to drink the medicine but you, you never fuss, you just make everything easy."

"Is that a compliment?" Adanna asked.

"I must tell you this I have never met anyone like you, you are just different."

"Guess you picked the words right out of my mouth because I was about to say the same things of you." Adanna said still wearing her new face which had smile on it.

The Herbalist had noticed it how she was smiling, "And I like the fact that you are now smiling." The Herbalist said with his own smiling face. Adanna simply nodded and said no words.

"I will be leaving now have some places to attend to okay, have a nice day."

"You too."

He left, walking out of the hut he met Nnadi coming in, he said no words to her as Nnadi greeted him, she knocked, before saying a word Adanna knew what it was all about.

"Let us get on with it." Adanna said as the girl marched into her hut the Herbalist went into his hut, picked up the herbs that needed to be delivered, he had a lot of people to visit today, but his first point of call would be Mama Adubi. He had made up his mind.

He stepped out of his hut, he must be swift in walking the day holds a lot, barely had he gone out of the compound amongst the barge of countless good morning coming from slaves did he meet with Bariye. His long forgotten friend who had wanted them to be farmers as youngsters. The Herbalist was the first to see Bariye from his steps it looked like he was coming to his place.

"Bariye" the Herbalist called out, walking to his old friend. "Hope all is well?"

"Herbalist all is not well."

"Tell me straight away." The Herbalist said.

"It is my slave, he is shriving badly and has a bad body temperature. It is not normal." Bariye said.

"Indeed it is not normal," the Herbalist quickly went back into the compound, down to his hut, with Bariye following. He took herbs, Bariye patiently waiting at the entrance of his hut. Quickly they marched to his home.

*****

Back at home, Adanna had not given up on her knees, she has been raising and lowering it as if it was a play thing, with each raising she found a fascination and with the bringing down she found another fascination. The compound seemed quieter now, except for the sounds from the animals. For a moment as she raised and lowered her knees on the bamboo bed, she felt it would make the knees heal faster. Sometimes ignoring the pain she would raise it up to a level that the knee was not yet

accepting. She was feeling her condition more seriously today, not only was she consigned to a spot, she couldn't take a look around to know what was happening in her environment. She was called back by a knock. She knew the sound of the clap, now she could distinguish it from her son's clap. It was Etiti.
"Please come in." She said.
A smiling Etiti walked in with a young boy following her both women smiled at each other, the boy greeted Adanna.
"I guess this is the boy." Adanna said.
"Yes he is."
"Dear how are you?" Adanna asked.
"Fine Ma'am." He was nothing like Adanna had imagined. She had sat thinking how he would look, for his parents to want to sell him. The boy standing before her looked frail, almost scrawny, he wouldn't have made it in the slave market. No one would have bought him, from the little she had seen, he didn't look like the type the slavers wanted. They went for those that looked strong and could work, with dentition showing they could work.
Again the boy was a bit shorter than his age, he was 9 and looked like a 5-year-old. Etiti looked at Adanna's face, if she was heartbroken for the boy she wasn't showing it. Adanna felt pity for the boy but didn't know she was. Her outward appearance had not changed, but she kept looking at the boy with his tiny arms and legs. Etiti when she saw him for the first time her heart felt pierced, such a young boy, with such misery. What would he be feeling? What was going through his mind? To be in such state it meant since he was born he had been suffering. Etiti had fought tears ever since taking the boy.

"The first thing I have to do for him is give him food and have him bath, I don't like the way he is looking so unkempt." She said.

"I think you should" Adanna said, "Young man you are welcome alright, feel at peace this is your place now and you are with the most beautiful and amazing people on earth, welcome." Adanna said.

The young boy nodded in agreement, from the hut, Etiti called out Nnadi's name who came running, she gave her orders concerning the boy, and he was led out by Nnadi. The two women sat together in the hut, "Just imagine that I sold my son the Herbalist, what would have happened to me, I am still trying to imagine what would have happened and how life would have been." Etiti spoke shaking her head in bewilderment. As Adanna stared at the woman beside her. "It is an unimaginable cruelty when a mother loses her child to death and then imagine when you willingly sell one, because of life's circumstances."

Adanna sat speechless as Etiti kept pondering on the matter, She had never been known to give advice or console anyone, besides Etiti's words, should be rhetorical, obviously she didn't expect her to provide answers. Etiti still speaking continued.

"I really don't know what this business of slavery is doing to us, it has made us to forsake our humanity up till now we still do not care."

Adanna was certainly lost now she had no words to say and obviously didn't understand Etiti's last statement. What evil was she talking about? The last she checked slaves were rejects who deserved their fate, but the thought would remain with her. Etiti inhaled sharply and exhaled, slapping her hands against her kneecaps she stood up. Adanna's knees tingled as she witnessed Etiti slap her's in that manner.

"I have women's meeting to attend, only the gods know how I loathe it, but I have no choice, it is go or be penalized for failure to honour invitation."

"Okay, go then." Adanna said.

"Take care my dear, I will be back soon." Marching out Adanna heard Etiti saying some words, she had heard Nnadi being mentioned, but couldn't hear the remaining words spoken. Presumably it would be words of order given to Nnadi as usual. Adanna now alone tried to reason out Etiti's words of how slavery was an evil, but from her perspective it just didn't register in. She stayed a while with nothing but the sounds she has now become accustomed to, she thought of returning to her exercise. Only to see a head, then a full body, it was the boy. Surprised, Adanna stared at him for a while not sure where to begin.

"Are you okay?" She asked.

"Yes ma'am" the boy answered timidly, he stood beside the door scared he might be chased away and making sure not to look at Adanna. Adanna couldn't remember the last time she was in such a position. In Akom the children were aware of Adanna's conk, children took to their heels when she approached. Because they knew their parents would do nothing but advise them to stay away from Adanna. While others cursed her in shadows hoping it caught up with her, without her knowing it was them that made the curses. Adanna looking at the boy if only he knew her reputation, he wouldn't dare near her hut even at death's point. After a while of hesitation.

"Do you want to sit down?" she asked.

As if pushed by wind the boy quickly went and sat on her bamboo bed, the good news was he sat where her feet were.

"Okay" she nodded. She had meant the seat in front of her bed and not the bed itself. The boy sat dejected, still not staring at Adanna, but something in Adanna told her he wanted to just be where he was.

"Hope you have had something to eat?" Adanna asked still picking her words, she didn't even know where to start from in attending to the child. In answering her question the boy simply shook his head slowly as if not only was he scared of speaking but was also scared of any form of communication. Adanna saw the shaking of head as an encouragement to speak on, though she herself didn't know what she was doing.

"So big boy," as she spoke she tried looking at his face but it was somewhat impossible. She could only see the right side of his face, the child sat backing her and trying his best to maintain as little space on the bed as possible. "What is your name?" she asked he took forever to answer, first adjusting himself, then his clothes, he scratched his right knee suddenly his eyes were itchy and he duly pacified them with his fingers, then he muttered a word. Adanna could barely hear and certainly was not sure of what he said leaning closer.

"Come again." She said.

"Are you scared?" He remained mute this time not even shaking his head. Adanna persisted "Do you want to go home?" No answer, "Don't you like here?" Still no answer. Maybe she had overdone it, before she was getting response, now nothing at all, Adanna caught the Scratching Syndrome, she scratched her temple then her right arm with her left, she felt helpless not only was she handicapped she couldn't talk to a child. Adanna sat looking at the child who was determined not to look at her. She heard Nnadi shouting Tiperi and she sensed the calling was coming from different positions in the compound intermittently; she looked at the boy who adjusted himself and sat motionless again, now there were more voices shouting Tiperi and there were chatter. Adanna could hear even a man's voice and the distinct high pitch of Nnadi's voice. She sensed chaos from the shouts and alarm.

"Is it you that they are calling?" Adanna asked. No answer, the child still sat motionless, gazing at the exit with his hands tucked between his laps. The calls still continued outside, Adanna considered her position she couldn't stand, she waited for anyone to get closer to her hut. Fortunately for her it was Nnadi who came close to her hut, shouting "Tiperi." Adanna beckoned on her, Nnadi heeded and came into her hut, she closed her eyes and exhaled when she saw the child.

"Is it him you are looking for?" Adanna asked.

"Yes ma'am" Nnadi said smiling. Looking at her smile Adanna wondered if anything ever made her cry, she seemed to be always upbeat with life. Never frowning, always showing her teeth. Adanna could tell she couldn't mistake Nnadi's voice. When she laughed it was like the birds sang. Adanna had never seen such behavior from an individual, nothing dampened Nnadi's spirit.

"Thank you ma'am" Nnadi said as she left the hut. Adanna could guess where she had gone to within a moment the shouts of Tiperi had stopped. All she could hear now was chatter, Nnadi re-emerged in her hut. "Come and eat" she said to the boy.

Adanna eagerly watched to see what would unfold, the boy still sat on the bed as if he didn't hear Nnadi.

Looking at him Nnadi gave out a laughter that meant 'this is unbelievable.' Nnadi went closer to him, placed her right hand on his shoulder.

"Dear come and eat the food is delicious okay, you will enjoy it." Nnadi said as sweetly as she could. The boy wouldn't budge.

"Do you want to eat?" she asked, he said nothing still looking down on the ground and, Nnadi gave Adanna a look that meant help me, and Adanna looked on. Showing she was at a loss too.

"Do you want to eat the food here?" Nnadi asked, looking at Adanna, "Ma'am I hoped you don't mind." Adanna nonchalantly quickly replied. "No not at all." Adanna continued looking at the two, Nnadi went to the exit and in one last attempt, beckoned on the boy to follow her, he sat on the bed and seemed as if he was not the one being spoken to. Nnadi gave up and instead left to bring the food to him. In about a moment Nnadi returned with the food it was a vegetable and water leaf soup, with fish and pounded yam. Adanna was surprised with the quantity but then again the boy needed all the food he could get. After placing it before him, "Dear eat you hear, it is your food." Nnadi said. Both women were saved the stress of trying to cajole him into eating as he quickly went to the food and began to rush it. Taking in huge chunks with every handful both women watched with delight. Adanna had already given up the thought that she would try to persuade him, leaving it to the herbalist, he would certainly know what to do. Nnadi stood a while looking at him as he ate then satisfied he would be okay, she took excuse from Adanna and left. Adanna with nothing in her mind, blankly stared at the boy as he ate. As he ate she began to wonder if he wouldn't need drinking water, surely the food must be inconveniencing his oesophagus in a way. The boy kept swallowing fast.

"Don't you think…" before she could finish the sentence, he reached out and took a water gourd and in same manner drank ferociously. Adanna decided not to finish her words but contently looked on at the child devouring food in her presence. She felt disgusted at his parent's ignorance, if they wanted to sell him as a slave they should have fed him well, not leaving him to emaciate. The child continued with his food trying to eat as much as possible. Adanna observing him now noticed what he was doing, he wanted to finish the food. There was no way he could do so. But then again he obviously felt there might not be another food coming. He was clearly exhausted and satisfied now but kept on eating.

"You know you don't have to finish it, that beautiful lady will give you another one in the afternoon and in the night or better still later on you can continue." Adanna continued. The boy turned and dropped the ball of pounded yam in his hand, gave a sigh of relief and then proceeded to drink some water. He washed his hands and sat back on the bed. Nnadi re-emerged again to see he had done substantial job with the food, happy she patted him on the shoulder. She didn't bother to ask him if he was okay with the food as the boy still sat rigidly even after eating. Nnadi picked the locally made plates.

"Won't you say thank you?" Adanna asked. Both were happy to hear a faint "Thank you" from him. At least he still talks. Nnadi picked the plates and left. Adanna was alone with him again, and she decided to probe further. All questions she asked returned unanswered, after a while both were silent and listened to the chatter outside.

CHAPTER 36

Since the morning unexpected interruption from Bariye, nothing had gone out of the ordinary. The herbalist's next visited Erika and gave her a fresh barge of herbs. Another that remained was mama Adubi, but that would be later she may be at the women's meeting hopefully she didn't discuss the matter with his mother. As he walked past people he kept receiving greetings both from those he knew and those he wondered if he had ever met. He went on to the compound of his mother's friend Okongi who was nursing a newborn, she and the baby seemed to be in perfect health. The problem was her older son he had been complaining of bad stomach and he had just the right herb for him. Getting to the compound, everywhere was deserted, the huts were all open and the ground was covered with dirt of all kinds. As the Herbalist approached what was supposed to be Okongi's son's hut, he looked to his right a basket was lying with its contents spilled on the ground and a precious content it was, who would waste cocoyam like that. The Herbalist apprehensive, couldn't determine what must have happened, he checked the huts and no one was around. He called the few names he knew and no one answered, what could have happened here? He had few options come to him the scene looked uncanny should he go and report to village authorities or could there be a more reasonable explanation to the state of things. One thing was certain: he needed to find out what happened, he had heard from Okongi a few days ago, should they be planning to leave without telling him. He shook his head in disbelief, turned and left the compound. On his way out he took his left to make his way to his next point of delivery, as he stepped out, he saw a woman coming from the opposite direction, seeing her he felt she must be from around there but then again the woman was looking at him like he was a ghost and he wondered if it was because he was coming out from Okongi's compound. He thought of stopping her to ask her about the Okongi's but decided not to, she didn't look friendly. He passed her, he could tell that she stopped to look at him, he turned back to look and there she was standing with her hands on her hips and looking at him with gaze that showed intrigue on her face. He wondered what could have happened in that compound to make someone who came out from it look suspicious. Hopefully no evil had befallen them. With the thought he went his way he would surely find out.

*****

Iwobo had been leading his team joyfully as they told tales and he felt he should tell them about the next village they were about to enter.

"After Fujiri is the people of Obikiti."

Obeli from behind, "What! The Obikiti I have heard about?" he said aloud.

"Yes that very one you have heard about" Iwobo said.

"Why, what about them?" Nne asked looking forward and backward hoping to get an answer from either Iwobo or Obeli.

"We have heard so many tales about the people of Obikiti and it is not very good." Obeli said.

"How do you mean? Nne probed on.

"It is mixed, then you won't know which one is true and which is a complete epic tale."

Obirika had a smile upon her face as she marched behind her daughter who was in a lost world, she had never heard the tale about Obikiti.

"Is anyone going to tell me, or will I find out for myself when we get to Obikiti? We are still in Fujiri are we not?"

"Sure we are." Iwobo answered Nne as sweet as possible. Since Nne was walking ahead of her even though the path was wide enough to contain at least two people, Obirika placed her hand on Nne's shoulder slowing her down. Definitely it would be better for Obirika to tell her.

"My dear" Obirika began with her voice down, "The tales surrounding the people of Obikiti is multifaceted, but what is generally known is that the people are known for their overzealous worship of their god." Obeli had heard the story before and Iwobo acted as if he was present when it all happened, or in the version he had frequently heard.

"But mama that is a good thing, for people to worship their god."

"Yes it is, Obikiti is different, in Akom we believe in sacrifice as much as they do, but then what others find disturbing is that it is said that during the third month of every year no one knows why, the elders by lot pick a pregnant woman they will kill her by opening her womb they will take her internal organs some say it is only her heart, others say it is her heart and other internal organs, then they will also take the unborn child from her womb."

Nne trying to comprehend more, "From the womb which means she doesn't give birth?"

"No she doesn't in fact some say it is while the baby is sixty market days others say seventy market days no one knows for sure, then they also open the unborn child and take out its heart."

"What will they do with them?" Hearing the question Iwobo shook his head and Nne could see he disapproved of it, she couldn't see Obeli he was behind them.

Obirika continued with her tale "They pound them in a mortar with pestle then they will pound the unborn child separately, in fact they pound all separately then they will take the mother into the forest and leave her there for vultures to feed on her corpse. Nne shuddered.

"What do they do with the pounded organs?"

"Some say their Chief Priest is actually the architect of the scheme and according to him they use it for protection and they do it mostly when they are going to war and against invaders who carry them away into slavery."

"And it works?"

"Who knows?" Obirika shrugged.

"It is also said that they bury the pounded baby's remains at the entrance of their borders, with other villages." Obeli added. With the stories Nne felt they should take another route. She had heard of human sacrifices before and knew about sacrifices but not this type. She didn't bother to ask how the lot was determined because it didn't make sense to her. It simply meant pregnant women were ill-fated in their place, because you would never know if it would be your turn.

"You know there are stories too because I have never really heard about the sacrifice itself from an Obikiti man or woman but strangers from Obikiti." Obeli continued.

Iwobo concurred "The victims are taken unaware, even their husbands do not know about the impending doom."

Nne feeling sensitive to the matter "Can I ask a question?"

"Sure you can." Iwobo said.

"Why is it that it is women they are using, most times I hear of human sacrifice, it is usually the women."

"My daughter that is how it is supposed to be." Obirika answered and with that they fell silent on the matter. They were not having problems as the morning sun met their new hats, Atibi had done great this time by giving them the hats as far as they were concerned it was a priceless piece of property now. They marched on passing farmlands and bushes with people walking pass them going to different places, every now and then Iwobo would cursorily glance black making sure he looked at Nne. He couldn't get enough of her shining ebony skin, and the satisfaction that he felt knowing she was now donning his gifts were indescribable to him. Thinking about her or even imagining she was behind him made his heart to ache. At the rear Obeli was feeling the same thing. Wishing Iwobo and Obirika evaporated leaving behind only him and Nne. He was certain in his heart that Nne should be his very own, all he needed now was to tell her how he felt. The four maintained their walking positions as it would take them time before they left the territory of Fujiri. Nne didn't know what it was but something made their prospective journey into Obikiti less enthusiastic.

"So are we going to march into Obikiti just like this?" Nne asked with her voice wavering.

"Sure why not?" Obeli answered trying to sound manly and give her the assurance that nothing would happen to her.

"It is just based on what we have heard." Nne said.

"I don't think you should be scared, nothing is going to happen." Obeli said. Nne wished she could take in the words and believe it, a reputation was not something to ignore, if you are known for doing something there was a chance you would do it again and even try to incorporate other acts and in this case it would mean killing travellers who dared enter their village of course they couldn't turn back, it was too late now.

"Iwobo is there no other way we can follow?" Nne asked.

With the question and at that point he felt like crossing his arm across her neck and gently whispering into her ears. "I will rather die than let anything happen to you."

But he thought better of it. Obirika may not have any weapon but one might mysteriously materialize and she would use it to slice off his arm. Then Iwobo had a better idea to just say the words.

"I will rather die than let anything happen to you, I can't lead you into danger please trust me, nothing will happen to you." He said turning back to look at her. Obirika moved closer to her and crossed her arm across Nne's neck and whispered to her. Iwobo smiled, exactly what he had thought of doing. Obirika and Nne were speaking in whispers now and he felt he was not needed anymore so he resumed his position of leading the pack. With Nne being persuaded by her mother, three damsels were coming from the opposite direction brandishing machete, all four were stunned at the sight, their faces didn't indicate they were coming with peace. They were not with baskets to show they were headed to the farm, they kept approaching, looking stern and serious. The three of them moved at the same pace, still holding their machete. Iwobo slowed down, contemplating whether they were coming for peace or not at least that was what

Nne thought when she saw him slow down. With the ladies a few yards from them a grasscutter ran across from the farmland to their right to the farmland at their left. Both Iwobo and Obeli had seen the rodent, and it ran across them just like the antelope had done in Dubiri, the girls were still approaching with their machete. Once the grasscutter ran across with every ounce of energy Obeli and Iwobo once again lurched forward after it. Leaving Nne and Obirika bewildered and scared again. Nne and her mother looked to their left to see Iwobo and Obeli falling on the ground frantically and standing to run some more all in a bid to catch a grasscutter zigzagging its run and wanting to escape its chasers. Iwobo and Obeli persisted, chasing the animal with little regard for things that stood in their way their hats had fallen a way behind them and they didn't care just like when they dropped all they were carrying and ran after the grasscutter. With what they had been told and seen Nne and her mother knew there was no problem for them in Fujiri. But the ladies with the machete were still a threat and struck fear into them. The three women continued approaching, Obirika and Nne left the path clinching in each other's arm. The ladies got to where they were greeted and with a stern face passed, they both continued looking at them as the ladies never turned but went on. Nne and her mother were called back to the scene where Iwobo and Obeli were by a hysterical laughter followed by jubilation coming from the two of them. Entering the farm they saw Iwobo and Obeli happily marching out empty handed. The two women could have sworn they thought they caught the game. The women waited as the two came forward, no need to ask them what was funny, both were bleeding mildly from minor bruises. That didn't concern them, the women thought better of it, no need to ask questions. The four left the farm, took their belongings from the ground and continued their journey. Iwobo and Obeli resumed their positions, Nne silently prayed that they didn't meet an armed group along the way, it wouldn't be this two defending them. All walked while Iwobo and Obeli shared blames as to whose fault it was that the grasscutter escaped.

"We could have had a delightful dinner or even lunch if not for your incompetence Iwobo."

"And if not for your stupidity I would have caught a grasscutter today." Iwobo responded. Nne and Obirika kept mute and listened to the two rant, from what it seemed the two of them rant at each other almost always but seem to be closer more than brothers could. And their exchange of words never caused animosity between them.

"I'm sorry my ladies, if not for this nincompoop here I would have made your day by giving you a nice meal served with grasscutter." Obeli said.

Iwobo not answering him simply shook his head and gave a soft laughter.

"Thank you Obeli we appreciate, but we are fine." Obirika said sounding like the mother that she was.

"But it still would have been nice." He said smiling. The sun was steadily warming up the earth and they felt it. If they marched along the great part of the day it would see them walk through Fujiri, they had walked on the path that had its bushes on both side cut down but now they were entering a path that had its bushes taller than them all. Though they had passed similar paths this one looked too narrow, and it unsettled Nne, before her mother was kidnapped she had heard tales of men hiding in the bush and jumping from it when the passersby were unprepared and pouncing on them, would completely overwhelm them, that was how some of the slaves were gotten and that was the most widely reported tactics used by those who kidnapped people for the slave coast. They entered the path and she felt she should say something concerning what she was thinking, before she could, Iwobo and Obeli unsheathed their swords.

"Good, very good," Nne thought, they must have heard it too.

"I think we should be very cautious here, this path stretches for almost 500 feet or so, we have no other option, the bushes have grown taller than I last remember it and stories about such areas is not in any way funny." Iwobo said. Obeli looking at the women in front of him felt they should have their own weapons. It was important for a time like this, he knew they had given them assurance of protection, but still it was important at such a moment for them to have weapons in case anything happened. Women should also be able to protect themselves, so they gave them daggers each. They walked a considerable distance not seeing anyone or hearing anything except the creatures that inhabited bushes. Obeli was at alert looking from side to side, but forgetting the most important which was to look behind, that was his job. They were walking as fast as possible the earlier they left the path, the better for them. "Obeli what will you do if another game should run pass us?" Iwobo asked teasingly.

"Pursue it hoping you don't follow, because then it would be able to get away."

"I would say the same about you, you run like a pregnant woman." Iwobo said.

"And you run like my great grandmother, I wonder how you have survived this far." Obeli said.

"See who is talking grasscutter that was just before you dive and catch it. Due to sheer incompetence you allowed it to escape." Iwobo continued.

"Who ran out first after it, you or me? And you were slacking till I overtook you." Obeli said.

Nne and Obirika just walked, ignoring the two as they went loggerheads against each other. They had moved a considerable distance down the path trying to focus on getting to where they were going. Obeli screaming at Iwobo.

"Iwobo look your left!" All were started and shocked, Iwobo quickly reacted, raising his sword ready to strike an attacker from his left, but nothing was there.

"Ah! this goat." Iwobo said calming his now rapidly beating heart, Nne and Obirika's heart were pounding too, trying to calm down.

"Obeli not this kind of joke, not in this circumstance," Obirika said.

Obeli, who was laughing now satisfied that his prank was funny even if it was funny only to him.

"Okay I'm sorry to you two, but that rat Iwobo deserves it."

With the words still coming out from his mouth they heard a voice from behind.

"Good day everyone."

Obeli was so terrified that he almost pissed on himself "Great 'Utte'" he screamed, dropping his sword on the ground. Turning back with the rest of the group, he saw a man with his family walking gently towards them. Obeli's heart almost popped out from his body. When he saw the man he placed his right hand on his chest as if that would calm it down. For now everyone's eyes were on the strangers.

Iwobo had seen Obeli's sword on the ground "Can you imagine?" he said smiling and shaking his head utterly amused, "Brave warrior of Akom at least pick your sword."

Obeli looked down indeed his sword was on the ground, he picked it up.

"Sorry if I startled you all, didn't mean to," the man said apparently the head of family.

Obeli brought out his hand for a shake, "A polite man he is" Iwobo whispered to no one in particular, handshake was a greeting form newly learnt from the white man. Nne and Obirika kept their place.

"The man shook Obeli and introduced himself "I'm Ekugo, and this is my wife Dinti." He said pointing to a very beautiful woman, with a ruby round face. Sparkling white teeth and elegant body. Her husband was as huge as anything Iwobo and his crew had seen. He looked like three men were put into one body. Towering above them all, Iwobo in his calculation saw it plausible that Ekugo could take them all in a fight with one arm, the man was just plain big. Then he pointed to a beautiful girl and introduced her as his daughter her name was Gotiu. She looked like her mother elegant and graceful. The load on her head hid nothing. Then finally he pointed to a young man who looked everything like his father "His name is Oduko," tall, huge and every bit a man. Iwobo was just wide eyed, Nne and Obirika seemed uncomfortable.

"I reckon you people must be heading to Obikiti." The man said.

"Yes we are" Obeli said, "And let me introduce my group here is Obirika." Obeli had apparently resumed position as the head of the group and his first task, as Iwobo and others looked on would be whether he would lie or tell the truth or what he would say while introducing them. "Obirika is" he pointed at Nne, "the mother of this wonderful, beautiful damsel and we are their countrymen." Obirika and Nne greeted him bending their knees, while Iwobo also greeted, while waving to the rest of his family. Obirika was pleased with Obeli's honesty.

"We better get moving," the man said, "I tell you this part is not for staying longer than necessary."

Iwobo and co. had noticed all the loads they were carrying.

"Are you people travelling or what?" Obeli asked sounding like he had long been waiting for a companion to chat with. Nne and Obirika still felt unsettled, they had been pleased with only the four of them walking. They didn't need any body to add to their burden or make them more uncomfortable than they already were.

"Yes we are. Why are you people headed to Obikiti my friends?"

"We are passing through, going to another place entirely."

"Oh okay, I and my family we are heading to Obikiti and we are never going back to where we are coming from." The man said.

Nne didn't mind him telling them all about himself and his affairs, but she would like their mouthpiece Obeli to keep their affairs private.

"Why sir?" Obeli asked.

"My brother it is a long story I'm not sure you want to hear it because it deals with the heartlessness and callousness of our people." Though he had said they didn't need to hear it, they were certain he was going to say it anyway. "I just met you people I know" Ekugo said as all now walked along the path Iwobo still leading the pack with Obeli and Ekugo maintaining the last position Ekugo was not only a huge man in stature his voice also showed it was coming from a huge body. Obirika wondered if someone would not detect them with the way his voice loomed. His family were marching behind Obirika and Nne, both wished they had more weapons, maybe they could protect themselves more. Nne in her haste while preparing had forgotten to bring a weapon but then again she didn't know what journey it was going to be.

Ekugo continued, "What will you do when the village you have resided in all your life turn against you?" he asked no one in particular, "I have stayed in Fujiri almost all my life now they treat me and my family this way."

Iwobo felt really uncomfortable hearing this, he had always believed that Fujiri could do no wrong. Maybe what his friends were saying was true, you cannot find a place that was completely free of evil people neither can you have a place that was completely inhabited by evil people. In a good place depending on how you see it there are bad people and in a place you see as a bad place there are good people. But then the question will be, what is the degree of good people to bad people or vice versa? In the case of Fujiri they had more good people than bad people, if there were bad people in it they were very few.

"Can you imagine" Ekugo said "Just take a look at my son, just because he had a swim at the sacred obekey river, we were asked to make restitution or be banished from the village, I wouldn't wait to be banished, no one can banish me from my own homeland, just because I have no title they believed they can treat me anyhow."

As his explanation continued Ekugo was deviating from it and now almost ranting "They are senseless village heads who cannot see that every of their decision is poisoned."

His wife sensing his anger rise, said words to soothe him "Our father, it is okay." She said, "Let us forget about the past and face the future." She said in a very cool calm voice.

"My dear I know" Ekugo responded. "People don't see that our world is rotten, where no one cares about the other, no one is considerate about the affairs of the other man and how he is surviving."

Iwobo wondered if Atibi was amongst the elders who gave the order. Obeli didn't know who to support in his mind, should he support the Elders for holding up the traditions and custom or was it possible that maybe the custom had gone too far this time around. Ekugo spoke like a man who had been more than hurt.

"Those men I tell you, they shall all see horrible deaths.

"Our father, don't speak like that." Dinti admonished.

"My dear do not support them in this matter." Ekugo said.

"I'm not supporting anyone." Dinti said.

"So you are saying I'm wrong?" Ekugo interrogated.

"That is not what I meant."

"But you said you are not supporting anyone?" Ekugo asked Dinti.

"Our father I'm not supporting the elders that is what I mean, you are my husband so I support you."

"So you are supporting me because I'm your husband?" Obeli wondered why Ekugo was taking it out on his wife at this juncture. Iwobo looked forward but kept his hearing behind, Nne and her mother were holding each other still uncomfortable with the new acquaintance. Obeli played on as the interested listener of Ekugo's ordeal.

"Listen my dear" Ekugo continued with Dinti who was now silent not even answering his last question. "You can't support me because I'm your husband, but because I'm the one with reason here. I'm the one the gods should hear, because I have not acquired wealth that is why I have been mocked." He was walking side by side with Obeli now, they had passed the narrow path and entered a wider path, but up ahead they would have to split and walk in single file again as the path became narrow once again.

"You must see beyond this, they didn't come up with the option to banish us, because my son had a swim in the sacred river, but because we are poor, no one to fight for us. My son." He called to Obeli "What is that your name again?"

"Obeli sir," Nne felt a wave of discomfort, with Obeli giving away his name they must remain covert she reasoned. To Obeli the man seemed harmless.

"I am leaving Fujiri to Obikiti to make a fresh start, it is not too late for me. My children will be respected more than anything. I will give them the good life they deserve." Ekugo shook his head in disbelief "Imagine Idiri calling me, a spoilt child, Idiri that I saw being fed as a child can now talk to me calling me a spoilt child because he has been titled. And as a titled man now, he expects me to bow to him." Ekugo had started speaking to no one in particular, but was sure his words were reaching the whole group. Iwobo heard a noise ahead but couldn't see anyone, he slowed his steps to listen more intently placing his hand on the handle of his sword. Surely they wouldn't be foes. Ekugo and Obeli had not noticed as Ekugo chatted away. Nne had noticed together with her mother, both clung to each other more closely now. The path they were on now was narrow and bent to the left, with that Iwobo couldn't see anyone approaching. Ekugo continued with his criticism of those he perceived had done him wrong. Apparently almost all the wealthy people in Fujiri had wronged him one way or the other. The worst criticism went to Ikife, the man he claimed to have laboured for all his life, working on his farm like a slave, so that he would pay him back with yam seeds so he could start his own farm. Indeed Ikife had also promised him a farmland but quickly turned against him when the elders threatened to banish him and his family all of a sudden he discovered how unfit and unhelpful Ekugo had been. They walked slowing down, unknowingly Iwobo was still with rapt attention when Ekugo asked Iwobo what the matter was he shook his head to signify nothing.

"Just heard voices that is all." Iwobo said.

"Don't be scared nothing will happen if anything we are still in Fujiri and nothing can happen, just walk on my brother."

Iwobo heeded his words and increased his pace.

CHAPTER 37

The Herbalist had given it much thought since leaving the deserted Okongi's compound, it had to be the right thing that he was doing, though he might not be rich as some of his contemporaries but surely there were some he was better off than. And now it was important that he visited Ekidu. Though his mother had worried about his relationship with Ekidu still he didn't see any problem with it. Ekidu had not been married before and probably never will, he was well advanced in age now. Old enough to be the Herbalist's father or even grandfather but still their relationship had blossomed. Ekidu was regarded in Mkpunki as the strange one. But still was one of the greatest musicians in Mkpunki. Not only did Ekidu not marry he had also decided to live alone both in compound and environment, one would have to pass through so many grass covered areas and hope not to be attacked by a wild animal, then march into an area with tall trees. You might as well be in the forest. The Herbalist had asked him several times about his choice of abode and he simply said "What good can living with other men bring but strive and hatred, unhealthy competition, envy and jealousy, it is better you stayed alone with no one to disturb you then you will know you have your peace."

Many still wondered what sort of relationship he had with Ekidu especially his mother, when they saw them together in the village square on those rare occasions that Ekidu came out to perform or when they saw him coming out or entering the path that led to his abode. They would never understand that Ekidu had a rare intelligence that he found wanting in so many men. Ekidu saw things differently from the way other men saw things, maybe that would account for his strange way of life and why he had decided not to follow the path that every man followed. Instead doing things that others couldn't imagine doing. Right from when he was a boy Ekidu had given him knowledge in ways he couldn't imagine and made it impossible for him to pay back. Other men marry many wives to have children so that they could look after them when they were not able to do so but not Ekidu he seemed to have it the other way.

"No man is obligated to have children," he had said. He lived alone, and only lately did he acquire a slave to help out, only reluctantly did he agree, when he saw that death was not coming and he couldn't even fetch water for himself, of course it was his siblings that prevailed on that matter. People would love to learn music from him, because of the place he was staying and the distance they backed out. Only the strong willed ones still made it. Ekidu was not what he used to be as a result of age, he still tried to do some things for himself a remarkable feat for a man his age, showing amazing strength. The Herbalist made it to Ekidu's hut grateful he was around, despite his age he still walked into the forest, disappearing only to reappear after a considerable time claiming to have gone to refresh. The Herbalist saw Ekidu sitting in front of his hut, when Ekidu saw him his face broadened with smile and wrinkles formed perfect lines on his face. His teeth were all brown now, the Herbalist was surprised to see none had fallen, his hairs were almost all gone, and they were all white those that remained, you could see his scalp. Ekidu's smile pleased the Herbalist, they had come far, both of them, sharing stories and finding solace in one another's company, their friendship had blossomed though the Herbalist had tried sometimes to call him Papa Ekidu. He would always denounce it encouraging him to call him Ekidu. Saying they were friends and making sure to let the Herbalist know that he didn't find the custom of respect to elders in any way enticing. His body was looking frail but it didn't show in Ekidu's posture.

"The greatest Herbalist in Mkpunki." Ekidu said. As the Herbalist approached with him now also smiling "Ekidu the Great" he called back.

"It has been a while, thank the gods you still remember me." Ekidu said.

"Can I ever forget about you, if not for anything at least I can hear your music." The Herbalist said.

Ekidu laughed, he liked it when people talked about his art and he knew they were not faking especially the Herbalist.

"Well I'm glad you still like my music and you know anytime you come and ask me to play you something I never refuse. You are welcome. Yatibi bring a seat for our visitor." Ekidu said.

"Who is Yatibi?" The Herbalist asked.

"My slave."

"I thought your slave's name is Chintuki."

"Yes and this is his wife, he is now married."

"No kidding, that is very nice." The Herbalist said wide eyed.

"My dear it is not."

"Is it because the thing you loathe so much is happening without your control over it?" The Herbalist asked.

"I guess you can say that, after so many market days living alone, now that I am closer to the grave, men that I have avoided almost all my life get to live with me."

"Indeed I can guess."

"My dear you must not get me wrong I don't hate humans, I never did, people say I stay alone because I hate people. It is not true, if anything I love people more than they know, the only thing is, I want peace. Yatibi here and her husband, I have told them and they are trying to live as if I don't exist and I the same, and with that we get along fine, having few intercourse, I'm an old man, soon I will join my ancestors, I have given the world all that I wanted to give, my music will speak for me even if our future generation will not remember me, the earth will remember me." Ekidu said.

"Great Ekidu!" The Herbalist hailed, "You know there is no way they will remember us it will just be like we never existed, all we can do is watch them from afar."

"You are correct my dear, age doesn't let me do a lot of things now, so it is also important that they stay here with me."

Yatibi brought the seat which the Herbalist sat on close to his friend Ekidu. Who brought out his snuff container and took a sniff before putting it back. "Yatibi" he called again "Bring kola for our visitor he is a special friend. I would have gone to bring it myself but it is better she does, I have not had a visitor in a long while, I'm very excited, before the kola comes you must listen to my new song I'm planning to teach it to the children that visit me, sometime."

"Children visit you?" the Herbalist asked sounding surprised.

"Yes, they do. You sound surprised?"

"Ekidu coming here is not easy, I'm just surprised they have the courage to make the journey."

"So you are still scared of that path even up till now?" Ekidu asked as he laughed and shook his head.

"Yes I am, I am surprised with what you have done with the place also." The Herbalist said as he looked around Ekidu's compound, "It looks different, I can barely recognize it." The Herbalist said.

"All you see is Chintuki, he did it all."

"I must say he is very talented" the Herbalist said looking at the beautiful mud walls and flowers.

"Yes he is, I guess he can't wait for me to pass away, whether he will stay here or not I cannot tell, but he is good, he cleared the ground, built a hut for himself and his wife, fenced the place, even built a new barn and so many others."

"You are blessed to have found him."

"I didn't find him my younger brother did, my younger brother always thinks my decisions are wrong and so has decided to act my father."

"Ekidu there is no one who does not think your decisions are wrong." The Herbalist said smiling.

"I know but if I live again I will make the same decisions that I have made in this life, I do not regret anyone."

Yatibi brought the kola and placed it before the herbalist.

"Go into my hut and bring the palm wine."

"No Ekidu I won't be drinking wine this morning." The Herbalist said.

"Nonsense it is fresh Chintuki just tapped it now it is still sweet you will enjoy it." Yatibi went to get the palm wine. "You will enjoy it." Ekidu assured him. While at it Ekidu brought out a drum that had been lying by his left hand side, "I must play you something, it is a song I just heard playing in my head, like I said I plan to teach it to the children."

He started beating the drum to a sweet melody, Ekidu's fingers were as slender as a woman's fingers and he gracefully played the drum, singing along.

There is a time in every man's life
Ndo ndo dim dim da da
When he must give account of his affairs
Ndo ndo dim dim da da.
The gods will ask,
Ndo ndo, dim dim da da,
Man what have you done with your days?
Ndo ndo dim dim da da
And man will answer
Ndo ndo dim dim da da
I've been fighting battles with the vicissitudes of life
Ndo ndo dim dim da da
And so I didn't have time to do anything else
Ndo ndo dim dim da da
The gods will ask man
Ndo ndo dim dim da da
Did you win the fight?
Ndo ndo dim da da
Death took me away before the fight ended
Ndo ndo dim dim da da
Ndo ndo dim dim da da
Ndo ndo dim dim da da

This time the Herbalist was nodding to the rhythm.
"Well that is the song." Ekidu said while still playing the drum and singing Ndo ndo dim dim da da.
"It is a good song just like all your songs."
"So should I teach it to the children?" Ekidu asked.
"Surely, it is a good song they will love it." The Herbalist said.

"Very well then I will go on to compose another but you must come back to hear that one it is not ready yet." Yatibi brought the palm wine and drinking horns and they proceeded to pour and drink, true to his word it was fresh and sweet.

"Ekidu I never knew you could play the drum so sweetly, I thought it was only the flute."

"I'm a musician I know how to play all musical instruments." Ekidu said.

"There are so many facets to you at your age you still are fresh just like this palm wine." The Herbalist said and both gave out a hearty laughter.

"What goes into us like this wine is a good thing, so is music. Like I told you I don't regret any of the decisions I have taken, and another one is to make sure only good things go into me, so that when I come back I will come back good, and it is also important so that you don't give out bad things. If you are a person who gives out bad things, it simply means you have allowed bad things go into you, it goes to all areas of life, the most important is that you should be careful to give out good things because there are already enough bad things giving themselves out freely to people, so you shouldn't add to it but be the rare light that they see in a world full of evil. Then from you like a firefly light is coming out. If good things are coming out of you it would certainly go a long way. These children that come to me, I always hope they learn all they can before I meet my ancestors. I am desperate to give out everything before I go."

The Herbalist nodded at the words and drank his palm wine while taking occasional bites at his kola. Not long after Yatibi brought roasted meat.

"My husband caught this yesterday." She said. She dropped the meat before them, greeted and left. The

Herbalist took a bite of the meat and immediately his taste buds were hit with a savouring flavour he took more bites and completely enjoyed it. "Ekidu you should join me this taste good."

"I think you should enjoy it all, I eat that almost every day. Chintuki is a great hunter, he has a lot of traps scattered everywhere and we get to eat different kinds different days."

"And I bet you are enjoying their company?" the Herbalist asked.

"My life is what it has been nothing changed, every day we wake up, look at the day, plan its affairs and hope everything we do makes it possible for our lives to be less painful. For me I know that there is no joy here. Everything we do, we do it so that we will find joy and satisfaction. There will always be a mystery. Do you hear?" the Herbalist nodded. "Things will always be mysterious. There is something always not known and there would never be an answer for it until the gods explain. As for me, whether I enjoy their company or whether you perceive that I am now living a richer life because I have people with me, all I can say is that I never had the answer and I was and will never have lived a perfect life, my choices are not the best neither are yours, but we must live on in the mystery called life. No one's life is perfect and no man has all the answers that is why we look up to the gods for answers to things we don't understand because we believe they predate us and will outlive us. But then again I'm a content man, I was when I was alone and I am now that they are with me, there are no hard rules about life, because none can be perfect. No one knows it all. When people see me they think I must be strange for living this way, well I think they are strange for living the way they do too."

The Herbalist understood what he meant sometimes he feels like that too with people. "You know saying that, I was going to tell you I'm thinking of getting married." Ekidu's face beamed with smile turning to the left he looked at the Herbalist who sat with his horn of palm wine in his hands.

"The great eagle!" Ekidu said amongst the smile, "And who is the lucky girl?"

"Guess." The Herbalist said.

"Hmmm this would be tough, you are one of the most handsome and sought after in Mkpunki."

The Herbalist gave out a laughter when Ekidu said that, "I don't think so but then we will allow it."

"Oh please I know who it is, it is the mysterious woman in your compound." Ekidu said.

"What!!" The Herbalist screamed "Why would you think that and who told you about her?"

"Oh so it is her?"

"No it is not, does everyone in this village know about her?"

"Mkpunki is a small place. And she is the only one I can think of, we have known each other for a long time and I should provide a better guess but that is all I know, I'm sorry."

"Ekidu you amaze me. It is Irima, Mama..." before the Herbalist could complete the words Ekidu cut in with pleasure in his voice now it was also his turn to scream.

"Adubi's last daughter, ah pardon me I should have thought of it." Ekidu now laughed. "Both of you used to dance around as children holding hands. Do you remember? Wow, this is really good, this is really really good, I should have known." Slapping his knee he gently placed his left hand on the Herbalist's right shoulder. "You are doing the right thing. I'm happy for you."

"Yes, thank you very much." The Herbalist said.

"Both of you used to play around the whole village as children, hah! How things turn out, I'm not surprised, I should have known she would be the one you would choose, hmm." Ekidu was still smiling, he nodded. "You have been a good man Herbalist keep being a good man, no matter what happens, give out good. As you marry give out good, bad times will come but still give out good, when the good come enjoy it and still give out good, there are no rules to follow to find perfection and happiness. But in it all just keep giving out good, it is better and I want to believe she was thrilled when you told her about your intentions?"

"Actually I have not it is her mother that I plan to meet, I believe when I meet her today, telling her my intentions, she will tell her and in turn get back to me that is what is on ground for now."

"It is good, it is as good as done." Ekidu started playing the drum and shortly followed it up with singing.

"Have you seen the one I see and my heart beats faster
na na na na hey hey na na na hey.
Have you seen the one I think about and I lose appetite
na na na na hey hey na na na na hey.
Have you seen the one I think about all day and cannot get enough of
na na na na hey hey na na na na hey
my good mother says such a one will bring happiness,
na na na na hey hey na na na na hey.
I won't let my special one go
na na na na hey hey na na na na ye
my special one stay with me under the great mango tree
we will eat its sweet fruit na na na na hey hey na na na

na hey,
I have found my special one life is no longer bitter na na na na hey hey na na na na hey
my special one our days shall be filled with laughter na na na na hey hey na na na na hey, na na na na hey hey na na na na hey,

the Herbalist smiled and swayed with the beats of the drum and the melodious song. When Ekidu finished he said "You have found the special one."

"I hope so."

"Indeed you have, now everything will be pleasant because you have a feeling that makes everything look alright, makes you forget about bad things" "How would you know?" the Herbalist asked.

Ekidu gave out a hearty laughter "Trust me I know, I know all about it.

"Ekidu is there anything you are hiding from me how do you know?"

"I just know just take it like that and leave it at that." Ekidu said. The Herbalist took the last piece of the roasted meat and threw it into his mouth, drenched his drinking horn, leaving only one kolanut remaining.

"I must take my leave" he said as he roused himself up. "I can see you are in perfect health, I shall visit soon again and I'm glad you have people taking care of you, it is a good thing."

"Do you know what I will do from now on?" Ekidu asked.

"No."

"Compose songs for your marriage. It shall be a great feast I hope?"

"Let us look and see what happens if it is going to be a feast I don't know yet." The Herbalist said.

Ekidu stood up, agile for a man his age in the Herbalist estimate, he approached the Herbalist and hugged him. "You are a true friend," he whispered in his ears "And I cherish today, thank you very much." Releasing the Herbalist. "I would also like it if you visit more often so that we can talk about many things, and I must say, I pray you don't find me unappreciative I'm happy you came but next time let it be longer please I beg you."

"I'm glad you feel so, next time it would be longer I promise, thank you for your hospitality." The Herbalist said.

Ekidu hugged him again, "I will have Chintuki bring you more roasted bush meat."

"Ah that would be great." The Herbalist said as he walked away.

"And fresh palm wine." Ekidu added.

"That would be good also." The Herbalist said now from a distance. He turned and looked at his friend from a distance now. Waved at him saw a stick on the ground picked it up and turned to his right, from there it would be the woods and the grassland. Soon it would be noon and he had one more place to go and get home to meet the people waiting for him. He hoped he had timed it well, Mama Adubi should be back from the meeting by now so should his mother. He hoped the information he had gotten was right because he knew that the women's meeting took almost all day but he had heard this would be a short one. He felt glad he had spoken to Ekidu about it. And he had given him the assurance that he needed, though he knew he was doing the right thing. As he walked along the woods he humed Ekidu's song. Nda nda dim dim da da. Soon he was out of the woods and unto the part of the journey he hated, the grassland area. He walked as fast as he could in this part, still humming the songs he had heard, he walked a while and soon was out of the area without any problem even though he had never had any problem since he started visiting his friend Ekidu. He quickly went on to Mama Adubi's. She must be expecting him, a woman called him from behind he turned to see a chubby woman with a cheerful face walking towards him carrying a basket on her head. He had not seen her when he came unto the path or maybe he didn't look well in her direction, he wondered if she was greeting but then she gave him a sign to wait, meaning she wanted to talk. He patiently waited as the woman hastened her steps, she came to him and greeted more properly.

"You don't know me." She said, "But my brother was once sick and you visited, just wanted to thank you because he is well now."

"That is good to know." The Herbalist said.

"Are you going home?" she asked.

"No I'm going to meet someone. I have something important that I want to do."

She brought down the basket and from it the Herbalist could see, avocado pear and coconut that was peeled, "Please I want you to have this." She said taking out the pear and coconut from her basket, "Please I wish I can do more."

"You don't have to give me anything."

"Please don't reject it, please I beg you."

Seeing her sincerity the Herbalist took the gift and thanked her she seemed glad as she lifted the basket, placed it on her head, greeted and went the opposite direction. While the Herbalist pleased, continued his journey to Mama Adubi's compound.

CHAPTER 38

Adanna sat on her bed, for a while she would focus on her knees, exercise them while still contemplating a way to approach Tiperi. If anything she felt he was comfortable staying with her, what she didn't understand was why he was acting scared and not speaking to anyone, for a boy his age he should be cheerful. But he was not, looking and acting so timid. Adanna looked at him she had given up trying to speak to him a long time ago. They both sat speechless Adanna thought of telling him stories or singing to him but that also would be a waste of time besides she couldn't even remember the stories or children songs that well. She had asked him to go outside and play with other children in the compound and the plea fell on deaf ears. The way things were they would both stay together for a long time without making any progress. Nnadi came in to check on him and Adanna noticed him make an attempt to get closer to her on the bamboo bed. As if he was scared Nnadi would take him away. Nnadi too noticed.

"Don't worry I'm not taking you away." She said. And the boy made a face as if he was going to cry.

Nnadi was only surprised, "I will leave." She said and walked away. Tiperi after a long while began to doze off while still sitting down, he would doze his head would sway, when he would almost fall, he would regain consciousness only to repeat the pattern. Adanna watched him without saying a word, until now her words had not been having any meanings to him. She watched him trying to sleep while sitting down with his back not resting on anything. He continued to doze, Adanna considered her options calling Nnadi, would rattle him, and she couldn't move freely with her knees, still making every movement ached her knees, if not she would lay him on the bed herself. She looked at the poor boy and decided to make the move, he was sitting on her bed on her feet area, she decided to help. With her hands she tucked her two legs, picking them and raising her knees, this time unknowingly she raised it higher and immediately it sent a powerful shot of pain which rippled through her body, firing its way to her brain. She winced in pain. The pain subsided, it had moved like a wave through her body. With determination she placed the legs on the ground, moved closer to him and gently holding him she laid him on her bed, and moved him inwards towards the wall. He didn't fuss, but laid quietly and Adanna watched him sleep off peacefully. No one knew his story but surely there would be time to understand him later. With her legs on the ground she could feel the cold earth, in her father's compound they had mats on the ground in their huts, well weaved mats. But then again she was grateful she could feel with her legs, before now they had been numb, but now that she could feel with them it was a good thing indeed. The activity in the compound had gone down considerably; she could hear chatters probably the people waiting for the Herbalist. She could see herself outside doing the things she loved very soon.

*****

The Herbalist had gone to Mama Adubi's compound and everything went well more than he anticipated. He walked into the compound only to see people waiting for him, he expected it. He quickly went to them and exchanged greetings, went to Adanna greeted her and checked on her knees.

"How do you feel with them?" he asked with care in his voice.

"The ground is cold, despite the sun."

"Ah, that is good very good, let me meet these patients. Is that him?" he asked pointing to Tiperi "Yes, so you don't know your cousin."

He laughed, "I know, my bad, I've actually never met him."

"Well you will, when he wakes up." Adanna said.

"Sure let me get Nnadi to carry him, he would be staying with her." The Herbalist said.

"No it is okay let him stay here besides I really think he wants to stay, so no need disturbing him."

"Okay if you say so."

"Hope he is not discomforting you."

"No he is not."

"Right let me meet these people I well be back." Adanna sat smiling to herself everything was beginning to make some sense now, soon very soon she would start walking, and the prospect of it elevated her disposition from gloomy to hopeful. Sitting, she applied pressure on her legs, and the knees tingled, soon she would walk, by tomorrow she would try to stand. For now she would let it heal slowly. The Herbalist was attending to the people who came for herbs when his mother walked in with a somewhat nonchalant, frowning face she went straight into her hut. The Herbalist thought of going to meet her, but then she always came back from women meeting with a frowned face and with time get over it, she would get over this one. Etiti must have taken a detour before coming home, she usually did. Mama Adubi was home a while ago and he met her before coming back. He attended to the man who had a shoulder problem, as a bone setter he was able to assure the man he didn't have much problem as his issue could easily be handled. Sitting before the Herbalist were almost eight people with different issues, and he had to attend to them all, and doing so would take a considerable time of the day. Attending to them all he was now with the last person, who had a muscle pull. Once he was done attending to people, the person made his payment and took off, some promised to pay on another day. It was almost evening, the sun was going down and he could now rest, he had treated the first batch and now he was with the last person he had massaged her with hot water, applied the local palm and assured her it would get better. She had gotten the muscle pull while farming. Pleased after attending to her, she left and he was left alone. He noticed his mother had not come out since she came back not even to ask him or his patients how they were doing. Usually when she was in the compound, she came around to greet. He would ask her why she was always so downtrodden whenever she came back from women's meeting and she wouldn't give him any reasonable reply. Getting all his equipment into his hut, he washed his hands and remembered he had not eaten all day except the kola at Ekidu's. That would have to wait, he went to his mother's hut and found her lying down facing up and gazing at the thatched roof. If anything her demeanour showed she wasn't happy and had a lot on her mind.

"Don't you think you should stop going to this women's meeting since it makes you so unhappy?" he said as he sat on the bed with her.

Etiti roused herself and sat up with a hiss. "You won't understand those women will make you feel you are worthless because you don't have what they have."

"What exactly do they have that you don't?"

"You won't understand my son." Etiti said and heaved.

"Then make me to understand."

"I can't stop attending the meeting then they will fine me."

"We will pay the fines then, is it not better you sacrifice money or wealth or any worldly possession for peace of mind, think about it, I don't want to see you in such condition, it hurts me, as your son I want to make sure you are always happy, it is my duty to make sure that happens."

"You are doing great at it, don't bother yourself with women matters."

"So how was the meeting?"

"It went well."

"Good then I went to your friend's place and everywhere was deserted. What happened there? Hope all is well with them?"

"Which of my friends?"

"Okongi."

"Hey!" Etiti exclaimed "You haven't heard."

"Heard what?"

"Things happen in this village and pass you."

"Nobody has told me anything."

"An abomination occurred there, things nobody should talk about."

"What happened, because even a lady who saw me come out of the compound was looking at me in a strange way."

"Where will I start, Okongi's husband's name is Afomtu and in my reasoning Afomtu is a cruel man. Okongi is always telling me of how he maltreats her, always beating her. She is the fourth wife not only her but other wives. Afomtu rules his house with a heavy hand infact his first wife has a scar at the back of her neck. He is always beating and fighting, his wickedness to his household is unparalleled."

"I never heard of it, so what happened his wives decided to all run away or what?" the Herbalist asked.

"Recently he was beating his first wife, they all gathered and beat him up." Etiti said.

"They beat up their husband?" the Herbalist asked.

"Yes" Etiti said.

"Where are the wives?"

"They finally did what they should have done a long time ago, they have gone home leaving his compound for him, I even heard after beating him they locked him in the barn."

The Herbalist shook his head, sat for a while as if thinking and then spoke.

"There is something else I want to discuss with you." The Herbalist said.

"Well what is it?"

"I've been wanting to make a decision and today after visiting Ekidu."

"Oh! Ekidu, you and that man again." Etiti said almost shouting and feigning tears.

"Calm down I know you don't like him."

"I just don't want you to end up like him, besides you two shouldn't be friends. He is almost three times your age, how many people do you see visiting him?"

"Mama it is okay, there are things you won't understand."

"As far as it is Ekidu I don't want to understand, they say we become like those we are associated with. I don't want you becoming like him." Etiti said.

"Very well noted then, the thing is I have decided to get married." The Herbalist said.

The word "get married" coming from her son went into her hears, reaching her inside spurred every organ into life before getting to her brain and sparking it, for how long she had waited to hear those words. Her discussions with him about marriage had yielded no result till she made peace with her god and gave it up. Etiti came down from the bed, savouring every moment, now looking into her son's eyes. "What did you say? Marriage?" she asked rhetorically. Then she stood up and began to dance in the hut, as she danced she sang, the Herbalist sat looking at her. She would dance and thank the gods. "So this good thing will happen to me, and my fellow women won't mock me any more in women's meeting." She said. Sang again and danced.

"Hey!" She exhaled "I knew you would go for her." She said laughing, obviously in celebratory mood. The Herbalist was certain he was lost, 'who could have told her so quickly,' he didn't see her go out or anyone come to visit her while he attended to his patients. "Go for who Mama?"

Etiti covered her mouth with her right palm, then she removed it, "My dear who are you talking about."

"But who did you think it was?" the Herbalist asked.

"Just tell me." Etiti said.

"It's Irima." The Herbalist said.

"But I thought…" Etiti was surprised.

"Thought what Mama? You better tell me what you have in mind."

"It doesn't matter now." Etiti said, Etiti too had thought it was Adanna. "Irima Mama Adubi's last born." She said in whisper. "We shall start preparations immediately." Etiti said, laughing she ran out of the hut and then the compound. She told no one where she was going. The Herbalist made his way back to his hut, in a while he would go to check on Adanna he had not seen her all afternoon.

CHAPTER 39

Adanna was now making progress with Tiperi. When he woke up the first sight he beheld was the face of Adanna. And Adanna was shocked to hear him greet. Nnadi came in and he returned to his former self, when Nnadi brought their afternoon food, for the first time in a very long while Adanna invited someone to come eat with her. She invited him to come eat with her and he agreed. Now answering all her question howbeit with a shake of head or a nod. It was good, he was warming up to her. When they were both settled, the Herbalist came in, handing over her medications, he proceeded to check her knees.

"I'm getting better" Adanna said.

Looking at Tiperi now "Boy how are you?" the Herbalist asked. He got no response.

"Is he alright?" the Herbalist asked looking at Adanna.

"I guess he is." Adanna answered.

"Boy what is your name?" the Herbalist asked to spur Tiperi. No response. The Herbalist proceeded to try touching him only for him to change his facial expression from a blank stare to tearful eyes. "Okay don't cry, don't cry." The Herbalist said, "at his age he is not supposed to be crying."

"Don't worry he was like that with me I guess he would come around." Adanna said.

"All is well," the Herbalist said, "Children you can never understand them, but I don't know, children love me."

"Oh! Really?" Adanna said with a smile temporarily forgetting her own history with children, children in Akom run away when they see her. Only the ignorant ones came closer to her. Nnadi came in and informed the Herbalist he had visitors, the evening batch of patients.

"I will be with them in a moment" he said, "I have to go, after meeting the visitors, I will start preparing the herbs for tomorrow."

"Okay no problem at least now I have company." Adanna said.

"Who? Him?" the Herbalist exclaimed pointing at Tiperi. "Boy you have to be a man, do you hear me, hope it is not shyness that you are displaying maybe it is something else." The Herbalist said, stood up and left. At the exit, "I will see you soon," he said.

"Okay" Adanna said, Adanna with Tiperi again, alone, she thought of telling him stories again or singing to him, that was what was expected, when she eavesdropped that was what she usually heard adults discussing with children, but in her case she didn't know any. She had never bothered to learn, of course she never knew there would be a time when life would require her to even think about it but here she was. Tiperi looked at her as she laboured to find words to say, for now she had exhausted all the questions she had to ask. Tiperi's disposition had returned to being a part lively and a part shy. After a while Adanna heard. "Ma'am let me tell you a story." Adanna's eyes widened at the words. A story! this ought to be nice. Adanna wanted to add 'it is as if you read my mind' but decided against it. The words would be lost on him.

"So what is the story tell me."

The somewhat shy but now coming to life Tiperi mused then continued speaking, "It is a story my sister used to tell me."

'Typical, it has to be sister, sisters were the ones who told stories only few fathers did.' Adanna thought. She couldn't remember the stories her mother told her when she was little, before here untimely death, just when she was about to become a woman, her mother was taken from her. Cautiously happy that Tiperi was warming up to her. "This is the story," Tiperi said clapping his hands together, became quiet and then started, "once upon a time." Adanna with smiles "Time, time." Tiperi proceeded to tell his story, at the end. "Ma'am what did you learn?" he asked.

"What I learnt?" Adanna asked, teasing him, "I learnt a lot if anything I learnt we should be courageous." They both giggled.

"Ma'am will you tell me a story?" The question caught Adanna off guard. She had to make a promise that was a lie, "I will but not now." She said, thinking she had survived a terrible point in her relationship with Tiperi the young boy made another startling demand.

"Ma'am can I call you mother?"

Adanna's lower abdomen tightened, as her heart pounded, with sweats softening her palms, for some reason she didn't comprehend the question but she was certain she heard the question, in her mind she had her own questions for him, like "Why would you want to do that," and the serious one "What made you think of such a thing" and so many others.

With quivering lips, "Sure you can" she said, her heart still rapidly beating, hearing the assurance, Tiperi now wore a smile and re-adjusted himself on the bed. Adanna could tell he felt comfortable, but then what else. They had stayed on the same bed, and eaten from the same plate in the afternoon, surely the young man was feeling welcome.

*****

The Herbalist as he attended to people, looked around for any sign of his mother. Ever since their discussion he had not seen her. What had she gone to do, announce the pending marriage to the entire village? He needn't worry because his mother would not do anything to hurt him, but then again she was a woman and could do the unthinkable. He attended to a woman whose newborn baby had a separated suture, the Herbalist, received a lot of this kind of case, a newborn baby with such a problem, but no need to worry. He took the baby and examined him some more. She would have to come back in the morning so he could mix the herb to be placed on the spot, with that he was certain he had done all he was supposed to do, the woman turned and left.

CHAPTER 40

Iwobo's apprehension did not yield any cause for harm. It was just another group of travellers who didn't wish to make acquaintance like Ekugo and his family. Iwobo relieved, hoped for nothing to cause harm to any of them. The path was a treacherous one, they passed the path with tall grasses and all gave out a sigh of relief even Ekugo. Who if he were to be kidnapped or an attempt of kidnap made against him his assailants would find it an enormous task. Such a task would require five men of Iwobo and Obeli's size, once again they moved into the woods and appreciated the tall trees with its canopy. The air was cool, and they could hear the distinct sounds of animals, mostly birds, some they could tell what sort of animal it was, others they couldn't they were still on guard, as far as you are in the open country you are not safe. After the woods they would enter Obikiti. They had walked the considerable part of the day, till it got to the cool of the evening and Iwobo brought the idea they should rest. It was a good idea, their feet were tired, and they badly needed refreshment. They had been walking since morning, they chose a spot under a large Oak tree, sun couldn't reach them, but evidence of its rays were showing on the ground. As its lights scattered throughout the woods, piercing through where the tree leaves allowed. The chilling air with its scent of fresh life gave a good reason to rest. Those with load on their heads brought down their loads and then brought out their foods. Nne and her mother brought out, their roasted plantain, and roasted bush meat. It was almost what they all had, they would have to eat it without palm oil sauce. Ekugo seemed more prepared with his family, his wife brought out the local plate which was in the basket her daughter was carrying. In it was coco yam with sauce, he also had roasted meat, him and his family proceeded to eat, Ekugo noticed that his companions were eating without oil sauce.

"Please you all should come and join me." He pleaded.

"Thank you we have ours." Iwobo said.

"I know but you all are eating without sauce, please come and join me, I insist my wife made it, it is delicious."

"We are okay sir, indeed we are." Nne responded "Thank you very much."

Ekugo vehemently refused, "I won't eat then, how do you think it would be that I eat with pleasure, while you gnaw a plantain, please I beg you all, come and join me it will be enough for us all." Obirika remained silent. "Please I beg you people come and join me, I beg you." Obeli feeling no need to protest any longer. Dipped his plantain into the local plate and took a huge bite, Iwobo looked at him with amazement.

"Thank you my brother." Ekugo said.

Seeing it would be rude to reject Iwobo joined. The women of course most times had to follow the men. They all ate sauce from the same plate, as they ate none of them felt relaxed for Nne and Obirika it was double jeopardy not only were they on a run from known and unknown foes they were also eating from a stranger's plate. Their mind was at war with the decisions they were making, but their tongue was sending a different message, the sauce was delicious. Nne was pleased with the unity Ekugo had with his family. Seeing it her mind went back to her father. Her father had once told her, she was the best thing to happen to him, as a kid she used to eat with him. When he went out she would wait for him to return just so they could eat together. He was the most peace loving man she had ever met. Each person took the sauce and waited for the next person, even Ekugo himself. Most men would choose to eat alone as a mark of respect for the man who was the head of the family, but not for Ekugo from what Nne observed Ekugo have been eating together with his family for a long time. Just like she used to do with her father even now she was grown. She wondered if Ekugo played with his children, her mind went back to when her father would come back from the farm bringing her a lot of fruits. She remembered him coming back on a certain day, he had spent most of the day in the farm, when he arrived at the compound she had been sitting with her mother, removing corn grains. She had been expecting him knowing fully well he would bring home something nice for her, sometimes he brought cloth. As a kid there was never a day her father came back without bringing back something.

"Just to let you know I'm always thinking of you," he would say to her.

On this day, she saw her father and ran to him, running to embrace his outstretched arm, she fell and bruised her elbow. Before she could look up with tearful eyes, her father was already running to her, he picked her up sang all the songs he knew how to sing, treated her wound, he had petted her. For a whole long week, he always carried her, rocking her sideways, then he would sing to her. He had a beautiful voice and used it to sing only for her. Nne didn't notice it but she had become distant, and oblivious of what was happening around her. Iwobo had seen a drop of tears from her left eye, Obeli then saw it, both were well enthused she was eating from the same plate with them but now weary. Then Ekugo saw it, Obirika had not seen it she was sitting side by side with her.

"Nne are you Okay?" Obeli asked.
Realizing herself, she quickly dabbed the tear with her hand. Not wanting to make a spectacle, she excused herself dropped the remainder of her plantain quickly. As she went out, she let out a soft wheeze, then the tears flowed. She was missing her father and yet again couldn't believe he was gone. Obirika was right behind her. She was a mother she couldn't read her mind but she could tell her daughter was going through a lot. Obirika hugging her let out her own tears and cried.
"Nne what is it?" she asked with tearful eyes. Both women cried alone away from the presence of the others. Iwobo and Obeli stood up to go and check on them, but Ekugo asked them not to, assuring them they would be back. Both women knew there wouldn't be a good place to cry but for the moment they couldn't hide what they were feeling they both dabbed their eyes.
"Nne it is okay." Obirika said, "What is it?" she asked trying to control her tears.
"Mama don't worry it is Okay." Nne said, both women in each other's arms consoled each other. They had been staying a few feet away from the rest of the group, with trees separating them, they heard footsteps, and calmed themselves. Iwobo and Obeli appeared. "Hope all is well?" Iwobo asked. Both nodded and they all headed back to the group, they passed and Iwobo and Obeli looked at each other as if to say 'do you know what is going on' both shrugged it off and went back only to see Ekugo looking bigger, going back to him as he sat on the ground, under the tree Obeli saw him and felt he looked bigger or maybe it was his eyes deceiving him. They sat down to rest, while those who were still eating concluded their business. Nne sitting back down took her plantain and wrapped it up.

"Dear are you alright?" Ekugo asked with concern in his eyes.

"Yes" she said "Thanks for asking sir."

"Why not finish your plantain."

"No I've had enough, will probably eat later." Nne said. Ekugo's wife seeing everyone was done now packed up, Ekugo's children greeted, thanking everyone. Obeli looking around noticed that everyone now was wearing a smile which made everything sensible. Ekugo proceeded to ask everyone how they were doing. "Very well," each person answered. He really was caring. Soon they resumed their marching.

The women in the group all remained silent as the men chatted away. Ekugo told of a brother who kidnapped his own brother's children and also the wife and sold. As the story lasted Obirika chased away a fly hovering around her.

"I hope you people know we are now in Obikiti." He asked. Obirika and Nne quickly looked around as if to find where such was indicated.

"You can never know it." Ekugo continued. "There is no mark to show the beginning of Obikiti, it is only those who travel much often that can know it." Indeed they had seen no mark, even Iwobo didn't know they were now in Obikiti. They were still in the woods; he would know they were in Obikiti when they reached the path that was well treaded. Ekugo sensing they will wish to know.

"Where Obikiti started in the woods, is" he said pointing. "You see those oak trees there, those two almost like they are one." Everyone turned back now to look for the trees, the trees were almost together as if they have been halved but they shared, it would also seem the same root, when he was certain they had seen the tree.

"That tree marks the beginning of Obikiti." They all walked now, content to have learnt a new thing.

"Obikiti, never knew I would come back to my father's land like this but Fujiri what can I say, it shall be well with all of us" Ekugo said.

"Papa we will be happy here." Ekugo's son spoke for the first time since they met the strangers. It was a huge relief for Obeli who had been looking at him.

"Papa left for me I don't think we should go back." The daughter added. To Obeli all was well then.

"My children this is our new home now, and is going to be for a very long time, let nothing ever trouble you people." Ekugo said. Obeli felt Ekugo's children feel liberated their countenance changed, as their gait changed to lively.

"I must make it this time." Ekugo said.

Obeli in his heart wished him well. Not long after they came upon the path, Iwobo knew. In Obikiti you couldn't march through it without seeing people, the path ran though the village. This was certainly what they did not want, but then they had no options of doing otherwise, they would have to wish the darkness of night to come quick and cover them, this time they had head lamps, Atibi had also given them that. Though they had not discussed it, but surely they would march through the night. In two market days they should be in Akom. They had arrived Obikiti in the cool of the evening, and soon darkness would be upon them.

"My friends we should go right." Ekugo said, as he anticipated Iwobo would pass a path that led to his right. Iwobo halted before he got to the path. "That would lead us into Obikiti" Iwobo said.

"Well yes, please you can't tell me you plan on continuing the journey." Ekugo said "You must rest for the night besides it is dangerous."

"We can't, we must keep moving, we can feel our land from here." Iwobo said.

"Akom is still two days from here and marching in the night won't make it any faster, if anything you would be weary and worn out to march in the day." Ekugo said he had guessed they were from Akom, nobody told him, Iwobo and co. pretended they didn't hear him. His children now joined. "Please it is dangerous."

Iwobo was still the one speaking for the group. "We will make it, we can't stay here we must move on we plan to take a break then continue in the morning."

"My friends come on" Ekugo said stretching forth his hand, "You can't have an offer to have a good place to stay and then go and stay in the open, in the night there are evil things creeping about even bad spirits move in the night you have got to trust me on this one."

"Sir we appreciate all you have done but we mustn't lay a burden upon you, I believe, I speak the heart of my group we must move on. We can't have a bad thing happen to us now that we are so close to home, thank you for the offer but we must move on."

"We never wish evil on ourselves neither should we even talk about them, but I must warn you the days are evil this is not a time people walk in the night. You must be very careful, even though the place we are going we have not been there for a very long time and don't know the kind of welcome we will receive, but it is still a better choice than walking in the night. So I plead with you one last time come with us."

Obeli feeling the need to speak up now, supported his friend, "Sir we will march on, we appreciate your kind gesture, you are truly a great man but we must move on."

"Hope you have refreshment" Ekugo asked.

"Yes we do." Iwobo said.

"Very well" Ekugo told his wife to bring down the basket on her head which she did, he uncovered it and proceeded to bring out roasted yams, plantains, the sauce, what was remaining, however the oil had coagulated a bit, but it could be warmed easily even by putting a torch under it. He also brought out dried meat, foods that could last a journey, he brought out fruits: Pineapples, oranges and handed them over to Obirika and Nne.

"Please you must take this." He said to her, "It is necessary for the journey."

Ekugo's wife, Dinti lifted the basket and placed it on her head. Ekugo gave them a shake, "I hope we see again someday, if only you had known my place or I yours, then that would have been a possibility but please anytime you come to Obikiti ask for Ekugo Obayi of Obikiti, by then I will be well known and respected."

"Sure will do sir." Obeli responded not bothering to reciprocate by telling their own names. Ekugo couldn't hurt a person unless it was necessary but then again they must be careful on giving out information. Ekugo meant no harm they knew. Nne and Obirika stuffing the gifts into their bags bent their knees and greeted before hugging the wife and children of Ekugo. When they had all greeted each other they resumed the march with Iwobo going straight and Ekugo and his family taking the path to the right. Walking a while both groups turned back to wave with smiles on their faces, then the tall grasses and trees cut out each other's view. Iwobo proceeded feeling a little bit forlorn he had become fond of Ekugo, Obeli too, the group once again, re-assured themselves that they were taking the best decision, they were so close to home that they must be focused. They all checked their lamps everything seemed okay with them.

"Iwobo how long till we leave Obikiti?" Nne asked finding her voice again.

"When the sun is at the highest point tomorrow we should, we will rest a while in the night, like Ekugo said, so we don't become weary, then we continue in the early hours of the morning because after that we will be in Ebemi."

CHAPTER 41

Adanna and Tiperi had been discussing all night the more he spoke the more liberated he became. Adanna wondered what made him mute and shy initially as they chatted away, they even laughed. After they had their evening meal, Tiperi seemed to relax even more.

"Mother," he said to Adanna, the name still gave her a chilling sensation, her spine froze and tingled as the hairs on her body stood. "I don't want to ever go back to my compound. Please don't let them take me back."

She was not in the position to makes promises but she had no options.

"Nobody will take you away, you hear me." Adanna felt at that moment she should re-assure him by at least patting his back, or holding him close to her. She was not used to being nice, so then she would pass, the thought was not a good one.

"Why don't you want to go back?" she asked, as if the question struck a nerve. Tiperi bent his head and spoke despite speaking in low voice Adanna could hear him, they were sitting on the bamboo with their legs on the ground.

"My father doesn't like me," he said, "And he is always beating me and my mother, and I don't know when my sister is coming back. When I grow I will take my mother from him. Please don't let them take me back."

Looking at him closely, she could see scares all over his body, no need to ask him what they were, his father had really been beating him. Those were scars from excessive floggings. Adanna didn't know she had not heard the last. "Mother," he called again "Can we leave here, let us leave."

"Why, where do you want to go?"

"Anywhere that is not here. I don't want to remain here, I want to become big so that I can help my mother, she is always crying, I don't want her to cry again."

"Do not worry, everything will turn out well very soon I can assure you that okay. You have had your bath and you have eaten, soon sleep will come so just relax okay, everything will turn out well."

Tiperi nodded at the words, laid down and waited for sleep, he would be sleeping with Adanna tonight no doubt. Adanna smiled at him, everyone in the compound was preparing for sleep, Adanna could notice the compound get quite in her hut. She heard a knock, it had to be the Herbalist, and sure it was. He came in with the balm and some herbs he gave them to her and she drank, he proceeded to massage her knees, inspecting them, the pain was decreasing, rapidly.

"You know I have to say," he said when he was done massaging the knees and applying the locally made balm, "I like the fact that you smile nowadays it warms my heart, gladdens me in no small measure."

"What do you mean I always smile?" Adanna said trying to sound serious.

The Herbalist gave out a laugh, shook his head "No you don't."

"Well that is your own opinion, I won't argue with you."

"It is really good. What is he doing?" he asked pointing at Tiperi.

"Trying to sleep."

"Here?" The Herbalist exclaimed.

"Why you don't want him to sleep in your hut?"

"No, not that, he shouldn't disturb you." He called out to Nnadi, "Please come and carry him to the visitor's hut he ordered."

Nnadi on her way, Tiperi had heard and started whimpering.

"What are you crying for, the bed doesn't have enough space for both of you." The Herbalist said.

Sensing the need to speak, "Let him be," Adanna urged, "We will manage."

Tiperi was almost crying now and it baffled the Herbalist. "You are crying, okay have it your way."

Nnadi who was almost at the entrance was made to go back.

"So everything is good?" the Herbalist asked.

"Sure, yes." Adanna responded.

Tiperi was sitting up now on the bed, with almost tearful eyes, did nothing but stare at Adanna. The Herbalist wished them goodnight and went to check the compound before going into his hut. His mother was a source of concern now, Etiti was not back yet, he went into his hut. A woman shouldn't be outside her home by this time, he waited in his hut, feeling uneasy he came out only to see Etiti walking into the compound. The moon shone the way, making her visible but not obvious, it had to be her the Herbalist reasoned he approached her as she entered the compound.

"Mama where have you been?" he asked her.

The gay Etiti, laughing now, "To make preparations of course, I went to the women leader's house, then I went to Mama Adubi's place to see our bride, they are preparing her, everything seems okay with them, then I went see your uncles and aunties. I met uncle Ujaki, I didn't meet uncle Akonsi but I left a message. Uncle Madibi will come in the morning he was as thrilled as I was, uncle Okonsi too and aunty Mentu will start telling others, my friend Akutu, will start the things I have told her to. We must hurry, I will meet the others tomorrow. It is not a woman's job, but I have to do it, your father is no more. You have to tell your friends or should I go and tell them. Do you think Ovemti will be around he has to know about it."

"Mama calm down you did all these this night?"

"Yes oh!" the lamp with the Herbalist illuminated Etiti's face. "I have to, in two days' time you should be married. I have told Mama Adubi and they agreed. There is no need to waste time, we must make haste. We will start this night."

The Herbalist shocked, "Start what this night?"

"Preparations, I have already started."

"Mama I'm tired, we are not starting anything this night, I need rest, maybe tomorrow, the marriage is not going to evaporate, it will still hold."

"Okay tomorrow morning then, but visitors should start coming from tomorrow morning, I will tell the village groups tomorrow, everything will go well."

The Herbalist couldn't believe his mother it was as if she was intoxicated.

"My son who and who do you want invite, for me the whole village should come, we can afford it, even your patients, I know you don't tell them but you have no start telling them, we can't waste time should we invite them all."

"Mama we will talk about this in the morning, I need to go and rest, I was worried about you."

"Sorry dear, don't bother yourself just go and rest I will handle everything, Okay. It would be a marriage unheard of before, those that mock me will be ashamed."

Believing he had heard enough, "Mama good night," he

said, with his lamp in his hand, he turned and left for his hut. Etiti followed him and then deviated to the left into Adanna's hut, the light in her hut was still on, she knocked and entered. Tiperi had dozed off, Adanna greeted and Etiti responded.

"I saw your light on and decided to come and see you, hope you are doing well?"

"Yes, I'm getting better. How was your day?"

"Very good, sorry I didn't come to see you in the afternoon, something very important came up." Etiti said sounding almost like a child.

"Really what happened?"

"You have not heard, my son is getting married." The words fired into Adanna, momentarily causing her heart to stop. Reclaiming her consciousness, she could only inhale, as her hands quaked. Etiti had caught the momentary lapse, she thought of telling her and then not telling her, Adanna felt surprised why she had reacted in such a manner. Why should it concern her that he was getting married? She didn't know what she was feeling and why she had reacted in such a manner, she was almost crying but fought it.

"Odabi are you okay?" Etiti asked. They still called her Odabi, in Akuma she was known as Mmerika. Though severally she had thought of telling them her real name seeing how nice they were. They had accepted her and hidden nothing from her. Adanna getting herself back, exhaled deeply, "I'm okay, what a great news, I was just caught unprepared. You can say I was surprised."

"I know" Etiti said, Etiti had been standing, "I was surprised too when he told me." She sat on the bed with her. "Just like you were, it is a news I never thought I would hear, the news shocked me to the core. Odabi you cannot imagine how happy I am, all his life he had never acted like a person who would one day consider getting married. His mates are all married, then you remind him of it, it is either he would change the topic or he would pretend he didn't hear. My ancestors have heard me, I would do all in my power to see him get married as fast as possible."

"Congratulations" Adanna said.

"Thank you very much. Hope you have eaten? I didn't even ask you before rambling on."

"Yes I have and it is a good news not rambling."

Etiti laughed shyly, "Let me go and rest tomorrow will be a busy day, as you already know, we are a people that do nothing else but fish and farm, only a few amongst us decide to farm, so most of us are fishermen. Which means, we are always out on the river. Tomorrow I will leave only to meet the people I want to meet." Etiti stood up. "Why is he here?" she asked pointing to Tiperi who was fast asleep.

"He wants to stay here." Adanna answered.

"He would disturb you." She called Nnadi to take him to the visitor's hut. Nnadi came and carried him to the visitor's hut and he slept through it. Etiti wished her goodnight and went to her hut, after a short while Adanna who was still looking down on the ground wondering why she was feeling so weak and unhappy all of a sudden. She had felt happy at the prospect of walking again, now she felt just sad, why did the news affect her in such a way? Before she could reason it out, she looked up after noticing a form at the entrance, it was Tiperi. He said nothing, he just walked to her bed, laid down and slept off again. The gesture made Adanna giggle, she pushed the unpleasant thought from her heart and in a short while slept off without putting out her oil lamp. The

Herbalist had stayed up a while, he had a lot to do and think about surely marrying Irima was a good thing. He couldn't have made a mistake, he had had a good life up till now and marrying should make it better not worse, then again marriage was a good thing. Since it made his mother this happy, surely it was a good thing everyone made the decision and now he had made the same.

*****

Iwobo led his group through Obikiti with their oil lamps still on, Ekugo and his family after pressuring them to spend the night in Obikiti had long deviated and went their way, they marched steadily. The night was cold, and they were feeling it, they used their extra wrapper to wrap around their body, not even the exercise of walking generated enough heat for their body.

"Iwobo I know you spoke for the group, and you meant well, but now I am feeling we should have accepted Ekugo's offer. Which one is better, staying with a seemingly nice stranger or freezing to death?" Obeli said.

"Why didn't you protest when I was making the decision?" Iwobo answered, feeling the cold himself.

"Are you not 'I know everything' and 'I'm always right'?"

"Since you know that, let us continue the journey then and don't disturb me again."

"Yes master I won't disturb you, just let it be you are doing the right thing, walking through an unknown place in the night."

Nne and Obirika had not said a word, they trudged ahead with sheer determination trying to ignore the natural elements working against them.

"I think we should rest for a while before we move on." Obirika said with a please. The request made an impact on them. She had always been the one requesting that they move on, for her to need rest was a good thing albeit they all needed rest. To be able to make it for the next day's journey by their calculations they should be in the very late part of the night.

"Let us find a good spot then we can't stay on the path like this." Obeli suggested.

"I'm telling you we should really have gone with Ekugo." Obeli said after they had walked a considerable distance looking for a place that could accommodate them off the path.

"You are free to go back," Iwobo responded "Ekugo will still welcome you, in fact he will thank you for the change of heart."

"Keep quiet there, running your mouth that is what you are good at." Obeli said sounding authoritative.

"Instead of being a stumbling block why not be useful and pick woods so we can make fire." Iwobo said pointing to dry logs on the ground.

"Are you commanding me?"

"Not at all master."

"Better."

Nne and her mother who were now standing as both looked around for logs decided to help but was quickly disrupted by Obeli.

"Don't worry we will do the picking, both of you just relax."

"Let us help" Obirika protested.

"Please you don't have to." Iwobo said supporting his friend Obeli. When they had gathered enough logs of wood, they had no option but to use the path. Obeli and Iwobo made the fire, when they were done, they laid their mat they have been carrying for the women, they all sat together not feeling hungry but out of necessity they all ate little from the foods they had. "Iwobo what will you do if a wild pig runs out?" Obeli asked.

"Why? Does it not sleep?" Iwobo said sounding unconcerned and uninterested.

"I'm just asking." Obeli said.

Feeling the need to say something now at least she supposed she would be helping, "For me I would say you people should take a break from chasing animals." Obirika said. And took a bite of her now cold yams.

"Will anything ever make us stop, one day we will make a big catch and you are free to enjoy it with us." Obeli said sounding as if he had ever caught anything before.

"Well till then, but for now, just try and take a day off." Nne added supporting her mother.

What the two women did not know was that Iwobo and Obeli had never caught any animal in their life, they didn't even hunt, they had never hunted before on their own. Whenever Akom went to war they never volunteered to participate even women went to war but both of them would rather stay home, and chat away the time. Iwobo knew the places he knew because he was under the protection of his father and half-brothers, the swords both of them were carrying had never been used for anything combat before. Both of them had depended on their father's wealth so far, doing only farming when coerced to, most youth set trap but then again their traps had never caught anything and they blamed it on bad luck instead of their lack of know how. The good thing about them was that they knew how to tell tales of other men's prowess.

"When will you two get to the point where others will praise you?" someone once asked them.

"Greatness is not meant for everybody only a selected few." Obeli responded with delight, and anyone seeing them would really believe it, they had lived there lives in the shadows expecting others to lead the way while they followed.

"You know we might even catch an antelope." Iwobo continued.

"Please let us go back to Akom then you can hunt whatever you want." Obirika said still trying to find a nicer way to tell them they were punishing themselves in the name of hunting.

"I think I get it Iwobo." Obeli said as if he had a revelation. "You people are scared when we run out that there is no one to protect you, don't worry we will always protect you." Obeli continued almost bragging as he said the word protect. He tapped the handle of his sword that was by his loins, the sword he had never used before. "This is not for play," he said still tapping the sword, he finished eating, being the man he now was, Obeli kept making bold decisions, "I think you two should get a shut eye, we will start marching very early tomorrow morning."

"What about you people?" Nne asked feeling concerned.

"We can't all go to sleep since we are in the open like this, Iwobo and I will keep watch, you two should get some rest." When he said the words, Iwobo went a little distance in the other direction to keep watch, he still maintained his position of leading the way, the point he was, was the direction they would be heading come daylight. Obeli maintained the rear. They stayed in a position where the women would be in sight while they also watched the opposite direction. After they had sat a while Nne approached Obeli.

"You haven't slept?" he asked.

"Not feeling sleepy but my mum is I believe sleeping or at least resting and it is thanks to you two, you both must know I really appreciate. Just wanted you to know, I will go and tell Iwobo the same." She said moving backwards while still facing Obeli she was also playing with her fingers, shyness it must be, as she made an attempt to face the direction she was to face, Obeli called her back. Sensing this was his opportunity possibly the only he might get, surely he was not helping Nne so she could like him, but rather the unexpected had happened. Every time he saw her changes happened within him, and his breath became a bit laboured, it could be nothing else but that he cherished her deeply.

"Nne" he called in a very low voice, almost nervous but he had to say what he wanted to say, cursed be the consequences. "Nne there is something I want to say." Nne who was closer to him now gave an attentive ear, with her attention his breathing became even more laboured. "Nne" calling her for almost the third time. "What I want to say is, I know maybe you will think this is not the right moment, but I don't know if there is ever a right moment."

The more he spoke the more he picked up courage and fluency. "Here is the thing, in your thinking you may consider my family and especially my sister to be the reason why you are having the troubles and hurting you are going through. To that I would say don't impute other people's sins to me. If given the chance I would make everything right and put you back in the situations you wish to be. Which are nothing but good and blissful. I know you are thanking me for assisting you, I can do more. I want to do more Nne." Nne who was standing did nothing but stand rigid. "All I'm asking is you let me do more. I would like to be the one you see as your one true friend and companion, that is all I want to say. Think about it I know it is coming wrongly but please consider it."

Nne had no words to say but nodded, with her voice waving "I will think about it." She said.

Satisfied he had made his point no matter how rough it sounded of course he was not a poet, there were poets in Akom who could do better. Nne walked off with her head bowed. Obeli watched her walk to the fire expecting her to walk past it towards Iwobo, she went to her mat and laid down. Apparently she wouldn't be seeing Iwobo anymore. Obeli sat not knowing what to feel the truth also being that he didn't know what to expect. In fact he had not carefully thought about it, everything was just by chance. With his new move he thought he would feel happy when he declared his intentions to Nne but now he did it he felt uncertain. Uncertain whether he had done the right thing. The thought of his actions kept sleep away from his eyes. Iwobo was dozing at his watch post, he sat on the ground, using his sword as a support for his forehead. He had hit his forehead on the handle of the sword countless times, each time opening his eyes only to doze again. He had not noticed the army ants marching across the path close to where he sat. One of the ants gave him a serious bite on the thigh that he jerked up like one in a bad dream. He regained consciousness and felt the pain permeate his skin to his nerves up to his brain, he felt the pain move through his body literally. As he dusted himself and scratched ferociously on his thigh, he noticed torches approaching from his far right. This would be the first time he was looking at that direction since he started his watch. He noticed the torches approaching still, luckily their fire was now only smoke and charcoal burning. He rushed to it and doused it, quenching it completely. Hastily he went and woke up Obirika he noticed Nne had not been sleeping but just laid on the mat, Obeli who was lost in thought turned to their direction then ran to them they quickly gathered all their belongings. The bush they had been avoiding was their only refuge now they quickly dove into it. Any person walking by this time couldn't mean well. Such a person or people should be avoided they possibly couldn't be travellers. And even if so should still be avoided. As they hid in the bush Iwobo had his hands occupied holding the mats Obirika had been sleeping on, while Obeli held Nne's and they weren't to make noise. The torches were close now as a result the ant bite felt more poignant, the thing was itching him badly, calling for a scratch and he couldn't scratch it, it was also swollen now. He had never been in such a situation before. He was greatly uncomfortable and he didn't know if it was fear, or his aching forehead or the ant bite. As they watched on, the torches got closer. They didn't know what they were looking at whether humans or ghost. They had the body of humans, mostly young men but their body was painted in stripes giving them a look of black and white. They couldn't see their faces, they were wearing masks of different designs and different shapes, they had weapons of all kinds, and they jogged instead of walking. They were chanting songs Iwobo and his crew had never heard before. As they passed Obeli prayed they didn't stop because it would mean certain death for them. Though he didn't know who or what they represented, all the promises of protection he made to the women haunted him now. His knees quaked almost knocking together in trepidation he could hear his own heartbeat. It was very loud and his eyes watered he held his sword not to fight but with the fear he was having he needed something to hold. He didn't plan to die on this mission, by his estimate only one of the men could knock him unconscious. Then all of them combined would simply trample him to death. They all watched from the shadow as the group of men or spirits passed, each with a hideous mask a sword or machete and a torch. Iwobo couldn't tell clearly if it was red colour or blood he saw on some of them. His ant bite was still tormenting him and he couldn't still scratch it, he eyes watered and was pure red. The men seemed to have a mission barely looking around quickly they moved and quickly they passed. When they were all gone, Iwobo and his companions waited a while in the bush, realizing the bush had its own danger they rushed out onto the path. Glad nothing had attacked them in the bush, they had to continue now. No more sleep or stopping till daylight when they can find a suitable spot for rest.

"Thank goodness you were wide awake Iwobo they would have caught us unawares." Obirika said. The proper thing was 'thank goodness an ant bit you Iwobo, now your forehead is saved.'

*****

Adanna had a bad dream again, this time she dreamt about Obeli and her father. The Herbalist was standing beside her in her hut holding his lamp.

"Are you okay?" he asked.

"Yes I am, thank you."

Tiperi slept through it, he didn't move.

"Sorry I disturbed you." She said.

"No it is nothing, you are sure everything is alright."
"Yes it was just a bad dream." Adanna said.
"They are getting frequent but don't worry, everything will turn out well." The Herbalist said, attending to her a little bit then he went back to his hut.

*****

Obeli had to drag himself along as they walked he couldn't remember being so tired or uncomfortable before. Had it been he was in Akom he would still be in the comfort of his bed by now, sleep came the sweetest to him in the early morning. Now not only was he missing the morning sleep he had not had much since last night and the base of his skull and also a part of his forehead were beginning to ache him. He felt like magically disappearing and then re-appearing in Akom, back to the comfort of his hut. With the somewhat heavy eyes he took a cursory look at himself and noticed he was getting lean. His father would never believe the lie he had told about going to his uncle's place. Iwobo was having issues of his own, the ant bite on his thigh was still acting up. As a result he had marched and crushed every creeping insect he had come across on the way. Even the harmless ones he would crush with the sole of his feet and then there was also sleep, he wasn't doing any better than Obeli, he desperately needed sleep too. Nne and her mother fared better having had a little rest. Obeli stared at Nne who had maintained her position since the occurrence of the early morning or in her estimate last night, he couldn't tell if she was pleased or not. If only he could read minds, he would certainly read hers. Nobody felt like talking between Obeli and Iwobo, they had sleep to grapple with. Their march would see them enter Ebemi by the later part of the day after that Odiidi which had a boundary with Akom. Iwobo in his sleep mood had announced. Glancing back Iwobo saw Nne and her mother wearing hats, it might help with the cold he reasoned and proceeded to put on his own hat.

*****

Adanna had woken up for a while. Tiperi snored away beside her. She was glad he was having a nice rest, how he found his way in the dark back to her hut after being taken away in his sleep last night still remained a mystery. Outside she could hear voices never before heard and wondered what was going on. The Herbalist's uncle had visited as Etiti said.

"It is your first time so I must put you through."

The Herbalist sat to listen to Okonsi like a child listening to his parents tell a tale, both men discussed about everything he should know and do.

Adanna had heard the greeting but then nothing else, now by her estimate the time for her medication had passed. All she wanted to do was stand, the knees were getting better and they were doing it speedily. She had to take her medications even more medication to hasten the healing. Tiperi had woken and they both had done the morning necessaries of refreshing for the day. Nnadi as steady as ever had brought food for them and they were eating, Tiperi now preferring to eat with her as Adanna warmed up to the plea of eating with someone else. As they ate Etiti had rushed into her hut with smiles on her face. Her face was radiating and beaming with happiness.

"How are you?" she asked.

"I'm fine." Adanna responded.

Tiperi gulped water and greeted Etiti. Etiti responded to him and he continued with his meal, he was enjoying the delicacy. Etiti wished them well, highlighting the chores and errands she had to attend to. The impending marriage of her son had thrown her life's activities into frenzy. Not long after she left, she went to her son to narrate again all the places she had been to since morning. The Herbalist narrated his conversation with Okonsi, and all seemed to have gone well. Adanna and Tiperi now sat with satisfied stomachs allowing the day to unfold. When they had relaxed a bit Tiperi resumed with his request that never got answered whenever he made them.

"Mother will you teach me a song?" he asked Adanna.

If she didn't know stories, was it songs that she would know. Adanna in a lost world searched her mind for a song, and none came to her rescue.

"Why don't you teach me one?" she said after frantically searching her mind to find a song and redeem herself as someone who cared about children for once. Tiperi with smiles.

"Okay there is this one my sister taught me and I will teach you. Mother do you know how to play the drum?"

Another question, Adanna simply shook her head the more the questions or request from Tiperi the more inadequate she felt.

"Here is the song," with no musical instrument he had to use his palms, clapping rhythmically with the song.

As Tiperi sang the last words, he heard the Herbalist join him to sing the song.

The Herbalist continued to sing, he knocked and walked in without anyone answering, Adanna was certain he was coming in anyway, still singing the song he was smiling and singing as he walked in.

"I missed the beginning of the song." He said. "Who taught you the song?"

Tiperi was mute and wide eyed now staring at the Herbalist who sat on the seat.

"You don't want to answer?" he said looking at Tiperi who was gradually shifting closer to Adanna.

"His sister taught him." Adanna said when Tiperi refused to talk or even answer.

"He is still not talking? But I heard you singing just now. Are you still scared of me?" The Herbalist asked with no answer. "I don't know what I ever did to you. Well it is good you two are bonding, here" he handed over Adanna's herbs which she gladly took and drank.

"I'm sorry to come late my uncle came, and I was with him," turning back to Tiperi. "The song you were singing do you know what it means?" he asked, still no answer.

"Okay fine since you prefer being mute when you see me. You know my mom taught me the song, though I have forgotten most of the words, but it is a song of encouragement." He explained.

"How do you feel?" he asked Adanna.

"Getting stronger."

"I'm glad, I'm glad" he repeated, "I will run some errands I have a lot on my hands right now, I will see you later." He stood to leave looking at Tiperi, "You should be a man. How many times will I tell you, you can't like a woman and hate a fellow man."

Adanna laughed at the words. When he left Tiperi came back to his old self, and continued from where he stopped, Adanna eagerly listening.

*****

The sun had relieved them from the chilling cold of the morning, however it didn't bring them comfort but rather its own rays, which when it touched the skin heated it up. They had been walking under it for a while toiling under the weather, as it threw whatever it had on them knowing fully well they had no options. When they got to a cleared spot under a tree the spot looked like what it had always been used for was rest, along the path it curved in around the tree, while the path remained, the path was considerably wide. Iwobo and Obeli cleared the grass around, the women wanted to help again the men objected, preferring to do everything themselves. When they sat they ate the only thing they had remaining dried meat and drank some water.

He needed rest and he needed it badly. "We can rest a while here Akom is no longer far by this time tomorrow we shall be close to Akom." With the words still in his mouth Iwobo dozed off.

Nne and her mother managed to do the same, however wearily. Obeli couldn't help but snore, they had a short time to rest and he would make use of every opportunity to get sleep.

The women were the first to wake up they took the position of the sun and reckoned they had slept enough and they must continue. After much consultation amongst the two of them, they left the men alone and went into the woods hoping to come back before they wake up. They had not been long gone when the men woke up. Obeli was the first to wake up, rousing Iwobo up when his heart almost failed him.

"Where is Nne and Obirika?" he asked. Both men alerted now, called out to them and prayed nothing bad had happened. Iwobo had advised they probably went into the woods, and would be back despite him having his own fears.

"You check this way while I go the opposite." Obeli suggested. But before they could move away, Nne and her mother appeared, holding bananas with enough in their bags. They came out from the bush they had passed before getting to the spot, the young men breathed and gave a sigh of relief.

"We were worried." Obeli said.

"We didn't want to disturb you people, we are sorry, you people should come and eat banana." Nne said.

They went back to the spot they had been, sat round and enjoyed the delicious banana produced and given by earth. They huddled round the banana and ate with delight. With Obeli and Iwobo arguing about who the tallest wrestler in Akom was, they had been mentioning names all afternoon, while stuffing bananas into their mouth. When they had had enough it was only natural that Iwobo would throw the question "Can we rest a while?" And suggest that they should spend more time, nobody objected. They sat under the shade of the tree. They greeted those that passed by as if they were people from Obikiti. After a while Obirika looking at her daughter gave her a nod and encouraged her without Obeli and Iwobo noticing it. Nne stood up they had been staying behind the tree, from the direction of anyone coming to the spot, they would pass the tree and find them under its shade. Nne stood and went close to the tree, "Can I have everyone's attention" she said, "I had planned to do this in a better way but didn't know which way best to do it, I mean on how to thank you both. I'm not eloquent but I must say something, we still have a long distance ahead of us but we have come a long way, for now all I can say is thank you to you both." At this moment Iwobo felt like stopping her and assuring her he would cross the evil forest for her, Obeli felt the same but they had to listen to her, it warmed their hearts, filled it with pleasure and took away discomfort from them. "Your bravery is unparalleled by any one I have ever seen, you both don't know what you have done for me." The word bravery made them feel like being in another world. Never did they imagine that someone would ever use the word to describe them. "You helped to bring my joy back, seeing my mother here is because of you two, so you will agree with me there is nothing I could have done without you two. I was in deep pit of gloom and agony and you both pulled me out, I'm eternally grateful. But there is an issue and on this matter I have had a headache because I didn't know what to do. I was confused and worried and had little peace till I related the issue to my mother whose guidance I cherish. I didn't have the knowledge to make a decision so I'm asking you both to decide on it, both of you have declared interest in me." Iwobo's heart raced like a pursued chicken, Obeli's ear canal burned, and his heart pounded in no small proportion his stomach churned and burned, Nne oblivious of their pain. "I am a woman and I can't marry two men, it is never before heard of or done, so you two should just know, and I see myself as not mine but to the man that would show interest in me. I will gladly be with any of you two, but I can't be with two of you." Obeli felt like peeing while Iwobo's bladder was being pounded upon by an unknown force, he looked at Nne she wasn't wearing any of the jewelries he had bought her. She didn't tell them who was first to declare interest, she didn't want to bother them with that. Informing the two of them she went and sat down, Obeli and Iwobo felt weak and confused. The little joy they had, had now been taken away, the situation was unpleasant to them, they sat gloomy with their hands shaking. After a while Obirika suggested they move on like little children without a say, they both stood up, ever since Nne made the revelation, they have not spoken a word. But they knew they still had to carry on with their functions, each man maintained his position while the ladies theirs. Iwobo at the front, Obirika, Nne and Obeli at the rear. Both young men didn't know if they were to feel anger for each other or not or call off the whole thing, or even fight each other for her hand. Both had never been so confused, and in such a complicated matter before. Now they also wished to find someone whom they may get advice from, but none. From here they were proceeding to the market in Ebemi to get supplies and Obeli was planning to buy Nne a gift, maybe that would have to wait.

*****

All through the day Adanna and Tiperi had done nothing but discuss, play games, eat, sleep and discuss some more. The more time they spent together the more liberated Tiperi became, Adanna was glad he had such an informed mind. His sister had done good by engaging him in a lot of discussions, but for his father she couldn't really tell. It seemed all his grieve came from him. With his presence she had been able to take her mind away from her predicaments, and focus on other issues of life. She had enjoyed the riddles with him, since he made her hut his comfort zone he had not bothered to go outside and check on the happenings of the outside world, rather he stayed with Adanna. The usual influx of people could be noticed by Adanna, since the marriage news, activities had increased in the compound. She could notice people coming and going. Thanks to Tiperi she did not bother herself with the activities, very soon darkness would come and now what bothered her was the fact that she was having nightmares. He was not complaining, that was the Herbalist, but then again he must be feeling it as a disturbance to his peace. She had never seen him complain or make a face to suggest he was angry and she wondered what it would be like. Tiperi must know how an angry man behaved with what he had told her about his father. Men are almost like animals, exhibiting the same characteristics when they are angry, but the Herbalist, he was a man that knew a lot.

*****

Iwobo led them into Ebemi and they went straight to the market. This should be the last market till they enter into Odiidi, when they got to Odubi market they went around, shopping for mainly foods that could last a day. Akom was a day away. Iwobo and Obeli were not talking to each other in fact they had nothing to say to one another. They all still stayed together, Nne and her mother noticed it and it crushed them, both of them had been good friends, it would be nice to see their relationship survive their current ordeal. The market was closing, people were rounding up their buying while the sellers hustled to sell their last bit of wares or merchandise. Obirika could buy the things she wanted since Iwobo and Obeli split their money to give her a portion. Obeli noticed someone hugging Iwobo and letting out a joyful laughter. It was Pimpi, getting closer, he overhead her asking for him.

"Where is your other half?" she shouted amidst raucous laughter, Iwobo looked back to see Obeli approaching, he could only smile and point towards him albeit a forced smile, he wasn't in the mood to smile. But this was Pimpi the most jovial woman they had ever seen. Pimpi was the smiling face of Akom, with her plump body frame, anybody who was having a bad day whenever you met Pimpi it changed.

"There you are you little mischief maker, come and give your Pimpi a hug." She said, with an outstretched arm.

Obeli now smiling walked to her and gave her a hug, she went on to hug Nne and Obirika when Iwobo had introduced them.

Nne had always heard of Pimpi, but had never seen her and she was feeling good when she saw her, everything she had heard about her was right and accurate.

"Where are you two daredevils coming from?" Pimpi asked with a hearty laughter.

"Pimpi from a far land with tales you wouldn't believe." Iwobo said. Trying to warm up to Pimpi's enthusiastic energy.

"I must say, it has been days now since I last saw you two miscreants, and I wondered what was up with you two. Hope everything is fine?" she asked.

"Everything is fine. Pimpi what are you doing in Ebemi?" Obeli asked.

"Business of course and a little bit of visiting, this is my grandmother's village I came to see her people."

Pimpi had nothing with her but a basket apparently she had finished selling her wares and was now on her way home.

"Pimpi, where are you headed?" Iwobo asked.

"Home my dear. What about you people?"

"We are marching onto Akom." Obeli said.

"My good gods even in the night?"

"Yes" Iwobo answered, "We have to get home as soon as possible."

"I don't think that is a good idea." Pimpi said.

"Why not?" Obeli asked.

"It is a dangerous time we live in." Pimpi said.

"I must say you two look quiet. Hope all is well with you two? It is not like your usual selves." She was talking about Iwobo and Obeli, "You two used to have a go at each other and yet remain close friends, more than even brothers."

Nne pretended she didn't hear the words just like Obirika.

"Pimpi we are fine." Iwobo answered.

"You don't know these two." Pimpi said turning to Obirika.

The three women were now walking side by side, Obirika offered no explanation for their coldness towards each other. They took a left turn, unto a path flanked by farmlands on two sides, inside the farm Pimpi noticed a grasscutter, "Look, look, look!" She said pointing to it.

Obirika expected Iwobo and Obeli to do their usual but they simply looked at the grasscutter and looked away.

They came to a path that led to Odiidi.

"This is it." Pimpi said. "I must take the right to get to my home." She hugged everyone. "You stay safe, I will soon be back to Akom and maybe then you will tell me what is going on between you two." She said pointing to Obeli and Iwobo. To Obirika and Nne she simply hugged and flashed her shiny white teeth before turning and walking away, they waved her goodbye. Like before they would have to walk through the night and find a spot for a brief rest and then resume their journey again.

CHAPTER 42

Adanna sat with Tiperi as their bonding continued not long after the Herbalist came in to give her, her drugs and message her knees, he came and did it with Tiperi watching in silence. Whether it was paining her or not the little boy couldn't tell. Adanna knew how to mask her pain, but then again the pain was reducing drastically. All around her kneecap she felt no pain, all she needed was for the knee to get strong again and recover from the shock she had felt. She couldn't tell why she was not walking already, the pains had gone down considerably. Tiperi watched on as the Herbalist performed his trick. He wondered what on earth the Herbalist was doing. In the process Etiti walked in into the hut, she was as enthused as the day before, and standing right now in Adanna's hut she felt like a complete woman. Almost everyone in Mkpunki had heard about her son getting married, after he was through with what he was doing she would like to give him a good countdown of all the things she had done. Likewise the Herbalist, as his uncle had made sure he was at the same pace with his mother. Etiti watched also as he massaged Adanna, or as they knew her Odabi. The Herbalist kept performing his tricks, with everyone watching. Etiti who was waiting for her son, heard her name outside and went to check who it was, she was expecting a lot of people. The Herbalist was certain it was someone who definitely must have something to do with his pending marriage, when he was through massaging the knees, he gave Adanna a smile assuring her soon very soon she would be able to stand. He greeted them and went out to meet his mother. Tiperi now back to life asked Adanna what it was that the

Herbalist was doing. "He is trying to make my knees better, so I can walk again. It has been a while that I walked on my two feet." Adanna answered.

The answer seemed to satisfy Tiperi, they spent a while asking and answering questions trying to get to know each other better. After that they would probably sing, tell riddles, jokes, and wait for sleep to come. After discussing a while Adanna applied pressure on her legs, sink them into the ground just to know how it would feel. Certainly very soon she would walk, then a thought came to her as they discussed, the day after she would try once again to walk and see what would happen. She must not be lazy she thought to herself she would try to stand the day after. Outside Etiti was done with her visitor and she went to meet her son, they had to plan for the day after because she had planned that in two days they will be done with the marriage, everything about it. The day after they would go for the introduction, as she relayed this plan to her son, he could only stutter with words. Who has ever done such a thing, who rushes a thing such as marriage?

"Mother let us take it easy." He pleaded.

"Don't tell me that, we will do it as I have decided I'm your mother." Etiti said as stern as possible.

The Herbalist recoiled, he had never seen his mother in such a mood.

"In fact all I want you to do is prepare to get married. Leave all the details and running around for me I will handle it." She said.

With no words all the Herbalist could say was "Yes Mama."

Etiti gave him a smile played with her eyebrows by raising them up and down, with a smiley face.

"Very soon you will be married," she said, she played

with her eyebrows again, and the Herbalist could do nothing else but laugh. "Soon you will be a complete man." She said again and smiled.

"I'm already complete, don't need a woman to complete me." He said it faintly with Etiti not hearing it.

"Goodnight" Etiti finally said. She walked to her hut singing a marriage song and dancing along the way. As she made her way to her hut with her oil lamp, the Herbalist could only laugh looking at his mother, after a while he went into his hut. Despite the marriage ceremony coming up he was not going to abandon his work, he went ahead to prepare some herbs for his patients. He would attend to them in the early morning, before the introduction and whatever else that came his way. The night was just as usual.

*****

Iwobo leading the way maintained his composure as if nothing was going on in his mind. But the fact that his bosom friend was also interested in the same woman that he was interested in made everything look gloomy. Obeli was almost a brother, and he was certain of it, he led the way knowing he had a duty.

Nne and her mother held each other's arm walked behind Iwobo not saying much. Obeli maintained his position of being at the back of the line, he was not doing any better than Iwobo, he had his own issues. Also which were not so much different from Iwobo's thought, but then he knew he didn't make any mistake in telling Nne how he felt about her. They walked through the night, hoping to find a spot like they had done at Obikiti, rest for a while and continue the journey later, hopefully they wouldn't meet anything unpleasant and unusual.

Iwobo and Obeli were showing bravery never before seen in them. In their respective families they were known as nothing but weaklings, who couldn't even farm, but since they embarked on the quest it had been a surprising tale for them. They had managed to survive though they had not met any real danger, the few that came their way. They either ran, or dodged in the bush whichever way they did it, they had been surviving and they planned to do so for a long time to come. In a day or so they would be at their destination, hopefully safe.

*****

The day began like every other day and almost becoming usual for Adanna, since she hurt her knees. The Herbalist came to check on her and did everything he was supposed to do as usual before leaving. Etiti also in her busy schedules had come to visit. Tiperi who had all night told stories and sang songs was still sleeping. When Nnadi came to wake him up Adanna pleaded he should be allowed to rest more, she was getting fond of him. Adanna knew the day was the introduction day, still the Herbalist had not mentioned it to her that he was getting married. He had not even acted like someone who was getting married but Adanna knew better. She felt he should tell her, why would he want to keep it secret? Everything in the compound had gone on as normal in the morning, except that Adanna could notice a fewer people visiting, they must have heard that it was the Herbalist's introduction day. Sitting alone for some time Adanna's attention went back to her knees within her they felt strong enough to support her weight. She wouldn't want to fall to aggravate her pain, after much consideration with her hands she brought down her legs from the bamboo bed. Now facing side of the hut which had the exit and backing Tiperi, she gently tried standing but she found herself hesitating. Something was telling her not to stand. 'It was dangerous,' the voice said in her head, 'you could fall and injure yourself' it continued saying. But she had to block out the voice. She continued, determined but a little scared, first she stood with her left leg, then summoning up courage she added her right, now she was bent, and she was facing the other direction. Using the bed as a support all she needed to do was leave the bed and stand. It took her a while, she closed her eyes, breathed heavily, tried to encourage herself. "You can do it Adanna, you can stand again." She said to herself. "Come on, just try it, you can stand." She continued saying when she opened her eyes she saw Tiperi staring at her with a sleepy eyes, both looked at each other, the boy wondered what she was doing, he sat up with his eyes fixed at Adanna.

"Good morning." He greeted.

"Good morning, how are you?" Adanna said, her hands on the bamboo bed, and back bent, she was bowing. Tiperi waking had cut off her concentration. She tried to encourage herself again to stand, but didn't find the courage. Now she was not sacred she could fall, she was scared that, she wouldn't be able to stand. In her mind she had believed that everything was right for her to walk again, but now it would be bad for her to find out she still couldn't stand. She couldn't remain bed ridden, it shouldn't be. She stayed in the bent position for a while not knowing whether to sit or try to stand. Tiperi kept looking on, she searched her mind for a voice, to spur her on, but none came after a while she gently sat down and breathed in heavily. Pushed away every thought of defeat from her mind, she would try again. After a while she called out to Nnadi who came and attended to Tiperi. When Adanna found herself alone, she sat on the bed and wished herself good. "I must walk again, I can't be in this situation," she continued saying to herself. She was now her own adviser and she knew she had to walk again, the things she has missed. How she would love to take her new gun and go into the woods and hunt. How lovely it would be, being in the woods, chasing animals and getting a good game, it would just be lovely. She couldn't wait to take her life back. In a little while her mind went back to Tiperi and she imagined what to do with him, she was getting fond of him. Will the Herbalist and his mother agree to let her take him to Akom? She would certainly love to. With Tiperi on her mind, the child walked into the hut with smiles, looking refreshed. Nnadi surely knew how to take care of people. She had heard in Mkpunki human sacrifices were rampant but she had not witnessed any. It was said that most often the villagers sacrificed human's to appease the gods, she had even heard that the people of Mkpunki also buried Slaves with their masters and Nnadi came to mind, she didn't deserve such fate. Mkpunki was not the only place that did such, but in Akom they didn't do it, human sacrifices were unheard of in Akom.

*****

Marching homewards, Obeli and company had been mostly silent. Since the night, they had been marching, the women refused to rest, suggesting it was better they walk, since by night fall, they should be at their destination. They didn't even stop to eat, rather each, ate as they walked. Sometimes Iwobo wondered who was the leader of the pack, whether the men or women. For the most part all he could remember was them making the decisions. Iwobo couldn't believe they would soon enter Odiidi. The women were scaring him the more, they had refused rest since the evening of yesterday. They had been walking and whispering together. Whatever they were saying they didn't want anybody to know about it. Nne and her mother had hoped that they would sit down and discuss it with each other but even the women would not know what to do if they were in their situation. What could they possibly do, it was a decision one should not have to take. The women felt sorry for them, of course they wouldn't kill each other, just to get what they want. It was a sorry situation for them. Nne and her mother had talked little about it and went on to discuss other things, like what the future held for them and how best to start a new life in Ebe, Ujuru's village.

*****

Still lying down and gazing at the thatched roof in the hut, a sight she was now familiar with, she still tried to encourage herself to stand up. With the thoughts in her mind she drifted into sleep unknowingly. In her sleep she dreamt she was bedridden and someone kidnapped Tiperi, she woke up, sitting up quickly and opening her eyes she noticed she had been dreaming again, she heaved. Tiperi was lying down beside her also looking at the thatched roof. Without thought, without words, she dropped her legs on the ground and quickly stood. She stood her eyes turned and it seemed as if her brain also swirled around violently she almost fell, it seemed as if all the blood in her body rushed to her brain. She staggered like a drunkard for a while and then caught herself, spreading her arms to balance herself she could only give up an anxious unsteady laughter. She was standing, indeed she was standing. Tiperi sat up to marvel at her, after a while her knees began to shake it wasn't shaking because it was unstable but rather because she was anxious, she stood for a considerable time, and then sat down again, laughing and congratulating herself.

"Yes" she said out loud, raising her hands, she could not describe what she was feeling, she would certainly walk after all, indeed she would walk. Tiperi did nothing but sit and watch, lost at what he was beholding. She sat and continued raising her hands in the air and laughing, sometimes she would clap, congratulating herself at her victory over fear that held her down, now she could stand. Moments ago she had thought it was impossible but now it was very possible, she would have to leave this hut she thought to herself. She had seen it but never knew it would be so soon. She believed it was the work of the Herbalist and would have to thank him specially. Tiperi smiled as he continued looking at Adanna laugh and clap for herself, Adanna now turned to look at him the only person that had witnessed her victory over her fears, she turned with a healthy laughter. They both laughed. She couldn't wait to tell Etiti and the Herbalist. If she laughed Tiperi would laugh together with her, if she smiled he would do the same. One thing was obvious he didn't know why he was doing them, and Adanna didn't expect him to understand. She had imagined herself unable to walk again. What would happen to her alone in a strange land with no relatives, others had their families to care for them but in her case it would be strangers taking care of her.

She planned to rest a while and then stand again. The whole day was going to be spent doing just that, when she felt she had waited enough, she called Tiperi, placing her hands on his shoulder she stood. Looking at the child all he did was laugh with her, she was feeling reluctant to leave his shoulder. The fear had crept in again.

"I just stood now" she said with laughter this time she didn't stand alone. "You know what?" she asked Tiperi who shook his head in the negation, he didn't know what.

"We will try again later, fear has crept in again." She admitted to herself and Tiperi obliged. They would stand again and again, till she could if possible fly, she wouldn't give up easily. Tiperi was ready to do all her biddings after all she was his mother now and would certainly like to see her walk.

After a while she tried again, all she was doing now was to try to stand on her own, walking would come later. They tried again this time she fought the fears and was able to remove her hands from Tiperi's shoulder, she gave out another anxious laughter.

"Can you see?" she asked Tiperi, "I'm standing." Though her legs felt wobbly she still stood with Tiperi close by he knew he would try his best to catch her, if she wanted to fall. But not Adanna, she was not planning to fall. Tiperi had joined in the celebration now, as if he was the one celebrating the ability to walk again, he clapped and laughed louder than Adanna. Adanna was certain those outside would be wondering what was going on inside her hut, Adanna herself was even singing.

"I'm standing, I'm standing" she would sing the words and clap, Tiperi joined, he had never heard the song before but it was a good one.

"I'm standing" they both sang, she stood for a considerable time before deciding to sit down again, she sat down, looked at Tiperi who was showing his teeth in what appears to be smiling, looking happier than she had ever seen him, he was laughing so loud that the laughter caught her she joined him to laugh, now they were laughing for no reason. Surely someone outside most have heard them. After a while they calmed down, she placed her face on her palms and looked down through her fingers, she was exhaling loudly a sigh of relief it was. Tiperi with smiles just sat looking at her, like he was seeing her for the first time. Adanna thanked her stars for showing her mercy and giving her hope, she thought she had lost all but now she could start a new life. She could certainly make things right and live happily. Once again hunting was the first thing she would do, she would hunt a game and prepare it for the Herbalist and Etiti, in fact the entire household.

CHAPTER 43

Still walking and with more energy, by their calculation they had passed noon of the day, Akom was in sight. Nne felt relieved but the journey still remained, they walked some more and got to a path that pointed to four directions. All these while they had been walking backing the east direction, when they got to this point they all knew it very well. Going straight ahead headed into Akom, taking the left was to another village and taking right would lead them to Ebe, turning back would lead them to where they were coming from.

"My good people we are now in Akom," Iwobo announced feigning to be happy or relieved, he was neither.

Without looking back after he made the announcement he continued walking towards Akom. Nne called his attention, they were still standing at the junction, Nne, Obirika and Obeli. Obeli was confused, standing behind them, Iwobo retraced his steps and came back. In his mind all he heard his inner voice say was "What again" hopefully it wouldn't be something that would make his burden heavier. How to deal with Obeli was still already in his mind. When he got close to them, Obirika spoke asking Obeli too to come closer. When they gathered together they had to ignore people that occasionally passed by.

Obirika had something to say, "My sons first I will speak as a mother, if I were the woman who bore you two and suckled you, watching you take your first steps and the feat you have accomplished. I would be the proudest mother on earth. In your thinking you might think this is nothing but I tell you, generations unborn will hear your story and thank the gods that once a while ago there were men whose pure heart marched their bravery and strength. As a mother you two are the finest a mother can ever ask for. Now as a woman, what could I have done without your strength and fearlessness, you risked your life and your comfort for me. In this life and the next life I can never repay you, never. And as a former slave," the boys shook their heads to inform her they would have done it no matter what and also she wasn't a slave. "Oh yes for a few days I was, all I can say is that you rescued me when all despised me. I had lost faith in men thinking all men were callous and wicked, who trampled upon their own kind. In my darkest times, I saw men as lost who would cover their faces in shame when their children remembered the evils they did. But you two have showed that there must be some who are still good after all. You have shown me, there is hope for the black man. That one day love will find its way into our heart and we will stop killing each other, but love and cherish each other. I and my daughter thank you." As she said the thank she tried to kneel before both men rushed to her and stopped her from kneeling down.

"Please don't," they pleaded after a while she heeded their words and stood up. Nne was dumbfounded, she stood rigid, Obirika continued, "We won't be going to Akom." Another arrow thrust through Iwobo and Obeli, they had hoped to see Nne sometime later, "We would be going to Ebe" Obirika said no need to hide anything from them. "My sons as you can see there is nothing left for us in Akom, we must go to Ebe to start a new life with my brother Ujuru. Once again thank you all very much for the help, we must continue from here to Ebe. May the gods keep you two, bless you abundantly. You shall know no pain, you will prosper in all you do, life will treat you well all your days and you shall go down full of age. You will lack nothing."

As she now prayed for them they concurred at every word. "You will know no sorrow, laughter all your days is your portion, oh how I am short of words, there is nothing I can do that would be enough to show my appreciation to both of you." She hugged them, first she hugged Obeli and then she hugged Iwobo. "To get to Ebe we must take the right, it is just around the corner, before nightfall we will be there, goodbye." She said.

"Not so fast" Iwobo said with a weakened voice, "I believe our job is to take you both to your final destination and watch you settle down, we planned to take you two back to Akom, to see the plan has changed, I don't know about Obeli but I will gladly lead you two to Ebe and meet this brother of yours Ujuru." Saying it he left the path and took the path that led to Ebe.

"I will also do the same." Obeli said "But I have one request."

"Please what is it?" Obirika said.

"I would like it that you people don't tell anyone that my sister Adanna was involved in your kidnapping. She is just misguided that's all."

"Very well Obeli we totally agree with you." Obirika said, "Besides what good will it do us? We didn't plan to bring it up."

"Thank you very much." Obeli said relieved, he pointed to Ebe, "So Ebe it is let us go then."

Momentarily everyone wore a smile as they marched towards Ebe.

*****

Adanna and Tiperi had been singing a new song Tiperi brought up, Adanna was quick to learn the words. Tiperi had told her one of the songs was a girl's song, as he did put it, to get the full rhythm of the song, 'you must stand, you clap with your hands and also tap your feet along as you sing the song'. Adanna had enjoyed the song, watching the boy perform the song he looked almost like a girl dancing, clapping and singing the song. When she told him he looked like a girl dancing, clapping and singing the song he burst out in laughter, and sat down. Since then Adanna had pleaded with him to do the song again and he refused, laughing every time he said no.

"I promise I won't say you look like a girl." She had pleaded; he simply laughed some more and shyly said no.

He proceeded to teach her other songs that didn't require him tapping his feet or dancing in any form like the one they were singing now, for now they sang and sang. Adanna's voice had gotten higher this time perhaps the joy of being able to stand was doing it. Both of them barely noticed when those who went for introduction came back. Without going to his hut first, after greeting everyone and settling everyone including those who came to congratulate him he went straight to Adanna's hut. As he approached he heard her singing. He knocked and entered, as usual Tiperi slid back into his shell, Adanna was laughing towards the Herbalist, Tiperi was mute now.

"Anything you see me you freeze." He said looking at Tiperi, "I don't bite and I won't hurt you, you must know that."

"He is just shy." Adanna said in Tiperi's defence and she said so with a lively voice, one that surprised the Herbalist.

"Okay let it just be that he is shy." The Herbalist said. Before he could ask Adanna how she was doing.

"Guess what I did today?" she asked smiling.

The question surprised him he looked around the hut hastily as if to say she did something about the hut.

Although the place felt strange maybe it was her energy that he was noticing was quite more today.

After a while thinking, "Beats me, please tell." He said.

"So you can't guess?"

"I'm not good at it."

"I stood."

The Herbalist widened his eyes automatically as his eyebrows reached their highest point. "No kidding."

"None, I did."

He burst out into his own laughter now.

"Aside from singing and dancing," she continued, "We have been standing." She said with smiles, even Tiperi was smiling.

"Please show me," he said.

Without much ado she did what she had been doing almost all through the day she stood with of course Tiperi assisting.

"This is awesome," the Herbalist said as he clapped his hands. Etiti who was approaching the hut hastened her footsteps when she heard her son clapping and laughing. She entered and the sight was an awesome one, she quickly rushed to Adanna and hugged her, "You are standing." She said.

"Yes I am!"

She hugged Adanna again and even proceeded to hug her son who was sitting on a log of wood.

"When did this happen?" she asked enthusiastically. "Today" Adanna responded as she sat.

Etiti almost started dancing, "I just heard the noise and wondered what was going on, hey! I'm so happy." As she spoke she heard her name called outside.

"I'm coming" she shouted in reply, "Congratulations" she said and went and hugged Adanna again.

The Herbalist was laughing as loud as possible he even patted Tiperi on the shoulder.

Etiti heard her name again, "I'm coming" she said this time, the "I'm coming" was to Adanna and company she dashed out of the hut. She left and they could hear her cracking a raucous laughter outside. Whoever it was she was pleased to see the person Adanna and co. could hear them, but later on their voiced faded. Adanna now seated looked at the Herbalist, who wore a beautiful smile.

"This is good, this is, this is really really good, I can't tell you how I feel right now, this is good." He said, "I just came to see you, give me a moment I will be back with your herbs, I prepared it before I left." And with that he went out and not too long after he came back with her herbs. She drank and of course all that remained was massaging the knee, with the locally made balm.

"You know the last I heard your people are almost close, not long now they will get to Mkpunki." He said as he inspected her knees and gently tried massaging it.

"Good for them." Adanna said nonchalantly.

"I won't lie to you, I don't think it should be such you know me by now, even here we sacrifice humans it gives me sleepless nights and breaks my heart. I don't think it should be such, it is just that there is nothing I can do about it, our children unborn will surely hate us for our behaviours and acts that is one thing I'm sure of."

Adanna feeling his pain, "Like you said there is nothing we can do."

"For now dear, for now, soon men like me, will have a say we must not continue this way, I cannot tell you the horrors slaves go through, at least the ones I have seen and attended to, they are broken beyond repair." He shook his head in disgust.

"Speaking of telling," Adanna interrupted "Why

haven't you told me you are getting married?"

The question startled him, his eyes darted from one corner of the room to another corner, without looking at Adanna instead he looked at Tiperi who was staring at the Herbalist sternly as if Adanna asked the question on his behalf, and to get an answer was his right.

"Who told you that?" the Herbalist finally managed to say his voice fluttering.

"Your mother."

He gave out a confusing laughter, "The truth is I didn't know how to, didn't know how you will take it, so I guess that is that."

Adanna didn't understand what he meant, but she continued "Still you should have told me."

"I'm sorry, I'm very sorry" he finally said, "I must leave now, have some things to do, we will talk more later on." He wished her good night, stole a glance at her and then left.

CHAPTER 44

Night was approaching, as they walked, it seemed to get darker with each step, Iwobo and Obeli had still not spoken to each other, not even their usual jibes at each. With every growing moment, Nne felt the need to do something to remedy their friendship. Alas!, she didn't know what to do. They got to Ebe in the evening and Obirika took over leading the way, with Iwobo now following. Not long after, they marched into a very large compound, Iwobo and Obeli could tell they were accepted, when they saw children running towards them with shouts of joy, some ran into the huts or into some corners to inform other people they had visitors, with all the noise, the children and some other women, girls and boys ran and began hugging them all. One woman who looked oldest also came and hugged them. Obirika with all the hugging and greeting and laughter tried in vain to introduce Iwobo and Obeli. Everyone's voice was still loud, "You are welcome, you are welcome!" They shouted. Iwobo was not counting, they must have hugged close to twenty people and still counting. After a while when they had hugged almost everyone, the woman presumed to be the eldest wife offered them a seat. Arrangements to prepare huts for them began. All the huts needed was cleaning, there were enough huts in the Ujuru compound. When they enquired of Ujuru they were told he was not back yet from a meeting.

They went on to refresh and eat a proper meal of soup, bush rat meat, dry fish and pounded yam. Resting in the huts, Iwobo and Obeli both in the same hut didn't talk to each other, although they had had reasons to. Nne and her mother had their joy overfull, the peace they sought was finally theirs, and the hut they were given was quite large. They were home, they didn't have any doubt that they wouldn't be missing Akom. Their hearts even elated more, when they heard Ujuru's voice.

"He is back." Obirika said. Not long after a servant came to inform them that Ujuru was around. On their way to his hut they met Iwobo and Obeli outside, who joined them as they went towards Ujuru's hut. When they got to it, Obirika knocked and heard a deep voice say "Enter" they all entered to meet a man as huge as Ekugo the Obikiti man they met along the way coming with his family. Ujuru was tall with a very handsome face, his body was still firm when they entered the hut, he was trying to arrange it and hang his animal skin bag on the wall, after he was done he turned around and flashed them a smile.

"Obirika darling" he called to his baby sister. He quickly went to hug her. "Sweet niece" he called to Nne beaming with smiles and hugged her too, then shook Iwobo and Obeli. "You all are welcome." They sat down as he bid them to on a long bench in his hut.

"My sister it is so good to see you, I'm thrilled." He said genuinely happy, "You all are welcome," he proceeded to bring kola and palm wine.

"This is fresh" he said, Iwobo was almost salivating, palm wine, it had been so long, now they get to have some feelings in the mouth. He shouted for a servant who came within a twinkling of an eye, the servant or slave left with instructions to bring drinking horns for the visitors. When he came back he poured for the men first. "It is tradition." Ujuru said. "Men must and should be served first." He did the same also with the kola nut. "There must not be favouritism," he continued. "A man ought to take first, he must be first because it is believed that if a woman should first the man, what awaits to attack him will attack her, then she won't be able to fight back." He said laughing.

When he had served all four of them, he poured a portion on the ground praying to the ancestors, "Ancestors take your own and protect us, may we always have plenty to eat." He prayed and they all concurred. They went ahead to eat and drink not minding they already had full stomachs.

"I hope you people came well, and you will be staying a while?" he asked no one in particular, but Obirika spoke for them.

"A very long time" Obirika said laughing.

"Tell me all my dear sister it has been a long time."

"You don't know the half of it, we are coming from Mpkunki."

"Agbala eh!" Ujuru shouted, "What happened?" he asked almost screaming.

"I was kidnapped by slavers."

Ujuru was wide eyed now, he dropped his drinking horn, surprised "My own sister?" he said, he bit his finger, shook it violently, bit his lips. "Eh in this time you dare kidnap? That is why in Ebe, anybody who doesn't get slaves the right way we kill them instantly." Ujuru said.

"The whole story is that I'm here, we passed through dangers and turmoil and thanks to these two young men. We are here, they rescued me." Tears were almost in Ujuru's eyes. "They are the bravest of men I have ever seen." Obirika said as tears formed in her eyes and her voice wavered, she went on to immortalize them, "Brother Ujuru, Obeli is Otukidikpo 1 of Akom, the brave and benevolent conqueror of all Akom land, the mighty warrior, giver of freedom, the Egunti Onapipo

Ekutororo, the man that dines with the gods as an equal, protector of the weak, the oracle amongst men," Obirika was all tears now. Everyone let her be and she continued "Iwobo is the Ekutidebe 1 of Akom, the majestic weapon of the gods, the benevolent benefactor of mankind, Arum Onachikpe kirodo, the greatest and mightiest." Ujuru concurred nodding to every praise. "No one has ever seen their likes before and I'm honored to have had an encounter with them. They are my saviours and to Nne I won't be able to praise enough, she is irreplaceable, never will earth know her type again, she is a mighty warrior and the greatest to ever set foot on earth..." Everyone received their praise soberly as Obirika had tears running down her cheeks. Ujuru patted her tenderly with Nne joining and she calmed down a little bit. Everyone was silent for a while before Ujuru started speaking again.

"My fellow men thank you," he said. "Please whatever your price is, as long as Ujuru is alive he would pay, I will pay in full please mention whatever you want." Iwobo and Obeli who were sitting silent till now waved it off." "We are fine all we wanted was their happiness." Iwobo said and Obeli agreed.

"My brothers I'm Ujuru, anything you want that I can afford is all yours, thank you indeed. Obirika you won't be going back to Akom."

Obirika still with tears and Nne consoling her, "I don't plan to." She muttered.

"Very good" he looked at Nne who was also silent, but content. "You people must have passed through turmoil, it is all over now, no evil will befall you in Ebe, I can assure you. Please feel free to do whatever you want. Brothers I have farmlands that no one is cultivating, I have land, I have seeds. Ujuru is a hardworking man and I have been able to acquire a lot, please I will gladly give you land to farm on for free, just to show appreciation."

The men thanked him for his kindness. "We appreciate," Iwobo said.

They continued their tale recounting all they experienced. Nne could notice Iwobo and Obeli still were not talking to each other. When they left Ujuru's hut to get back to their huts after talking about all they could, she met them.

"You two should talk," she said, "You have to talk to each other, being silent won't solve the matter." She said to them and went with her mum to their hut.

The men went into their hut and both continued to ignore each other.

*****

Early in the morning, when it was still dark Obeli woke up, he had little rest, his mind had been in turmoil. Looking round the hut he couldn't find Iwobo, he packed his belongings. Once he refreshed he would leave, stepping outside the hut he saw Iwobo sitting in front of the hut, no doubt he too also had a restless night like him. It was bad omen to start a day without greeting a friend but instead holding grudges, the day would be unpleasant. But that was not what was compelling him, Iwobo was his friend, once he saw him he knew he had to talk to him. Iwobo too noticed his friend was close, both at the same said "Good morning." They had same intentions; again they both said "Morning how are you." The same time, so that they wouldn't repeat it the third time, Obeli with a smile came and sat beside his friend, as he sat, "What are you thinking about?" he asked sitting down.

Iwobo shook his head, "I would be a liar if I told you I have a reasonable thought in my head right now. Just anxious about the next step to take." He said relieved that his friend was asking him how he was doing.

"You know we are supposed to talk about Nne, but I've made my decision," Obeli said. "We are friends and can never be enemies. She is determined to stay here, and I believe here will bring her happiness, but not me I'm going back to Akom." Obeli said, "Besides even if she had accepted me, what would she do when she remembers about Adanna? I need to get back to my father and family."

Iwobo laughed. "For me you know there is nothing in Akom for me, I'm really considering Ujuru's offer, take my time and do farming, besides I would give up much more for Nne just to be with her." Iwobo said.

"Wow, not only am I losing my interest in a woman I get to lose my friend also."

"I am not your friend Obeli, I am your brother, besides you can never lose me, we shall visit every now and then."

Both hugged each other, holding each other for a while, almost to the point of tears before releasing each other, "It will be well with you." Obeli said.

"You too" Iwobo said.

Obeli left to prepare himself, he must get to Akom, a lot had to be done.

*****

Adanna awoke in Mpkunki with no nightmares this time, the noise outside had woken her, it was the marriage day. How Etiti made a marriage happen in three days was unknown and unprecedented.

Today the set mark to attain was to walk and if possible run. While others celebrated their happiness and new things happening to them she had to celebrate hers, she looked to her left, Tiperi was still sleeping and would be for a very long time, his sleeping antics reminded her of Obeli her brother, they never wake early. Her heart felt heavy and gloomy as she remembered Obeli, she was certain that by now he was dead. She had killed her own brother, she had always fought the thought, the only thing that was different now was that she had no justification for his death. She had no reason to tell herself she had to do it, just like she had no reason now for Nefari the girl she broke her ankle, in fact her ankles. Nefari had disciplined Obeli while Obeli was a child and Adanna avenged Obeli in her own way. She had to be her own adviser and that meant not letting the past deter her and her resolve to have a better future. This would take time, she had always triumphed in the fight of the mind ever since she became bed ridden, her past had been trying to inflict pain on her. Triperi stretched himself, moaned, changed position and continued his pleasant sleep.

Adanna got confused by him, a child that should be up and about, playing outside and seeking for new adventures with his mates, rather he would stay in the hut with her. Stepping outside only for necessaries and returning immediately. She was fond of him, she had never really seen that person that she couldn't do without, if she survived her mother's death she would survive anything. Some people can't be replaced and her mother couldn't, her mother saw her through the most difficult times of her life. Giving her all the forms of support she so badly needed. Fought her battles and protected her and now for a very long time she had been doing that for herself but people didn't understand. She heard a familiar sound, it was the Herbalist and Etiti. When they stepped in Adanna saw in Etiti's eyes what it was meant to be, 'happy.' She had changed considerably, her attire made her look like a new person. Above all smile never left her face.

"We are ready." The Herbalist said, trying his best not to sound excited. If he was happy or not you wouldn't know, his face wore no emotion.

"I can see I wish you well" before Adanna could finish the wish you well, Etiti came and hugged her.

"We will soon be back," Etiti said. "How do I look?" she asked Adanna, turning round for her to see.

"Mama, I have told you, you look fine about five times why not let it rest." The Herbalist said.

"Shush your mouth, I didn't ask you," Etiti snapped back "My dear answer me."

Adanna had never praised anyone to make the person feel happy in her life, never but she remembered she had heard somebody who was asked the same question "How do I look". Answer "You look rather ravishing" and to her this would be a perfect time to use it. With a pleasant smile, "You look ravishing" Adanna said.

Etiti giggled and hugged her again.

"There you have it, let us go." The Herbalist said.

"Warn him, I will deal with him." Etiti said to Adanna pointing at the Herbalist. "This is my happy day, allow me to enjoy it." She continued.

"Fine just let us be going." He said again.

Etiti for no apparent reason laughed again, clapped her hands, made miniature dance steps, waved at Adanna and left.

The Herbalist handed over her drugs to her "We will soon be back take care of yourself." He left.

CHAPTER 45

This time the journey felt different, at most he was confused, this time making the journey he was not sure of his decision. He didn't know what to expect and he was scared. The people he left behind had hugged him and promised to be in touch. Then he felt leaving Nne was a good idea now he wasn't so sure. Walking the paths alone made the journey more odious, he walked as fast as he could, when possible he would run. Seeing people on the path didn't make it any better his hand never left his sword. Walking alone these days was as dangerous as going into the evil forest, the deepest part of it. Obeli jogged consciously aware that he was afraid. A while ago he felt he could take a life to protect Obirika and Nne even Iwobo, he was so sure of himself, that it earned him being called brave. A name he never knew would be used for him, now he wished he was brave. Any unfamiliar sound, whether by man or animal triggered him to run faster. With what he had heard and seen the worst thing that would happen to him was for people to jump out from the bush and turn him into a slave, it would be the worst fate imaginable. He needed to get back to his father and he needed to do it fast. If he ran fast enough he would get to Akom in the evening.

*****

Adanna had been standing for a while now, Tiperi looked eager to make sure, she actualized her heart desire of walking. Today he was serving as the moving support, Adanna placing both her hands on either side of his shoulders, his job was to move slowly and then she would follow. She was learning to walk again as such she had to start with baby steps.

"Should I move?" Tiperi would ask.

"No, no, just wait I'm not ready." She would say and exhale looking up at the thatched roof, trying to motivate herself. No motivation came, after standing for a considerable time their legs began to ache, they had been standing at a fixed point and no progress.

"Tiperi you know I'm getting tired let us sit for a while and try sometime later" Adanna said.

"Why?" Tiperi asked.

"I'm tired, aren't you tired?"

"No" he said though he was.

"Well I am, if you are not."

"Don't you want to walk again?"

"I want to Tiperi, but I guess I'm not ready, let us just sit okay." Adanna pleaded. The boy obeyed, and assisting Adanna, she sat back down, exhaling heavily again. Tiperi sat beside her, staring into her eyes with the concern of a child, who would also cry if he should see his mother cry. In Adanna he found peace and protection for no reason known. Adanna made him most times not to miss his own mother or sister. In her estimate they had rested enough. She must try again, they repeated, the very same routine until she sat again. This was the second time and time was going by Tiperi's calculations.

"Okay let us try again," she said. "This would be the last for today, if it doesn't work we will have to try again tomorrow." She said with a saddened voice, her fears were having a better part of her. Tiperi the reliable support he was, stood. She was able to stand again, but to lift her legs from the floor and move it, seemed impossible. Using her toes, she first raised them, they were okay as far as she could notice, pressing them into the floor, she dragged her foot her foot moved at the pace of a snail. Still she was not able to raise her leg up from the floor, drawing her feet with her toes was not a good alternative. She had to give up, she was going to give up for the day.

"Tiperi let us sit," she said. "We will try sometimes later." "Don't you want to walk?" Tiperi asked again. She rolled her eyes in disbelief, a question she had heard again and again, but she had to answer.

"Tiperi there is nothing I want more now, but to stand and walk okay, I really do want to walk, I do, but you can't force it, that is why I think we should rest and try again tomorrow, we won't give up, we will keep trying and trying till we make it happen, it is going to happen I can assure you. So it is better, we be patient and achieve it, than hurry and ruin it." With the words still coming out from her mouth, she still had a lot of preaching to do. Tiperi had heard enough, not informing her in any way as he had been standing rigid listening to her, took steps forward dragging her along.

Adanna could only blurt out "Tiperi! Tiperi! Tiperi!" wild eyed as Tiperi walked, she had to walk to stop from falling face down, "Tiperi" she continued screaming but she was walking, indeed she was walking, she was taking steps.

"Tiperi stop I beg you," she pleaded, the boy simply laughed and with her hands still on his shoulders he walked out of the hut, into the compound.

"Oh my goodness, Tiperi I will fall, Tiperi please I beg you Tiperi." He laughed some more. The both of them were walking, "Oh my goodness at least slow down." Tiperi chuckled. Adanna was walking, she clutched Tiperi's shoulder, the child had no option they continued walking, almost to middle of the compound. Adanna had all her attention focused ahead, not looking to the sides. Nnadi was out of her hut now with other occupants in the compound who had not gone to the marriage ceremony. They applauded and cheered, congratulating Adanna, she could only smile and laugh now.

"Thank you, thank you" she said laughing. She felt like waving, if only she could. "Madam Congratulations" were coming from every corner. Nnadi jumped, clapped and celebrated like Adanna was raised from the dead. Tiperi took her to the entrance, with her congratulators following, those by her side and those behind, even the do-gooders who picked harmless pebbles and stones on the ground from before them. Those around numbered up to nine, smiling and saying nice things. Tiperi was the hero, Adanna the inspiration. Adanna was not certain she heard right, but she believed she heard a faint voice saying they would do their own party right in the compound. Since they couldn't make it to the marriage ceremony, on account of her healing and ability to walk. As they walked back to the hut. When they got to the entrance of the hut, Adanna expecting that would be it for the day, anticipated rest, but she didn't know the mind of Tiperi. The young man leading her almost into the hut unexpectedly turned around.

"O Tiperi!" Adanna shouted sounding defeated, "You are enjoying yourself isn't it?"

The boy gave his chuckle again.

"Tiperi walk round the compound." A male voice suggested from the crowd.

"Oh please not yet." Adanna pleaded.

In the crowd a woman asked "Is his name Tiperi?" another voice answered, "Yes. Were you not around when they brought him?"

"I have never even seen him, this is my first time."

They continued their discussion.
"This is a miracle." One said.
Thinking they were marching to the entrance of the compound as usual, Adanna allowed Tiperi lead on, again he had his own design, Tiperi took a detour, leading Adanna to the corner of the compound.
"Tiperi, where are you going?" Adanna demanded he pointed to his destination. Adanna couldn't see any discernable destination.
"Where are you pointing to Tiperi?"
"The corner, we are going round." Tiperi said.
"I think we've done enough, Tiperi take me back and I mean it."
"Just this last one, it is so that your legs will be strong."
"Since when did you become the Herbalist Tiperi?"
He chuckled again, "This is the last one I promise."
"Tiperi go round the compound, after that you people will go to the village square," another male said.
"Please stop encouraging him, and giving him ideas." Adanna pleaded. If she wanted to be free, she could easily release her hand from Tiperi's shoulder but fear wouldn't let her. Tiperi did as he was determined to do. Nnadi marched alongside him giving him the encouragement he needed. Adanna could only protest childishly. The day's breeze graced itself upon their skin, it was a good thing to feel once again. They have only felt it for short periods of time for so long, it was nice they were feeling it now as it gave them the notion of tasting freedom once again.
"Tiperi we are going round the compound?"
"Yes" he said.
"Do you want me to fall?"
"You won't fall I will catch you."
"With which hands?"

Tiperi stretched out his hands. "These ones, I'm very strong." He said assuring her. Adanna laughed in disbelief, shaking her head "There is nothing I won't hear."

"At least slow down" she demanded, and he did.

"Like this?"

"You may as well stop waking all together, walk a little faster." Adanna said.

He increased his pace a little, "like this?"

"Yes better, just like this."

Walking round the compound would see them go behind huts in the compound, they walked as much as they could. When they returned and ready to enter the hut, the crowd had gathered in front of her hut, giving a standing ovation as they approached. Of course Adanna couldn't identify who had said they were supposed to celebrate. The word got round and they concurred to it, putting their words into agreement. Adanna could hear drumbeats, they were expecting merry making, they just needed a trigger, and Adanna walking was a perfect excuse. Adanna had never known such a thing before, she laughed and smiled, Tiperi attempted to start dancing with her hands still on his shoulder.

"You better not try it", Adanna warned.

He wouldn't have any of it he laughed and continued his miniature dance.

"You just want me to fall, that is just what you want" Adanna said.

"Okay fine I will stop dancing." Tiperi said raising his hands up in surrender, "I don't want you to fall" he said and he was true to his word. When they approached the hut, she decided against entering the hut, rather asked Nnadi to bring her a log of wood for sitting, which Nnadi did. The crowd had now fully immersed themselves into the music, everyone was dancing, while those who could sing did sing. Adanna sat on her log of wood, with Nnadi and Tiperi on either side of her like a queen with her bodyguards. Tiperi stood looking at those who danced, Nnadi also stood, her jaw on her palm. She looked at those dancing like something bad would happen to her if she joined them, she knew her place, she was a slave. The most beautiful slave Adanna had ever seen.

"You don't want to dance again, right?" Adanna asked looking at Tiperi. Tiperi found the question funny he laughed and shook his head, before saying no. The three stayed together, while others toiled under the sun in the name of dancing, looking at them, and the way they were going about the merriment, they wouldn't be stopping any time soon. Adanna thanked her stars, that she was sitting down, it would be hard to leave them and go inside, after all they were celebrating on her behalf. Adanna couldn't deny it, she was flowing with the music, they played for a very long time before one of the drummers asked her to try and join them to dance. He must unarguably be the oldest man amongst them. Adanna knew she had seen him once or twice before but couldn't remember the details of their meeting, she knew he was family.

"Come and dance, just try," he continued pleading, though to Adanna it sounded more like a command than a request.

"I don't dance, I don't and I don't think I'm even in the condition to, even if I wanted to."

"Don't worry you can." He said. Again to Adanna he sounded something like, "You must dance, you have no option." Before Adanna could protest some more, she was lifted up by unknown men, who led her gently to the centre where they gathered, Tiperi sprang into action, making himself available as the man to provide support. True to her word, she did not dance, and had probably never danced before, as far as she could remember, she just did not dance, her dance moves were so very pathetic as she shook her body awkwardly, like one having a seizure. Nnadi's jaw dropped. It was horrible! Others who also noticed her sorry state dancing, rationalized it, by excusing her, believing it was her recovering knees. The man who had invited her to the dance floor in all his years on earth, had never seen such dancing before, it was mind numbing and unbelievable. Right there and then he prayed to the god of health never to allow him have a knee injury in his remaining days on earth. He felt sorry for Adanna. As for him he played the drum harder almost injuring his fingers. Those around and passersby knew there was celebration in the Herbalist compound, but didn't expect it so early. Uninvited they trooped in.

*****

Obeli had been jogging almost the whole day for him fear was a powerful motivator. Luckily for him he was close to Akom, and he thought he could take a breather. He drank from his water pouch to quench his taste, picked some dried meat to relieve hunger. He wouldn't be stopping for food, he had to make it home as quick as possible. If only Obirika could see him now, she was serious when she was praising and he was certain she meant the words, calling him the bravest, Otukidikpo 1 of Akom the Egunti Onapipi Ekuntoro, the man that dines with the gods as equal and so forth. The words were still in his head, he even smiled and congratulated himself when he remembered the words. Sometimes he would make war steps as a warrior he was. He had his meat in his hand, his mouth was open all that remained was for him to throw the dry meat into his mouth, his hand was very close to his open mouth when he heard a branch snap in the bush, the wind rustled also in the bush. In his mind it was kidnappers. Otukidikpo 1 of Akom the brave raced off dropping his meat on the ground, he ran like the wind, he didn't even look back to ascertain if he was being pursued, right now he was the fastest runner in Akom. Obeli ran without any caution in the world after running for a very great distance, without seeing anyone he took a sharp turn to the left he was very close to Akom now. Five girls saw him coming, and for them one thing was certain a man running at such pace meant grave danger and certain death was lurking around, they didn't wait for Obeli to get closer they dropped their baskets and hoes and ran off screaming as they did so. Obeli saw them run surely there was danger somewhere for them to run, he ran even faster. Obeli the protector of the weak got to the girls and pushed one of the girls down and didn't even stop to say sorry or care, he overtook them running past them like a shadow. Obeli ran all the way into Akom without looking back for a split second, a new record. In Akom still in full sprint he took a turn to the right, colliding with an unsuspecting path user. The man was coming from the opposite direction, with the impact, both men saw themselves on the ground. Obeli quickly stood up without apologizing he started running again, the man too stood up, he must have hurt his waist because he felt a sharp pain there but that didn't deter him, he turned around facing Obeli's direction and ran also limping as he did so, there was no need waiting for what was pursuing Obeli to catch up with him.

    Alas! Obeli did it, he ran from one village to another, later he planned to justify it by claiming he had an urgent message to deliver that would aid his beloved sister. He ran into his father's compound. Startled Odika could only stare in disbelief. "Obeli" he shouted dropping his fresh roasted yam, yet to be scraped. Obeli was panting, clutching his stomach, his throat was severely dry with hands on the knees, he tried to stabilize himself before speaking. The ground was spinning fiercely, Obeli felt strange, his father was nowhere in sight then he fell to the ground and blacked out.

*****

Immediately Adanna greeted the last well-wisher, just standing in front of her hut, the Herbalist and his entourage came in. By now everyone had dispersed, all those who celebrated with Adanna. The sun was about to go in for the day, entering the compound Etiti gave out a joyous shout to indicate they were back. The good thing was that people who saw them coming back followed them. When Etiti gave the shout, those in the compound came out, but with only smiles at first, Adanna was also out now gently walking towards the Herbalist with Tiperi leading. The Herbalist noticed her, he stood transfixed, looking at Adanna walk towards him. He felt the world complete, his great masterpiece. The good feeling that came when see your work come to fruition, he had nursed this strong, most beautiful, bold, and simply mesmerizing woman back to good health. His new wife was standing shy beside him, with her slaves. Etiti had stopped shouting now, she had seen Adanna. The tired compound people who had expended their energy gyrating all day, sensed the need to celebrate again. Of course they were expected to dance and celebrate. The old man who played the drum ignored his blistered fingers. A new set of instrumentalists had begun a music. As Adanna walked, towards them while also dancing as much as she could, her face beamed. She wore a beautiful smile, oh she was beautiful. The Herbalist had to call himself back to consciousness, he was drooling. Etiti ran to Adanna and gave a very tight hug. Tiperi could only smile, Etiti and Adanna held each other for a long while, there Etiti was sobbing.

"Etiti are you crying?" Adanna asked with all tenderness in her voice.

"No dear" Etiti answered amidst tears, "I'm just happy, so very happy."

The merry makers continued, eyes fixed on Etiti and Adanna, but body moving to the music. Herbalist stared on, beside his wife Irima could only wonder who the woman was. Etiti released Adanna who had also been hugging. Then she faced the crowd, raised her hands up gave a melodious screech, everyone's spirit got lifted. She gave the melodious screech again, joyous celebration ensued fiercer. The people hugged, danced, no need to wait, drinking also started. The old man had an exiguous part of his inner self tainted with regret, his aching fingers didn't allow him hold his drinking horn properly as a result he wasn't enjoying his drink. It was senseless to enjoy with pain he wished for freedom to enjoy literally and with every gulp he gave Adanna a malevolent eye as if she caused his pain. Irima had had enough dancing, but it was expected, she did the little she could, she had to impress her in-laws especially harmless Etiti. The elders came and congratulated the Herbalist, relatives hugged them both with screams of "welcome my beautiful darling, the precious one, amazing girl" and so forth, they also congratulated the Herbalist and Etiti "You have done well" they said. "Congratulations now you will know true happiness," others said. Adanna showed unwavering support to the best of her ability, the Herbalist believing he had shown enough detachment from emotion approached Adanna with smiles.

"You will have to tell me everything. How is it possible that you didn't crawl but went straight to walking?"

Still displaying her perfect white teeth amazingly set together.

"No problem I will tell you all." They embraced.

The celebration went on for a while more people would come and some would go, it was an open invitation to anyone. 'Come drink, eat, dance, greet, congratulate, give gift if you had any'. After a while, when it was well into the night the Herbalist took a bow and went into his hut with his wife. Adanna and the ever-dependable Tiperi followed suit. The whole world belonged to Etiti at that moment as such, she must please all men, it was her day, she barked orders and made the attempt of greeting almost everyone even greeting some twice or thrice, especially the women who attended the village women meeting. Those she would see going, she would tell to come again as if she had another son that she was hoping would get married. When the Herbalist sensed visitors had reduced, he went straight to Adanna's hut gave her, her herbs and went on to massage the knees.

"So how did it happen I must have missed a lot." He said smiling.

Adanna who had now forgotten what it meant to have anger in her heart, pointed to Tiperi. Who as usual had turned to a carved wood in a shrine, emotionless, motionless and almost blank. For now only Adanna brought out the best in him, pointing to him he smiled but not as usual.

"I never knew this boy is mischievous."
Tiperi smiled more facing down and listening to all Adanna said.
"I was struggling to get myself together, unexpectedly, this boy triggered me, it was either I walked or fall face down flat on the ground, imagine me falling?" The Herbalist was getting the gist he had to laugh.
"I told him we should sit and rest of course I was standing and he was the support. Do you know what he did? He moved." Adanna said stretching the move, "Without even warning me."
The Herbalist with a satisfying laughter, "So he is the hero?"
"Hero!" Adanna said clapping in disbelief, "You are calling him hero, he punished me, was walking up and down, he took me round the whole compound. I don't even know what to say." Tiperi only chuckled, while playing with his fingers still faced down not looking at either her or the Herbalist.
"People came out then one of your uncles I don't think I know his name made me dance, the elderly one."
"Then or now, when we returned?" the Herbalist asked. "Then" Adanna answered "We have been dancing almost all day."
"No wonder," the Herbalist said, "saw your dance moves this evening, was mesmerized. I knew you must have been training, you danced so amazingly."
A temporary shyness caught Adanna, "Thank you" she said shy.
"Wow, Tiperi well done my man." The Herbalist said. "He is still shy," he added pointing to him.
"Enough about me how was the marriage ceremony? You are the one who should be telling stories."

"Oh it was pleasant, everything went smoothly."
"Tell me everything." Adanna demanded.
"Well okay…" The Herbalist went on to narrate all that occurred in a very detailed manner plus he revealed to Adanna the fact that Irima was his childhood friend. "We played together a lot as kids but I never really imagined marriage, I remember going to swim with her in the river one day it was totally her idea we both almost drowned but some fisher men saved us or was it when I took fruits to them we sure played a lot as kids. We were also close when we grew up then she left later she came back and now we are married" he concluded.
"You two played as kids?"
"Yes we did, you don't believe me?"
"I believe you, since you are saying it but I didn't see it in you two today, she acted like this stranger to you and all that."
"She acquired the shyness newly, I too noticed it but give her time. As kids we were fearless, honestly. There is this one time we went into the forest it was also her idea." The Herbalist emphasized on "It was her idea," saying the words as slowly as possible. "We stayed home because then both our fathers were alive and our fathers took us wherever they went but that day her father brought her to our place and the two fathers went out leaving us alone so, we went into the forest and got attacked by a wild monkey, we can't tell what we did but that day, don't laugh, I discovered she could run faster than me. Yeah I said it."
Adanna chuckled "An open confession it is."
"Yes it is." The Herbalist continued. "Again there is another one I can remember, don't misunderstand there are a lot of stories just don't want to bore you with our shenanigans. Here again what happened was her idea that

caused it. My father attended to the king's servant, as a reward the king gave him a bottle of the white man's drink it is a very violent drink."

"How do you know it is violent?" Adanna asked teasingly.

"Well listen to the story." The Herbalist said. "So my dad came back with the drink I had never seen such a thing as the container before, my father when he returned told us the king had a magical instrument from which you can see yourself just like the water. It is also breakable like the container of the violent drink. Anyways my father came back and showed us all this strange drink and its container, he tasted it and informed us all not to touch it, it was only for men. When my wife visited," when he said "Wife" his heart warmed with pride and contentment, "I told her about the drink, she became so fascinated that I didn't rest for any period, she told me all she wanted was to see this container I was talking about, so we sneaked into my father's hut, this very one you are staying in right now."

"Hmmmm," Adanna hummed raising her eyebrows, "really?" she asked.

"Yes this was my father's hut."

"I figured it has got be, anyway continue." Adanna said. "Okay, so we searched for the drink everywhere, there used to be a shelf made with bamboo trees tied together at this corner of the hut," he pointed to his left, "The top there, but I removed the shelf, as kids we were of course short but then all we needed was how to get the breakable container, we were certain it had to be up there, we searched the whole ground and didn't find it, we piled logs of wood on top each other, stealthy I made it to the top." The Herbalist smiled. "I found what we were looking for, we erased every trace of our act, and then by her suggestion, we went into the bush, the one behind my mother's shrine, and opened it, we listened if it would talk or something too strange to happen, Irima caressed it, and caressed it, looking inside it, she took a long pause then she drank, her face distorted, I was scared I had seen my father's face do likewise, but then she pressured me and I couldn't resist, so I drank too. It was just discomforting, the sensation, the taste, was just eerie, but we continued drinking until," the Herbalist grabbed his knees, "Until we finished it. Then we began to feel really strange and disoriented, well I can't remember more, but we were later told we were found the following day, because I woke up with a terrible pain in my head and I remember throwing up, both of us. I heard my father ran to the king but he laughed at my father and told him he had had similar experience himself. That we would get over it and we did, bottom line we were drunk." Adanna could only smile, removing her gaze from the Herbalist only to check Tiperi who was in deep sleep now she was not a stranger to the white man's goods.

"As kids we shared everything, every gift given to us."
"Wait, wait, wait, what did your father do to you two when you two recovered?" Adanna asked.

"He was more happy than angry, grateful no harm came to us, he never even scolded us, such was his love."

"And you are exactly like him," Adanna said.

"You think so?" the Herbalist asked.

"Pawpaw tree will only bear pawpaw."

"If you say so, I really felt it when she left, it was not our faults, there was nothing we could do."

"Wow! Tell me about your father."

"He didn't stay around much, he left this world while I was a bit very young, but then again, long enough to teach me all I needed that would guide me through life. I just pray to the gods that I would do the same for my children."

The Herbalist went on to share the little he knew about his father, and his death almost ruined Adanna's day but with the Herbalist help, she was able to shake it off.

"My father taught me all he knew, not minding my age, took me along wherever he went. I know you are aware about my displeasure with the slave trade, it is from my father too.

"Yes, I know his death was quite tragic." Adanna said, trying to console the Herbalist.

"Not even that, about his death, you know, long before I was born. When the slave trade bloomed, the slavers were carrying slaves on a canoe across for embarkation. The canoe was over-burdened, just overloaded, it capsized, my father was at the bank of the river, shouting at the slavers, cursing them for their heartlessness and atrocities. They promised to kill him if he did not shut his mouth. He dared them, this was while they were going, before the canoe capsized, now when the canoe capsized, the slaves had the white man's rope, very strong, they call it chain or iron shackle, impossible to break. I heard it is their god that made it himself for them. They were about thirty slaves, women, children, men and most didn't know how to swim, they were from the hinterland, the slavers could swim, they quickly swam ashore, abandoning the slaves. My father saw it all, he panicked, he looked and the slavers were swimming to the shore saving themselves. He dove into the river swimming as fast as he could, trying to get to the slaves, who were now completely submerged, as you know the river is not clear. Sensing he was at the spot he submerged into the river almost reaching the bottom he had thought the slavers would rescue their merchandise but they didn't.

Searching and staying under water for as long as a man could, he felt something with his hand, it was human. He tried to swim to the surface with the body, it was impossible, they were about thirty people tied to the same shackle, by this time he was on the surface of the river with the first body but others dragged them down but those still struggling almost at the bottom of the river, the first person he raised was a girl. He looked at her neck and noticed how the shackle could be opened. Though this took him a long time, he tried splitting the metal but no success. When fortunately he had seen how to unlock it, he unlocked it, and carried her to the shore which was quite a distance. Do you want to know something shocking? My father was not the only one at the shore, aside the slavers. There were villagers, fishermen. They refused to help when my father called for help. Not a single person jumped into that river to assist him, not one. All the slaves could have been rescued, if not all, at least most. Nobody helped, not one person. Instead they stood and watched like they were witnessing a drama. When my father called for help some more he swam back. He was able to carry about eighteen people. He swam that day till his bones quaked. His eyes were blood shot and veins popped out in strange places on his body. His muscles were as if they had withered. He tried to resuscitate them, still no one came close to help. He started from the first girl he brought ashore. Thankfully she came back to live. It was an act of the good gods. Amongst the eighteen, only four survived. My father took the four, but before then the remaining fourteen he lined them at the shore, and cursed any man that would come to try to bury them. He said that their corpse would decay and the stench would pollute the air and every man would breathe in the stench of their filthiness and wickedness. The stench he said would fill their stomachs. After he had arranged the dead on the shore, men and women, he couldn't find the children. It haunted him. Then when they had recovered their strength a little, he marched them to his compound. To his astonishment, the slavers came back and challenged him. The same slavers who were in the canoe with them and abandoned them to die."

"These are our property," they claimed. They accused my father of being a thief. "We demand what is ours" they said. "You are a free man that is why we are respecting you."

"They are not your slaves anymore," my father argued. "I picked them from the bottom of the river by my own strength. I released their shackles. From now on they are free men and women. You abandoned them to die. Go to the river or to the shore and take those ones lying there, but these ones, you can't have them. Over my dead body." My father said.

"And over your dead body shall it be" they said.

"By now, they had lost their weapons in the river, but still they attacked my father without mercy. The slaves were three men and a woman. Being men, they were able to evade capture and they escaped. It remained only the woman and my father defended her with all his strength. Glad that the others had escaped, he knew that the girl's life rested on his shoulders. By then, my father was a chief, albeit, he being young. They attacked him with caution. After much tussle, they got hold of the woman, grabbed her and ran off. My father, weary, both from the exercise in the river and fighting off five men ran after them. The girl screamed as loud as she could. My father ran after them. They would push him down, he would stand up and pursue again. He got a club. This time he had an upper hand. When he had attacked them with the club, they dropped the girl. Angered, they frantically searched for their own clubs. They couldn't find any. They cut off tree branches, formed a circle and was ready to attack. A man who was in the woods who had been observing the whole thing then approached with the white man's gun. He didn't know what was happening but was certain that my father and the girl were victims. He made them all surrender and that was my father's salvation. He would have died that day, or at least both of them. The man surrendering them patiently marched them to the king, to report what he had seen. The king ordered the woman seized. My father protested and challenged the king. That would have meant death for him but the king was not in the mood. He had learnt about what my father did at the river and what had transpired. The girl was locked up, still to be sold as a slave. My father was broken. For days after he returned he couldn't eat, or sleep. Every day he would go to the king to solicit on behalf of the girl. After much entreaty, the king gave him an option. If he wanted her free, he may as well buy her, not by offering agricultural produce, but by paying the price that the white man would have paid in full. My father sold a lot of things he had, some of his lands and he purchased her freedom. The slavers were furious at this. They petitioned the king for my father to also pay for the escaped slaves. They would have died anyway, my father protested. But his plea fell on deaf ears so he was made to pay for the 3 escaped slaves, not the tiniest part was left."

"Should I also pay for the dead ones and children now turned food for the animals in the river?" my father asked the king and his chiefs.

In anger, a fellow chief got up and slapped him as hard

as possible. "How dare you speak to the king in that tone?" he asked.

"For the second time you escape the death sentence", the king said. He was stripped of his chieftaincy title and he was made to go through the shame parade as punishment." The Herbalist exhaled. "You must know, my father continued as a herbalist still healing the people of the same village even the king and his chiefs like I told you before, till his death which I have already told you about too. Please I beg you, you must not tell anyone about this story, about my father. Please I beg you, you wanted to know the kind of man that he was and why he died the sort of death that he died. Plus you are, or you used to be a slaver, so I thought you should know about him and about me. I believe in love, the kind of love where you are happy that good things are happening to other people, and you yourself try to make good things happen to people, giving them smile, and laughter. Life is too short and ordinarily filled with pain for another man to cause you more pain. Being a slave, you can't dream, you only exist, and life is too short for that. I believe in love."

Adanna was lost for words. Their discussion had taken a greater part of the night and they both knew that it was time for rest. The Herbalist got up, "I must leave you now."

"Wait," Adanna said. "What happened to the girl after he paid for her, and where is she now?"

The Herbalist looked at her with a smile, "her name is Etiti, my mother. Good night."

Adanna felt numb. Trying to say good night she could only move her lips, no sound came out. The Herbalist walked to his mother's hut to check on her. He knocked and no one answered. He went into her hut only to see

Etiti spread on her bamboo bed, with her food set on a raised platform in front of her. She even had a ball of pounded yam in her hand. The Herbalist could only smile. After arranging a marriage ceremony in three days, walking round the whole village and doing all manner of jobs, the body had its limit and hers had reached it. Hopefully she didn't have any in her mouth as she exhaled like one in a deep sleep. The Herbalist removed the food on the platform, took the ball of pounded yam in her hand. She would wash her hands in the morning or maybe afternoon. Assisting her, he raised her legs and aligned them straight on the bed, satisfied that she would be okay. His heart had a doubt he checked her mouth to see if food was inside so that she does not choke. He checked her mouth and it was empty. He looked at her hands again, no problem too, she would wash them tomorrow. He took a cloth and covered her. On his way out, Etiti muttered some words, "Dance, dance, Herbalist dance." He turned and looked at her once again. He was happy, even in her sleep, he was in her heart. He left. As was his custom he went round the compound and checked everywhere to make sure that all was safe as the man of the compound. He passed the old man's hut, the man that Adanna had described, only to see him lying outside his hut, the noticeable things about him being his protruding stomach awkwardly on top of his lanky frame, and a gourd in his hand, with his loud snoring. It was a common sight. The Herbalist ignored him sure that everything was okay went to his hut and called it a night.

CHAPTER 46

Otukidikpo I of Akom was lying face up in his hut after downing about one clay pot of water and food for two. He had been resuscitated and left to rest for a while. His legs and upper body were numb. Darkness was already visible, so then again, he had a feeling he had failed again, his father was sitting beside him, waiting for him to utter his first words.

"How long was I out?" Obeli asked.

"A while, the sun has gone down completely," his brother answered. His brothers were all with him now. His father still stared at him without speaking. A moment of silence reigned. With much effort like a woman delivering a baby, squeezing his face, as oddly as possible while hissing in pain, it was not fifty men that beat him but running, that was the reason he was numb and in pains. Obeli sat upright on his bed looked at his father. How would he start his tale? He had not personally witnessed his father act violently but then he had heard stories, how Ubiakwa was a hard man. Ubiakwa still looked at him intently.

"Obeli," he finally said. "What happened? Has my brother become so callous that he can't take care of you people? I heard you ran in, what was chasing you?"

Obeli nodded, swallowed hard, "We, I went to Mkpunki."

Ubiakwa frowned his face. He was in fact pouting. He would look at Obeli, then every corner of the hut. He did so moving only his eyeballs, his face remained rigid.

"Mkpunki," he said skeptically.

"I went after Adanna."

Ubiakwa re-adjusted himself on the seat, mute.

"Father, this must not leave this hut." He was even giving orders. Nothing Ubiakwa would not see, "Father I found out that Adanna had kidnapped Obirika and planned to sell her. She also released Oja the Akuta warrior. He was the one who led them to Mkpunki. I went after them because I believed I could reason with her, talk her out of it since she is my sister. A lot happened but after we rescued Obirika, Adanna chased after us. Something must have happened because we lost her, and we concentrated on coming back. I believe she is still back there, or maybe something happened to her. I really don't know."

"I felt it," Ubiakwa said, "As a father I just knew." Immediately he got up, went into the compound, called on his slave. "Go to Amatokwu, tell him I need nothing less than 300 warriors, trackers, ready to leave for Mkpunki immediately. Fly now, fly."

Amatokwu was the right man. In moments, three hundred and fifty something men had gathered at Ubiakwa's compound, well-built and agile with their assorted weapons. It was the middle of the night. Soon it would be morning. The weather was crispy, soon to change and become humid.

"You all know Adanna? I want her back here, no matter what. You people leave immediately, go into every corner, known and unknown, starting from Mkpunki. You would neither eat, nor sleep, not even rest, till Adanna is back here. If you don't find her don't come back to Akom, I'm Ubiakwa and I have spoken." With the final words the men dispersed, running off, into the darkness with their torchlights.

*****

The Herbalist had been introducing Irima in the morning, though she was not a stranger to the compound, at least to the new people in the compound. After the introduction to the people, the Herbalist attended to Adanna, excusing himself by claiming he had errands to run.

"You just got married won't you at least stay and be with your wife." Adanna had said.

"I'm a herbalist, I attend to the sick. I can't enjoy while others nurse pain."

Etiti had come to visit her as usual before also leaving for who knows where. To the surprise of almost everyone things were changing, in fact, have changed, Tiperi woke up early today.

*****

The men sent by Ubiakwa to go after Adanna had covered a great distance that in the latter part of the morning they were at the border of Akom. At such pace in days they would be in Mkpunki. All were men of valour, great warriors of Akom, strong in every sense of the word, and capable of bringing the result Ubiakwa demanded. At least each of them had tasted battle and knew what it was like to take a life in a bid to protect loved ones.

Obiagu the leader halted them, "Men of Akom, I greet you." They hailed and greeted back. The leaves on the trees seemed to rattle at the sound of an explosion of baritone voices. "We have a mission to go to Mkpunki and return the lost daughter of Akom back to the open arms of her darling father, who is a chieftain. My warriors and men of great courage, we must accomplish this task. To be qualified to be called a man you must do the impossible. There are two known routes to Mkpunki. We shall split into two groups. We will search to and fro. What do I mean by that? We will enter every known village on our way to Mkpunki and we will repeat the same on our way returning. Until we find her, we shall gather here on the sixth day, and must wait for two days for everyone before returning. If your group finds her, return with her and wait here for two days, for others. If your group do not find her, still wait here. The mission is to return with her, no other option. Never split yourselves into a group of less than 10 so that you can withstand any attack and defend yourselves if the need arises. Nuhu, you will lead the second group." They hailed again. Each was properly and heavily armed, chanting their war songs. They shared themselves into groups of two with plans to split further. They, having done that, dispersed.

*****

Adanna was sitting on her bed as usual. Tiperi occupied the sitting log, waiting for action, but Adanna was taking her time. She had no job to do but walk around to strengthen her bones some more. Secretly she wished to do solo today. If she danced yesterday then certainly it was possible. As usual, she had a bad night. Nightmares were becoming a common occurrence for her. In her dreams she kept seeing bad things happen to the people she knew, and most times she wouldn't be able to help them, always incapacitated. Last night it was Tiperi she saw getting drowned in the river. She couldn't swim, as a result she couldn't help him. In real life, one thing she was certain of was that she wouldn't let any harm to come to him. Tiperi slept through most of her night turmoil. Her ever present help came from the Herbalist and Etiti.

"Tiperi, why are you so quiet, hope all is well," Adanna asked.

"I'm fine," the young boy said with smiles.

"Okay, good. You seem overly quiet, that is why I'm asking."

"I'm thinking about so many things." Tiperi said.

Adanna who had been inspecting her knees abandoned it and stared at Tiperi in disbelief, pondering if she heard him correctly. Then she gave Tiperi a suspicious look, with one eye wide opened and the other, half closed. "You are thinking, as in thinking?" Adanna asked.

"Yes" Tiperi said with all seriousness.

The next thing that came to Adanna was to gape. Adanna had seen and heard so many things in her short time on earth. She considered herself adventurous and fearless. But here Tiperi was presenting a serious dilemma for her. When a child told you he was doing serious thinking, it was either you become scared, really scared, or you become filled with curiosity, itching to find out what the serious thinking was. Then again it could be something to laugh over and forget, or a shocking revelation that could alter one's course of life, changing it completely. She had to do something.

"Is it something you want to share, maybe I can help?" Adanna asked with genuine care.

And it got worse. Tiperi sighed, scratched his head, wiped his face with his palm, and rested the hand under his jaw. Adanna was truly worried now. It was as if she was looking at a 50 year old man who had a terrible harvest and now couldn't feed his fifteen children and four wives, considering whether to abandon his family and abscond, or go into begging. Tiperi maintained his posture, erasing any doubt in Adanna's mind that he was not really thinking.

"Okay, Tiperi, you are kind of scaring me. Just tell me what it is already."

Tiperi hesitated, not knowing how to put his words. He hesitated again. Adanna depicted calmness outwardly, but inwardly, was apprehensive. Tiperi took his time, flinched, cracked his knuckles. Adanna cleared her throat.

"I have suffered," Tiperi said.

The voice in Adanna's head was screaming, "You should have been scared." Adanna felt her heart sink deeper. Should she hear the next words or run out from the hut? What does a child know about suffering? Unfortunately for her this was a child that found solace with her.

"I, I don't want to suffer again," the poor boy said. "Please promise me that I won't suffer again."

This would have been a perfect job for the Herbalist. He always knew when and how to say the right thing under such situations. Though it felt like lying, because somehow, man always suffered, but she needed to do as requested. "I promise you won't suffer," Adanna said. "But if you start walking won't you leave me? You will go to your place, and leave me. Then I will be here alone and suffer, or go back to my father and also suffer. Please don't leave me. I will do anything you want me to do," tears bubbled in Tiperi's eyes. "Please, mother." The word "mother" pierced through Adanna's heart, breaking her last stronghold, and shattering every of her defence against having emotion for another creature. Her life had been altered forever. Lack of love had made lack of feeling easy, making regret less severe and giving assurance that she wouldn't get hurt for any reason, giving the pride that she made her decision with reason and not emotion. Then again what life would you have afterwards if you deny this innocent child a simple request of just loving?

"Tiperi" Adanna said coolly, "If we ever separate it is because you left me. I have no intention to ever leave you, or hurt you no matter what. I'm your mother, I will protect you, fight for you and give you the best life has to offer."

Tiperi as swift as a peregrine falcon rushed and hugged Adanna. He had his tears but he was laughing now. They held each other for quite a long time. When the hugging ended, Tiperi sat down with a burden apparently lifted off him.

"Okay when are we going?" Tiperi asked.

"Go?" stunned Adanna asked.

"Yes," said Tiperi.

"Let me get well first."

"Will I be a fisherman?"

"Ahh! We don't really have rivers in Akom."

"You don't have rivers? What do you have?"

"Streams."

"So what will I be?"

"How about choosing between, maybe hunting, farming, or maybe, I can't believe I'm going to say this, because I belittle my brother that does it, but you can weave mats, and baskets, and hats, etc.?"

"Yes, that is the one I will do," excited Tiperi said.

"Sure, why not, why not?" Adanna said, scratching her temple.

"Or maybe I will farm."

"That is my boy. Farming is good honey."

"Okay I will decide later." Tiperi said.

"Take your time my darling."

"Are there other things that I can do?" the boy asked.

"Hunting." Adanna said.

"You have said hunting before."

"Okay then I will remember others later and tell you. Yes, we have cloth making."

"Is that not for women?" Tiperi asked.

"Thank goodness you know. What about animal husbandry?" he had to think hard about this one. While in the process, they heard a knock. It was a strange knock. Both had never heard this pattern before. "Please come in." Adanna said.

The newest bride came in. She was an adequate competitor to Adanna when it came to beauty. She greeted with warmth. Adanna reciprocated. Tiperi got up to offer Irima the seat.

"No, don't worry dear. I will sit on the bed," Irima said. Sitting down she glanced to her right, to the top corner where the Herbalist's father's shelf used to be. She seemed surprised and the look was on her face.

"It has been removed," Adanna innocently teased. "I know you are looking for it."

Irima beamed. "So he told you?"

"Yes, we talked a little about you."

"I'm sure he made it appear I'm always the architect, and initiator."

Adanna had to laugh. "You two really were a couple."

"I was just following him, every bad idea came from him. Even the day we got drunk with the white man's drink, he told me about it, so that I would suggest we should go after it."

"Really?"

"Yes. Really." Both women had a hearty laugh, instantly they had clicked like sisters.

"But if you would ask me I would say you were the leader." Adanna said.

"I said it, he always made it appear so. Okay listen to this so that you will judge." Irima told more stories of her adventures with the Herbalist. Adanna listened with rapt attention still wearing her 'I'm a friendly person' smile. Tiperi had excused them now, choosing to sit outside while they discussed. As a child he had been trained to excuse himself and leave when adults were discussing.

"It is always him. He is the leader, but whenever, even if he is sleeping and you wake him up to recount tales, he presented me as the initiator." Irima continued.

Adanna chuckled. With Irima stories she noticed she had never had such powers over a man though she had killed one or two.

"Yes, that is the way it is. Did he tell you about when we hijacked a canoe?"

Adanna's eyes widened in surprise. "You guys were really adventurous." Even Irima chuckled. "It is him," she said abashed.

"But he doesn't act like one much into activities as such." Adanna said.

"Even as kids he would do something and you wouldn't believe he was the one that did it." Irima countered pleasantly.

"So you people hijacked a canoe, literally?" Adanna probed on.

"Hijack is the only word I can remember and use. I wouldn't use steal. When we got into trouble he would be saying gbakurube, gbakurube."

"What does gbakurube mean?" Adanna asked.

"Nobody knows. It is only him that does, and when you initiate it and say it then he would be giving you his, according to him, 'wicked eyes'. He says people give 'wicked eyes', why shouldn't he, and since then, if anything happens, he is scared, excited, frightened, agitated, he would exclaim 'gbakurube!'."

"I have never heard him say it." Adanna said.

"Maybe he has stopped. But he used to."

Adanna cracked up. She couldn't control the laughter. As Irima continued the stories.

"When I told him he was reckless, he called me Niaturikipa."

"Hey!" Adanna exclaimed.

"You will never know, he has a lot of names, and most times it is me that he calls them, he will call me or use it as an exclamation, I can't remember all names." She gave it a time to remember another one, "When he finds something funny then he would say 'O ma gad I kant bili dis' that one I asked him he said the white men say it, that, that is what someone heard from someone, who had it from another." Irima slapped her laps, with excitement. "If he is displeased and wants to get at you, he would say "daa negoro." Another one from as he said people say the white man say, or "stuupi negoro' so many, he had so many, I don't know if he still remembers them, he had his own and others he learnt from people. If I remember more I will tell you." Irima assured.

"You know I have heard someone say "o ma gad" but the person said it outside and I think it sounded like his voice, I wonder what it means." Adanna said.

"If you ask him he won't say." Irima responded, sounding perplexed. "And at first he started with "gbakurube" then he went over to 'o ma gad'." Both women had a laugh.

Tiperi sitting outside as far as he was concerned just did not care.

"How is your leg?" Irima asked.

"My knees, and it is getting better, at least I danced yesterday."

"Yes I saw you, please you must know, you are a wonderful dancer."

"Mmm" Adanna hummed and hugged her with tenderness, "I can't wait to start walking freely." Adanna said.

"Sure you will certainly walk, you are almost there." Irima said.

"I have not even started exercising for today and when I start walking the first place to go for me, is hunting." Adanna said with assurance.

"And you will escort me to visit friends." Irima said.

"So which one first, hunting or visiting friends?" Adanna asked.

"Hunting, then visiting, then fishing and we will rotate it like that."

"Do you think your husband will be okay with that?" Adanna asked.

"Why shouldn't he, we would do a lot," Irima said, "I know you have not gone round Mkpunki that much, so I will show you around. Have you seen my mother?" Irima asked.

"No I haven't."

"You will, she has this very mean, fish sauce, it's a killer."

"On that note I will prepare for you my bush meat pepper soup, you will be dumbfounded." Adanna said.

"Okay it is an agreement, you will give me your bush meat and I will take you to my mother to eat her fish and fish sauce, and don't tell anyone this one, there is a place that only girls in Mkpunki know and we will go, believe me it is a secret only known to girls, I can guarantee you, no man knows, and will ever know, so I will take you there." Irima said, in a low voice.

"What do you people do there?"

"You will see, and then you will know, when I went away, anytime I came back, I didn't miss going there and you will be pleased, trust me."

"Okay, I trust you."

"And to do all this you need to walk, I'm not sure I'm strong enough to carry you on my back." Irima said and laughter followed.

"You won't, I will walk." Adanna said.

"Alright then to achieve that I think we should start practicing." Irima said standing up and stretching forth her hands to Adanna to grab and stand. Adanna gladly did, when both were standing, Adanna's legs were numb and tingly, she had to shake it off, and walking would do. Irima went to her side to help her this time, she would still need support, before walking on her own. Adanna called to Tiperi who quickly ran in like his name was screamed in fear and he came to protect and kill the danger.

"Where have you been?" Adanna asked.

"Outside."

"That is a new one, I'm happy for you." Adanna said.

Irima added "We are going to exercise a little bit, so that she can get stronger, as you already know she is trying to do, we will be back soon, okay."

Tiperi would have none of that, tears began forming in his eyes, he couldn't imagine what was about to unfold.

"But aunty it is me that leads her." He protested, holding Adanna firmly now.

Adanna stuttering, "Well, eh, he is, he actually is correct, he's been doing the job." Adanna said clearing her throat.

"Alright no problem." Irima said.

"Thank you." Adanna said.

"Sure, over to you sir," Irima said,

Tiperi's face beamed, he was a pro now, assuming position he was ready to do what he knew how to do.

"She is calling you sir, you better don't do what you did yesterday." Adanna said poking his head.

Tiperi gave out a healthy laughter, that was contagious, Adanna joined to laugh.

"What did he do?" puzzled Irima asked.

"This boy! Ask him, made me over work myself."

Tiperi was still laughing. Irima wouldn't be far, the three set out from the hut. The still very cheerful ones came and greeted them when they came out. This time there wouldn't be any reason for celebration by eating drinking and dancing. When they got to the entrance of the compound Tiperi asked if they would be going out like Irima had suggested as they walked.

"No, no way." Adanna refused vehemently, "I won't be going out like this, I have some feelings too you know." An Akom indigene would shudder at those words, Adanna have feelings? She was resolute and her decision held ground, they moved round the whole compound, went to the back and again.

"Tiperi hopefully you won't be the one to get tired today, because I intend walking on my own today and I am certain it would happen." Adanna said.

The walking exercise had taken them the whole day. Now in the hut, in the cool of the evening it would be nothing more but for them to rest and then continue the following day.

Etiti, Irima and Tiperi were the ones in the hut occupied by Adanna. Etiti and Irima sat on the bed Etiti was arranging Irima's hair, playing the mother to a daughter. One of the things she had always wanted. "Tomorrow I will adorn it for you, I have beautiful ornaments." Etiti said.

Tiperi could only watch with glee, Irima had the same glee definitely Etiti did too but hair wool was clinched between her teeth. Still in the process the Herbalist knocked and walked in. What he saw was strange, at such, he had to re-adjust himself, he looked around in the hut again. Usual but somewhat unusual occupants, he greeted with anxiety to his mother as his wife greeted. All he wanted to ask was "What is going on?" before he could ask Adanna walked in on her own slowly but strongly and steadily. She was coming from the bathroom on her own, alone, the Herbalist could only look at her, he was speechless. Staring at Adanna who looked at him, gave him a smile and raised her eyebrows.

"Wow!" the Herbalist exclaimed "You are just like a magician, how do you do the things you do?" he asked.

"I'm an Akom woman." She said and winked at him "Akom woman," she repeated like being an Akom indigene gave superpowers.

"Really it has to do with Akom anyway, because you people are famed for so many things. Akom woman, okay, good to know, I will note that, my maternal grandmother is from Akom." The Herbalist said.

Etiti was gaping. The Herbalist continued "I never met her, I'm sure she must have been as strong as you are I heard she was awesome and all."

"Hold on, hold on" Etiti interrupted. "Who told you your grandmother was from Akom?" Etiti asked still in shock. "You told me she is from Akom, when I asked you, have you forgotten?"

Etiti laughed in a way that said I can't believe this, "How is Akum and Akom the same thing, I said Akum a stone throw form here. Have you not been to Akum before?" Etiti asked surprised at her son. The Herbalist was in a strange place right now he had thought he heard Akom. He even accepted Adanna the first time because of it. Etiti shook her head and continued making Irima's hair. He had to correct a lot of things. He looked at

Adanna who was smiling at him and the fact he was searching for words.

"Okay so Akum it is good to know."

"And I'm sure you have been telling people your grandmother is from Akom?" Etiti asked.

The Herbalist scratched the back of his neck and didn't answer.

"Well sometimes we hear things wrongly," he said he turned to Adanna "So you are perfectly okay now, no pains, aches, none whatsoever?" he asked.

"I still feel this sensation like everything is still soft inside or so, I don't really know how to describe it but aside that I'm really strong." Adanna said.

"It will stop, you really have a good body system, very strong indeed."

The Herbalist looked at the three of them sitting on the bed, they looked more like sisters, beauty was all he could see sitting on his log of wood.

"I'm happy that the three most special women in my life are happy, I'm a king, I'm really taking good care of you people."

Adanna and Irima smiled.

Etiti gave a protracted sigh "Who is this one?" she said.

"But I'm trying, am I not, I am amazing, most perfect, good, wonderful man to women," he turned to Irima " 'daali' am I not?"

Irima gave Adanna a look that says "didn't I tell you" while Adanna reciprocated with "I believe you" look. "What is 'daali' again?" Irima asked.

"You don't need to know." The Herbalist said resolute.

"I need to know what you are calling me."

"I'm not telling you."

Adanna looked at him and said "Akinputukido kuru di kwa o me nunu" with smiles and then waved at him. "What does that mean?" the Herbalist said to Adanna "I'm not telling you, tell us 'daali' and we will tell you, Irima also knows the meaning." Adanna said.

Irima was surprised. She looked at Adanna shaking her head. Adanna patted her shoulder. They did all with body language and no words.

"So this is a gang up, as the man I demand to know the meaning at once. And it is an order."

"And if they don't what will happen?" Etiti asked.

"I will raze down this hut and show anger."

"Look at this one." Etiti said pointing at him in contempt, "My darlings if he does anything, we will all beat him up, we will give him a serious beating like they did Afomtu, Okongi's husband."

The Herbalist feigning anger, "If fifty of you come to fight me, and I'm one handed, I will still defeat you all. Ten times over."

He must have forgotten only Adanna could give him a serious injury, a scar for life, both inwardly and outwardly.

Irima looking at him into his eyes, "Just tell us." She said sounding like a three year old girl, who wanted her mother to carry her. The Herbalist's defence was gone, he was about to talk, then hesitated, a man has got to be resolute. Adanna looked at him and said, "Akinputukido kuru di kwa o me nunu" again, smiled and pointed at him.

The Herbalist was challenged "Now seriously what does that mean?" he said.

"Tell us and we will tell you ours, 'O ma gad'" Adanna said.

The Herbalist looked at Irima she had to be the one that had told Adanna 'O ma gad' even though she used it out of place. So you people have been gossiping he thought in his head. He had no option, he had to know what this woman was saying. He may not remember the words again. And then he would have sleepless nights trying to find out or wonder what it meant and what message it carried.

"Fine 'daali' does not mean a bad thing, slave merchant who was learning the white man's language saw him doing some strange things, the black slave merchant said the white man told him he was 'riting' and he was 'riting' to his wife his 'daali' and he said his 'daali' is his wife, that is why I called you 'daali' maybe it means wife."

Irima smiled, first time he was explaining and opening up. "What of 'O ma gad'?" Adanna asked.

"That is also from the white man, it means he is calling his 'god' and saying he is surprised."

"What of…"

He didn't let her finish, as he cut her off "I'm not telling you another one, if you don't tell me the meaning of 'Aki potaku did wa mumu' or whatever it is you said."

Adanna hesitated, cleared her throat, "Actually it does not mean anything, it's senseless and meaningless, I just made it up to… you know, stimulate you, kind of." She said sounding unsure of the Herbalist next action.

"Really, it has no meaning?"

"I'm telling the truth, it does not, I'm sorry." She said respectfully.

The Herbalist shook his head. "I brought your herbs, okay finc it has no meaning," he said. "Please let's do the real business." He adjusted his seat to Adanna, gave her, her drugs and went on to message her knees, doing his job he turned to Irima "You are looking charming." He said.

"Thank you," Irima said.

"And me?" Etiti asked, menacingly.

The Herbalist was now certain, she meant it when she said she would beat him, "Mother you are the most precious and adorable, the love of my life."

Etiti gave another protracted sigh, got up, patted Irima on the shoulder and went for the exit, passing the Herbalist she slapped him at the back of the head, playfully. The Herbalist was satisfied and content with the slap, she meant it and she did it. Etiti assured Adanna she was coming back. Into the compound now they heard Etiti singing and they could also imagine she was taking dancing steps as she went to her hut. That was one happy woman. The Herbalist continued to do what he knew how to do, with delight. Tiperi had found comfort on the bed a long time ago, choosing to ignore all that was going on. Whenever the Herbalist would look up, and look at Adanna and Irima, both would become mute. He would bend down his head to concentrate on the knees and would start hearing whispers. He would try to make out what they were saying, but would only hear whispers. He would look up and they would become mute and blank again. His heart quivered, he was in trouble he thought, the two were already in alliance. Done, Adanna felt an instant impact on her knees, the relief was better. With all happening, Adanna was really considering staying in Mkpunki, there would be a lot of misery in Akom. She was really considering doing and acting in a different way. Etiti came in with Nnadi behind her they passed round, the locally made plate, each containing a fish pepper soup. She handed it out with smiles, sure they were surprised. The aroma was precious. Adanna tasted it, and her taste buds came to life. She thought of waking Tiperi. She couldn't believe he was missing this.

Everyone was concentrating on Etiti's special treat. A meal that created a memory that would last forever.

"I have something to ask, I thought of asking you privately." Adanna said looking at the Herbalist, "But I think anybody can contribute, the question is," she paused, then she spoke again, "To be a man, that has hate and a man with love, who will survive in this our world? Okay let me rephrase it, hate and love which has more advantages? The two should be saying the same thing. I really don't know."

The Herbalist's mouth was stuffed full with fish, which he gradually masticated, allowing him time to ponder on how best to answer. Etiti and Irima believed they had something to say but the man should answer first. Still chewing, he made sure to grind every last bit with his molars then he swallowed hard. "Hate and love, I really have not given it much thought because I have been leaning on one side, our elders would say love is life and hate is death, and I believe that sums it up. A wise man is not the man that knows proverbs, searches out the deep things of life but the man that loves. Love is Life. That is what I think."

"Thank you for the answer" Adanna said to the Herbalist, "Etiti" Adanna called, "Do you have anything to say?"

"My son has said it all, we all have troubles, if you love it makes it better. If you hate it makes it worse even though it may look easier, but most times in fact all times it is not the easiest. Love brings life hate brings death, that is all I know."

Then Irima spoke. "They have said most, my mother will say love is better, hate will birth hate and more hate, it never gets satisfied, if you hate this person because he has a land you want, you will kill him, you will get the land, then you will need farm instruments, and seeds, you will resort to hate again at the end it will consume you totally. Both in this life and in the next, that is what I believe, so for me it is love."

Adanna could have sworn there was a time in her life hating made much sense. But then she had more problems and more problems they never ceased coming. "Okay" she said, "Thank you all very much, means a lot to me."

The Herbalist who by this time had another mouth full could only nod in response. Etiti too nodded, Irima gave a smile. Adanna eating half of her fish and pepper soup, took excuse to go get Nnadi so that she could help her, get a cover for the plate, to preserve the remaining.

"You don't like it?" Etiti asked.

How is that possible the Herbalist wondered, wide eyed.

"Oh, it is lovely, superbly delicious I'm remaining for Tiperi, he likes fish and I think he would miss a lot by not tasting this one." Adanna said.

"Please, don't worry yourself, there is still some more remaining in the kitchen. He would eat his tomorrow, okay, enjoy yourself, I even thought you people would want extra." Etiti said.

"Who said we don't, please fill this plate." The Herbalist said, handing her his plate.

"Sure, sir, it is your favourite." Etiti took the plate and headed towards the kitchen. Adanna had made some decisions, she would tell them her real name and if they liked tell them a little about Akom and her family. She had sensed they didn't want to probe into her life, giving her enough time, and now she would be a woman who practiced love, even though she believed she had a very good reason to be a woman filled with hate. Etiti returned and handed the Herbalist a refill, and he attacked it. Adanna had also resumed with her own.

"There is something I heard today" Etiti said as she sat, "I was with a friend today and we were talking, then something happened she said her husband gave her a riddle, if she got it he would do the unthinkable and cook for her. But if she didn't, she could wave the offer good buy forever. She told me the riddle and I told her I didn't know it, then later as I was about to leave, her daughter met me and told me the same riddle with the father also making a promise to her. I was lost and helpless." Hearing that Adanna was like, 'Tell me about it.' It was the same feeling she got with Tiperi.

"And you have never really heard the riddle before?" The Herbalist asked.

"Yes!" Etiti exclaimed.

"Mother why not tell him I'am sure he would know." Irima said pointing to her husband.

"My mother is the king of riddles, there is none she doesn't know, she is the one that thought me all I know." The Herbalist said.

"But still let us hear it." Adanna said.

"Okay what does not walk, and does not have body parts but gives birth sustains life, reproduces, breathes, eats?"

All looked at Etiti, the Herbalist gave it a hard thought, surely something did he had it at the back of his mind. "I will ask around," he said.

Adanna was still on her fish pepper soup. Irima ate delicately no matter how delicious the food may seem.

"I would like to know the meaning. It is good for people to know the meaning of these things," Adanna said. Actually it was good for her to know of these things, she had paid little interest to them.

"So now it is two riddles that I have heard and don't know the answer." Irima said gently mouthing, fish bone.

"Which one again have you heard?" The Herbalist asked. "Actually two, making it, three" she answered. "The first, I am something, I'm not living but I support life, and every man and woman becomes me."

Adanna continued with her fish, it was pointless to try to even think about it, the good thing was she had never heard the riddle before. Etiti too had never heard the riddle before. Which was surprising for the Herbalist. Irima looked around to see if any of them would furnish her with answer, none did.

"Okay so two, what is the second one?" the Herbalist asked.

"I have been trying to remember it, but it is something like this, what is the thing you cannot see, cannot touch, it does not have hands, but can carry almost anything up, or around."

Etiti smiled "At least I know this one, but I won't say till others have attempted to answer."

Adanna focused more intently on her fish. The Herbalist knew all attention was on him, "I have never heard the riddle before." He said.

"Wind," Etiti said "This is actually too easy, if not the easiest, I don't have hands, but can carry things up."

"Is it only hands that can carry things up?" The Herbalist asked.

"It is the primary and in one way or the other assist in carrying things up."

The Herbalist still gave the issue a serious thought, there obviously must be something else, one can't always trust all these riddles and its answers, after a while he took a breather and drank his pepper soup, while also cutting a portion of the fish and putting it into his mouth.

"It is good we know the answer of one now, remaining two," Irima said "how do we find out the answer to others?"
"When life gives you tough questions, go to gods," Etiti was singing now.

Ejambiri
When life makes you cry, go to the gods.
Ejambiri.
At this juncture the Herbalist sang the ejambiri with his baritone voice, Etiti was up now and making dance steps.
When you want something, beloved go to the gods.
Ejambiri.
When you can't sleep go to the gods.
Ejambiri.

"Ejambiri" Etiti clapped, as she sang the last words. "I have so many songs I can teach you people," she said to Irima and Adanna. Both sat smiling at Etiti.
"My son knows a lot of songs too but you can hardly hear him sing."
"I do sing." The Herbalist protested.
"Hah!" Etiti exclaimed. "When have I ever seen or heard you sing. Please you don't sing, let us just leave it at that. Even now that you are married you are supposed to be singing to your wife. My days now speak of unending joy I have found a companion."
"O yes I have.
My cherished one, said it is us forever,
O yes it is.
Let my story be told, I have found the one that says I'm special.
O yes I have.
Come all and see I have someone, that says life is

meaningless without me.

O yes it is.

My cherished one and I are forever together.

O yes we are" Etiti sang the song. Irima and the Herbalist gave the responsive part. Adanna simply looked on.

"Sing the next words." Etiti said to the Herbalist.

After shyly refusing he smiled scratched his head and sang the next words.

"Please my dear one never leave me."

"Please never leave me." Etiti sang.

This time Irima was silent smiling and looking down. Her posture made the Herbalist chuckle, as he continued singing.

"In you I have found solace, never let my joy end.

Never let my joy end.

I have gone through the world to seek you.

O yes to seek you.

When I saw you my heart leaped.

O yes it leaped,

I knew then I was meant to be happy for forever,

O yes forever."

Then Etiti took over, "My days now speak of unending joy I have found a companion."

All sang "O yes I have." Adanna inclusive, she had picked up some words.

"Irima it is your turn." Etiti said clapping to the songs, Irima was still faced down, looking at her toes as she played with them.

"Irima" Etiti called again, "It is your turn to sing."

She laughed and ignored them still staring at the floor. Tiperi woke up, looked around changed position and slept off again.

The Herbalist stared at Irima, Adanna had her

attention and focus on different places. She was trying to memorize the words she had heard, she looked at the Herbalist and Irima intermittently while also trying to smile, clap like Etiti and imagine the next words. After much hesitation, Irima looked up still smiling and of course shy, she looked at the Herbalist and started singing, smiling as she did so. Etiti was singing the responsive part.

"Since I found you, you have made my life complete.
O yes you have,
Please in my next life come look for me,
Please come,
This joy we have found together we must keep it by all means,
Yes we must,
My world is complete with you in it,
O yes it is,
And I will cherish you for ever"

"O yes I will," Irima chuckled looked at Adanna and faced down again. Etiti continued, "My days now speak of unending joy I have found a companion,
O yes I have."

This time it was only she and Adanna that sang, the two newly married couldn't find their voices. "This song you people just sang, is just one of the songs newly married sing. I will also teach you people more. Maybe Odabi will also teach us, Akom people have songs too, I'm sure." Etiti said. Adanna simply nodded, she couldn't remember even one song, on that day she would simply say the truth.

"And I must warm you all." Etiti said "We have sang songs, which means we intend to keep it and be happy for as long as is possible. But then again truth be told, there will come a time when trials will come, evil will knock but we must gird ourselves. To be able to repel it with the love we have for each other. Our anger will die an infant. Herbalist you are the man, I expect that when feud comes you will rise above it and call your wife, making her feel just the way she feels today. As a family, if it is to go forward in love, if it is to prosper, if there is to be peace, if kindness will reign, if laughter will never cease, it is the responsibility of the man. It is how you want us to be that we will be. A man can marry any kind of woman from anywhere, of any background, status, stature, disposition, character, looks etcetera and still have a happy home. Because he would build it the way he wants, after all he is the head. But we advise women to look carefully, search, enquire and inquire because the man she marries can make or mare her. She can follow but who she is following is important, a woman cannot marry any kind of man because he will decide her fate to a large extent. That is why sometimes we find it an unfortunate occurrence for us women. So I beg you, my son be a worthy father, leader, husband, make our days happy and we will gladly follow." Etiti said.

"I will try my best mama." The Herbalist said.

"Mother if he maltreats us, we will beat him up like you suggested." Irima said delicately, looking at the Herbalist who shuddered.

"Yes of course I have even planned it, we will tie him up, use sticks and start from his fingers." Etiti said.

Adanna's mind came back to life, she had a lot of tactics for that. However her muscles felt weak. She was not sure, if called upon, she would deliver. The Herbalist simply looked on in silence, even his wife had thoughts of beating him up.

"Let me tell you people a story," the Herbalist said and told a story of a man who said some words and called it a slip of the tongue. "You people are making jokes of beating up a man and the worst part is that, it is the man's mother and his wife that are making the plan. All I can say is that it is in the inner recesses of your minds. As such guide and guard your heart."

Adanna smiled, she had a thing or two to say about slip of tongue, but one thing was sure, it was still a word uttered. Etiti looked at the Herbalist, as he continued his speech about guiding one's heart, she heard her name outside, it was the old man, he too had been treated to the fish pepper soup and he probably wanted more. Etiti got up from the bed, gave the Herbalist a nonchalant look. Irima sat feeling scolded and it showed in her demeanour. She sat as quiet as possible, including Adanna. When Etiti went towards the exit, using the back of her hand, she gave the Herbalist a soft smack on the temple, the second time she was hitting him. Irima chuckled, relieving herself of some stress of being serious minded. With the smack the Herbalist went mute, his sermon had bounced off their shells, in fact he was speaking into a whirlwind. The women of his generation, he thought, a fearful prospect it was. They remained silent.

Etiti didn't waste time before coming in again. "The answers to the riddles are plants for the first riddle and dust for the second riddle." The Herbalist looked a little unsure, "I asked your Uncle, besides the answers make sense." Etiti said. Looking at them she had her heart filled with joy and pride. She was content and fulfilled. The future was certainly sure to carry more blessings soon it would be children, grandchildren, and soon she would be the great mother overseeing a clan of worthy elect, and useful individuals. Things may start awry but would always take shape she believed. She had nothing more to say, she wished them all good night and left. Tiperi slept in peace. Adanna had a grateful heart, things made sense now. The Herbalist knew his work for the day was done, he stood greeted Adanna. Offered his left hand to Irima, assisted her up, and they both left, arm in arm to their hut.

On the way out, "It is tomorrow," Irima said turning to Adanna.

"What is tomorrow?" the Herbalist asked.

"We plan to go out and do a lot together tomorrow, hunting and so much more."

"So you people are planning to have fun?" the Herbalist asked as they went along to their hut.

Adanna heard their voice fade as they walked on, she looked round about her, the night had a sweet smell, and the weather was cool, promising a sweet sleep without heat. The dungs did well at repelling the biting insects, in all, sleep would be sweet. Except for the nightmares which she prayed should not come, at least not today. She planned to have a very happy sleep. Tomorrow she would be able to fulfil all she had dreamt of and thought of, for a very long time also being propelled by a new force. They called it love. Adanna has decided she would be led by love no more hate. Adanna the woman that loves and loved it would be said of her.

CHAPTER 47

Etiti was a proud happy woman. She doubted people would see her as weird now her son was married and had done valiantly like every other man in Mkpunki. The Herbalist had resumed fully in his work as village herbalist, though to Adanna he never really showed any difference. The two ladies walked hand in hand with each other like they were sisters, and Tiperi their kid brother. Those who invested themselves with the happenings of the village, could guess who they were. They came and greeted, news about them was not new. Some even said Irima was second wife of the Herbalist, while Adanna was the first but had a child outside wedlock, of course the child being Tiperi. Another had sworn Adanna was Etiti's child gotten in adultery. Unknown to the husband, now he was dead, she had brought her back. The person peddling the information had sworn with his life he knew what he was talking about. They both walked, still sharing their stories, in no time they felt they had known each other since birth. However they were learning the two different ways, two different women had lived their lives. One thing that was corroborated on both sides was that the men dominated and made them feel and realize that they were second tier to them. But Adanna despite the limitations imposed by men had had quite an adventurous life, doing what most fantasized about. She was about to show Irima one of such activities, hunting. Do all Adanna, then tomorrow it would be all Irima. Adanna had spent considerable time thinking about where women go to together that men don't know about.

Irima had an innocent face, not showing any sign of being involved in any nefarious act. What exactly do they do there? They had followed a narrow foot path with bushes by both sides. Tiperi couldn't wait to see an animal shot, he was carrying the little he could, Adanna was with the Dane gun. She carried it with pride and most men that saw her wore a strange look, because they were looking at a strange happening. A woman should not be carrying a gun, it had never been heard of. Adanna returned the strange glance with hers. Most of the men had only machete, so no need challenging a strange woman with the white man's magic. If something bad happened, what would you say you were trying to do? To correct an unruly woman and make her know her place? Not many people did that from the land of the dead and no one really wanted to find out how that worked. Adanna somehow managed to give Irima a smiling face, making her at peace and also at the same period gave the strangers 'don't try me face'. They had made a considerable advancement. Irima knew where hunting could be done in the forest at this time. Though some men chose to also hunt in the night. Adanna was aware of all that, she had been teaching Irima all the hunting techniques she had learnt and developed or discovered by herself. Marching beside a shallow stream, along the part that led into the main woods, she had taught Irima also, how to make traps, explaining it to her and promising to give her a practical demonstration when the time came. Adanna dipped her feet into the stream as they marched along its bank, the cool sensation to her feet was chilling. Tiperi had seen and been around a lot of water but still followed suit to dip his feet like Adanna did. What did he know she was his mother? He had dutifully followed them, giving less worry, he was efficient and dependable already becoming the man he was supposed to be. All Adanna planned now was to get a kill, a very nice one and prepare it for the whole family. One thing was certain she was not going back to the way she was before. She was going to want peace and happiness and get the little life could pass out. It was never too late. Change had come and it would stay. She had seen the Herbalist laugh and smile, she had seen Etiti laugh and smile, she had seen Irima, one thing was certain they laughed with contentment. No care and no fear, secured and at peace. She was going to keep on, on that path of life. Irima still held her hand and she clutched it a bit harder now. She had never been this far into the forest before, not even during her forays with the Herbalist as a kid. She was scared, Adanna had sensed it, warmth grew in her heart, Irima was still marching on with her, it meant she trusted her and was comfortable with her. Adanna was certain of one thing she would die if she had to, to protect Irima and Tiperi. Passing large tall trees, scattered around the path, Irima held her more. Adanna patted her and gave her assurance, she was in safe hands.

Adanna patted her Dane gun giving her assurance they were ably protected. They both laughed like little girls playing in the stream with Adanna's gesture.

"I have been wanting to ask you." Irima said, "What is the tattoo on your arm, what does it mean?"

Adanna smiled "That's my family's mark, only a member of my family can have it, we do such in Akom." Adanna said.

"We do too in Mkpunki" Irima said. "But ours is erasable, not permanent like yours and is mostly for beautification."

"So is ours too but also it is a mark."

Mkpunki men were not hunters as such, Adanna would be famous. They were mainly fishermen and as such, they had their focus on something else. There were so many inlets into the forest, however, most preferred a particular route not because it was peculiar in any way but rather because it was used. Adanna could see traces of footprints on the ground. Irima felt a sudden calm come upon her when she saw three men emerging from the opposite direction. It surprised Adanna, competition for her it was, but the men only had machete and nothing else which meant they must have set traps or they didn't go to hunt. You don't hunt with machete, most animals were faster than humans. The three men saw them in each other's arm marching deeper into the forest, with Tiperi diligently following. They greeted the men as they were supposed to. The men responded as the ladies passed and continued on their journey.

One of the men looked back. "Are those not the Herbalist's new wives?" He asked.

"Wife" another corrected.

"More like wives," he said. "There is something shady going on in that family, besides I don't trust the one by the left." The man said.

They all looked back now he was referring to Adanna, "There is something strange about her, I even heard, she works with the white man and she is a slaver, words are that she kidnapped people of "Mkpunki" and sells them." All shuddered "Why should someone who tramples on Mkpunki indigenes be allowed to roam about freely?" one asked.

Not that they were any better off, they had also engaged in slave trading, but claim never to trade Mkpunki indigenes, but indigenes of other villages. Their hate for Adanna glowed, of course they had a confirmation, she was carrying a Dane gun. Mostly a Dane gun was gotten when there was an exchange of slaves. Even, it was only the chiefs and their wards who possessed a Dane gun, how a woman had a Dane gun, it was unheard of. Having a Dane gun meant she had something about her most people didn't have. They had been walking but now slowing down, they could start from here to hunt. The men moving a little further decided to stop and do their gossip instead of walking on, also they would use the opportunity to rest. Irima and Adanna were out of sight. Irima scouted the area, while Adanna unslung her Dane gun from her shoulder and prepared to fire.

"Should we tell our rulers about this woman and her gun?" one of the men asked.

"Why should we involve ourselves with what is none of our business, who cares what she does," another said. "I'm only saying this because I know they are from that Herbalist's compound and if you ask me, I will say they are shady, I don't trust that Herbalist, he is a pretender, and believe me he is planning ill for us, a green snake under the green grass." The man said.

"And what makes you think so?" another asked him.

"Well you see because of what happened to his father, do you think he has a clean heart, I tell you the man is shady and full of evil. I hate him and everything that comes from his compound." The man continued.

They gave it a thought amongst the three, two have been predominantly in the discussion, one who had been silent all this while joined in the conversation.

"But you have gone to ask him for herbs before?" he said, "I remember that should be when" he gave it a little thought, looked up into the sky in a bid to remember when exactly, Eureka! He remembered, "When your mother was seriously ill, and if I know anything that your mother is alive till today, even now as we speak." The stout one among them, who had dominated the discussion so far, looked at his plump friend as if he spoke out of ignorance.

"He is the Herbalist what else, who was I supposed to get the drugs from, besides that does not change the fact that he may be harbouring some ills towards the people of Mkpunki. The man is a disaster waiting to happen. I don't trust him one bit. And yes I will say it I hate him and anything that comes from his compound. Because they act like they are good people, always showing off, as if they are the only kindhearted people in Mkpunki. It annoys me." They called their discussion to an end. When they heard a loud bang, the gun had gone off. Birds swiftly flew away from the treetops. They themselves were stunned, they had almost run away. They had heard the Dane gun go off before, amongst the three two were plump and they sat on a ridge, while one was stout and was standing. All three were stunned with the loud noise, but then something unexpected happened. They heard a loud cry, a screech even, it was coming from Adanna and co's direction. Then a heartfelt scream, from the same person again, the loud cry was missed with a nervous repetition of the word "No." The men ran towards the direction, the closer they got the louder and more piercing the cry. They could also hear a distressed boy's cry, the boy was in great confusion. The men ran with reckless abandon, not minding where their feet stepped on, on the twigs, branches, leaves, etcetera of the forest, on their way, each ran with machete drawn, as the loud piercing wailing continued. The men ran and got to the spot where the cries were emanating from. Irima was lying motionless on the ground. Adanna knelt beside her, her hands all bloodied. Tiperi sat on the ground and cried. The Dane gun was a little farther away from Irima's head. The men got to them, there was blood all around Irima's head. Adanna was dazed. The men not wasting time picked up Irima, on their heels now, they rushed towards the village. Adanna was only acting on reflex, she didn't know where she was or what was happening around her, she saw the men pick up Irima's motionless body, and she followed them. The men moved with a fast pace, despite carrying Irima. Getting to the well-treaded footpath, any who saw them exclaimed, asked questions, some cried, some felt pity, but all followed them not knowing where they were going, they abandoned all to follow. While others continued asking 'what happened' the paths they followed showed one thing they were going to the Herbalist's compound. Adanna's mind was still blank, but her body was moving especially her legs. On their way to the Herbalist's compound they had amassed all and sundry that they met on the path. All were sympathizers now. On getting to the Herbalist, there was good news, he was around. He had just stepped in to attend to those in his compound who came for one form of medicine or the other. Some young men met on the way to the compound, had been sent ahead of others to go and get the Herbalist. If he was not around to go and look for him. The Herbalist had met them, and they had relayed the information. The Herbalist was a man, but he was also human, on hearing about his wife's state, he became disoriented. His bowels moved abruptly inside him, they were extremely hot and he was certain his bowels were coming out of him. His heart was beating so hard that his ears chimed and his vision became blurred. He wobbled about, in his hut with shaking hands as he searched for herbs. He actually didn't know what he was looking for, containers of herbs, prepared and unprepared, tumbled and spilled as his unsteady hands kept groping about. His muscles ached, and he couldn't move them, they had lost all strength. Still in the hut, he heard a commotion outside, they were in now, he ran out empty handed. Pushing one or two people aside he got to the men carrying Irima. He had wished it was not true, they had mistaken Irima for someone else, but it was true. His Irima was now on the ground, eyes shut, and motionless. He got to her, and was lost. He had held this woman in his arms this morning, as she gave him a beautiful smile. Weeks ago she was happy and safe now she had met danger under his care. What went wrong? The Herbalist lost his calm he screamed to Irima but his voice was but a whisper, he had lost his voice, the throat had more sorrow in it now than vocals. He tried calling again but could only whisper, he looked at the people gathered around him, clutching Irima in his arms.

"What did I do?" he asked them in a husky voice, tears rolling down his cheeks.

"What, what did I do?" he asked again scanning their faces for an answer.

"Who did I wrong?" he asked, still with a husky voice, the people remained silent. His hands were trembling terribly now, he tried searching for Irima's opening to stop the bleeding. Etiti was oblivious of what was happening, she had been approaching the compound with her friend, laughing as loud as ever. Getting to the entrance of the compound, she noticed a commotion and apologized to her friend, she excused her friend and promised to visit, her friend turned back. Etiti entered the compound, the sight was not a new one, people always come to her son in such manner. Etiti entered the compound, greeted.

"What is going on?" she asked.

No one gave an answer but stared at her in a way that frightened her. The look on their faces meant something. "What is wrong, have you people seen my son?" she asked.

No one answered but looked at her pitifully, Etiti edged closer, now at alert. There was something in the centre where they were gathered that they were looking at. She didn't push anyone, as she approached, any one on her path gently gave way, one by one they gave way. Etiti getting closer, saw a female leg on the ground, the leg was the first thing she saw, she knew that leg, but just must see who now owned it. She got closer and few more people gave way revealing Irima's body bit by bit. Then she got to the centre she saw her son, frantically trying to fix something with quaking hands. Boys were running up and down from the Herbalist's hut to where they were. The Herbalist had not seen his mother, Etiti looked at Irima's body on the ground, she saw the blood on the ground, she saw her son who looked lost in mind but present in body. Etiti lost her breath, she collapsed on the ground with full force. No one could catch her as she fell. No one expected it, Etiti's body was more motionless than Irima's. The Herbalist had not seen his mother but had heard the thud; he turned and saw his mother on the ground. Her eyes were open but not moving, there were no words to describe the Herbalist's state of mind. He was much higher than just confused. During a jovial discussion someone had asked him, when they were still teenagers. 'If his wife and mother were in trouble and in need of his help in a life-threatening situation, who would he help first? he had laughed and without thinking then had said his mother. No one should ever be asked such a question. Right now he didn't know where he was. Everyone in the compound was out already and doing the little they could to help both women. Every man has his weakness, every man has a breaking point, the Herbalist was far past his. He was certain he had stopped breathing, he went to his mother and checked her, he was functioning on something he didn't know what it was, his body moved, but his mind had gone off, he screamed "Mother" at the same time he screamed "Irima" running up and down. More helpers were coming now to his aid everyone was barking orders and attending to the women.

The men who had brought in Irima had gone out to the king a long time ago to report what had happened. They returned swiftly searching for Adanna. They saw her farther beside the entrance, curled up with Tiperi all over her with tears and in confused state he too was trying to help Adanna but didn't know where to start. Adanna on the ground was shivering terribly. She was not just shivering but was having a serious epileptic bout. Her entire body quaked violently, as she sobbed. The men got to her seeing her in her pathetic state each grabbed her. She couldn't even stand, they had to drag her by her arm with the legs dragging on the ground. Her quaking didn't stop, she didn't know where they were taking her to in her subconscious she could hear Tiperi's screams of "Mother." His voice was getting farther and farther away. She couldn't mutter any word, she was going off, she had promised Tiperi never to leave him. The poor boy just didn't want to go back to the life he was living before. Not only that he really saw Adanna as his mother. Tiperi had tried biting, or scratching with the fingers even kicking and punching but the men who held him were so much stronger, as they easily contained him. The little boy had lost his voice screaming for his mother Adanna. Where were they taking her, he wondered? With that he screamed the more. His convulsion ridden mother was dragged farther away. Tiperi was himself getting fatigued he had screamed more than he could bear. He knew nothing else to do but to wail. The Herbalist was oblivious of all the happenings with Tiperi and Adanna.

CHAPTER 48

"I'm sorry I came late." The Herbalist said as he knelt on the ground looking at Adanna. Adanna was almost unrecognizable, she was still convulsing her eyes had gone into her skull and were blood shot, almost dark red in colour, her complexion was as dark as charcoal, her hair entangled with dirt of all kinds. The Herbalist looked at her and was awed at how much she had changed. The woman was suffering.

"I didn't know what to bring, so I decided to come see you first, then know." The Herbalist continued while looking around. Adanna was kept in a cage made with bamboo and reed, properly dug into the ground, it was a holding area beside the king's palace, the holding area was for criminals and any other who had contravened the laws of the land, there were several barracoons in this area but, Adanna was kept separately since the Herbalist had not made a case against her. The area was properly guarded, with armed guards who served the king personally and took care of the justice of the land. The place was nigh impenetrable. Adanna stared at the Herbalist like he was some strange creature never seen before.

"Odabi are you okay?" the Herbalist asked, she still said no words.

"I'm sorry I'm coming now, a day before yesterday I was in a strange place, with all the happenings. Yesterday was not so much different, but was better. That was when I realized I had not seen you and asked about you and Tiperi then…" the Herbalist felt he was speaking to the wind as Adanna only stared at him, shivering. The only sound coming from her was a laboured breathing, a groaning that sounded somewhat like a hiccup. She breathed like someone without enough air. The Herbalist called to the guards, one of them answered.

"Please help me with water." He said, she needs water."

"I'm sorry we don't offer such services here." The guard said and returned to his post. The Herbalist could hear groaning emanating from behind the palm fronds wall the entire area was fenced with palm fronds and materials obviously from the shrine. He easily guessed those were slaves in chains and pains. He couldn't see beyond the palm fronds wall. On the side Adanna was kept there were about seven of such cells lined up, but Adanna was the only one occupying one. More lands had been cleared farther down, which meant they were planning to build more cells. She needed water, and the guard was not going to bring any. The Herbalist took out his water pouch it wouldn't be enough, but it was something. He would have to come back again. Immediately with his water pouch in his hand he called to Adanna, her eyelids were moving she looked at him, but still didn't move. The cell was shut and the Herbalist knelt outside the cell before her, there was no way he could get to her. He called her again, Adanna remained where she was. The Herbalist called to the guard again, the same man answered with disinterested face, he asked "What?" "Please open the cell I want to go in." The herbalist said.

"I should open the cell?" the man asked sarcastically.

"Yes please open it." The Herbalist was firm.

"Let me understand one thing. Just who do you think you are?" the man asked.

The Herbalist got up with a clinched teeth, he looked at the man in the eyes "Open the cell, she is my family." He said firmly.

The man still looked unconcerned; he sighed, cocked his head to the side, stepped away from the Herbalist, and went and opened the cell. He motioned to the Herbalist with his hand. "There you go," he said pointing at the cell nonchalantly. The Herbalist breathed in heavily, he stepped into the cell got close to Adanna, he sat beside her and took her in his arms like a mother who was to suckle a newborn baby. He had an extra calico on his shoulder good he brought it. It was part of his dressing. He removed it and wrapped it around Adanna to help with the shivering. The guards had seen her shivering but didn't bother to cover her up. Gently he opened her mouth, gradually putting drops of water, after about two attempts Adanna was not drinking the water, the Herbalist decided to let her rest. He whispered her name but, she said no words, he still felt like he should explain. "Odabi I'm really sorry," he said. "If I had known earlier I would have been here a long time ago." He said, "I just got to know yesterday, besides you will be home soon." Adanna reacted to that, blinking her eyes repeatedly "Irima and Etiti are recovering," the Herbalist said, "It was just a flesh wound she had, maybe the shock made her to faint, the same with my mother. Etiti may take longer to recover but, in days they both should be fine. They are asking about you. Tiperi is still crying but I promised to bring him later so later you will see him, that got him to keep quiet. Do not worry you will be home soon, now take some water." The Herbalist said.

Hearing the words Adanna rolled away from his arms faced the opposite direction and let out a good cry, she cried as loud as possible. The Herbalist's manhood had been tested severally these few days this time it was him fighting tears. He felt like joining Adanna to cry, he swallowed hard and maintained his posture. Men don't cry in public or in front of a woman. Adanna's convulsion had stopped but her tears flowed freely, the Herbalist got close to her and picked her up in his arms again. She avoided looking at him but kept her face on the ground as she continued wailing. The same guard came in, looked at them with derision written all over his face and stepped away.

"Odabi drink some water," he said again, "your voice is cracked, you really should stop crying, if not for anything do it for me." He said.

The last words had an impact. Adanna stopped crying instantly, but couldn't stop the sobbing. The Herbalist turned her face towards him. She obediently turned but still looked away, he brought the water again this time she took little by little. The Herbalist continued slowly until she emptied the pouch.

"I will go and meet the king and elders now but it may take the whole of today. I can assure you by this time tomorrow you will be home and everything will be back to normal. I will come back with Tiperi, just so that he will have peace and also because I promised. By then, I will come with Nnadi too and they will bring you something to eat."

"I won't eat till I see Irima." Adanna said with quavering lips. Her first words in two days.

"Irima is fine you will see her tomorrow, to be able to do that you need food for strength." The Herbalist explained.

"Please don't force me, I have already planned to join my ancestors but now I have taken water, I won't eat and drink without seeing Irima. I already feel bad drinking water but then, I did it for you. Please don't make me eat before seeing Irima. Please I beg you." Adanna pleaded, drops of tears streaming down from the corners of her eyes.

"All the same I shall come back when I'm done with the king and elders. Then we shall see, like I have said it may take the whole of the today. But I will see him surely." The Herbalist assured.

The two sat together for a while the Herbalist sensing Adanna was calmer now, assured her he would be back, once again and he took his leave. Sighting her tenderly as he marched away, when he got to the narrow entrance covered with palm fronds, he waved at her and promised to return. Adanna felt tremendous weight lifted off of her, thank the gods she had thrown her Dane gun away that thing would never come close to her again. With the Herbalist exiting the barracoons, he met the guards, one he had confronted, the other he didn't even remember what he looked like when he passed initially. The Herbalist gently informed them he was leaving before he could say "I'm coming back to see her." The other one he had not encountered spoke to him.

"Herbalist," he called nicely. "What should we do, we should move her right away?" he asked.

The Herbalist was puzzled, he edged closer to the man, "What do you mean move her?" he asked.

"Ah Herbalist you always claim innocence but it is your type that are very dangerous. Anyway it does not matter I'm your brother, so I will assume you don't know. I meant we should sell her off, without joining her with the others. It will be our own profit the king does not need to know, we do it all the time. So you won't get into trouble we will split the reward fifty-fifty. I'm your brother and all I can say is welcome to the brotherhood.

If you can supply, we will be rich, we will outsmart the king and chiefs, just think about it, besides she is strong and we will sell her for a high price. So should we move her immediately? It won't take long, the transaction will be completed and you will get your own share effortlessly." The man said.

The Herbalist was furious but showed restraint. "So now you think we are brothers? When it is time to come together and take life, you people come out to claim brotherhood, I don't remember seeing you come to me when it was about helping to sustain a life. Isn't it funny that you criminals and cut throats, evil men of the underworld claim brotherhood? You even go as far as making blood covenants, because you are about to carry out your wicked acts. But will never know each other when it comes to helping sustain a life." The Herbalist edged closer till their skin almost touched, he looked into his eyes like he had done his companion.

"If so much as one hair leaves that woman because of you or your group you may not live to tell the story." The Herbalist said sternly.

"Are you threatening me? you slug that will turn his back on his own kind." The man asked even sterner.

"Try the slug." The Herbalist said and walked away with strong steady steps, not looking back.

"I told you he will not agree." The other said.

"Who cares? She is gone is a fact. Whether he likes it or not, he just lost his opportunity of making a gain out of it. Which is unfortunate for him, go and check her we will move her this night. We are getting richer tonight and it is certain."

"What if he talks or raises an alarm?" the other asked. The one apparently the leader, spoke "He will go just like his father which is also unfortunate," he said yawned unconcernedly and chuckled. "Go and check her and try not to harm one hair." He said and chuckled again maliciously. "I really feel pity for him," the man continued "when you are trying to help people they will see you as a bad person. You saw how he challenged me because I wanted to help, just to help him. It is alright, let me see how I will not live after this. What are you still doing there go and check her. I've said it like a thousand times." He snapped.

The other left grumbling "You were talking to me that's why." He said. In a few moments he came back and gave a report. "She is okay, not much work I think."

"Very good I was worried of her state yesterday and today, I guess he has done his magic. Just like his father used to do."

"What really happened to his father?" the rookie asked. The man obviously a veteran in slave trade business chuckled. "Trust me you don't want to know, but all I can say is, he was an obstacle that needed to be removed, it does not matter how he was removed. Unfortunately his son is following his footsteps, destined to meet the same fate. It is just sad like I said you try to help people they turn against you. This is what is tenable in our time, everybody lives this way. So I don't see any point being different. Just be like others and you will survive. It is good he rejected my help, he is simply not man enough and he does not have the heart of a man." The veteran said, widening his eyes as he said 'man.' "You must be tough." He said to the rookie. "I've seen your demeanour change because of the groaning you hear every day coming from these unfortunate ones but it is life and you must man up. If you follow the way of the Herbalist you lose, because majority is on our side. She is even being treated fairly supposing we kept her together with the others. I wonder what state she would be in. You are sure she has stopped shivering?" he asked. "Yes she has." He replied.

"Very good, just very good, all is working according to plan."

They sat a very long while discussing so many things.

The Herbalist reappeared again, with Tiperi beside him, but no Nnadi. Why stress her. He went in, through the entrance made with palm fronds. He retraced his steps, bringing out his head, "come and open the cell," he said to no one in particular but he made sure both of the guards heard him. Tiperi was already clinching the bamboo sticks with smiles. The Herbalist walked and joined him. Adanna was sitting up and looking at them with a plain relaxed faced. She was calm also. The Herbalist could tell she was relieved to see them. The guard of course the rookie took his time to come open the cell. Tiperi dug his feet into the ground in anticipation. Taking all the time in the world, the guard finally opened the cell. Tiperi rushed in, flew to Adanna and hugged her, almost unbalancing her with the force. Tears were free to Adanna now, and as they hugged, it flowed freely and unrestrained. The Herbalist gave them a moment to re-invigorate their bond which was magical to him. Tiperi laughed as he hugged Adanna, Adanna cried with Tiperi in her arms. The Herbalist smiled. Holding each other for a while, they disentangled from each other's embrace like every mother does, Adanna began inspecting Tiperi, to determine if he was okay. "How are you?" she asked with a tearful voice.

"I'm fine." the boy replied and hugged her again.

Adanna resumed her tears, the Herbalist stood allowing them all the moment they needed. This time the rookie stood and was witnessing everything. They separated from each other's arms again, and Tiperi sat down beside her, holding her left arm, they were okay now. The Herbalist approached, and sat to Adanna's right.

"I don't know how to start but the king is unavailable, but once I leave here. I will be going straight to his palace. I met a very good chief his authority and position is very high in Mkpunki, you can say he is even the second in charge in Mkpunki. Chief Afimi, he is well respected and known. I don't want to scare you but keep a sharp eye and be very alert don't leave this prison for any reason, any reason at all never leave it. Nobody is supposed to tell you to leave for any reason, remain here until you see me, especially tonight. I couldn't find men to stay here besides it is not allowed, it has never been allowed in Mkpunki, if not I would have gotten at least hundred men here to guard you."

"Why what is wrong?" Adanna asked.

"One of the guards told me something fearful I don't want to scare you, but be on alert. By tomorrow you will be out of here if possible tonight, I can assure you that. I'm going straight to the king, besides Chief Afimi is aware of everything I have explained all to him and to some other people. So I have a strong case, nothing will happen to you. I would have met other chiefs but chief Afimi informed me it was a waste of time, rather I should make haste and go to the king again. With the situation of things, we may leave here tonight even but the king has to sanction it, you are in his cell."

After the warning, they chatted about Irima, Etiti and all in the compound. The Herbalist did the talking mostly, Adanna was a work in progress. She still had an aftershock but was relaxed now. However her tears resumed when the Herbalist told her Irima wanted to come and see her.

"She has been asking of you?" the Herbalist said, "Odabi stop crying, what happened was nobody's fault, and thank the gods we are all alright."

The Herbalist thought this would make her smile. "When Etiti woke up and heard everything; she said I shouldn't come back without you." The Herbalist said and chuckled. "So we are all waiting for you."

The Etiti part produced the opposite result, it brought more tears to Adanna. She had a lot to say, him calling her Odabi was another reason to cry. She had tears, a confused mind, she also had a torn heart, accompanied with a bruised body.

"I have a lot to tell you." Adanna said with whispers, "Starting from my name." She looked at the Herbalist. My name is…" She was interrupted when a group of armed men marched towards the cell, all armed, a pot bellied man was in front, without a weapon. He did not need any, he was obviously guarded. Their entrance had rattled all three in the cell, abruptly ending their conversation. The man pointed to Adanna as he and his group discussed. All three in the cell watched in apprehension, they didn't know what was happening. The Herbalist recognized the man, he had seen him at the king's palace earlier in the day. Which meant the king must be available now. The men were still inaudible to Adanna and co.

"I will be back," the Herbalist said to Adanna assuredly. He left the cell they were in and went and spoke to the man, the man gave him an audience. After a short while discussing the Herbalist ran back to Adanna, "I asked him, if you were being released, he said the king needs to sanction it. He also said the king is available now, so I must hurry. It is no longer tomorrow I will come back tonight, you will be free tonight. Tiperi let us go." The Herbalist said.

Tiperi looked at him, then at Adanna like the Herbalist was speaking an unknown tongue or he had gone deaf.

"Hurry Tiperi no time, we will come back."

The young man played deaf, he simply refused. Shaking his head in negation, the Herbalist grunted. There was no time.

"I'm coming back." The Herbalist said, and ran out. The men had come for evening inspection, they inspected the barracoons, at least three times a day. In the early period of the day, when the sun comes out and when it has gone down, then during darkness. It was more of checking up on the occupants, than inspection and reporting. The men discussed with each other, went around the whole area and paid little attention to Adanna and Tiperi in the cage. The two guards remained outside of the enclosed space, the groaning, sobbing, cries from the other side was more poignant now. Most wished for death, to relieve them of the anguish, Tiperi heard the groaning but could make little sense of it. Adanna felt greatly disturbed, who knew what Oja Dike and his countrymen had passed through and will pass through. The slaves from Akuta had a detour and as such had been held up, and would take a longer time to arrive to this very place in Mkpunki. Definitely this was what awaited them and it was just the beginning. They did not know what awaited them in the white man's big house on the sea, neither did they know their fate should they get to their destination, this was just the beginning. Adanna looking at Tiperi imagined him in chains, starting at this age. Till when would the chains fall off? And his life redeemed. A man shall be born to such fate, and when he closes his eyes in death, he knew not what awaited him. There also, trying to focus on their own issues, they talked about prospects and what was befitting to them. How to go about things and make sure there was a good permanent change. Their deliberations took a while with Tiperi doing most of the talking. He had planned how he was going to find something doing and become wealthy so that he could take care of his mother Adanna. Make her happy as much as he could, their talk had taken them into the night. The entrance to the cell was left open the guards felt the two were no threats and had nowhere to go, every now and then one of the guards would pop in to check on them. In all his visits he had seen them in the same position and paying little attention to what was happening in their surroundings, he would return and give report to his co-guard, obviously his superior. Sitting still in the bamboo made prison, Adanna and Tiperi heard voices greeting and exchanging pleasantries, a voice almost sounded like the Herbalist's. Tiperi put on a smile, they were going home after all. Adanna exhaled with relief. Tiperi with the excitement, decided to go welcome the Herbalist and witness whatever it was they were doing. Adanna told him to wait in the prison for him to come but Tiperi had another plan. The little boy wanted to wait for the Herbalist at the entrance, he would crouch, monitor him come in and then frighten him from behind. When he had explained to Adanna his plan, she didn't know if she should allow him play in such an environment but then he was a kid and wouldn't understand. So she allowed him, Tiperi with delight at the permission stealthy on his toes went close to the palm fronds fence, just close to the entrance. Getting to the entrance, the voice had faded and moved farther down, away from the entrance where they were initially. He went on all fours crawling now he peeped through the entrance, the place had only one torch and he could see only one guard. The Herbalist was not there, farther down, close to a tree from which cutting to the right led to the path away from the barracoon. Tiperi could see four men, surely the Herbalist was one of them. He thought of returning to the entrance and waiting, no need he would scare him right there and then. Tiperi thought of leaving. Adanna had her face down on her palms, she was not sobbing but perplexed, what was she going to tell Irima should she meet her tonight? What will Etiti say and how are they going to treat her from here now on afterwards, she was lost in thought. Maybe after seeing them she would head straight to Akom. Tiperi making attempt to crawl towards the Herbalist had a rethink; they were coming back to the entrance. He resumed his position, the one remaining guard, had not looked back as such had not noticed him. His attention was on his colleagues and their discussion as they approached. Tiperi no longer crouching but on his hands and knees, peeped out again and was greatly disappointed at what he saw. The men approached and when they got close to the light, the Herbalist was not amongst them. He recognized all four of them, three were the men who had arrested Adanna and dragged her away, he had first seen them in the forest, on that day the troubles started. The other man he could remember was the man he had seen at the entrance when he came with the Herbalist, earlier in the day. The young boy's countenance changed abruptly from gay to despair, they had expected the Herbalist so much they thought they heard his voice. Those days when his sister left him and no one cared, he would cry and wait for her return. He would see people from afar and they would look just exactly like his sister only to be called back to reality when the people got closer. Now they had anticipated the Herbalist so much, that they heard his voice in their heads. The men approached and got close to the entrance, Tiperi could hear them clearly now. Adanna couldn't. It took him time to regain his composure, despite being a kid, he knew what a bad disappointing news was. He would have to tell Adanna it was not the herbalist at least not yet, he had assured them he would come and Tiperi was certain he would. He decided to crawl back to the cell, but was stopped cold, when the other guard approached and looked towards the prison, it was just a glance, he didn't look down he would have seen Tiperi. He didn't return to his former position but rather stood in between the entrance. Turning right and looking down he would see Tiperi, any move or sound from Tiperi he would be caught, the boy had to play dead at the spot, he breathed as light as ever. If only the guard would move so he could return to his position. Adanna had seen them both her heart ached but she had to control herself. She had seen Tiperi was in trouble, there was nothing she could do, she stared in disbelief. The Herbalist was not coming in and she had stopped hearing his voice, at least she thought she heard his voice. She hoped the Herbalist to see Tiperi before the guard. It was either the guard ruined Tiperi's plan of playfully frightening the Herbalist, or reacted violently before understanding the situation. Adanna felt her forehead pound violently; she sat transfixed staring at Tiperi on his knees, with a fearful face. And the unkind guard blocking the entrance, the Herbalist better come fast Adanna thought or Tiperi would be in trouble before they could explain. The four men who were now close, stood a while then Tiperi heard one say "Should we wait or do it ourselves?"

The guard who was with them clearly disgusted with the question asked him what they had just discussed.

"What did we just discuss now?" he said in a hushing voice.

"The other continued "I'm just unsure." He said, "This one has taken a different turn."

Tiperi could hear all they were saying but was still a bit confused.

"Listen," the guard continued "Chief Afimi has been doing this for a long while."

Tiperi's heartbeat increased, the Herbalist had mentioned Chief Afimi as a man helping their course, he remembered vividly. The scared colleague continued "I know he is, but now the Herbalist may have told someone about our plan since you have approached him earlier and he refused." The man said.

"Listen carefully, our quest is just and right and we have never gone wrong. We do this only in the night, all we have to do now is gag her. Fortunately a young boy is with her now, so gag them, tie them up and join them with the others, they will move out immediately. Chief Afimi is the king's right-hand man and we too will testify against the Herbalist. I thought I explained all this for crying out loud. Who is the Herbalist? We have sold more important people into slavery, why should she be an exception. Who is the Herbalist that I should be scared? The both of them are sold already all we need is to deliver them, this is how we survive, the king knows nothing about this. Why must he be the only one making money out of the trade, this is how we survive. Chief Afimi knows what to say should the Herbalist raise alarm. We frame him for helping her escape. This time his silence for his life and that of his family. No gain of money anymore he has lost that opportunity because of his foolishness. Imagine he threatened me, I don't know why I'm repeating myself, let's be quick I heard he went to the king. We would have done this already, even yesterday, if not for you worthless and stupid people and your delay."

The last words hurt the feelings of the three, "Who are you calling worthless and stupid?" one challenged. The three wore a frown now, "and you have forgotten your father is an invalid," another said. The guard was also furious now, an altercation arose amongst them. Tiperi was having short breaths and tremor on his hands, the guard at the entrance, left to separate them. That was the opening Tiperi needed. Adanna was still anxious and frightened; Tiperi moving fast opened the cell bamboo door, ran in and banged it shut. He dashed to Adanna's side who caught him in her arms and tried to calm him down. Almost immediately the men all five of them came in, they had heard the noise from the banged bamboo cell door. Looking at Tiperi and Adanna, one of them, the veteran went close to them, he had regained his composure; they looked at them, that is Tiperi and Adanna. Sure nothing was out of place, they moved out again.

As soon as they left, Tiperi wide eyed now "Let's run," he said looking at the entrance and at Adanna, one after the other. Adanna had never seen him in such mood, his words were misplaced but the word "run away" kept coming out, then another was "sell," "slavery."

"Tiperi slow down and calm yourself, then you can speak."

"Chief Afimi has sold us," the boy said.

"Tiperi he is helping us," Adanna said.

"Those men," the boy continued, "have sold us, they are lying, Chief Afimi has sold us, they want to come and take us, you must believe me. They have sold us, they will kill us, we must run now. I heard everything they said, they are bad men." The boy continued in trepidation. Adanna understood now, one thing was certain; they had to run to the Herbalist or find a place to stay and wait for him. Adanna tried calming Tiperi, they needed an act of the gods now to be rescued. The men came in again but this time only four of them, the one regarded as the rookie had maintained his position outside the entrance to the barracoon area. The men came in and the man who had spoken before still addressed them, getting close to the cell, he held the bamboo bars, looking at Adanna and Tiperi, he being as calm as he could muster.

"We will be moving you people out very soon, don't worry, we are taking you to a better place, where you will be comfortable. From what we've heard you will be home soon very soon, so we want you people to be comfortable." Turning to Tiperi "Boy how are you?" he asked with smiles. Tiperi didn't answer. The man was not bothered.

"We are ready, give us a moment and please you can start coming out, nobody is harming you, in fact you can follow behind us or ahead as we will direct you, but please relax and be comfortable, it is all good now, okay?" He rubbed his palms together, wiped his face and motioned for his men to follow him out again. When they were gone, Adanna and Tiperi looked around frantically for an escape route. The men outside now, the veteran continued to speak, "I didn't explain this part but I'm sure you people understand what I'm trying to do, do not make them suspect anything, let them be free and let them trust us. Let us lead them out of this area quietly so they can be no witnesses; there are other guards behind this fence. Should the need arise, nobody will say I heard a scream. When we are far, we will have to tie them, that's the only way they can be made to enter the canoe bound for the ship. That's all, let's move out and make it quick." They returned and went to Adanna, and Tiperi. "Alright," the man said, holding open the cell door. "Let's go. I'm sure you are tired and weary, do not worry, where we are going you will relax and be comfortable." Adanna and Tiperi were still sitting, looking at them with fear. "Stand up let us go." The man said.

The two did not move the veteran entered the prison, went to them with all the softness of voice, he looked tenderly at them. "Are you scared?" he asked, he didn't wait for them to answer. "Don't be, no one is going to harm you, because I'm here, but you have to be obedient because to be honest with you both I'm the kind person here, in fact I can say the only kind person here." He said pointing at himself "and I'm trying to help, stand up and let us go, believe me it is for your own good, if you don't okay listen, listen attentively." He stopped speaking and with his left hand he made a suppressing gesture while with the right he pointed at the palm fronds wall. Adanna and Tiperi knew what he was talking about, now they could hear men and women in great pain, groaning, children crying with a tired voices, chains and shackles clanging. Some shouted in frustration having tried to break loose the chains but could not. The man was sure the message was clear.

"That would be you people in a few moments, if I don't move you out of here immediately. Our turn is over and another set of guards will soon take over, you don't want them near you, trust me, now get up and let's go, please I promise nothing will happen to you two. You are under my protection and care, besides we are all one."

The message had registered, it would be smarter for Adanna and Tiperi to do their bidding, being stubborn wouldn't help. He helped Adanna to her feet, though she was reluctant, Tiperi held Adanna's left hand and moved when she moved, and stopped when she stopped. Slowly they left the cell. The men each winked at each other while maintaining a straight face. Adanna and Tiperi had not observed this.

"You are safe." One said.

Their job there was done. As they had planned, they all went ahead, leaving Adanna and Tiperi behind, they wanted them to feel safe and fear nothing. They had not considered that maybe the Herbalist may have told them anything. Why should he? There are things you don't say but must keep secret, they had reasoned. The man had inspected them, if they knew, he thought, the Herbalist wouldn't leave, and they would be very agitated, more than they were right now. Marching on, the entrance of the prison was still in sight, one brought out, a dried fish from his animal skin bag. They all shared still trying to win their trust. The veteran took his, and went to Adanna broke it into three, threw one into his mouth, chewed and swallowed and handed the one to Adanna who also took chewed and swallowed, thanked him, with Tiperi doing likewise. That was it, the veteran was certain they had their trust now. "Try to keep up." He said and returned to his position. Adanna knew what they were trying to do, they took the right turn, it was the only path, out of the barracoon and it was narrow. All these areas were fenced with bamboo sticks and palm fronds, on both sides. Adanna had looked straight ahead they cannot outrun the men here. The man again brought out his water pouch drank from it and gave it to Adanna, who drank gratefully again, she had taken a small quantity. Tiperi took the pouch and emptied it, the man smiled. "You must be thirsty" he said "Why didn't you talk, the water you drank a grown man can't even finish it," the man said and smiled again, taking his pouch from Tiperi. Their plan was working, Adanna didn't even have a plan. At the end of the path was a T-junction.

"We will take the left", the man said, they couldn't see it clearly, the night was bright, the moon was doing a great job, but night was night. They had two torches and those that held them, marched ahead. Adanna wished the Herbalist would emerge before they made it to the end of the narrow path, they made it to the end of the narrow path and the Herbalist didn't show up. She knew one thing, they couldn't outrun these men. They took the left turn as had been said this path had no palm fronds it was just a forest path. The man had been making small talks asking her questions and sounding genuinely caring and kind. To most of his questions and jokes, Adanna nodded to some, though in the dark. One thing was certain she made him believe he had her attention. The man had gone on to tell her stories about himself which were all lies, at least his colleagues knew and Adanna suspected. Their tales continued until Tiperi clutched his stomach. "What is it?" Adanna asked.

"My stomach." The boy said.

"Just hold it." The man said, "We are almost at our destination, then you can do anything you want."

The boy listened and obeyed. They continued a while again and Tiperi complained, yet again, he clutched his stomach, this time almost in tears.

"Just hold it," the man said. The young boy slowed down and tried dragging himself along, the veteran asked one of his colleagues to carry him, the rookie, he made the move.

"Carrying him won't stop the pain, he is a kid." Another reasoned.

After a while the man agreed. "But we are almost close," he said sounding frustrated. "Alright you," the veteran called, pointing to his colleague, who had reasoned carrying him wouldn't stop the pain. "Take him to the forest to relieve himself." Tiperi was already undressing on the path.

"Boy not here, enter the bush, this is a path people pass."

The man took him in and headed for the forest.

"Can I join, I think I'm pressed too," Adanna said.

"Fine," the man gave up. "Go with him, we trust you and you trust us, so go, no problem."

He ordered his colleague to standby, give them space, but watch them, was the order. The two entered the forest, hand in hand, the man stood at the edge and waited, others remained at the path. Adanna and Tiperi could hear them, laugh and chat, their chat was inaudible, the men with the torches patiently waited. Tiperi relieving himself discovered he was only pressed but he was certain his stomach had ached him terribly. Adanna gave him a space to relief herself also while on her own she put her finger into her month down to her throat she vomited violently. She wouldn't eat and she meant it, till she saw Irima, but taking the fish was a way to her freedom, a necessity. She did all she could to make sure every drop of water and particle of fish came out of her. The men stayed and chatted for a while until it became a while too long, the men didn't suspect a thing. One of them, the one standing guard on them, checked in on them, first he called no answer, then repeatedly he called still no response. Then he went in to search for them, it took him a while, he came out alarmed.

"They are not here anymore!" he said to the group. It took them a while to comprehend the words, first they stared at each other with no words. Then like an explosion, they dove into the forest, all with full force. Searching the area no sign of them, they converged and made plans on how to find them, all five together now. The veteran who was now the leader spoke, "We will search for them all night, if we find them or not we must meet here, this exact same spot in the morning. When any of us find them, wait here for the group, we will find them certainly but if we don't, we get more men involved. Still if we don't find them, the Herbalist will have to pay for this with his head, I am not going down for this. How much are they worth? I will not. Now let's move it."

They all dispersed scattering into different directions, some with light, others without, they would have to make do with the moon. Adanna and Tiperi ran facing the way leading to the Herbalist's compound, all they did was guess work, there was no way of making certain they were facing the right direction. But they had to move, not only move but run. Rushing through the forest with its thickets, Adanna and Tiperi lurched on in desperation not minding the fatiguing of their body. They ran all night. When they looked behind, they did not notice anyone following but was certain any could be. For a very long while they ran, till they couldn't anymore. Their legs became wobbly due to fatigue, and they were badly bruised. Especially the legs, they had been slashing it against, branches, twigs and any form of low-lying plant. Adanna would continue but Tiperi was just a kid, he had stumbled and fallen about four times and had slowed down considerably. Adanna herself was fatigued, for long she had not tasted anything. No matter who it was hunger weakened the body. Right now she had a thing propelling her and pushing her forward, keeping her going and that was pure adrenaline. She picked up Tiperi placed him on her shoulder and continued running, this allowed them to cover a great distance. Even adrenaline gives up too. She was tired more than she could bear, in her mind all she knew and believed was that they had covered enough grounds and should be far from their chasers by now. Looking around all she could see were, wet forest leaves, tall trees, fog. She heard chirping of insects and the rustling of leaves by the wind, strange animals' sounds, but no sign of human. The popular held beliefs of the forest being an abode of spirits in the period of darkness mattered little, the two slumped and sat on the ground, each resting their backs on a tree while looking around for any dangerous predator. They wished to move on, and only rest when they were in a safe place, but their body proved otherwise. The muscles were sorely fatigued, neither could move his or her body, they had not sat for a moment to breath in, when Adanna noticed a touch approaching from her right. Tiperi had not seen it, she roused Tiperi up and they set out again. This time they ran a few distance before slowing down and walking. Trudging forward, the torch was still approaching, Adanna was not seeing the torch but a reflection of its glows on the area it fell and its glow showed it was coming directly for them fast. Tiperi was face flat on the ground and sobbing, his body couldn't take anymore. Adanna again picked him this time for her, it was like pulling a fully grown palm tree from the ground. She still managed, her muscles quaked, lifting Tiperi up, they trudged a further distance before crashing to the ground. She crawled to Tiperi, looked around there was no place large enough to hide, it was all tall trees now and because of the canopy, shorter tree did not grow much, the trees were impossible to climb, they were at least 20 feets tall before getting to any branch. That was like a hut, placed on top each other ten times. At this moment they had daylight Adanna tried climbing one her hands couldn't go round, the tree was out of options. The torch was still approaching, Adanna had to reach to her inner self.

"I'm not dying today," she said. She stood up again, picked up Tiperi and put him on her back and started trudging, pain shooting through her body with every step. She was not giving up at least, she opened her eyes after a few steps, they were still facing the village area she believed. Tiperi was breathing heavily on her back. Adanna walked a few feet more and saw her help to her right. She could see a small trench just big enough to fit in Tiperi, with her last strength she hurried to it. Brought him down from her shoulder, not checking if there were snakes or scorpions or any poisonous animal in the trench, she began to lay him into it. Tiperi was aware of what was happening, Adanna laid him in. "Now lie down Tiperi, I will cover you with leaves." She said, glancing around. The glow was not visible anymore, maybe they had lost the person or he was not after them or maybe it was the daylight that hid the glow. It was early dawn, the birds had begun to sing.

Tiperi confused, "How will you now come in?" Tiperi asked.

Adanna hesitated, "I won't." She said tears, forming in hers.

"But mother why, where will you hide?"

No need to lie to the boy at least not this time and under the circumstances.

"Tiperi" she said cupping his jaw in her hands "Just lie, let me cover you. My time is up, now stay here till daybreak then find your way to the Herbalist, if I die now, I truly deserve it but my son, you don't. At least I know you will be safe. They are tracking us, so I will continue and divert them, I'm sorry Tiperi, I truly am." She was sobbing now. "Now lie Tiperi, please lie let me cover you don't make a sound," she said amidst tears, with her finger across her lips, Tiperi was already climbing out, on his own. "Tiperi" she called "No time, get back in." Tiperi would have none of it with one attempt he was out of the trench. The trench was only deep to his belly bottom. Out now, he shook his head in negation. "You are not leaving me again," the boy said, "My sister left me, you won't leave me, I am not a reject." The boy said. "You won't leave me, I deserve to be loved too." Tiperi had his own tears now. "If you die, just know I'm right behind you, whenever, wherever." Tiperi got up and gave his hand to Adanna. "Get up mother," he said "We won't die today."

Adanna wiped her tears, took his hand, got up and they resumed their walk but not run, they walked for a while, until they had a reason to run, they heard a rustling of leaves, and twigs snapping as a result of being stepped on, that was enough. Mustering all the strength they had, they ran but was certain, someone was in heavy pursuit and the person was gaining on them too fast and at an alarming rate. Adanna ran wishing that the next step she took would see her at the Herbalist's compound. They had stopped hearing the footsteps behind, could it be they had outrun the person? They wouldn't be stopping to find out, just when they thought they had escaped and there was hope after all, a man jumped from their left-hand side, to their front, cutting of their route of escape. He almost caught Tiperi, with his left hand but the boy was quick enough to stop and scamper back to Adanna. This was the same man they first saw in the forest when they went to it with Irima, she could recognize him. They couldn't run back, he would easily catch up with them, also should they go right or left, he was agile even for his body structure. That was not the only problem, he looked at them evilly and with all nefarious intention, he was not trying to capture them, his machete was drawn and raised up, ready to cut, or slash as he approached them. Adanna grabbed Tiperi and put him behind her, she looked on the ground, only twigs not good enough to even kill a lizard. She took her stand and faced him with bare hands, the man had a weapon but Adanna was ready to fight with bare hands. She would rather die than see her son die. That was the extent of a mother's love. On Adanna's face was the expression of resignation to death, fear and courage to defend Tiperi to the death. She was certain the man would slice them to pieces but she took a fight stand, despite she had no weapon, tears were dropping from Adanna's eyes, but she still stood with Tiperi behind her.

"Come" she said with a tearful voice. "Come," motioning to the man with her hands, both she and Tiperi were shedding tears uncontrollably now. Yet she maintained her fight stand. "Come and be fast about it," she said, still sobbing. "Please I dare you, come and fight." Her words were almost inaudible as she spoke with tears dropping like water from her eyes. The man still had his machete and stared at them, Adanna was weeping with a wheeze now. "What are you waiting for? Come," she said.

This was not the first time the man had seen a woman ready to fight with bare hands against a man with a weapon, just to save her child's life. A very long time ago when he was very young, younger than Tiperi, he had gone to the farm with his mother they had dropped their farm equipment and was resting when slavers about six of them came up against him and his mother. They had gone alone that day, his mother put him behind and faced the men with bare hands. That day she had cried, screamed, pleaded with the men to take her alone but still took her stand with bare hands against six men with weapons. His mother had cried like a baby that day. Today he was like those men, doing exactly what they had done. He was also the same who the Herbalist had helped to treat his mother and she recovered. He knew Adanna and Tiperi were with the Herbalist, he also knew letting Adanna and Tiperi escape meant death for him and even the Herbalist. The man stood and stared at Adanna and Tiperi behind her, Adanna's tears still flowed in abundance.

The man's machete was becoming too heavy, his arm weakened, "Go" he said, in a defeated voice, he moved aside from the path, "Just run." The man said again. Adanna and Tiperi were sceptical at first not believing the words, the man smashed the tip of his machete into the ground, causing the machete to sink into the ground. Adanna and Tiperi had started making small movement towards the right direction.

"Don't go to the Herbalist, they will frame him, even if I support and then they will kill us all. Very powerful men are the ones involved in this, in the meantime I will be the Herbalist's alibi but you must leave Mkpunki. Run to Akom when the dust settles, we will come for you."

He reached to his side and brought out a small knife (dagger), he gave it to Tiperi. "This is all I can do, I still need to think of a lot of things but you must run. Now please run, the gods will give you the strength, you must run."

Adanna nudged Tiperi forward pushing him slightly with her eyes still fixed on the man, getting a little distance she turned and both in no long time disappeared. The man had little time to reflect, drops of tears had formed on his tear duct. He was contrite. He shook it off, maned up, inhaled and exhaled heavily, took his machete with contrition and went the opposite direction. Covering as much footprints as he could, should someone decide to still track. He turned, he had forgotten to tell them something about the dagger but it was too late, he sighed and moved on. There was something about the dagger. He would meet his group at the designated rendezvous point. Then he would have to find the Herbalist, they needed a brilliant plan to be able to keep their heads on their shoulders now.

CHAPTER 49

The day had gone far by their estimate, but then it was still morning, though the sun was out, the day still had its freshness about it. The men had gotten to Akumi, not to have any regrets, they searched thoroughly and asked almost everyone. They asked question, both making promises of great wealth as a reward should anyone tell them the where about of Adanna. None seemed to recall. The only glimmer of hope they have had, was in the person of Akintu. The slaver in charge of the slave market in Akumi. He could recall all, as he confirmed and corroborated of all description of Adanna.

The warriors were glad and continued their search.

*****

Following the direction of the sun, which was heading west ward now. The sun had risen from the east direction. Adanna and Tiperi kept to their right heading straight forward, that was the way to Akom. Slightly to the left, surely would take them into Mkpunki. Adanna was hungry now to a point she couldn't help. Coupled with the running which had taken much out of her, Tiperi too felt the pangs of hunger, both trudged on for a while. They had run since evening of yesterday to daybreak of today, they had kept to the paths in the forest, when there were bushes, which meant they couldn't go through it, they came out to the paths, and hurried off it as soon as possible. Making sure not to be seen, the journey had been a bit favourable on that aspect of not being seen. With it meant no witnesses. They would be easy to describe and spot. A woman walking with a young boy, in Adanna's mind she had other worries but if anything she was trying to convince her mind to accommodate the situation. She wouldn't be seeing Irima anytime soon should she continue, she may also fail Tiperi because definitely her body would give up, sooner or later. Her vision was already hazy, they were in the forest now, keeping sight of the path, to their left. This was her second time on the path, the first time Oja Dike the Akuta warrior led her and her companions, now she was trying to think clearly, stand on her feet, with her body proving otherwise. Tiperi had never been outside Mkpunki, this was his first time.

"I have to be reasonable." She said out loud, to no one in particular. Tiperi looked at her, he wanted to ask her what she meant. But couldn't his mouth seemed to be shut by another force unknown to him, he held Adanna's left hand as they walked slowly. After a while, Adanna stopped, she requested the knife from Tiperi who willingly gave her. She took it, with her last strength she made a weapon she knew she could only make, a spear. She made a smaller one and gave it to Tiperi, they walked at the same time searching for a kill. None was available. Adanna looked around, any animal now would be just fine, as if her wish came true, birds and arboreal animals emerged, she couldn't get to them, they couldn't be hunted with spears. Maybe she should have wished well, a slow terrestrial animal that lived in the forest was the new wish, that wish didn't come true. They got to a point that had four directions, Adanna's throat was dry and her heart laboured, all corners of her head pounded and her eyes were heavy. She was certain Tiperi was feeling the same. They wouldn't make it to Akom, with an empty stomach and in the condition they were in. What was worst she was losing concentration, trying to think clearly proved difficult. She studied the sun and knew any path seemed capable of leading to Akom, but could also be the wrong way. She looked at Tiperi both were at the junction now, but couldn't see, the end or even farther than a few miles of each path. Adanna thought for a while.

Tiperi was sure of what was going on, "Let us go that way." He said, pointing to the right.

Adanna exhaled, with smiles and a weary face, "Why?" she asked.

"It is on the right." The boy said.

"We will have to come back, if it turns out to be the wrong way, you know. Unless we see someone who knows the path. I think we should wait here for someone to pass, then we will ask." She said.

"What if those men catch us."

"They won't" she answered.

"Is it because that man helped us?" Tiperi asked.

"Maybe." Adanna said and shrugged, "But you are right doing something is better than doing nothing, so right it is."

They took the turn and went right, "But don't forget patience is a virtue also and working smart with the right choices is better than just being hard working. What we are doing now is just working hard, without patience also." Adanna added.

"My mind said we should go right." Tiperi said.

They made progress and Tiperi was right, at least to himself, to his left was a large cleared land with evidence of life and lively activities going on in it. A lot of huts were in the somewhat clan or large family. Tiperi pointed to it with delight his stomach rumbled and he salivated, smokes were going up from at least 5 spots in the area. Adanna was holding him. Tiperi didn't need to say a word, he dragged Adanna towards the direction. Adanna drew him back. "We won't be going there." She said, Tiperi couldn't believe his ears, he looked at Adanna expecting a very good reasonable explanation, why they should not. But she said no word, after a while she looked at Tiperi.

"Those are slavers from a place farther hinterland." She said, "They are the major slavers and slave dealers known, you can say, they are here because of slave trade, and that is what they are all about, they are known or rather their village is called Aro, farther inwards, so I don't think we should go there. We are trying to be as far away from slavery as possible." She explained to Tiperi. As they passed the area, she drew him closer, rubbing his head gently to soothe him, before crossing her left hand, across his shoulder and holding him closer. That was the first time Tiperi saw or heard such.

"Don't worry they have settlements everywhere, you will see many on many paths," she continued. With her left hand on his chin. She lifted his face up and pointed forward, Tiperi had delight again, it was a hamlet farther ahead, he breathed in relief. Adanna held his right hand again, and they marched on. The sun was about to depart for the day, it just stayed on to lead Adanna and Tiperi into this unknown hamlet. When they, having taken a long while for a distance so short, finally made it. The huts in the hamlet were not like the ones they had seen, at the end was a forest which they could see, by the sides of the path all the huts were lined up. With none in clusters they wouldn't be more than 150 huts in the hamlet, all lined up, getting to the first one, Tiperi stared in delight there was a hut to his left and to his right. He was aware now, they were in the wrong path as far as Akom was concerned. Adanna had told him, all they needed to do, would be done shortly, so they could return to the right path. Tiperi pointed to the hut by the right, Adanna smiled, shaking her head, they went for the right again, they got to the hut and called out, no one responded. They could hear voices coming from behind the hut, maybe they were not shouting loud enough, they made more noise. Tiperi screamed, Adanna was not sure where the strength was coming from. A young boy, younger than Tiperi emerged from behind the hut, through the side. Another problem was, what language do they speak?

Adanna said hello in the languages of Mkpunki and Akom, the boy responded to Akom's greeting with a different variation of the Akom language, she knew not but still understandable. She asked for help from him and he went on to get an adult. When what seemed, a member of the family, the head maybe, came out seeing Adanna and Tiperi he made enquires asking a lot of questions from them.

"We just need little food and water and we will be on our way." Adanna pleaded. "Kindly help us master." Tiperi didn't see any harm in the request and expected a return of kind gesture.

"You said you are from Akom the man said but you are lost," the man pointed to the direction they were backing, "That way is the way to Akom," he said. That meant they should have gone straight, "That is all I can do, now please leave." The man said. Adanna and Tiperi were stunned, they stood rigid.

"Don't make us push you out, leave. We don't have food to share."

Taking the rejection, rather well, they turned and left. "Maybe this time we should check the left for a change." Adanna suggested.

When someone from the hut on the left-hand side came out he asked them to check another hut maybe those ones would help. Men of all age grade answered, women of all age grade, met them and answered. None gave a helping hand, Adanna was certain, they had checked almost all the huts in the hamlet, no one agreed to help. One had asked her if they sold food in their hut. Another requested she handed over Tiperi when she could pay back, she would come and redeem him. Tiperi had asked Adanna if hunger killed and she said 'yes' he was very scared. They were at their wit's end, Adanna sat down without a single thought in her head, her head was empty. They had located an empty space, at the end of the path on which most of huts in the hamlet were located. They were not properly covered they had no weapons or shade, they couldn't explain what had kept them on their feet, they had no shelter and they were in a strange place. Darkness was upon them which meant, they couldn't, should superpowers come upon them, even move about. They also had no torches. Deciding to lie down and sleep till morning may be impossible and difficult. With all their difficulties, no one walked around, worst to Tiperi was that he could perceive delicious aroma from the huts close by. Trees were almost everywhere as they could see the forest, not a single one was fruit bearing at least the ones they could see.

"The ocean's water is undrinkable and the forest trees most do not bear edible fruits," Adanna said out loud. "Why?" Tiperi asked.

This time, they were both lying on the ground both facing up and looking into the sky, as noises from mortars and pestles and animals raved round about them.

"I don't know, even the Herbalist doesn't know," she said "The white woman told him about the oceans, how it is mighty big, bigger than we could think, but for the forest, I have seen myself majority of the trees are just too tall, without fruit, and that I don't know why."

Tiperi struggling with his right hand pointed to the sky. "Look" he said. It was a shooting star, he marvelled, the first time he was seeing such.

Adanna chuckled, "Do you know what that means?" Adanna asked, Tiperi shook his head in negation, Adanna didn't see it but guessed his silence meant no, "The gods have birthed a child."

Adanna sure Tiperi didn't understand. "Which means there is a newborn baby god, They always watch us from up there, he is going to take his place."

Tiperi exhaled, "Mother," he called.

"Yes."

"Are we going to die tonight?" the boy asked.

"Do you remember the song you taught me?" Adanna asked.

"Yes."

"This is the time we sing it in our heads, we won't give up, Tiperi, no we won't and we shouldn't. We will see a new sun tomorrow and the next and the next. Do you want to sing it?" Adanna asked.

Tiperi managed to shake his head in negation again, again Adanna didn't see it. Tiperi was not sure he would see the next day. He was cold, the night brought its chilling power, his muscles ached, his stomach was empty and his bruises itched, there would be no tomorrow for him. He took out the knife that was gifted to him, he struggled and sat up, called his mother "I want to give you something," he said, "It is the only thing I have, I wish I can give you the world with all its riches, but I can't, this is all I have so please take it to remember me by." Tiperi said with a faint voice.

Adanna took it with smile and wiped away the tears at the corner of her eyes, "Thank you," she said, "But we won't die tonight." She hugged him, laid him on her laps, "Just try to see if you can sleep, it may be difficult, but just try tomorrow will be better." She said, caressing his head. She took the knife, she had barely inspected it earlier on when she took it. It had a beautiful sheath, must be a priced possession of the benefactor. She unsheathed it, the blade glittered with the moon but there was something else the point of joining of the blade with the handle had small round sags, open by one side, which was shining. Adanna had thought it was decorations on the knife earlier on, there were three of such sags, two on one side, one on the other, one sag was empty. It could be opened. Adanna searched around if anything fell but none. With shaking weak fingers, she tried to bring out what looked like a shiny ball from the sags, hopefully it was what she thought it was. Finally one was out, she took it in between her fingers lifted it up and laughed in unbelief nervously. Tiperi got up from her laps to look at her holding a shining white ball between her thumb and index finger with a smile, traces of tears were on her face still. But would soon dry, Tiperi didn't know what it was but smiled because his mother smiled holding a white something that was shining. Adanna took it, "Get up Tiperi." She said hurriedly.

"What is that?" he asked.

"It is called a 'pearl'" Adanna answered, hurrying to the man who had requested for Tiperi in exchange for his help. When she got to his compound, he answered. Seeing it was them, he was irritated and snorted in disgust. He just looked at them cross armed not saying a word.

"I want food all you can afford and borrow. A hut to sleep in with my son and food for travel for at least two days. Water to bath, drink and travel with for two, for at least two days. A bow and arrows with quiver, machete, new clothes, how about all necessary things for travelling for two as much as we can carry. I also want balance in cowries, I will think of other things, and let you know. Can you supply these things?" Adanna asked.

The man said no word, Adanna lifted the white ball, so he could see for himself. The man exclaimed and salivated, reaching out to take the ball.

"We have the ball, supply all and do all you need to and then you can have it." Adanna said.

The man quickly let them in as they entered "The gods are with you as they are with me, I have just what you need." The man took them past about three huts, they entered a part well cleared, walking about 100fts, he showed them where they would lodge. He called it new huts they had finished building 6 remaining one, he led them to the largest already well finished one. "This was supposed to be my new huts as I intend to move in here, you will be the first to grace here, with your blissful presence. No one can disturb you here and all you need is here, the gods have directed you here, I will have my servants guard you. Everything is new we are relocating from the old ones, the ones you passed, as you can see I'm the man you want." Without wasting time, foods were brought those available and many more to be bartered for. The man began running helter-skelter calling as much servants as he could, there was a pearl in his compound and it could be his in no time. Within a twinkling of an eye he became an obedient servant to Adanna and Tiperi, willing to do just about anything to please them. The word pearl kept repeating itself in Tiperi's ears, till they dined like kings and slept like such.

*****

In the morning very early with the first light for the break of dawn sipping through, and the crispy chilling air Adanna was awake. She looked at Tiperi who slept so dull, they needed to move out. Adanna didn't know her way around, she called out and a servant answered the one who had stayed guard. Only a few in the compound had seen Adanna with Tiperi. The man who had met them, was known as Woyo in the hamlet, and had given Adanna and Tiperi his hut in the new quarters which was the biggest in the compound and was in isolation. Despite also being far from the old ones. Everyone had the same pattern, "I will be different." He had boasted, prompting him to build farther in land in the hamlet. Only his personal servants who were four in number had attended to Adanna and Tiperi the night before, when Adanna called and made her demands again, Woyo left with his men all four of them promising to return with all the supplies needed as requested by Adanna. Adanna went into her hut to wait for them and Tiperi. She had sleep for not too long and her strength had returned fully. Tiperi would take days to recover from the stress. Adanna went with them to the old quarters where the exit and entrance was, before turning back. Immediately the men of Woyo and himself left. Those that knew Adanna, Akom warriors, emerged into the hamlet. They started from the first hut, in the hamlet, they were about 25 in number they started asking questions concerning Adanna. None had seen a woman of her description with slaves and four men, with one maybe bond, and a slave woman bond for the slave market. But many agreed to have seen a woman of her description with her son, heading towards Akom. However they also agreed to have turned her away and were certain they left the hamlet the night before. The Akom warriors heard the same story, everywhere in the hamlet, they searched all areas, they got to Woyo's compound, knocked and shouted, in the hamlet's dialect. Adanna heard the shout but the dialect's sounded like those of people from the hamlet she had heard. She made her way back to the hut in the new quarters. The Akom warriors had shared themselves in such a way that those familiar with a particular territory, searched the area, those in the hamlet were from Akom, but knew the hamlet ways too well, they shouted and screamed, no one answered. The Akom warriors thought of going in first to see but they were in a foreign territory with no one responding. They started shouting Adanna's name, by this time Adanna was in the hut and could hear nothing. A woman answered them, later on, usually it was the men that answered the calls from visitors, certain no one was going to, she did. She had not seen Adanna or a boy. The Akom warriors screamed Adanna's name some more, no one responded. They went into the forest nearby, checked for footprints of a woman and a boy but already there were too many footprints they went around some more. Adanna in the hut took her time to sharpening her spear and Tiperi's. The men shouted and shouted, no one answered, they left and headed towards Mkpunki their final destination. Coming back they would search again from Mkpunki. They got to the junction, they split into equal members some headed towards Mkpunki others towards Akom entering the forest, should it be the missed them on the way. No need going to the left, it led into the forest where people of the hamlet threw in their dead and all manner of waste. Adanna felt pity for Tiperi, he looked so peaceful sleeping but would have to disturb him once Woyo came back, they need to move out as soon as possible. It took a long while and Adanna was getting upset and annoyed, the man had taken too much time, Adanna stood up and paced around the huge hut. She was running out of patience. She needed to get to Akom as fast as possible. Once again she needed her father's help, his words could cause Akom to go into war. She needed to know what was going on with Etiti, Irima and the Herbalist even Nnadi and certainly everyone in that compound. With the situation of things, sleep wouldn't be sleep and food wouldn't be food, water would be less satisfying too. As if they felt her vibe she heard Woyo's voice, she exhaled and went to the entrance of the hut, she had only brought out her head, when two men grabbed her by the arm. She struggled to get free, they were stronger, two more men, rushed into the hut and yanked Tiperi from the bamboo bed covered with mats and calico. Tiperi didn't know what was happening, he was struggling to wipe his eyes to even see. He heard Adanna struggling, opening his sleepy eyes it took a while for his eyes to adjust to the daylight, sun was out now. The boy struggled to recollect himself. Was he dreaming? He was dreaming. When his vision had clearly returned he was outside in an unknown place, with a lot of people standing before him and Adanna. Shouting and chatting noisily. Adanna and the men dragging her were in front with Tiperi dragged along behind her. Adanna was looking back, shouting Tiperi's name, the boy was still confused, he was crying to wake up from the nightmare. Tiperi's greater fear was, he was conscious that he was trying to wake up but couldn't. He got scared, could it be he was stuck in the dream world,

Tiperi engaged all his energy towards waking up, the more he sobbed in frustration, the more they got dragged along. They stepped onto the village path and threw them down violently. Another set of men came upon them. When they tried to stand they were pushed, others held clubs, others stone, demanding to end their lives. Immediately the men of the hamlet restrained them arguing that may come later, they poured mud water on them a sign they were filthy people. Tiperi staggered to get up, Adanna made attempts to get the clay water out of her mouth another splash came upon them. Pushing Tiperi down causing him to bruise his forehead against the ground, the spot peeled. The boy let out a shriek, still staggering. Adanna rushed to him to hold him up but was not allowed, they pulled them apart and she felt the pangs of pain when a cord made with reeds slashed across her bare backs. The cord wouldn't disfigure or leave a mark or scar but could cause considerable pain, if applied well. Those who held stones, had their fingers itch, they wanted to stone them so badly. The men authorized to beat them, continued to slash them with the cord.

    Farther behind two men were approaching, they had been discussing about the good luck of one, who had gone to spend the night with another man's wife. When they saw commotion and mud water on the ground, they shouted in excitement. "A thief has been caught" they both said in unison and ran towards the crowd. On their way they picked stones, they ran even faster getting to the crowd, they made their way pushing others aside, immediately at the sight of two people covered in mud. They hurled their stones, one caught Tiperi on the thigh, the boy screeched. The other stone bounced off Adanna's head and stunned her. Immediately, the men were restrained by words.

"No stoning yet." A voice shouted at them.

Still searching for more stones he shouted 'why' and got no response he turned to his friend, who had dropped the second stone he picked.

"You are saying, I went to meet another man's wife, that it is bad, that is nothing because we love each other. This one is a crime and you are dropping your stone, this people should be killed for stealing, because stealing is evil." He said in anger, "Why are they having mercy for them?" he asked in disgust "Our generation is ruined and lost." He wailed, "Thieves that deserve death now get mercy." His friend agreed with him, they picked more stones. "Thieves deserve to die," they protested. "Kill them," they shouted.

"Not yet" another said, they took more stones and sought a better hitting angle so that when permission was given they wouldn't hesitate to strike. Adanna and Tiperi were whipped mercilessly some more, they were forced upon their feet, Tiperi was not able to stand, any attempt by him to slump to the ground earned him a whip on the back. Struggling to stand straight, a ring of decayed things were made especially decayed foods like yam and plantain, cocoyam, dried fish and meat of all which attracted housefly were made and hung on their necks. With it they paraded them round the village, singing the songs of ignominy for them, and forcing them to dance along. Not dancing attracted some more whips with the houseflies in hundred or even thousands buzzing around them. They were paraded round the whole village amongst those parading Adanna and Tiperi were, the thieves, murderers, adulterers, gossips, those that believed in dark magic and attempted using them to cause harm on their neighbours, slanderers, backbiters, disobedient and the hateful. Tiperi received more of the whipping as he stumbled often, it had been a long while since he was dragged from his bed while asleep, a part of him still felt he was dreaming, but the pain was real. He felt spikes shoot out from his body. Dazed Adanna was not sure where she was, another person who didn't know about the restriction on using stone had stoned her and it caught her temple. This time it was a girl who had poisoned her mother. Adanna and Tiperi were thoroughly disgraced and then were marched to the elders who were awaiting their arrival. Taking a turn to the left the men got to a hut at the extreme. Some old men were standing and were expecting their arrival. Adanna and Tiperi were forced to remove the ring of shame and cast it away. The men dragged them to a circle enclosed with red cloths and palm fronds. Adanna looked around almost the whole village had gathered round about them, one of the men emerged all looking thin and pot-bellied. They had the swords round their waist, the white man's swords and it made them look ridiculous the more, swords tied on wrapper, while naked on top. He motioned to Woyo, who came out. He greeted the people and they responded.

"You all know Woyo, in our peaceful village." He said gesturing as he spoke, "He brought a report which I think is very patriotic of him. Woyo tell them what you told us." The man said.

Woyo took over, "My people I greet you," he said. Tiperi could understand nothing which compounded his woes, he only stared in disbelief still expecting to wake up.

"I was in my hut yesterday, when this woman came with her son. She made a request, the first time she came and I did the right thing and turned her away. I went back to my activities indoors, later was ready for sleep, when she came back the same night, with the same request, the first time she said she had no money, that she was a traveller and was heading for a far country. I looked at this woman, she had no single luggage for a traveler, she had nothing on her, both of them. She didn't look like one who had been attacked by robbers on the way, she claimed to be from Mkpunki and heading to Akom. It is easier to head towards Mkpunki and get supplies, than head towards Akom. However the second time she came, she presented a pearl as payment."

The word pearl sent everyone into a frenzy and various exclamations.

"As payment" the man continued amongst the chatter. "Silence!" the leaders ordered.

"As payments for the services she requested, she asked for accommodation, you all know I am building a new compound, she certainly knew about it, all I ask is how did she get the pearls, this woman I say is a thief."

More noise erupted, the elders asked Adanna for an explanation to defend herself, Adanna exhausted with every kind of pain imaginable attacking her, sat and said nothing. That attracted more whips, she still kept mute and said nothing.

"Whip the boy" the elder commanded.

"I am not a thief," Adanna said amidst tears, before they could lift their cord against Tiperi.

"How come you own pearls?" the man asked.

"It was given to me by a penitent benefactor."

"That doesn't make sense."

"You must know something, I am an Akom woman and I'm going to Akom with my son and you can't stop us."

The man smiled, the crowd raised their stones, ready to strike "you must defend yourself and you must do better than this or we will use our wisdom to pass judgment." "Is this your mother?" he asked Tiperi who was sobbing with laboured breathing. They asked Tiperi again and he didn't respond. They moved to whip him.

"He does not understand your language," Adanna protested with tears running down her cheeks.

"Very well" the elder said he motioned and an Akom man approached and asked Tiperi the same question in Akom language.

"He is from Mkpunki, born and bred in Mkpunki." Adanna said.

The man laughed in disbelief, "But you just called yourself his mother and bragged of being an Akom woman. We need no further proof, it turns out she is also a liar, not only a thief." The man said to the crowd.

They all concurred.

"You lie," Adanna said.

"Do not insult the wisdom of the elders," the man warned sternly "What an elder can see sitting down, even if you climb the highest tree, you cannot see it."

"You see nothing," Adanna said and chuckled in pain, revealing her bloodied teeth with quavering lips she continued to speak. Adanna looked unrecognizable, she had lost every sign of beauty, she did not look human anymore. "You are as blind as a bat in the daytime, and your foolishness is as deep as a bottomless pit. Just look around you, who do you not have in this crowd? Including you yourselves, you all are as dirty as I am. In this crowd are, murderers, thieves, slanderers, adulterers, and so much more despicable people. You claim wisdom, the wisdom I know is to love yourself and to love your fellow men, that is the wisdom I know. So take it from me, you are blind, ignorant and exceedingly foolish. Because you have refused to learn and will forever be blind, living in darkness while others see and choose to see some more."

The men moved to hit her, "Don't" the elder said, "She has taken too many hits to the head." He brought out the three pearls from the knife. Who owns the pearls?" the man asked.

"That is mine and will always be mine." Adanna said. Woyo protested, "She lies, she is a liar" he shouted and spat on the ground. "My people," Woyo said "When this woman returned with these pearls, I knew something was wrong, terribly wrong they must have stolen it because I also saw them with that knife this morning when I came out to report. I met three of my brothers who can support my story and confirm it is true. We went around and asked if anyone was looking for his or her pearl that was when we met this woman." From behind Woyo's men, an elderly woman emerged with her walking stick, she may as well be the oldest woman in the hamlet, when she walked out, Woyo's men went to her, assisting her to the centre of the crowd. Producing the emotions of pity on the woman from the crowd and that of approval for showing kindness on Woyo's men from the crowd. "This woman when we asked her, assured us she had a pearl hidden in her hut, under her bed, but was not aware if they were missing, we helped her to check, lo and behold her pearls were gone and underneath her bed ransacked, and scattered. She cried in appreciation to us, and we felt this people must suffer. Most of you that know this woman in our hamlet knows she is a poor woman and she has been living in poor conditions since she lost her four children. So you may ask why has she lived in poverty all these years? The answer is simple, the pearls were given to her by her husband before he died and she has kept them. Waiting for her children's return just so that she could give it to them, she was sacrificing her comfort for her children's comfort but this heartless two, stole her labour of years and sought to squander them all. Requesting for the biggest hut in my new compound and food that can feed us all. You can see the woman here, these are my servants they also went with me and these are men of this our peaceful hamlet, who also went with me. Thank you my people." Woyo said and stepped aside. Adanna looked at them, stunned at the performance. With her heart torn to shreds looking at the old woman, whom age has bent making her walk bent. How long would she enjoy the wealth she would get in this manner. "I guess you are tongue tied now because the evidence is overwhelming. Some Akom warriors were in our hamlet today looking for someone just like you. I'm sure you are also wanted in Akom. I'm sure it is you they were looking for." Adanna quavered looking around for a sign of them.

"Oh it is you."

Adanna's reaction showed it was her and the elder observed it.

"They are long gone, I never saw you, so I never knew you were in our village, I'm sure it is you, because they are looking for a criminal." Someone must have let her secret out Adanna thought, this couldn't be good, she was wanted almost everywhere.

The elder continued, "With my wisdom I have reasoned things out and have come to thank the white man for helping us dispose of such filth amongst us. The white men are filthy and so they prefer these filthy ones. The best part is we get to make gain off of it. In the times past our ignorant forefathers would have stoned these two to death, but I say let us not stone them today, let us dispose of them because they soil our lands and causes us reproach. So I say my people let us sale them, drink wine with the money made off them." The crowd cheered at the proposition, most dropped their stones so that they could clap. Woyo wore a smirk, so did his companions, they would get to keep the pearls and would get to drink from the sale of Adanna and Tiperi.

"You call the white man filth, yet you marvel at even the soil they step upon, but will still open your mouth to call them filth." Adanna said with a tearful voice as they were both dragged away, Adanna struggled and fought to find a way to hold Tiperi. She was certain there would be death should they be separated, the men allowed them. Grateful, they didn't scar them much, which meant the price wouldn't be reduced and they wouldn't be rejected, all that was needed was for them to wash out the mud. Adanna and Tiperi walked the path, they would have been carried onto the forest of the dead, had it not been for the option of slave trade. The slavers from Aro were close to the people of the hamlet, in no distant time, the men got to the slavers and handed over Adanna and Tiperi. Who were immediately chained and taken to the prison where other slaves were. Woyo was present for the payment, the Aro men paid in copper bars to the people.

"What of the white man's drink?" Woyo requested smiling childishly.

"That is not available now." The Aro slavers responded.

Woyo was disappointed, "I have not tasted it before, but I heard it is magical."

"It is." The Aro slaver answered.

Woyo took his payment, "I guess I will bring more slaves, but please keep the drink for me, it is what I want. In the meantime, I will manage our local drink." He said.

Woyo's companion were already far gone and he ran to meet up with them galloping, as he ran like an excited child despite his bulky frame and pot belly.

CHAPTER 50

The Akom warriors made it to Mkpunki in large numbers about 200 had gathered in Mkpunki causing panic for the people of Mkpunki. The least they wanted was war, they searched the whole of Mkpunki and most pointed to the Herbalist. They had gone to the king of Mkpunki seeking permission and was granted with the king offering his own warriors to assist them. They had described Adanna, with the king having no knowledge of her, despite receiving a disturbing request from the Herbalist seeking for a release of a lady. The Akom men had told the king of how the Herbalist was the person everyone said should know her. In all the villages the Akom warriors had gone to, they met its leaders first for permission before starting their search when they had gotten the permission they did spread out to every corner of the village and many had the Herbalist on their lips. The warriors got to the Herbalist's compound and described Adanna to him, without wasting time he affirmed to knowing her.

"What happened?" a warrior asked he was the leader.

"It will take the whole day." The Herbalist answered.

"No my good sir, the warrior responded "Where is she now? Where can we find her? her father wants her."

"Who is her father?" the Herbalist asked.

"Ubiakwa" the warrior responded.

"I've heard that name before," the Herbalist chuckled, "I've been having Ubiakwa's daughter under my roof."

"Yes you have."

"She was arrested after, what my wife says was a mistake."

"What happened?" the warrior asked, "To your wife." He added.

"They went hunting and Odabi mistakenly shot her but it was not fatal she is alive and well, my wife I mean."

The warrior closed his eyes in disbelief, "She hasn't changed," he said in his mind, he had shame on his face, but kept his composure. "Her name is Adanna," the warrior said.

The Herbalist chuckled again.

"Are you surprised?" the warrior asked.

"No" the Herbalist said.

"Why not, you know her by a fake name."

"She tried telling me her name, but there was no opportunity when she was arrested she was taken to the barracoon, however I went to the king to ask for her freedom and it was granted. When I returned to take her home, she was gone, her cage was empty and the area was empty with no guard. I knew the guards had done what they wanted to, they told me they wanted to sell her into slavery but when I reported the matter, they told me she was released and led to a path, which pointed home with Tiperi my relative. I told the king they were lying and called out the man who had offered me a share of the reward from the proceeds, should she be sold. The man denied it and claimed I misunderstood him. I have no alibi because I also reported that he said they did it all the time. The king investigated and found all his slaves bound for the great-ship intact and not tempered with, neither had anybody reported a prisoner missing to the king. The man claimed he mentioned reward and sharing of reward with me in his discussion with me, but was talking about his cousin who was interested in marrying her. And he also claimed to have said it as a joke. He had an alibi, I did not. Now I'm confused because I believe I heard right but his evidence proves to me otherwise."

The warrior breathed in heavily. "She has been seen in a village down, the first route to Akom and those who saw her said she had a child with her and both were headed to Akom." The Mkpunki warriors present, became excited Akom and Mkpunki's relationship would continue.

"So are you saying Odabi absconded and abandoned us?" the Herbalist asked sounding downcast.

The warriors of Akom knew her too well, the man maintained his composure still.

"I believe so." The man said and moved out.

With the crowd that had gathered also dispersing. Before the sun had moved a considerable distance the news that Adanna had been released and she absconded with Tiperi was rift throughout Mkpunki. All heard it and was disgusted at her, believing the Herbalist had gotten what he deserved. The Herbalist lost his appetite, and felt the world was too cruel for Adanna to have treated them in such manner. He cancelled all his plans for the day and retired to his hut not wanting to see or talk to anyone. The guards who had purported to sell her and Tiperi also had the news and the fact she had slipped through their fingers and was headed for Akom. They were agitated and scared, the veteran mocked their stupidity.

"She escaped and is headed for Akom, since the Herbalist's story of us wanting to sell her has been discredited. Should someone catch her and she says the Herbalist tipped her off, so she escaped. She too will be discredited. Everyone believes our side of the story so we are free and have no cause to worry, we never harmed her or made her feel she was being harmed. The Herbalist gave her wrong information that is all. Because I'm sure he must have told her. Brothers that is it. Chief Afimi has warned us to lie low, till the heat dies down and the king's suspicion goes down, now it is aroused. So I say let us go back to doing legit things just for now."

They celebrated at the words and went their separate ways. Adanna and Tiperi's benefactor, Sikpa had a mission to pass the right information but was fearful for his mother and sibling and relation should he make a mistake. It may cost him their lives and even his, it may be better to be mute.

*****

Ekidu the loner, who lived in the woods alone, had also heard the news and made haste to the Herbalist's compound, the first time he had ever done so, when he got to the compound it was deserted, he called out and no one answered, a certain gloom had descended in the compound. Etiti was indoors, oblivious of most of the happenings and the recent developments, she was still recuperating. Irima sat beside her husband and stared at him, saying no words, he had given specific orders for no one to disturb him. And she already violated one by being in his presence. A servant came out, and directed Ekidu to the Herbalist hut, when Ekidu got to his hut, he knocked and called. The Herbalist was surprised to have him as a visitor, what could have chased the rabbit out of its hole in the daytime. The Herbalist was not in the mood to help anybody. Ekidu called and called and yet no response. Ekidu called the servant and the servant confirmed the Herbalist was in but rather do not want to be disturbed by anyone. Ekidu laughed, "He is downcast and distraught," he went to the Herbalist's hut's entrance.

"Old friend, you know what it takes to get to my place and imagine it, what it takes for a man my age to get to this place from my place. Old friend I have heard the news and I can tell what you are thinking, I came to tell you something. Though you won't let me in, to tell it to you to your face, I will still speak hoping that the wind direct it to your ears, whenever you open them. Yesterday I saw a god birthed to, and it showed across our sky. I wasn't impressed, the gods? They are all the same. But I was content within me, that I have seen a god with my eyes and that god is you. My dear old friend, you exhibit what the gods claim to have, if we have more of you, we will be better off. So I tell you my friend, you are a god to some of us, do not be downcast or distrust. Because what you give has no foreseeable reward, but the world still stands because of it, keep loving my old friend, keep loving. I'm off to my hole, I hope to see you soon, before I join the gods. Hopefully the gods won't seek to punish me by bringing me back to life on the earth." Ekidu chuckled, "I have a question, old friend think on it and try to give me an answer when next you visit. We shall talk about it extensively." Ekidu was almost on top of his voice now. "Why do people pray for long life on earth despite most of it is spent in misery." Ekidu smiled "And I also have a new song," he shouted again "I will be going now, I'm even getting scared of going home late nowadays, see you soon old friend," he said laughed and hummed a song while walking away.

Irima heard all Ekidu had said, the Herbalist heard all too, he closed his eyes and motioned for his wife to come relax on the bed, she obeyed lying down, "Adanna didn't abandon us, and absconded." Irima said.

"I know." The Herbalist said and he slept off peacefully.

*****

Akom warriors left Mkpunki and headed towards Akom. Now they knew where whom they were searching for was headed. This time, they expected to find her though it seemed very unlikely. They thought it necessary, they split even more and many delved into the forest, others to the path. Should it be they had in any way, come into the forest. This time they were certain where their journey started, after the last hamlet where she was seen. They split themselves in such a way that they were three groups on the same path or direction what that meant was that, the first set would pass, then the second set. If there was anything the first missed and the second, definitely the third would see it. They would move with haste and still ask the necessary questions. Most of the groups went effortlessly without rancour or obstacle. Except the group headed by Obiagu, they had been attacked by the professional head hunters. Obiagu's group was the third group following the forest trail to Akom while also keeping sight of the path. The head hunters had outnumbered them. The Akom warriors expected to be attacked but that was when going to Mkpunki, they had believed a misinformed village may take their approach as a declaration of war, having gone successfully they least expected an attack returning. Seeing that all knew their intentions. The head hunters had heard of the Akom warriors and were informed of a great reward should they deliver the heads of Akom warriors. The group headed by Obiagu was the best option for them. They had monitored their movements and infiltrated especially by two Mkpunki head hunters who were also amongst them. The Mkpunki head hunters were dressed in war clothes worn by Mkpunki warriors which disgusted Obiagu. Who felt it was an insult for a head hunter to wear a warriors garment. Obiagu looked at the Mkpunki warriors and was certain he would attack them first because he disliked them more. The Mkpunki head hunters were two amongst the 25 and stood side by side they had found out, attacking the 3rd group meant attacking the last that could not call for help, or expect help. They were 25 in number and taking their time, came upon Obiagu's group. Obiagu and his group were only 8 in number, that meant that the professional head hunters had 3 men against one of the Akom, and also had one extra. Akom warriors were outnumbered, not with lanky men, but strong, muscular men, that could match the Akom warriors in height, strength, experience in battle, and any area necessary. With the Akom men surrounded, everyone brandished their machete. In no time, the forest would witness blood flowing on the ground and vultures would gather to feed for days. The men of Akom felt angered that the battle would hold in the forest, away from the prying eyes of people. With that who would tell their stories about the battle, who would sing songs of lament for their heroic death. The professional head hunters laughed derogatorily which angered Obiagu the more.

"Leave them to me." Obiagu said, "One thing I'm very sure of is that death by itself only will defeat me, not death caused by a worthless dog with a weapon."

This angered the head hunters and they attacked. Blades clashed together releasing sparks as they did so. Flesh began to tear, with few disembowelled. The unfortunate few had their heads taken off at one swing of the machete. Blood splashed, limps fell off, some fought with machete on the right and a fist on the left. Heads spun, all shouted in anger to intimidate one another. There were gasping for some as the blades met their necks. The fight raged on in no time many were unrecognizable on the ground with body motionless. A few moments ago these ones were full of life, just within a twinkling of an eye they were no more. Two warriors from each side were fighting it out with the hands and legs, raining heavy punches on each other, lifting and smashing on the ground. They had clashed their machetes, and the iron broke into two. A few others clashed their swords and it still broke, chaos reigned supreme. The longer they fought, the more souls left their bodies, leaving it lifeless, the sun had its rays on the ground when the fight started, when it ended it was four feet on some of the trees in the forest. Now the fight was over, the men standing had their heartbeat raising their chest to an unimaginable point. Their body was now painted with a mixture of sweat and blood. The professional head hunters had thought their plan was foolproof. They were wrong, the last group was the mightiest amongst them. The soup at the bottom of the bot, when settled has lots more. The fight was over and not one head hunter was standing. The only Akom warrior not standing had bent to bind a wound on his leg. Obiagu only had killed 11, he had cut off six heads, 2 of the heads belonged to the Mkpunki's head hunters. Disembowelled 2 and pierced through 3, piercing one, through the head, the other two, through the neck. When the other was done binding his wound to prevent blood loss, they looked around and laughed with pride. Giving Obiagu a thumps-up, Obiagu frowned his face, his garment was soaked with blood, and it dripped from it like a cloth soaked in the stream and brought out to be wrung. The Mkpunki warriors looked neat, their heads cleanly taken off, with their body dry Obiagu undressed them and took their garments and wore. When he was done, the men cheered.

"Move out," he commanded.

At once they ran off, no outsider had seen his accomplishment here, but it did not matter much. Many had seen him do more. "Today as we go to battle, leave half for Obiagu and focus on the others." The war leader would say, "Remember if you forget Obiagu may use you to make up the half, stay out of his way!"

They would cheer and move out for war. Women sang about it all the time. Today they had not seen, but would surely hear the story.

It would go something like, "We were outnumbered by fighters today, but Obiagu was with us, so we shared the enemies into two. Today he took 11."

The men ran faster this time they had been delayed and needed to cover a lot of ground with the other group. They may not wash the blood off their body, till they get to Akom, should they not see a stream. They wouldn't leave their mission to go and wash, they were warriors. Running through the forest, after a long while the Akom warrior whose ham was injured had been running with a limp, he enjoyed the pain as it shot through his body with every step. He was a warrior and had never been prouder to persevere through such pain. But this time he had to adjust the cloth he was using to bind the wound, to make him freer and faster. Obiagu was the last man, as they ran in a straight line, the injured warrior was before him, the man slowed down, called to his comrades and stopped. They all stopped and waited for him, trying to adjust the cloth used on the wound, when Obiagu got to the man, who was bent and working on his wound. Obiagu went down on one knee and from behind looked at the wound, the man was backing him.

"Let me see the wound." Obiagu said.

The man hearing the order, removed the cloth completely, Obiagu inspected it.

"Tie it loose, it is not too bad, should even heal on its own." Obiagu said.

The man obeyed and began to tie, Obiagu on one knee watched as the man did the binding. Obiagu took his left hand to his left side in preparation to get up, the man was almost through. Obiagu with his left hand to the side, there were shrubs there, felt a sharp piercing pain at the back of his hand. He reacted immediately, lifting his hand up, and taking a swing, with his machete at that direction.

"Obiagu, what is it?!" everyone asked drawing their machete and approaching Obiagu's position. Obiagu himself knew what it was by mere looking at the back of his hand. He saw two dots, with blood sipping through. He searched the area lifting the shrubs there, it was a cobra it was still wriggling and twisting. It had been cut in two by Obiagu's swing. Obiagu's men lost all strength in them in all ramifications. It was going to be told as a story, that a worthless, spineless snake ended the life of Obiagu the Great. Who would tell such a story? They were far from any village and the cobra's venom took effect before 10 steps could be completed. The men were stunned, how would they say it, Obiagu was no more, he was killed by a snake. The snake had been cut into two but still moved twisting itself. Obiagu looked at it again and took off its head. Causing its new severed body to dance around some more, the longer part moved like it still had life in it, as it rose and threatened to strike, however its head was gone and its tail shook violently.

"Juokwu" Obiagu called.

The man answered.

"You are the leader now" Obiagu said.

Obiagu sat on the ground and stared at his hand, clutching it strongly to stop the blood flow. The men cut a cloth and did bind his hand, to stop the poison spreading upwards.

"It won't do any good," Obiagu said as they tied it he felt his left hand go cold and rigid. The blood had stopped flowing and it felt like it would burst any moment.

"We are a long way from help."

Juokwu looked at Obiagu bent towards him and went on one knee, "Use your machete Obiagu, it is faster, the pain is not worth it, use your sword. We will meet in the afterlife soon, together we shall fight side by side again. Greet our warrior forefathers, farewell Obiagu the greatest amongst men, your story will be told for generations." Juokwu patted Obiagu on the shoulder. "Move out." He commanded and they all turned and ran without looking at Obiagu again. Obiagu sat on the ground hundreds of warriors couldn't kill him, not even sickness, but a spineless animal, now he wouldn't be buried, but would rot away and be food for more worthless animals. He looked around and saw trees, he had thought he would have his generation of warriors round about him, when he left this world, now it wouldn't happen again, he watched them run off and disappear behind the trees. Obiagu took his machete and smiled, he would end his own life with honour.

CHAPTER 51

Adanna and Tiperi had seen it all and didn't feel the new situation was new. Adanna was busy trying to stop herself from having thoughts in her head and it frustrated her in no small proportion. Making her discover man was a slave to his own mind, and really had control over nothing. If it was possible to stop your existence and start it when you felt like she would in the present situation. Her body ached, smelled, itched and irritated her. Her mind had been troubled just too long, in both worlds she had lived, she had known trouble, just didn't know which was greater, her only solace for herself was, in one of the worlds she had known peace. Tiperi sat in great confusion, somewhere, sometime in his past, someone had called him "Cursed", he couldn't remember all, but was certain the word had been used for him. He really did not understand the meaning of the word, but knew when it was said the person meant a bad thing. The slave house was just for business and nothing else, and the only business was selling slaves. The settlements were started for the purpose and only that. Adanna was in a cage, similar to the one in Mkpunki, the only difference being the one in Mkpunki was bigger than this one. This one was used to keep slaves, who had fallen sick on the journey, they were allowed to recover and gain weight before resuming the journey. Adanna and Tiperi had only stayed a short while and the slavers had already taken out 3 dead. They were being attended to, still death, was not relenting. It took them in great numbers, gradually and steadily. What was before Adanna was horror unimaginable, weak, disoriented, emaciated men, women and children. Their bones almost visible, the children were extremely scrawny, almost in coma, each waiting for his or her turn to die. Adanna could feel it, the heavy presence of death upon them all. She didn't also want to breathe, she could perceive death. Tiperi was not talking, not moving, not even crying, there was no way to tell what he was thinking, he simply sat and stared. They stayed a while when Aro slavers came in and took both of them outside. Separating them without explanation, Adanna struggled to resist them but they were stronger. She didn't make a sound, only a tearful face, she struggled with whimpering. She had lost her voice and will to cry. The men kept shouting at her and struggling with her. With threats of a beating, she didn't heed their warning both Adanna and Tiperi now were struggling to hold onto each other. The whimper from both continued, after much struggling with the men, from nowhere, Adanna felt a heavy hand, violently landing on her temple. The swollen temple and her eyes. The pain shot through her body, she lost her sight for a moment as she staggered, by now she was on the ground twisting in pain. Unaware of where she was, still moving she groped around like a child, she sought for Tiperi. "Tiperi" she called in a whisper her vision was blurred.

"Tiperi" she continued.

"You will be calm now" a voice said, scolding her "Is this what you want?" he asked.

The man that had hit her was the man in charge of the slave depot, they simply called him 'Catin,' he likened himself as the 'Catin,' saying "The white man too is 'Catin' because he is in charge him too is 'Catin'." However he had refused to wear any of the white man's clothes, rather he argued the black man's dress was better. The whites knew him as the 'Brutal captain,' and it gave him so much satisfaction. He was broad chested and bot bellied.

"The white man calls me Bruta Catin," he would remind his colleagues whenever he was doubted.

He had been in the slave trade for as long as he could remember, and always delivered whenever demanded to. He ruled with a heavy hand making sure all feared him.

Adanna still made an attempt to find Tiperi, moving in the direction she imagined he was.

"This one is stubborn," another voice said. Adanna crawling around, in pain, felt another heavy kick on the left side of her belly, making her gasp for breath. She opened her eyes, it was still blurred. She laid on the ground, turned to see the heavens for the last time before her soul departed her body. The evening sun didn't allow that to happen, peering through her eyelids and making sure the pain escalated. Adanna lying on the ground battered, laid still waiting to wake up in another world. The slavers wouldn't have it, they forcefully pulled her up, legs on the ground and scratched along as they dragged her. She was taken to an area, presumably the bathroom, but it had no cover, there, they doused her with water. To clean the mud and dirt of rotten organic material on her skin, a woman scrubbed her roughly and hastily. More water was poured on her, she had to breathe with the mouth and her whimper continued. Tiperi was receiving exactly the same treatment.

*****

Back in the cage again, what they had to contend with this time was the shivering. The slavers had used cold water. The acrid smell of death still hung in the air, coupled with the nauseating feeling, Adanna laid her back against the bamboo cage, she would surely like to lie, to help relieve the pain and stress but there was no space, the cage was overcrowded. Tiperi had curled himself allowing him rest his head on Adanna's lap. The boy waited for death too, he still felt he was in a trance. His senses picked everything, but he wasn't so sure of reality anymore, all he wanted to do was just wake up. Adanna had never known such discomfort, she was surviving now by the things she had learnt and felt in the forest as a hunter. All her life she had, had plenty and comfort, now she had nothing and couldn't even afford to lie on a ground covered with sand, to ease the stress on her aching, battered body. The longing to relax and be covered with a warm cloth haunted her now. Those days she had taken such things for granted. Then she had a hut all to herself with any imaginable cloth, the bed, the best materials, a lot of food to eat, now she wished if only she could lie down and rest her back on the ground. She was not the only one in this position, others sat too. While the very frail laid with their emaciated bodies and made no movements, those ones were before death and was just waiting to pass on into the other existence. With her head swaying, blood sipping through bruises all over the body. Adanna too was going into a trance, she did stay in a trance for a few moment, then she passed out because of exhaustion.

    When she opened her eyes, the night was already heavy, with cold. It also meant they had gone far into the night. But something was strange, it seemed they were in a new cage as she could see new statures and face shapes. The four burning torches kept at the four corners of the cage, illuminating the cage a little making it possible to see some of the faces. What had called her back to reality, was the voice of a young girl singing. Not only was she singing, she was also making melodious sounds with the chains with which she was bound. Adanna stayed awake but didn't feel much different.

Looking at the girl, the girl stood up, stopped her singing and attended to a child, who was obviously having a bad cough. From the child the girl went over to another child and laid her properly on the ground. Making her way back to her position she met a little girl while dodging legs and arms in the crowded cage, she patted the girl on the head and made some encouraging words to the girl, who instantly felt calm. The minstrel returned to her position and started singing again. Everyone listened. Her songs were only four lines but she repeated them in different ways.

"Dear travellers never get weary your journey has started

Hope in the end

The end is not the end but the end of a phase

The only joy dear traveller is the hope.

Hope For the end of the journey."

Adanna looked at her and was certain she was looking at Nnadi. All the beauty in Nnadi was in the minstrel. Amongst all in the cage, she didn't seem troubled with the perils they were in. Her face was bright and full of hope for a better tomorrow. Her motions alone energized those who wished to be energized.

For Adanna the reasons she passed out still stayed, she was getting weak and may be too weak should she be called upon, to be active to work in any capacity. The beautiful girl continued to sing, she didn't reveal much with her body motions. She sat on the ground quietly, staring at it, and sang, she sang and she sang. Adanna heard the slavers, who acted as guards, discuss. One of the men who stood afar off discussing with a colleague. Adanna didn't see him completely, but the much she could see made her jolt sighting him, her anguish knew no bound. Could that be Obeli her brother?

"Obeli" she muttered her voice too frail to speak. The man oblivious of her, continued chatting, his voice, his gait all reminiscent of Obeli. Adanna gazed upon him, not knowing what she wanted. Did she want it to be Obeli the innocent and kind, that she knew, doing this heinous trade? Or let it be true it was him so that she could be unchained and unshackled. She kept looking at him with only one eye functional. The other eye where she had received the slap earlier on was swollen with the possibility of getting more swollen. The man chatted away exploding into fits of laughter, mirth, surprise, beating his chest and making gestures of swearing at something with assurance, he was lost in his chat. Adanna kept calling but could barely hear her own voice.

"Obeli is dead" she heard a voice say in her head and the tears returned. She would be truly tormented now with regret.

"Obeli." She kept calling, no one heard her. She rattled her chain but was too weak to make any meaningful sound out of it. The man must have had enough chat, as he walked away happily without looking toward Adanna's direction. Adanna tried in vain to get his attention.

"Why not save your energy," a male voice said, "You are going to need it."

Adanna looked beside her to her right and saw where the voice was emanating from. A medium built man with gentle features, sat dejectedly, beside her, he didn't look at her but seemed like someone who knew a lot. Adanna returned her sight to the slavers and the man with the same semblance as Obeli was gone, and had not returned. Adanna took his fellow slavers advice and kept calm.

Tiperi's temperature was rising and he had remained still for too long now. Adanna would wait for a while before she would think of calling for help for him. Her tail bones were on fire, now she had been sitting for as long as she could remember.

"What is your story?" the man asked Adanna.

Adanna breathed for a while, shook her head, "I have no story," she said.

"We all have stories, I just noticed you this evening when we came in here. I have not been seeing you all this while so I figured, you must be new. We share our stories so that if any of us, should in any way survive, we will pass on the stories of our fallen brothers, so that their names will not be forgotten. I am Okonto, should you ever find freedom tell my story to my people."

The people in the cage numbering about 60 in number were all quiet now, the children about 10 most had gone to sleep, the men were 15 while the women 35 in number. All remained silent as Okonto shared his story. Some of them had heard the story before others had not, Okonto sensing he had everyone's attention raised his voice, so they could hear him clearly. The slavers still guarded the cage and seemed attentive to their stories, but showed no remorse. They were used to the stories, and the activities, the death, the groaning, the crying, all were familiar now. They couldn't relate with what the slaves were going through, they had never been chained before.

"I am Okonto from a faraway country known as Aro, I have walked and travelled through many moons, reaching countries I never knew existed, I never knew, our world was this big. Now I realize how insignificant I am but then I say, let us tell our stories so that the birds can sing about them to others in the morning. Let us tell our stories, so that the trees can whisper to each other about it. I was in my farm, on a very hot but peaceful day, weeding my farm in preparation. My brother approached me, I have had no ill against my brother, he informed me there was a terrible, problem at home. I left all I was doing and ran home. No one was seen on the path to my home, when I got home. I saw his first wife foaming in the mouth, we tried all to save her, but it was too late, she was gone. Trying to control ourselves and find out what had gone wrong my brother suggested we go to the Chief Priest to find out the best cause of action to take. When we were being questioned before the great Ibiniukpabi, I related all that I knew about my brother and his wife. Some of us here are aware of Ibiniukpabi and its prestige and important to the Aro man. It decided every step of an Aro man's affairs. While making our pleadings after entering the cave, we passed through tunnels, my brother while giving his pleadings quickly turned against me, and alleged I had killed his wife in colluding with my sisters. My father gave birth to multiple children but from my mother we are 5 and in this cage, four of my mother's offspring are being sold. So please tell my story, tell the world that Ibiniukpabi is a sham. Men created it to deceive other men. I am innocent but my brother connived with Ibiniukpabi to sell me. I am not alone on this, we have often witnessed the blood flow, from the river of blood and have been told the gods have executed judgment and the person was gone. Because the person was guilty. It is all sham, man colours the river red with the blood of animals in place of man's blood. Now here I am with my sisters and wives not knowing what is to become of my generation. Are we to be wiped off from the face of the earth, with no seed to preserve our memories and bloodline? Half of the children here are mine, we must tell our stories. Do you know what it means to be so powerless and hopeless?" he asked looking at Adanna. "Knowing you are nothing but chaff, have you ever sat and wondered why you are so powerless. We actually do not have power to change anything or control anything. You cannot decide what dream to dream at night, you cannot turn back time to revisit the past. You cannot go into the future, you cannot stop rain from falling neither can you decide to stop the sun from shining. You cannot decide who your parents will be, when you will be born or when you die, you cannot choose if you want to be born male or female. Endless as to how man is powerless, then you add it to the fact that they come to put you in chain and make you a slave. You fight against unseen forces, then you fight the seen forces, while in chains. Won't you wish not to be a rational man? Because you realize you are just another animal. We must tell our stories." Okonto said sounding weak and tired.

"All I want, is to get my hands on these people they call Balkie (white men) people, these people are the cause of our pain, they are the ones enslaving our people turning each of us against ourselves, corrupting our minds with their evil ways and destroying the goodwill we have towards each other. I am Doji I used to be a warrior, I still am, and I will avenge." He said.

"I am a woman, and I am not allowed to speak amongst men, but the case is different here, so you will forgive my affront, I too want my name, to be remembered. But I say I am not against Balkie's (white men) people. My husband and I with my daughter here, who is a minstrel, we were returning from my mother's village. When suddenly men appeared form the bush, with machete and clubs. They surrounded us, they attacked us and now here we are. My husband is a chief but that day, chose to be with his wife and decided to do it alone. His other wives we know nothing about, but sir permit me to say this. The men who came out from that bush were no Balkie's (white) men." she sobbed. "I didn't see any of them. I have never seen Balkie's (white) men trample upon our kind. These men had the colour of their skin as dark as mine. They didn't look any different; we were taken to a slave market. This was not the only slave market we were taken to. The freemen and the men in chains those with the guns and hats and those in chains were of the same colour. When we were brought here I saw no Balkie's (white) men. We marched so many nights with pain, and blisters, and cold, and the heat of the sun, famished and weary with the constant lashing, I turned to see who had lashed me and I saw no Balkie's (white) men. I saw men of same skin colour they lashed the men and women and children just the same. Each of their strike was to kill us, that didn't surprise me, what confused me was why they whipped us with so much hatred and anger. But we are the same skin colour, they whipped us like we were the scourge of the earth, but we are not. At every stroke, I didn't see any Balkie's (white) men. We have travelled, so long a distance, entered and rode upon a big body of water, Jam packed together. We have passed Aro through villages, to a point where we entered this water carrier. My husband said is a canoe till this detour, and to this point I have not seen a white man, yet. Why then is this going on? Why should we sell ourselves and cause so much evil upon ourselves? My name is Rodin, I am the 3rd wife of Chief Afimtu, and the girl who has been singing is my daughter Noli."

    The woman's husband remained silent, lost in thought, he certainly knew what had happened. A fellow chief had sold him into slavery. Doji the warrior was silent now and his anger had been re-channeled.

"Please brothers and sisters I will like my story to be told, I am the least here because I am a girl and I'm alone from my tribe. All I can say is that my mother who bore me, connived with my father and brothers to sell me, I am the only girl in the family and my parents have reiterated how unimportant a girl was to them. I was little when I last saw my sister, I was told by my mother that she had been killed but now I know what became of her. My name is Gikee, please tell my story, that I died because I am not wanted by the only people who should want me should others reject me. My mother tricked me, promising me I would return, she took my hand, and led me to a slaver, handed me over, in my very presence collected the reward and promised to return and take me, but she never did, I want my story to be remembered." Gikee said.

"I do not want my story to be remembered," a voice said from the far corner of the cage, "But I want my fellow slave's stories to be told, I know of two of them. We were all raided and ambushed, the three of us were sold together I never got to know their names, but whilst we have walked several days and toiled under our brother's whips. We had planned on overcoming the struggles together but it didn't work. Whilst we journeyed to this place with yokes on our necks as we were all bound together, our hands tied. We patiently waited for our rescue. Due to the heat, right before my very eyes my fellow in front of me slumped and never woke up again. His body was left for the vultures.

"Why waste food for animals." Our slavers had said.

We were two remaining of our group. And for my brother behind me, I only felt, the pulling force of our bonds, as my neck, dragged me to the ground. My brother behind me had fallen too, and I didn't see his face. Before and behind me men fell, women fell, children slumped. Only half of us made the journey. Tell the story of these men who had fallen. The slavers didn't stop lashing us, seeing we were dropping dead, rather they flogged us harder and more severely so that we will stop dying.

"If you think of dying I will deal with you." They will scream. And flog us harder, so that we won't slump and die. And believe me they meant it, a woman slumped up the line and they kept hitting her to wake her up from death. They kept hitting her till she was mutilated, her flesh smashed and torn into shreds, still in death they kept hitting her, for dying. I want these ones remembered, I am Himberu, but the name is not important."

All thought about this one for a while, then Adanna felt she should speak. With all she had heard death was the end for her she was sure.

"Who will survive?" Adanna asked. She was barely audible, but any who wanted to listen will hear, it was the dead of night, and sounds were loud.

The minstrel looked around, "We may die or we may live, tell your story so that the birds will sing it into the ears of men, as they sleep and as they walk about. Our salvation may come tonight and tomorrow will be a brighter day." Noli said, "My mother has spoken, my father is still too shocked to speak, because of the betrayal that has been wrought against him. But I believe in things turning out for the better always."

Noli felt emboldened. She stood. "My brothers and my sisters, let us not despair, we are in chains today, tomorrow we may be free. We have not always been in chains and we will never always be in chains. Things will change, new situations will come, and there will be a change. Let us not forget that. Let us not also fear for anything. Whether the slave or the master or the free, death comes for all men and there is no escape from it. No one is greater, no one is lesser, we were all born, we shall all die, and no one is different. So why despair, have hope I will say, this woman will tell us her story and the birds and air shall carry it, to other ears. We are all travellers, and have nothing else but hope." Noli the minstrel said and sat back down. Looking at her parents and giving them a smile. Chief Afimtu didn't see a reason not to cry, he had not spoken since he was captured with his family. Adanna, looked on with one eye, the other had swollen and had closed completely. Her temple was swollen and bleeding still, so were the bruises under her chin, and the scars some would have clotted, had it not been for the rough bath which re-opened the wounds. Adanna groaning and quacking in pain having gently laid Tiperi's hot body on the ground, grabbed the bars of the cage one at a time, one at a time, until she stood erect. Dragging her left leg along, while limping with the other made few steps forward, just so that they could see her, she continued, "I do not want my story to be told, for all I can say, only worthy songs should be sang, only worthy stories should be told. To do bad is easy but to be good is difficult. Those who have done good should be praised. Those who are not worthy like myself, should only be remembered as a blight and reproach. All of you here, wherever you find yourselves, sing your songs and also sing the songs of the Herbalist of Mkpunki. He showed me light, I have done things in my life, all of you can only hear of and shudder. My father is wealthy and unlike other men gave me freedom. Other men believe a woman shouldn't speak, but should worship them, my father gave me freedom and I utilized it all. Albeit not in a good way. This man despite his story showed me light. I do not know his name, I never got to know his name, his wife's name is Irima, and his mother is Etiti, they showed me light. I had justified myself so many times for my actions but he showed me, I had no excuse. When I was little, I was not a popular kid. I can say people picked on me and taunted me but now I know they were only joking, and meant no harm. My mother will always tell me then but I didn't understand. My mother was my refuge and last resort, a shelter for all my needs. I was pampered and I was her favourite, as such I rarely ventured far from my mother. My father was often busy but I expected little from him, he was like all fathers. I was content because I had my mother, she bathed me, beautified me, and always told me I was beautiful. She gave me every happy moment I can remember of as a kid. When the world was cruel I found solace in her bosom, and she sang me to sleep and to sweet dreams almost every night. We were inseparable, one day she encouraged me to play with my siblings and I agreed. That very day my mother left home to visit friends and relatives. The next time I saw my mother she was carried home. Later on I found out she had been poisoned. My mother was poisoned to death. The world was cruel to me, people were cruel to me. I had to give them back cruelty in any way I could. I believed I had no other option. That is my story as a child, I don't want that remembered. I want the Herbalist childhood story to be remembered, his father was everything my mother was to me, he taught him right from wrong. He showed him light. His mother was a slave drowning, his father showed love, and married a former slave. His father was against slavery, he didn't like the story of the black man killing, kidnapping, stealing a child while he or she slept, to sell just so that he could buy wine and guns and other worthless things.

He was against the business of living things sold for non-living things. It is an evil trade, he was against our chiefs thinking they own all even human lives. For the Herbalist, the men of his village didn't respect him or consider him, rather right before his very eyes, despite he was a child, they used clubs and clubbed his father to death. Right before his very eyes he watched as his father screamed for his dear life. He saw his father leave this earth, his father was beaten to death right before his eyes. But he still had light in him. He saw these men arrested and that is all he knows. If they should be killed it wouldn't bring back his father. I tell you all one thing, tell the story of the Herbalist. Minstrel, sing the song of the Herbalist. Doji fight should the Herbalist ask you to. Please I beg you all to sing the song of the Herbalist, to your children and make them sing it to their children. I was a slaver once, but now I am a slave. However am in the light now, as for me I will sing the song of the Herbalist." Adanna dressed back still whimpering with each movement. She laid herself low and sat back down in pain. Breathing heavily as the pain all over her body clogged her chest.

Noli stood up and spoke again "I am a minstrel and now I will sing the song of the Herbalist. With people like him we will have light in us and we will ourselves be transformed and will become light."

She was interrupted when 'Bruta Catin' approached, surprised that stress and tiredness had not forced them to sleep. With a heavy stick in his hand he banged the stick against the cage.

"Close your eyes and snore." He commanded, "Want you all lying as still as a dead body, you worthless waste." He shouted.

Few in the cage re-adjusted immediately and went to sleep.

Noli looked at him, and still sat, she made no attempt to sleep but was silent now, 'Bruta Catin' looked at her for a while, then opened the cage with a force not needed and banged it shot as he entered. The bang reverberating and rattling the cage. He stared at Noli with dead cold eyes, barely visible. His eyes had almost sunk into his skull, and his extremely dark complexion didn't help. His palms were dark and scared, he looked big and unkempt and had a terrible body odour. Making one wonder who was the slaver and who was the slave.

Noli lowered her head, and laid on the ground. Everyone now was eyes closed or lying. He went round the cage, re-arranging everyone's sleeping position, making sure everyone laid on his or her back and well stretched. Adama's eyes were still open, but he couldn't tell, he forcefully dragged her and laid her on the ground. Adjusting the people beside her, who had made it impossible for her to lie earlier on. Bruta Catin dragged almost everyone around cruelly. When he was certain, they were all well lying on the ground, no one was sitting or squatting. He looked around. They needed all the rest they could get. In a brief moment they would all journey to Mkpunki, to the "point of no return". He waved his club in rotation round his wrist, pounded it on his palm. Looked at the bodies, satisfied, he walked away. Banging the bamboo cage door, rattling it again. Noli laid on the ground, but could hear the slavers, chat, definitely making plans about their journey to commence soon. The chat lasted for a long while with Bruta Catin sounding the loudest and harshest. Noli couldn't hear anything said, but the sound of their voice, showed they were close by. Violation of their orders brought punishment,

punishment that contained so much hate. After a long while their voices died down, Noli was relieved but still waited a while longer before getting up. She sat up and looked around, she felt a pang of sadness, but waved it off, she must be strong now.

"Brothers." She called.

Few opened their eyes, she looked around. The birds chirped, and the air was very cold, and fresh. It was morning in no time the daylight would take over, that meant they had no time. One of the slavers had informed them they would arrive at their destination on that day. Whatever she had to say, she had to say it now, "Brothers rise up." Noli called again.

Doji was the first to sit up, he was a warrior, seeing Doji, others followed suit. When Noli had gotten an encouraging number, she spoke, looking at her father and mother who was also sitting up and listening to her.

"I want us to sing a song, as I laid I thought of the song and I think it would be good if we should learn it. It is a short song, it is so that we can always remember it. We have shared our stories, for those who are new, Sokido had shared his story before, all I can say is that his entire family is in this cage, not even one of his family members were left in his village. His entire clan is being sold off, many have died along the way, and we do not know our destination yet. Also, Rimtu, she was sold by her husband on her marriage night. She went straight from her marriage ceremony to a slave market. In all these we all here have seen terrible darkness. But we must get, keep and give the light, like the Herbalist. We must not give up, we must not break down, we will smile, because everything changes and there will be an end to our chains and bondage. Our minds cannot be chained by humans,

it cannot. To the gods maybe they can but no man can. This is the song.
    Hold a brother's hand when all is calm.
    Hold a brother's hand when it rains.
    Brothers are brothers, hurt comes to all.
    Leading each other to the light is all that matters.
    Always help a brother up, hurt comes for all.
    Be the Herbalist and heal a brother whenever, wherever in anyway.
    Hurt comes to all."

Noli introduced the song to a tune and began to teach them all how to sing it. Those still strong sang it, Adanna memorized and sang by heart. The pain was shutting down her body as almost all areas felt numb. Bruta Catin heard them singing and gently walked to the cage, each stopped singing when they saw him. He walked into the cage.

"I see you all are awake, you shouldn't have. You only wake when I ask you to, and speak when I ask you to, you eat when I allow it and you die when I want you to. How dare you sing when I have not asked you to?"

Almost all tooth in Bruta Catin's mouth was dark brown. His massive body odour permeated and saturated the air in the cage.

"But sir can't we just sing to mourn our fate and raise our spirits." Noli asked innocently.

Bruta Catin looking down saw Noli seated on the ground, he was close to her, with a swing of his club he caught Noli on the head, cracking her skull, blood spurted out with a fizz, spraying on the ground and on those close by. Noli in a twinkling of an eye was lifeless. She dropped on the ground like a falling tree, cut in the middle.

Bruta Catin had hit her on the right side of the skull and she fell to the ground landing on her left side. Her eyes blood shot and wide open.

"I own you." Bruta Catin said and immediately left. Getting to the exist he gave a command to his men. Chief Afimtu, couldn't believe what he was seeing, he rushed to his daughter's side, with his chained hands. He took his daughter up, and seeing she was dead, Chief Afimtu roared in pain and heart break like a wounded beast. Veins popping out everywhere, wide eyed, muscles stretched and tears from an old man who just saw his daughter murdered right before his very eyes, no one can explain the pain. Afimtu tried snapping the chains into two but he couldn't. He roared some more in pain, roaring at the top of his voice. His wife lost her mind, she closed her ears with her palms and prayed for a different reality. Begging the gods to whisper into her hearing and tell her, it was all a joke. She stared at Noli to stand up and laugh and tell her, she fell for the joke it didn't happen rather Noli's blood soaked the ground and flowed like a stream. Still in shock, Catin's men entered the cage, and began kicking and whipping everyone.

"Get up!" they shouted.

"You don't want to sleep so why not move earlier," another said, as he kicked and slapped, anyone close by. Those dazed were dragged up and out of the cage and tied together in a single line, chief Afimtu, needed six men to drag him, he pushed, and struggled with any and all. Bruta Catin looked at him from outside the cage with a smirk. He could easily kill him, but if he did he may not meet up to the quota. Rodim, when she was dragged from beside her daughter's corpse, struggled too. With tears in her eyes, Rodim looked at the men before her, while others dragged her.

"You all will pay for this," she said, "Our blood will be on your hands forever. Your children will be hated by other race, and will curse your grave. You all will be spitted upon, and hated, your lives will be worthless, and you and your generations will die young. Suffering, pain, shame and poverty will accompany you all. Your leaders will continue to subject you to pain in all areas as they do now. They will trample on you and you children's children, so will they always do. You will be known as the cursed race, with darkness hovering all over you. Noli's blood will hunt you even in the afterlife." She continued cursing while being dragged, her tears flowed. "You will continue to be backward, all of you slavers, you that have the same colour with me, light will hate you, and you will terribly suffer. You will suffer and know no joy, till ages come, you will suffer in all areas. You will suffer, and good things of life will be far from you. Death will always visit you." As she spoke, the men laughed. They had heard similar words before, and had seen similar things. Bruta Catin's smirk was gone now, he moved out to make final arrangements, they had to set out now. Adanna was tied in between a group, with Tiperi beside her, the poor boy's temperature was on another level now, he was not shivering but could barely stand. Adanna, was carrying him with her right hand, he held her waist and she dragged him with a limp, should she leave him, Tiperi would drop to the ground.

Seeing Adanna, Bruta Catin, commended her, "I want you all to be like this woman," he said, "Carry your brother, before or behind you if you have to, and we will make this journey, in peace, don't and you receive the whips. Now move it."

Weary and tired they marched out, Adanna struggling to hold up Tiperi, she did not want the lashes for him, Adanna was before Himberu.

CHAPTER 52

The Herbalist had, had terrible nights since Adanna's disappearance. He must take action. He with his men running now, glanced from left to right, in every direction, just to make sure they didn't miss a thing. When they left Mkpunki under darkness, they debated which way to follow. The Herbalist led the way, with two men behind him, he had told Ekidu about his plan, and Ekidu had given him two versatile, dexterous men he could swear for. "They are very useful," Ekidu had sworn. These men, now accompanied the Herbalist on the journey to Akom.

"Which way are we to take?" one asked.

"This way," the Herbalist pointed. It was the same way he was sure Adanna had followed while coming, besides it should be the only one she knew. They ran with the Herbalist holding a sword, he had never used the sword before, but was certain he would use it now should he have to. The men with him had spears, a quiver full of arrows, a bow, a knife, money and a machete, they didn't need other things not necessary for a fight. As they ran they looked and listened but regrettably it was still dark. The plan was to make a light search on the way to Akom. If she was not in Akom find mercenaries and then thoroughly look for her. They ran and got to the path that if followed straight, a point would be reached and taking right would lead to the hamlet, and the Aro's slave depot, straight would be a way to Akom. The Herbalist sighting the path, having ran a little stopped, before entering the path, the left was the forest, the right was also a forest and straight was a well-treaded upon path.

"Which way now?" they asked again.

"We go right," the Herbalist said.

"But that is into the forest," one said.

"I know, right is right" the Herbalist said.

Tiperi had also said that. They dove into the forest and he felt he made the right decision. Adanna wouldn't want to be seen, and she was a hunter, and "Right is right," taking the forest and being on the right-hand side was better. Feeling sure, the Herbalist with his men ran off, again they had covered a long distance. When with the first break of light, for dawn, they came upon slaughtered men, it was the head hunters killed by Obiagu and his men. Much flies buzzing round the corpse, there was presence of scavengers, and they looked newly killed. The Herbalist looked at them and felt no pity, he knew they were professional head hunters. His men drew their bow and was ready to shoot. They looked around for a sign of life then they ran off again. Spitting on the ground, and denouncing the curse that came with death being the first thing you witness. It was bound to bring terrible bad luck. The men looked at the Herbalist for direction, should they go back certainly this event was a bad omen. The Herbalist ignored them, and moved on, they had no option but to follow him. They were bound to him, running with determination and purpose, they covered more distance. When they came upon a man reclining on a tree, with his machete beside him, and it seemed he sat on a pool of his own blood. The Herbalist drew his sword, the man also looked fresh. His head bowed, his leg stretched out, the men watched him intently, ready to shoot anything that moved. The Herbalist thought of helping him, but decided against it. He had helped so many people in his life, that he deserved this one chance not to help. It wouldn't stop the fact that he had helped a lot of people, another thing being that the man was an Mkpunki warrior. His garment though stained with his own blood, still clearly showed it was the Mkpunki warriors colour of garment. The Herbalist now despised Mkpunki warriors and wished them evil. Once he saw the man was an Mkpunki warrior, he looked away from the man. He thought of running off, when he remembered his counsel to people. Who had said things like.

"In this case, I just had to kill him to get him out of the way, that was the only way I could have peace, it just had to be done, it was the only solution."

He had always disagreed. Also he had always been asked if man must always do good? And he said, "Always, no vacation or break, always till death", he had also said, "Never feel entitled to do a bad thing, because you have done so many good." His heart pricked him, and he turned. That was when he saw what he didn't see initially the man had only one hand, his left hand was lying beside him, and looked dead and shrivelled. The Herbalist got to the man. The point where the hand had been cut off, was charred. The man breathed, without looking up, at the Herbalist he called out.

"Herbalist is that you?" he said in a low voice, breathing with labour.

"How do you know my name?"

The man, chuckled, "Is Herbalist your name?" he asked.

"Who are you?" the Herbalist asked.

The man looked up. "Obiagu!" the Herbalist muttered in surprise, "What happened?" the Herbalist asked, scared of the answer.

"I was bitten by a cobra in the day light, could have sworn they were nocturnal, maybe I disturbed its niche." Obiagu said and smiled. "Maybe, I thought you will pass, why did you come back?" Obiagu asked and coughed slowly.

"I came to help you." The Herbalist answered.

Obiagu laughed, "The way you help it simply means you are a man who knows too many troubles, helping will always get you into trouble." Obiagu said.

"Trouble comes for all men, no matter what."

Obiagu nodded, "Picking herbs brings you this far from your village?"

"I'm headed to Akom to find Adanna."

Obiagu mused and smiled, "You are a man who knows too many troubles."

"We all know too many troubles."

"Woe betide us, I don't even know how many days I have sat here." Obiagu said.

"It can't be more than a night, yesterday was the last I saw you."

Obiagu was relieved, "Give me some water, to quench my thirst and I will be on my way to join my brothers."

"I am coming with you," the Herbalist said.

"No need this is a journey for men, the brave hearted, I can still use my right hand to take heads off."

"Taking heads off is not a sign of bravery or courage, it is surviving despite opposition, no matter what area or sphere." The Herbalist said.

Obiagu now mean "I am supposed to be dead, to my brothers I am dead, I was bitten by a snake, I took my own hand off, I burned my own arm while it was still part of my body. I just conquered death, I am Obiagu, now go back to your worthless herbs while a man does what men do."

"You think it is worthless, yet you are sitting beside leaves, that could have strengthened you, and made you regain blood. I guess you didn't know and you still think it's worthless. Wake up my friend, bravery goes beyond force."

"Watch your mouth I can still take your head off." Obiagu said.

"I will slit your throat like chicken before you can move." The Herbalist retorted.

Obiagu chuckled, the Herbalist handed him a pouch of water which he gulped down and requested for more. He was given and this time he drank a bit slowly, before returning the pouch.

"Do you need food?" The Herbalist asked.

"Not yet, it will slow me down." Obiagu said.

The Herbalist plucked some leaves, washed them, "I could have pounded them but no equipment, chew them and spit out the leaves but try to suck the water (sap) from the leave as much as possible."

Obiagu opened his mouth, with every bite, he witnessed his brain get alive again and again. Obiagu rested for a while, "Go back Herbalist, I will send word, this is a perilous journey, as for me I can go alone, I am immune to slavery now." He said raising his left hand, to show the charred hand, "I must move on now, it is good that there are people like you still in our race, you are a light for our race. What it means for me is that I will continue to be a warrior just so that your type in our race can survive. If you can wish to go to Akom for such a person as Adanna, you amaze me." Obiagu said, and tried standing. His body felt heavy, his legs were numb as he stood, he staggered and almost fell, he in fact fell to one knee. He used his machete to support himself, ensuring he didn't reach the ground. "What did you put in that water?" he asked.

"It is just water" the Herbalist said "You need rest, that is what your body is telling you."

"I will rest when I die." Obiagu said, and attempted standing again. The second time he did he stood and looked up into the heavens and breathed out heavily. He caressed the handle of his machete and marched on, the Herbalist followed.

"No wonder you two like each other, you are just as stubborn as Adanna." Obiagu said.

"I can't rest," the Herbalist said "I need to know what has become of her."

"It is all the same." Obiagu said, and kept walking, he had noticed the bow men, but didn't say a word. Men with children's play thing in the name of weapon. The four set out with Obiagu leading the line, with progressing steps each getting firmer and firmer. The Herbalist looked back and wondered how a man who lost so much blood could still walk.

*****

Adanna and her fellow slaves struggled and had made little progress, the line was too slow, and the lashes, didn't help the slavers. Many preferred death than take another step. The slavers whipped and dragged them along, Bruta Catin watched on, thinking of what to do, Afimtu walked but in his head planned how to get his hand free and kill as many as possible. Rodim was propelled with cane and had been dragged along, she wept uncontrollably, screaming, with so much pain in her voice. Adanna had so far dragged Tiperi along her hands lost all strength. They had passed the 4-way junction, and turned to their left now facing Mkpunki, she was unaware when Tiperi slipped from her hand, to the ground and was motionless. Not long after Himberu witnessed Adanna collapse in front of him. Should they continue, the person behind should be the next again. He thought and wondered when it would be his turn to collapse and pass from this cruel world. If Noli could die he too could and deserved it more. "Bruta Catin" walked to Adanna and inspected her, his men came to whip her to wake her.

"She is extremely lazy." One said.

"She has passed out." Bruta catin said "Unchain her." Himberu was on his knees now, so were the people before Adanna. She had dragged them down while falling. Bruta catin counted his men as if he didn't know how many they were. He called on one "Carry her back to the cage and treat her, do not take her to the cage of the sick. Death comes faster there. Make sure she is ready to move in two days." He said.

"Will this number be enough?" Bruta Catin's second in command asked.

"They need 55 to complete and set sail, we had 60, we have lost 3 and still have 2 extra they are more than enough. These two will be moved next tomorrow with the next badge arriving later today. Take them back." He said to the man. "Let's move out." He said.

They resumed their journey with Adanna and Tiperi lying on the ground motionless. With only one man to carry both of them. Bruta Catin needed more men to protect the 55 than protect 2. The 3 which comprised his man Adanna and Tiperi he left behind can perish, he did not care. The man struggled with the two of them. Carrying them one after the other, he made little progress. Then he tried carrying the two at the same time, and it was impossible. Dragging them one by one he was able to get them to the 4-way junction. He saw the futility of it, he left them and went to call more men from the depot. It would be faster and more sensible that way.

*****

Obiagu was the first to burst out at the junction from the forest, followed by the Herbalist and the two men. Obiagu and the Herbalist looking around saw a woman and a boy lying at the junction both not moving. The four men all pulled out their weapons once again and were ready to fight, they all turned their backs towards each other and came together. Looking in every direction to see if it was trap, no one was approaching. Obiagu told the Herbalist to dress towards the bodies, with him scanning everywhere ready to pounce on anyone. The two men had their bows stretched to its limit ready to release at any point. The Herbalist got to the bodies and couldn't recognize them, but everything in him told him that was Adanna and Tiperi. He just didn't believe it.

"It is them," he said in faith. All men still looking around, waiting for an attack. Obiagu wanting to verify told them to watch his position, he looked at the woman and didn't recognize her. He took her hand and looked at it, though bruised but he saw what he was looking for. He saw the tattoo for Ubiakwa's family.

"You speak truth," he said, "It is truly them."

The Herbalist exhaled in relieve, more relieve came for him when Obiagu suggested they head back to Mkpunki. "I have Men in Mkpunki," he said. "We didn't trust your report of her absconding, so we told some Akom warriors to do undercover." Obiagu said.

The Herbalist was not surprised, warriors have a way of reasoning. With every man still in battle stance, the Herbalist ordered his men to carry them, one picked Adanna and placed her on his shoulder. Another picked Tiperi, as they prepared to move the slaver who had gone to call his colleagues to help him approached, with three men with him making them four. When they saw Obiagu and his crew they ran faster and stopped them. Obiagu and the Herbalist were ready to fight.

"Go with them Herbalist, all of you should run now." Obiagu commanded.

The men ran off with Tiperi and Adanna on their shoulder towards Mkpunki.

"Those are our slaves," the men shouted, "We will kill you all." They shouted. They made an attempt to run after the men, Obiagu blocked them, still wielding his machete.

"Go it's a command." He said to the Herbalist.

"They are four and you need all the help you can get and besides you are one handed."

Obiagu laughed, "If I need help not against these ones, these are cowards and worthless, their blood will only stain my machete, and I will have to take weeks washing it off, because it is a reproach. They are cowards. Get one of them alone and he will lick the earth if you command. Their only strength comes when they are in a group of other cowards. Now go." He said "Save Adanna and Tiperi."

That one caught the Herbalist, he had to save Adanna, his men were far gone into the forest now. He hesitated some more, then wished Obiagu good luck and ran towards his men. Obiagu turned to the men,

"Children, do you know who I am?" Obiagu asked with a smile.

"A dead man." One said and they encircled Obiagu.

"Very wrong my child, you should pay attention when an elder teach you, I am Obiagu the death conqueror." He said and laughed mischievously.

The men attacked.

The Herbalist had caught up with the men and urged them to run faster, he was a little behind obviously concerned for Obiagu. When he looked behind him, he saw a man running towards them looking more closely, it was Obiagu and his right hand with a bloody machete. "Quickly" the Herbalist said with smile on his face "so fast," he thought. The Herbalist increased his pace and commanded the men to run faster which they did, Obiagu was enclosing faster.